BOOKS BY ANNE CA

No Virgin
No Shame

Looking for JJ
Finding Jennifer Jones
Moth Girls

NO SHAME

ANNE CASSIDY

HOT
KEY
BOOKS

First published in Great Britain in 2017 by
HOT KEY BOOKS
80–81 Wimpole St, London W1G 9RE
www.hotkeybooks.com

A CIP catalogue record for this book is available from the British Library.

ISBN: 978-1-4714-0678-2
also available as an ebook

1

This book is typeset using Atomik ePublisher
Printed and bound by Clays Ltd, St Ives Plc

Hot Key Books is an imprint of Bonnier Zaffre Ltd,
a Bonnier Publishing company
www.bonnierpublishing.com

PART ONE

One

I am Girl X and I was raped. My real name is Stacey Woods.

It happened in an apartment near Oxford Street, in London. The man who did this to me was arrested and charged. That was nine months ago and now his trial is in seven days and I am dreading it. Patrice, my closest friend, wants me to write about it so she bought me a beautiful book. It has got a purple leather cover and creamy lined paper and I was to use it when I was away from my laptop. *It's just for notes, Stacey*, she'd said, bossily. *The real story you put onto your computer.* The notebook had a leather marker for me to keep my page and it fitted into my bag perfectly.

Patrice also bought me a heart-shaped pendant from eBay. She loved to buy things that other people had already used. *It has a history*, she said, holding it up for me to see. The silver chain was resting on her fingers and the pendant hung in the air. It was lovely. The heart was just an outline, so I could put my finger through the space in the middle. *This is to show that you have people who care about you*, Patrice had said.

I'd worn the heart every day since.

The man who raped me was looking after the Poole Place

apartment for someone else. I had fallen out with everyone in my life and I found myself staying there – just for one night. I hadn't met him before. As I was getting ready to leave he came into the bedroom and forced me to have sex with him. Afterwards he gave me money to get a taxi home. I took that money. I know that was wrong but I was confused and shocked. Perhaps he thought he had paid me off and the price of forced sex was a taxi ride home. He was wrong, but I still took the money, so I was wrong as well.

I tried to picture what the courtroom would be like; the judge and barristers in wigs and gowns and the jury sitting on straight-backed chairs deciding whether or not I was telling the truth. I had a vision of myself on the stand being questioned and shrinking a little each time I gave an answer until I was a tiny girl peeking over the wooden bar barely able to see anyone.

My rapist kept his shirt and boxer shorts on. He'd pulled my pants off and then lay on top of me. The buttons on his shirt dug into my skin and he'd reeked of cigarettes. When he finished he let out a cry and rolled to the side. I slid out from under him, picked up my pants and scurried away to the bathroom like a frightened puppy.

Now I sat in my room and thought about what was to come. I had lots of people on my side; my mum and dad (and Gemma, my dad's partner), my sister, Jodie (and Tyler, her baby son), and Patrice. I had Annie Mulligan, my personal policewoman, and Mr Parvez, my solicitor. There would be a barrister too but I hadn't met her yet.

In among all this there was something else on my mind. A boy that I had been thinking about more and more as the trial got closer. He had given me a heart once. He'd drawn it onto a card and handed it to me. I'd thought it meant that I was special, but I wasn't the only girl he'd done this for. This boy had given his heart all over the place. I just hadn't realised.

I fingered the pendant around my neck.

It had been a long time since I'd seen this boy.

With the trial looming I found myself longing to see him again.

Two

The next day I was walking along a street in west London. I wasn't supposed to be there, I was aware of that. I got off the Tube at South Kensington and walked up the stairs to the street outside. I used my phone for directions and passed a parade of shops. I turned a corner at a crossroads and walked past a church with a spire and then saw some tennis courts. All at once I was in the street that led to his school.

All the way there I tried to imagine what my policewoman, Annie Mulligan, would say if she knew what I was doing. *Are you off your head, Stacey? This could jeopardise the case. What were you thinking of?*

I couldn't explain it. I felt *driven* to go.

The school had a high brick wall around it. On the opposite side of the road was a long terrace of houses with railings. The front doors were solid, glossy and expensive-looking. I stood on a corner by a Tesco van that was delivering a weekly shop. The driver was unloading plastic boxes of groceries onto a trolley. I watched him for a moment and then looked back at the school. The brick wall was solid and uniform and high above it was a wooden sign that had the words *Montagu International College* printed on it in gold lettering. Behind that was a three-storey building. It was smaller than I'd thought but then there were only one hundred and sixty students. I'd researched it on the internet. I'd also seen that parents paid thousands of pounds each term for their sons to go there.

The Tesco man was coming back.

'Can I help you?' he said, pointedly.

'No, sorry,' I said, stepping away from the van.

It was just after two and I guessed all the students would be inside in classes. It might be different with the sixth form, but still I imagined if they had free periods they would be doing 'prep' or sports or one of the other many extra-curricular activities the school offered. They would be busy and no one would be looking out of the window for a girl from a school in Stratford.

I hadn't seen Harry Connaught in a long time. Now he was just the other side of a wall. I stared at it and wondered if I had gone mad and what on earth had propelled me to do this. As I walked along the length of the school it started to rain and I put my hood up. When I got to the corner of the building I crossed the road to a row of shops, the end one empty, the windows boarded. I stepped into the doorway, avoiding the piles of rubbish that had built up in the corners. I stood there and stared further up the road at a pair of wooden double doors that were embedded in the brick wall of the school. Adjacent to them was a wire fence along the edge of the pavement and yellow zigzag lines on the road. I was guessing that this was the student entrance.

In just under an hour Harry Connaught would come out of

that gate. I had no intention of letting him see *me* there; that was not part of any plan. I just had to see him.

I'd made a decision to come here a few days ago, after I'd been at my dad's apartment in Shoreditch. He and his girlfriend, Gemma, are having a baby. Gemma was hardly showing but she'd already bought lots of baby things and they covered every available space in my dad's tiny apartment. I had coffee and a piece of chocolate cake with them. The three of us sat on the sofa balancing the cups and plates on our laps. Between mouthfuls I'd asked them, *Where will you put the baby's cot?* And Gemma, without taking a breath, had said, *Oh, we'll have to move. Out of London. The prices are so high and we need more space.* I'd looked down at what was left of my cake and thought of something Jodie had said as soon as she heard about Gemma's pregnancy: *Now they'll be getting married and moving to somewhere miles away, you bet.*

I didn't say anything. Gemma was doing most of the talking and I could hear Dad mumbling agreement. Later, when I left, Dad put his arms around me and said, *You're not upset, are you? It'll be six months, a year, before it happens. And we'll make sure there's a spare room just for you to come and stay.* I looked him hard in the face. Since the pregnancy he was even more besotted with Gemma, his glance constantly veering towards her tiny tummy bump. He was on his way somewhere and I wasn't going with him. I hugged him back and left.

I'd walked towards the Tube feeling distracted, thoughts running through my head about how everything was changing. Dad would live in a house far away from London where he and Gemma and the baby would have lots of room and I would hardly see him. I slowed down, reluctant to head off home where I would have to tell Jodie she'd been right. I paused on the corner of the street where the cafe Katie's Kitchen was. I looked along and expected to see the blackboard that sat in front of it. I'd often eyed the cafe from the main road when I was going to Dad's or going home. The blackboard wasn't there though. I walked down the street towards it and could see that the shop was shut up and there was a notice on the door:

We've relocated to Finsbury Park.
See website for details.
Thanks for your custom.

Underneath was the web address.

The windows were covered with metal mesh but I could still see through. The counter was flat, stripped of its coffee machine and displays of cakes and pastries. The tables and chairs had gone. There were some packing boxes stacked at the back but apart from that it was empty. I felt sad looking at it, even though I'd only ever visited the cafe once.

It was the day I first met Harry Connaught. He'd come in and we'd got talking. The cafe hadn't been busy, but still he'd sat at my table with his cafetiere and croissant. I'd been sketching and he'd asked me if I was an artist. It was an innocent picture. Two young people attracted to each other chatting across a table; girl meets boy, the stuff of romcoms. *I'm Harry*, he said, holding his hand out for me to shake as if I was a businessman and he was doing a deal. I don't remember anyone else in the cafe at that moment, at other tables or in the queue or even

10

behind the counter. I was in a bubble with this boy, the two of us in a world of our own. When he left I'd stood watching as his taxi disappeared round the corner and the colour seemed to seep out of the day and I knew then that I had to have him. It turned out that he had to have me as well but not for the reasons that I thought. The memory of it made my heart twist.

I knew it was mad but I wanted to see him again before the trial.

A little after three thirty some boys started to come out of Montagu International College. They spilled onto the pavement in twos, talking intently to each other, walking a few metres before whipping mobile phones out of pockets and bags. The further away from the gates they got the more physical they became, spreading out, pushing and shoving other boys, running, jumping and shouting out. Not so different from any school in Stratford, I thought. I noticed a couple of large black cars idling by the pavement, waiting to pick up some of the students.

I moved and stood in front of a newsagent's. There were stands along the pavement with foreign newspapers on display. I turned and pretended I was looking at them. Then I moved around so that I was partly hidden by the stand and looked back across at the gates. Some older boys were coming out and I watched with trepidation.

What was I doing? My memories of Harry had drawn me there. From those first few moments in the cafe I had been sucked into his world. I'd wanted him. And when he held out his hand for me to shake, the events of the next two days were settled. I would have done almost anything for him.

My phone beeped. I picked it out of my pocket and saw that it was a missed call from Mum. I thought about ringing her, then I decided not to. When I looked back to the school gates Harry was there. I was momentarily startled by the sight of him, as if he was the last person I expected to see. He was on his own. I pulled my hood up and turned my back to him. My heart was punching, my hand trembling, as I picked out a copy of a French newspaper from the stand. I looked at it and then glanced back to the school. He was on the other side of the road but had walked in my direction. He had his phone out and was reading something from it as he went slowly along.

He was holding his jacket over his arm. He looked thinner than I remembered and his hair had been cut very short. His face was gaunt, his jaw moving as if he was grinding his teeth. His tie was at an angle and his shirt had come untucked. He stopped abruptly and I thought for one awful moment he was going to glance over and see me.

But he was just searching his bag and I was able to study him. There was something different in the way he held himself. Last year he had been so smooth, so confident, but now he looked all fingers and thumbs, clawing into his bag for a book or some other item that he couldn't find. He pulled some papers out and they slipped from his hand and floated down onto the pavement. Exasperated, he dropped the bag and squatted down by it. A couple of younger boys passed and he spoke sharply to them, which made them hurry their step. He finally stood up and slung his bag over his shoulder and continued walking. I couldn't help myself, I felt this flood of something for him; sympathy perhaps, because he seemed agitated, unhappy.

After what he had done to me was I allowed any feelings for him?

I replaced the newspaper in the stand and walked a few steps along to keep up with him. From behind me I could hear a beeping sound. I looked round and saw a black Mini. I recognised it from last year. Dom, Harry's friend, was driving it. He overtook Harry and pulled in alongside the pavement.

I wondered why Dom hadn't been at school.

Harry bent down to the car and spoke to him. A conversation went on and I walked back to the far corner where the boarded-up shop was. I paused as I saw Harry walk round the car while Dom leaned across inside and pushed the door open. He stood for a moment by it and looked around the street as if searching for someone. I turned my face to the shop window, afraid that I might be spotted. I heard the car door shut and realised that he'd got in. As it drove off I remembered that day months before when he came to my school to find me. Dom had brought him in the car then and they'd waited across the road for me to come out of the school gate; just as I'd waited this afternoon for him. He'd been so sweet. *I like you*, he'd said. *I've come all this way to find you.* Then he'd looked relaxed, his voice as smooth as honey. Now he was all frowns and sharp angles.

How could I help but have some feelings left for him? After those two days in Oxford Street when I seemed to be the centre of his attention. Was I not allowed that? It wasn't *Harry* who assaulted me.

13

I turned and began to walk towards South Kensington Station and my thoughts argued back. *No, Harry didn't do anything,* a voice in my head said. *He just arranged everything so that his brother, Marty, could rape me.*

Three

In the days leading to the trial I became irritable at home, being sharp with Tyler when he only wanted to play; biting Jodie's head off when she asked me if I was all right. I stayed in my room a lot and looked at myself in the mirror and frowned at my hair. Patrice had talked me into a henna treatment and now instead of mousy brown it was a defiant red. It was all part of her project to make me feel stronger. She laid great faith in a new hairdo, and even though she was my friend and she meant well, I felt annoyed every time I looked at it.

When I wasn't being angry I thought about Harry Connaught a lot. Not the Harry I knew last year, but the gaunt and perplexed boy who'd come out of the Kensington school that day. I began to wonder whether there was a chance that Harry had not only changed in appearance but, maybe, he had changed *inside*. Then I pulled myself together. In movies people change; in real life they don't.

My head of year asked me to come and meet her in her office after school on Friday. I'd had no class last period so I was early. I sat on a soft chair in the sixth-form common room until most of the other students had left. It was a non-uniform day, so I'd paid my pound and was wearing skinny jeans and a giant orange jumper that I'd found in a sale bin. On a seat beside me was a copy of the *Metro*, a free newspaper that someone had picked up on the Tube on their way to school. I was leafing through it and could hear the sound of a single guitar strumming mournfully from one of the music rooms. Otherwise, the place was empty.

The newspaper was wrinkled and someone had cut a square off an inside page. A nearby headline caught my eye: *My Brother Made Me Rob*. I was about to read it when I heard my name being called. I looked up and saw Ms Harper in the doorway. I put the newspaper down and followed her along the corridor.

Inside her office she looked pointedly at my red hair.

'Goodness, you look *different*. What's happened to your hair?'

'Just some henna . . .'

On a side table were two china cups and saucers and a matching teapot. Behind them was a kettle which had just boiled and there were wisps of steam still ribboning out of the spout.

'Do you approve of my new crockery?' she said. 'Charity shop in Ilford.'

Ms Harper was always buying chinaware from charity shops. It was her hobby. She said she had shelves of it at home and every now and again she brought some into school. They were old-fashioned, thin porcelain with scalloped edges and tiny handles only big enough for a thumb and forefinger. The amount of tea they held was small, so Ms Harper was constantly refilling them from the pot.

'Now,' she said, sitting on the other side of a coffee table, 'how are you?'

'I'm good. I'm pretty much OK.'

'I can't get used to your hair. You look so, well, different.'

I tucked some strands behind my ear.

Ms Harper was wearing one of her many dark suits; a knee-length skirt and single-breasted jacket. Underneath she had a grey shirt, the cuffs sticking out of her jacket sleeves. She wore no jewellery or make-up and her hair was cut neatly into her neck and round her ears. In contrast, the teacup she was drinking from was a pale yellow with blue flowers and the rim looked as if it had been dipped in gold.

She was sitting on a hard chair, straight backed. I was perched on the edge of an old armchair that seemed to droop the moment I sat in it. I had to look up at her and it made me feel like a year seven.

'The trial starts on Monday, correct?'

I nodded.

'And you have your story straight for next week?'

'I'll be off sick on Monday and Tuesday. Those are the days when I will be definitely giving evidence. After that I don't actually *have* to be there so I'll pop into school and get some work from my teachers and say I'll do it at home. I may go back to the court, I don't know.'

'I doubt there'll be much publicity attached to this trial but it's best to have a story worked out. And it will most certainly be over by Easter, correct?'

'Yes.'

'So,' she continued, 'when you come back to school after Easter you will have your exams to prepare for. I know that at this moment the exams are the last thing on your mind

17

and I understand that. You have more important things to think about, but I will keep them at the forefront of *my* mind because I do not want this thing that has happened to you to destroy your future.'

Ms Harper drained her cup and then replaced it on the saucer. Without taking her eyes off me she picked up the teapot and refilled it. She was about to go on but I interrupted.

'Actually, I've made a decision about that.'

'Oh?'

'I've decided to defer university for a year.'

Ms Harper's face went slack. She pushed her cup and saucer away and stared at me. She looked as though she was on the brink of telling me off. I carried on speaking, though my voice was a little high.

'I . . . I've thought about it a lot and realised that I'm not ready to leave home and live in a different city among people I don't know. I'm just not ready.'

'I see.'

I couldn't blame her for being put out. We'd been meeting once a fortnight since the day I first told her about the rape, the previous September. She and the head teacher were the only two people in school who knew (except for Patrice). These meetings were important so that I could keep on track with my studies. So every two weeks she looked over my work and my progress. She gave me pep talks and if my grades were slipping she spoke to my teachers. She'd spent a long time with me choosing courses and universities and she'd given me lots of help with my personal statement.

'You didn't mention it at *our* last meeting.'

'I just decided over the last few days.'

'You have offers from Reading and Birmingham, correct?'

'I don't feel in the right frame of mind for university.'

Ms Harper sighed. It was what she did at sixth-form assemblies when she had a particularly difficult problem to discuss; personal safety or sexism or racist jokes.

'But you are still going to take your exams?'

'I'll get the best grades I can. Then I'll defer my start for a year. Lots of people do it.'

'Yes, they usually do it to go and work with a charity for a year or go abroad and travel. They don't do it so that they can stay in Stratford and work in Budgens.'

I flinched at her words.

'Well, of course I didn't mean that in the way it sounds . . .'

'It's OK. I understand.'

'No, no, Stacey. I spoke out of turn. I apologise. There is nothing wrong with having a part-time job in Budgens. There is nothing inherently bad about taking a year out and staying at home so that you can decide what you want to do. There *is* something wrong with doing these things because a crime has been committed against you. Don't let the actions of this man push you into hiding away.'

'I'm not hiding . . .'

'Aren't you? Really?'

I didn't speak because I felt a tightening in my throat. I'd made this decision and would have preferred to keep it private until after the trial.

'Will you do me a favour? Will you leave this until after your exams? That way you keep your options open.'

I stared at her with frustration.

'That's my problem. I've got too many options. I need to know *what* I'm going to be doing in September. I can't deal with the uncertainty. I might be doing History and English at Birmingham. I might be doing Communications at Reading. I might be in halls or sharing a house. I can't *picture* myself anywhere. Who will I be with? I don't make friends easily. If I stay here – just for a year – then I know exactly what I'll be doing.'

'Working in Budgens.'

'And I'll go to university the following year!'

'If you make this choice now you will view your exams differently. You will lose momentum.'

'I can resit if necessary . . .'

'It sounds to me like you've already given up, Stacey,' she said.

'No, no, I haven't.'

She stood up, picked up her cup and saucer and the teapot and put them back on the shelf beside the kettle. I wondered if the meeting was over, if she'd had enough of me. Six months of plans and discussions about university and now I'd let her down. She continued talking, her voice sounding weary.

'I've seen boys and girls say they're going to have a gap year so their grades plummet and a year later they're working in McDonald's. I don't want that to happen to you. Will you at least put this decision off until after the trial?'

'I've made up my mind,' I said.

'But you'll do *me* the courtesy of waiting until we meet again before you let the colleges know. Just so that I can be sure that you're doing the right thing.'

I nodded. It was pointless arguing with her. Her suits and mild manner covered a will of steel. The only fragile thing about Ms Harper was her china. I stood up. The meeting was over for me. As I opened the door she spoke.

'Good luck, Stacey. Just tell the truth and let justice work its course.'

'I will,' I said, 'and . . . thank you. I really am grateful for the trouble you've taken . . .'

'My pleasure, Stacey. I'll be thinking of you on Monday.'

I left feeling out of sorts. On my way out of the sixth-form block I picked up the free newspaper I had looked at earlier. I glanced over the article *My Brother Made Me Rob*. Then I tucked it in my bag and headed to the supermarket for my shift.

Four

It was busy at Budgens. I started at five and faced a wave of weary commuters dropping in to buy last-minute groceries. When that died down there were people on their way somewhere, dressed up for Friday night out, buying wine, beers, crisps and confectionery. Later I spent a lot of time wheeling the cages in and out of the storage area and restacking shelves.

While I did it I thought about the article I'd read in the *Metro*.

It was about Jeremy and Heather Morton, a brother and sister, who lived in Cornwall and had befriended an elderly lady who lived next door to them. They were accused of stealing thousands of pounds from the old lady, Mrs Joan Rider. It happened over some years. The brother admitted he was guilty but the sister was pleading not guilty and had said that her brother *made* her steal the money from the pensioner. The case was still going on. The article was short and gave no more details. I knew that the report had caught my attention because of the headline *My Brother Made Me* . . . The words stayed in my mind as I worked.

At eight I had a break. My friend Dan was already in the tiny staffroom, sitting down, his legs splayed, a can of Coke on the floor. He was looking at his phone, scrolling through something rapidly.

'I've just stacked enough tins of soup to feed an army,' I said.

'Good for you, physical work. Keeps you fit.'

'You should try some.'

'Look at this . . .'

Dan held his phone out for me to see. On the screen was a GIF of his dog. Every week he had some new set of photos or footage of Woody, a black mixed-pedigree dog.

'I've just had him groomed,' he said.

I looked at the screen and saw a leggy black dog staring at me, its eyes dark and shiny, one ear cocked, the other out of sight.

'Great,' I said, pretending a yawn.

'Here's my sister with him.'

I sighed and looked again. There in the photo was a blonde girl kneeling beside the dog. They were outside somewhere and the girl's long hair was blowing across her face.

'Right,' I said, 'I think I've seen enough photos of Woody today.'

I took a plastic cup from the water dispenser and poured a drink. I sat down beside Dan and for a minute neither of us said anything. We'd both worked there since the previous Christmas and I was comfortable with him and didn't feel the need to talk. I pulled my phone out of my pocket and googled the names Jeremy and Heather Morton. Several links came up and I read over some of the articles. Heather Morton hadn't been physically threatened by her brother. She just said that she and her brother had always been very close and if he asked her to do something she usually did, she always had. She had been worried about taking Joan Rider's money, she'd felt terrible about it, but her brother had told her that he needed the money to pay back a loan.

As I was reading their story a message icon came up on the screen. It was a text from Patrice. She'd been off school that day so I'd not seen her. I opened it immediately.

Come round tomorrow at 11
for chat xxxx

I texted back.

See you then xxx

Dan stood up, picked up his can and tossed it into the bin. I'd been so engrossed I'd almost forgotten he was there.

'What's with the hair?' he said.

I touched my head, remembering the henna treatment.

'Felt like a change,' I said.

'It's OK.'

'Just OK?'

'It's all right.'

'King of compliments, you are.'

'I'm being honest. I liked it the way it was before.'

'OK, I'll let you off.'

'See you . . .'

The door closed behind him as my phone beeped with another text. I expected it to be from Patrice but when I looked

25

at the screen I was surprised to see the name *Bella* there. I frowned and opened the message.

**Would be good to see you. Coffee in
Costa's? Sunday morning?**

I read the words over and felt odd. I hadn't heard from Bella for months, as far back as January. My finger was poised to send a reply but I didn't. I sat there for the rest of my break and wondered why Bella wanted to see me again. She must have known somehow that the trial was coming up. Did she know it actually started on the following Monday? Or was her text just a coincidence? When my break was over I put my phone back in my pocket and went out.

The store was narrow but stretched back far enough to house a lot of products. I was lucky to have a job there. The pay was good and there were half a dozen other kids who turned up on my shifts from time to time so I got to know new people, like Dan, who went to an all-boys' school in Ilford. And there were a couple of chatty girls each called Sue from a school in Plaistow who were always asking me stuff about my life: boyfriends, school and clothes.

The supervisor, Mrs Bakhtar, asked me to sort out the shampoos, so I went into the storeroom, filled up a cage, wheeled it back out and spent a while stacking the bottles and tubes and tidying up the nearby mousses and lacquers. With just under an hour to go to the end of my shift I went on the till. Only a trickle of people came in.

I thought about Bella; hearing from her so soon after seeing

26

Harry was weird. I patted my pocket where my phone was and tried to work out why I hadn't immediately answered her text.

I had met Bella the previous June in the weeks after the rape. She had been Harry Connaught's girlfriend some weeks before I had met him and I'd gone looking for her to find out whether she had experienced the same thing that I had. I had clicked with her right away. She was small, like me, and young-looking. Right from the moment I met her I could tell she was in pain because of Harry and his brother. We'd talked about what had happened to both of us. I hadn't been sure whether to go to the police but she had been definite that she was going to keep her assault secret.

We kept in touch over the months. I met her for coffee at Liverpool Street a few times and after we'd talked through our anguish about what happened we began to talk about other things. She was just starting her A levels and had plans to go to university, but she also had singing lessons as well as belonging to a choir. She told me she wrote her own songs and had recorded a demo.

I liked her. She was creative and I admired that. I had thought, at one time, that I might be creative in a different way, but those ambitions had gone. After the first few meetings I stopped feeling sorry for Bella because I could see she was a strong person. I began to think that maybe she didn't need to get justice in the way that I did. She took me to her house once in Dalston and introduced me to her mum, who was a theatre nurse in a hospital at King's Cross. She baked a chocolate cake for my visit.

The last time I saw Bella was after Christmas. She'd been wearing a red velvet coat that came almost down to her ankles.

We talked about school. She was doing English literature and so was I and we argued about the set text, *Wuthering Heights*. She loved it but I did not. She talked about the romance of the doomed couple in the book but I hadn't been convinced by them and anyway I'd written a ton of essays on it and I was sick of it. I remember saying to her, *You're still a romantic, then?* She'd looked at me sadly and nodded. Even after she'd been raped she believed in love. *Don't you believe there's someone out there for you?* she'd said and I had shaken my head. *Maybe there is but I've got a lot of other stuff to do first. The trial, my exams, university, career.*

That was long before I decided to defer my university place for a year.

I'd texted her a few times after January and suggested we meet up again but somehow we never did. She replied to a couple saying she had a lot on and would get back to me. I had stuff going on myself with schoolwork and my personal policewoman, Annie, preparing me for the trial. Weeks passed and then it was a couple of months and I did think about contacting her but I left it. The thing we had that linked us probably wasn't a good enough basis for a long-term friendship.

Now I had this text from her wanting to meet up. I didn't know whether I wanted to go but then I thought, *Why not?* When my shift was over and I was getting ready to go home I sent her an answer.

**How about Sunday morning
at 11, Liverpool Street?**

Seconds later I got a reply. As if she'd been sitting waiting for my message.

See you in Costa at 11.

I replied with three smileys.

Five

I wanted to talk to Patrice about Harry. We were in her bedroom and there was music playing. She was standing on a chair singing along with the song while I was on my knees taking up a dress she'd bought. I had to tell her to stay still several times while pinning and measuring. She rotated slowly as I checked the length of the skirt to make sure it was even. I tried to fit some words together to explain what I wanted to say. I cleared my throat.

'Do you think . . .'

I couldn't quite get the sentence out. *Do you think that Harry Connaught's brother put pressure on him to do what he did?*

'What?'

'Nothing.'

'Can you do this dress now? You can use Mum's machine,' she said.

'You wearing it tonight?'

'Yep. Sure you won't come?'

I shook my head.

I wondered what she would say if I just blurted the words out; *Harry Connaught's brother had an emotional hold on him.*

31

Do you think he made him find a girl? I had good reason for thinking this. I'd remembered the things Harry had told me about his brother. He had a strong bond with him. Marty had got him out of several scrapes and helped him with advice and money. I'd thought, when listening to him, that Harry had loved and admired his brother. Was that enough for his brother to put pressure on him? To ask him to do unpalatable things?

Patrice was staring at me.

'Duh?' she said. 'You're not even listening!'

'Sorry.'

I tried to look attentive.

'The party's not starting until ten or eleven. You could dash here straight from your shift. We'll be getting ready, having a few drinks and maybe pizza. I could do your hair.'

'I'd be too tired.'

I glanced up at her and I could see her lips were pursed in a comic way. She knew I was lying about why I didn't want to go but she wasn't going to say it. I knew she knew but I went along with it. It was a kind of game we'd played for some months now.

'Whose house is it in?' I said.

'You know Shelly's mate, Roxanne?'

I stood up, rubbing at a tingling sensation in my knees. Patrice got down off the chair and unzipped the dress, letting it drop to the floor. She stepped out of it, picked up her jeans from the bed and climbed into them. Pulling on a shirt, she sat down at her dressing table and tidied her hair back off her face.

'Her mum's away for the weekend but she knows about the party. Roxanne's gran and granddad will be there on duty but they'll be in another room.'

'Sounds good. But you know I'm not keen on –'

'You have to start going out again some time.'

'I will.'

'When?'

'Soon.'

'After the trial?'

'Maybe. I'll be a few minutes sewing this.'

I could feel Patrice's eyes on my back as I left.

I went into the spare room, which her mum had turned into a work space. The sewing machine was on a table in front of the window. I checked the spool and the bobbin and then lined up the hem of the skirt. I threaded the hem under the foot of the needle as Patrice's mum had shown me and rested my toes on the pedal. Then I began to sew.

I thought about our stilted conversation.

Patrice was desperate for me to be part of the gang again. I had been for a while after the rape. I enjoyed meeting up at her house to get ready. At first it was just her and me, but then other girls joined, Shelly and Roxanne. The four us would chat and try on clothes (Patrice had masses of stuff in her wardrobe and was always willing to loan any garment out). We'd do our nails and each other's hair and drink freezing-cold white wine. Eventually, between nine and ten, we'd leave her house and head for the pub or a club or someone's house where there was going to be a party.

That's when I stopped enjoying it. As soon as we got wherever it was we were going, I found myself shrinking back into a corner. I'd never been an extrovert, never someone who wanted everyone's attention, but in those days, after the rape, I found myself slinking along the walls, finding a seat behind a table, making excuses when I headed off home early. After a while I stopped going and Patrice and the others went on their own. I hung around with them during the day and sometimes at weekends, but in the evening I wanted to be at home.

The hem was finished so I stepped over to the ironing board and switched on the iron. As I lay the dress across the surface I thought about what to say to Patrice. *Do you think Harry may have been pressured into helping his brother?* I picked up the iron, pressed it onto the fabric right at the edge, making sure the hot metal didn't imprint on the stitching. As I was doing it I could hear Patrice coming along the landing talking to someone on her mobile. She was saying '*NO . . . Nooo . . . Never . . .*' Then she finished her call.

'You know that kid, Donny, friend of Roxanne's sister?'

'Yes.'

'He told Jessie – you know that girl who lives near Roxanne, the one with the dragon tattoo on her forearm? He told Jessie that he thinks I have a passion for him. What a cheek!'

Patrice picked up the dress from the ironing board.

'I mean, a *passion*! Who uses words like that? Donny Martin or something, his name is. Lower sixth. What a nerve! As if I would be interested in someone like him!'

She flounced back off to her bedroom and I unplugged the iron, tidied things up and followed her. When I got there she was standing in front of the mirror pulling the dress over her head and looking at her reflection.

'It looks good,' I said.

'It does,' she said, with a crooked smile. 'But maybe I'll wear my black sparkly jeans and a jumper.'

'Oh.'

'I'll wear it another day,' she said. 'Or one of the others might. Roxanne will. She said she liked it when I showed it to her.'

I was looking down at the fabric, pulling the threads away from the edge, and I felt my throat tighten up. I was never going to be able to ask her about Harry. Then I realised that she was looking at me. I heard her swear under her breath.

'Oh, Stacey. I'm going on and on about this frivolous stuff and you've got much more important things on your mind.'

I shook my head.

'No, it's fine . . .'

'But we could talk about it . . . If you want . . . In the past you've always been so keen *not* to talk about stuff, so I just prattle on . . .'

'I like talking about normal stuff and I think Donny Martin does like you. I heard him talking about it in the common room last week.'

She gave a sneer.

'Donny Martin is . . . No, no, I'm not going to talk any more. I'm shutting up. You talk to me.'

'There *was* something I wanted to ask you,' I said, forcing the words out.

'Right. About the trial. Right. What? Ask away. I'm all ears.'

She pulled a chair over and sat right in front of me. Our knees were almost touching. I'd have laughed at her but I didn't want to lose the moment. I ploughed on.

'It's not really about the trial but it is related.'

Patrice nodded. She was looking at me in an expectant way, her lips tightly shut. I knew she was trying to give me the space to speak.

'Do you think Marty Connaught made Harry do things for him? I don't mean by threatening him but because he knew Harry looked up to him?'

Her eyes seemed to glitter when I mentioned Harry's name as if some tiny alarm had gone off inside her. She still didn't speak. She let a silence settle. I went on.

'It's just that I was thinking that maybe he wasn't all bad. Maybe his brother *made* him do what he did.'

I looked at her. I could see by the hardness round her mouth that her answer wasn't going to be what I wanted to hear. She seemed to take a breath before she spoke.

'He was a total scumbag. He was the worst kind. He manipulated you and put you in a position that you couldn't get out of.'

'I know, I know . . .' I quickly said. 'But what if he was under his brother's control? If, over the years, Marty had worn him down so that he didn't know whether he was doing right or wrong?'

'Of course he knew. *Oh, Harry, can you bring some nice young girl to the apartment so that I can shag her whether she wants to or not!*'

'I don't know . . .'

'Why are you asking this?' she said with a hint of exasperation in her voice.

'I was just thinking about it, that's all. Just wondering . . .'

36

'That's the worst thing about you! You always want to see good in others. Course that's the *best* thing about you as well.'

'People can change.'

'No. Some people are just *bad*. Harry Connaught picked you up off the street and pretended to like you for two days so that his brother could come along and rape you. He's a bad person and no amount of excuses can change that. The only worse person that I can see is his foul brother, Marty.'

I didn't know what to say, how to answer her. She was right but she was wrong at the same time. Harry hadn't pretended to like me. He *had* liked me.

'No, Stacey, don't give him any sympathy. Harry Connaught is as bad as his brother. Pity he's not in the dock as well.'

I didn't say any more. I let it drop and made myself busy. I picked up the dress that I'd just shortened and put it on a hanger. Then Patrice made me sit down so that she could do my hair. She played some music and turned it up loud and sang along with it. She was trying to look happy, unconcerned, but I could sense a tension in her. She pulled the brush through my hair a little sharply and then using a tail comb parted it with geometric precision, moving strands of hair to one side or the other. I knew she was still riled by the things I'd said. I waited until the chorus came and I sang along with her.

Later, just before I was due to leave, we talked about the trial.

'So Monday's the big day.'

'Yeah. Are you still OK about coming?'

'Course I am!' she said loudly.

As Patrice was the first person I told about the rape she was to be a witness for the prosecution. Her version of what I said would back up my story. Annie Mulligan told me she was called the 'first complainant'. Patrice had rubbed her hands together when she heard that title.

'You don't feel you've been dragged into this?'

'Bring it on! I'll just tell the truth, that's what I'm going to do. Remember I believe in the concept of justice. It's what I want to do with my life. *Patrice Randall, Barrister-at-Law*.'

'Is your mum going with you?'

'Yes. We've been told to get there about eleven. Who's going with you?'

'Mum and Dad.'

We sat quietly for a moment.

'You are going to be all right, Stacey?'

'Course I am.'

'I'll be there on Monday to hold your hand.'

'I know.'

How could I not be all right with a friend like Patrice?

Six

I got to Costa a couple of minutes before eleven and bought myself a coffee. I sat at one of the tables near the window and watched out for Bella. The coffee shop was busy, most of the seats full, so I put my jacket across the back of the next chair. Outside the concourse seemed quiet, the weekday commuters at home with their families.

I looked at my phone. It had just gone ten past eleven and I'd been in this situation before. Bella wasn't the most punctual person. The last time we had met there, in January, she'd come rushing in apologising for being late. I remembered that she had rosy cheeks from running and her hair seemed frizzy with electricity. While she was queuing for a drink I noticed her red velvet coat, and seeing me looking at her she spun round to show it off as if she was a model. She carried a hot chocolate back to the table and sat down opposite me. She had lots to say. We'd chatted for about an hour. I'd told her about the job I'd started in Budgens and she said that she'd stopped volunteering in Oxfam at Shoreditch and now worked at weekends in an artisan bakery next to Hoxton Station. *I make some of the bread!* she'd said delightedly.

She asked me when the trial was and I told her I wasn't sure.

We had walked away from the cafe, and before she headed for her bus she gave me a hug. We hardly knew each other really but that hug was all about what had brought us together. We'd both fallen under Harry's spell. Before the rape she had known him for some weeks but I had only known him for two days. Even though we both felt we'd been naive and silly to trust so easily I always felt that it was me who had been the most foolish.

Maybe that's why I made the journey to Kensington to see him. Perhaps I wanted to see that old swagger of his, the confident trickster who had made an idiot out of me. Instead, whatever Patrice said, I'd seen someone different.

I was beginning to think Bella wasn't going to turn up. I tidied my bag out to pass the time, picking old receipts out and finding pound coins in the bottom. At eleven twenty someone asked if they could have the chair I was saving so I lifted my coat off and placed it on my lap. I got my phone out and looked at Bella's message just to check that I had the right time and place.

See you in Costa at 11

I found myself tapping lightly on the table, getting slightly annoyed. I tried to push it down because I did like Bella. I scrolled back through my messages since January.

You fancy meeting up?

How about a coffee in Costa?

Are you OK? Haven't seen you for a while.

**Long time since we had a chat. How about
a quick coffee?**

There were a couple more but I didn't bother to read them. I realised that it had been me who was doing all the asking. She replied to most of them briefly, saying she was busy working or at choir. She never once texted me to ask to meet up. I hadn't registered that; I'd always thought of our communications as a two-way street. It had been but since January it had dwindled and yet, out of the blue, she had texted me to meet there.

And here I was and there was no sign of her running across the concourse to see me. At twenty-five to twelve I got up and decided to go home. I left Costa Coffee and headed for the Tube but then changed my mind. I decided to walk out of Liverpool Street Station towards Spitalfields Market. I liked the stalls there. Many of them had vintage fashions and some were run by people who designed and made their own clothes. It was something I once thought I might do but I'd let it drop. Being a fashion designer had been a pathetic dream and I remembered my sketchbooks: page after page of fashion designs which I'd thrown away months before. I still like clothes though, and decided that a browse among the stalls would take my mind off being stood up by Bella and the fact that I had the trial hanging over me for the next few days.

But the oddest thing happened.

I walked away from the cafe, leaving the station behind, and while I was waiting to cross at some traffic lights I saw Bella on the opposite side of the road. It took a few moments to be sure. She had her back to me but I knew it was her because of her red velvet coat. It stood out among the puffa jackets, parkas and denims. She was standing in front of a shop window. At first I thought she was looking in but when she turned slightly I could see she was doing something with her phone. My first reaction was delight. She hadn't let me down but as usual had let the time get away from her. Possibly she had come via the market and had been distracted by the stalls.

I had to wait for the lights to change before I could cross and I watched her jabbing at her phone. Then I got a beep from my own phone. I pulled it out of my pocket and saw *Bella*. I opened the message immediately.

**Sorry I can't get there. I'm staying with Mum
because she's sick. Hope all goes well with
the trial xxxx**

The lights changed and I could have crossed but I stepped backwards, dismayed at the blatant lie in the message. Bella turned away from the shop then, and for a moment she looked in my direction. I tensed up because I didn't want her to see me there, reading her text. Her eyes drifted across me without any recognition though, and then she turned and walked away towards the market and I stood there, mystified. She had come to meet me and then changed her mind.

'Excuse me,' a woman said, bumping into me.

42

'I'm sorry,' I said, turning awkwardly around as if I didn't know where I was or what I was doing.

I looked down at the ground as I made my way back to the Tube. My feet kept going, one footstep after another, but I felt as if the rest of me was dragging behind. When I got my train I sat down, my shoulders hunched, and stared at the screen of my phone even though there was nothing on it.

Bella wasn't even a close friend, but to arrange to meet and then lie about why she couldn't come seemed like a slap in the face. It felt like a rejection.

Seven

When I got back to my street I saw a familiar car parked near my house. It was a dark blue VW and it belonged to my personal policewoman, Annie Mulligan. She was standing alongside it, talking into her mobile phone. She turned as I came along and I saw her do a double take and point at her hair. I knew she was referring to the henna treatment I had had. I had forgotten that my hair was red but people were still noticing it.

Annie finished her phone call.

Her real job title was S.O.I.T. Officer (Sexual Offences Investigation Trained Officer) which sounded very formal; she was anything but that. Today she was wearing jeans and a jumper and I could see she had her usual long earrings dangling. The front of her hair was a light pink. I'd last seen her a couple of weeks before and I was sure it had been blue then. She often fished out a small spray can from her bag and showed me whatever colour it was she'd used. Since I'd formally gone to the police she'd been to see me every few weeks to make sure everything was OK and often she'd toss me a tiny a bag of Haribo sweets as she left.

I liked her. She was quite different from anyone else I had ever met.

'Hi,' I said, walking up to her car.

She slid her phone into the pocket of her coat and stood facing me. She raised her hand and touched the edge of my hair.

'Nice colour. Not as good as mine but . . . Fancy a drive?'

'Sure.'

I got into her car. I wasn't feeling anxious or even curious. Her visits often started and ended in a drive. It was a way she could talk to me out of earshot of my mum and sister and generally away from my home. Those drives seemed to push away the fact that she was a policewoman and I was an abused girl. Today, as soon as we set off, she turned the music up loud. I moved my feet around in the well of the seat, dislodging empty water bottles and a spare pair of shoes. She didn't say anything much as we drove along but I recognised the route and saw that we were heading for Victoria Park. I looked out of the window and watched the grey streets go by and thought fleetingly of Bella and how she'd lit up the street in her red velvet coat while she was lying so casually to me.

We found a parking place near Victoria Park and we got out of the car and started to walk along the path that led towards the children's playground. It was a walk we'd done several times before. In the early days, when the hurt of the rape was still raw, we often went and sat near to the swings and climbing frames and watched the parents and children. While we talked, there was lots going on. Small children were swinging and sliding around; joyful one minute, upset and crying the next. There was plenty to look at as we trawled over the details of my rape.

This time we took a turn away from the playground and walked towards the pond. Annie got straight to the point. She never bothered much with small talk.

'Trial, Monday. You all set?'

'Yes.'

'So you arrive with Mum and Dad and go straight to the witness rooms. There you'll meet your barrister, Ms Gardner, who is absolutely brilliant and has prosecuted many of our cases. Mr Parvez will be there too. Ms Gardner will go through some of the proceedings with you and then you, as a witness, will have to stay in those rooms until you are called to the stand. Your parents will be able to go into the court if they wish, although they may want to stay with you.'

I knew all this; we'd been over it before.

'The examination by Ms Gardner will be hard. You remember that your barrister will take you through it detail by detail. She'll have to go into embarrassing stuff, yeah?'

'I know that.'

Annie had shown me transcripts of old cases where the barrister focused on every intimate detail.

'And if you think that's hard, you wait until you're cross-examined. Then it'll get ten times worse.'

'Right. I know that too.'

'Yeah.' Annie sighed. 'You think you know it but you don't really.'

'Are you trying to cheer me up? I thought this was meant to be a last-minute pep talk.'

'It is. I just want you to be on your guard. I'm not going to lie to you, Stacey. These people, like Martin Connaught, they will stoop to low levels to persuade the jury to believe them.'

I'm not going to lie to you. It was one of the first things Annie said to me when we met at the Rape Crisis Centre. I'd been sitting in an interview room that looked like an IKEA stand. The sofa was soft and I found myself hugging a cushion while looking at the pictures of skyscrapers on the wall. Annie came in and sat on the corner of the coffee table in front of me. I was startled by her forwardness but I was also confused by the way she looked. I'd been expecting a policewoman and I'd got some sort of hippy.

'I'm not going to lie to you, Stacey, this will be one of the hardest things you'll ever do. I'll help you as much as I can.'

She paused to let me speak but I had nothing to say.

'This man who raped you must go to prison. Not just because it stops him raping other girls but because it sets out a deterrent to other men who might think it's OK to have anyone they want. And I'll tell you this, I'll say – no, I *guarantee* – that he's done it before more than once. Let's face it – you, in the apartment at Poole Place – him turning up at the right moment. That was no accident. It sounds to me like a well-oiled plan.'

I thought of Bella. How right Annie was even though she didn't know it. I had trusted her straight away. Over the following months she talked it through with me. I couldn't have done it without her. There were times in those months when I got cold feet and considered dropping the case but she always turned up somewhere in her car with her brightly coloured fringe and talked things through.

That first day, in the Rape Crisis Centre, she pulled out a packet of sweets and gave it to me. Initially I felt embarrassed as if she thought I was a child but then she got a similar bag out for herself, tore it open and began to pop one jellied sweet into her mouth after another.

Now we were at the pond. Annie went right to the edge and stood staring at some ducks. It looked as though she might be about to arrest them.

'I've got something I need to tell you,' she said, sounding downbeat.

'What?'

I was instantly anxious. The tone of voice was all wrong *for her*.

'Let's sit down.'

We sat side by side. The bench was slightly damp and I put my hands under my thighs. I stared at the wildfowl on the water as she spoke.

'There might be more press interest in the case than we first thought.'

'Why?' I said.

'Ok, so you know that rape cases go largely unreported. I mean, they might make the local paper or something but they only hit the national press if the defendant is well known in some way or perhaps in a job where they could be a danger: teacher or social worker, doctor or police officer. So a rape case involving a footballer or a pop star would be on the front page of every newspaper. But this Martin Connaught is a stockbroker, no big deal. We expected the case to have some interest because of the unusual circumstances; two brothers and one girl. I told you that, yeah? At the beginning, when we first met?'

I nodded.

'Now something's come up that we haven't expected. The apartment you went to. Poole Place? Martin Connaught said he was looking after it for a fellow stockbroker.'

'Yes.'

'The stockbroker was called Richard John Mason,' Annie said, 'and he had a six-month stint in Singapore. On return he was interviewed and he agreed that he'd asked Martin Connaught to look after it and said he also knew that Connaught might use it for what he called his "lady friends".'

'OK.'

'The problem is – and we didn't know this until a civil servant got in touch – this Richard John Mason is the stepson of a junior government minister. His name is Michael Fitzwilliam and it's a recent appointment, last couple of months. He's in the Treasury somewhere. No one's ever heard of him really but when this trial starts the papers might make something of the connection. Picture the headline: *Minister's Son's Apartment Used for Rape*. Of course it's nonsense, the guy has nothing to do with what happened to you, but the press will hone in on your story because someone in the government is loosely attached to it.'

'But they won't be able to name me?' I said, suddenly fearful.

'No, no, course not. That's against the law. I've told you before, you are *Girl X*. But as well as the papers and TV the story will spread on social media which, as you know, can be a cruel place.'

'Maybe they won't be interested? I mean, if the stepson has had nothing whatsoever to do with it.'

'These headlines sell papers. *Government Minister's Stepson*. People love to hear about politicians with skeletons in their closet. It could be bad.'

I waited for some follow-up, some reassurance, but Annie pulled out her phone and looked at it, using her finger to casually flick from one page to the next. It wasn't like her to be so quiet. Eventually, after what seemed like a long time, she spoke. There was a hint of anger in her voice.

'No one in the courtroom will give two hoots for any of that. In court it will be you telling your story, yeah? And this man telling his. It will be about truth and justice. I believe that, Stacey. Otherwise I wouldn't do this job.'

'I know,' I said. 'I believe you. I'll be OK.'

The court case was like a train coming towards me. I was to get on it, go on a journey, make things right. Why did it feel as though I was on the rails in front of it, standing waiting for it to knock me down?

Eight

My mum and I got out of a minicab at Snaresbrook Crown Court. My dad was due to meet us there. As the cab pulled away we stood under an awning alongside a couple of people who were smoking. There was a stiff breeze making me feel cold.

The court building was like an old country house in the middle of substantial gardens. Annie had told me that the building had originally been erected in Victorian times as an orphanage surrounded by greenery. Now it was a place of law and the dormitories and dining halls had been changed into courtrooms. There was a long driveway that led back to the road and the local shopping area. I kept my eye on it for a glimpse of Dad.

I'd worn my school skirt and jacket over a white shirt. I was presenting myself as someone sensible, someone whose experience had taught them to take care. My mum was wearing a mac over some dark trousers and a top. Her hair was pulled back into a tie at the base of her neck. Around her neck was a decorative chain that held a pair of glasses that she'd recently been prescribed. *I'll probably be doing loads of reading or making notes*, she'd said to me that morning. The glasses hung there, ready for any emergency. My mum had made sure she was well armed for the trial ahead.

I could see my dad turn into the gates of the court grounds. He was waving and I waved back. He was wearing a suit and carrying a small rucksack.

'Here's your dad,' my mum said, needlessly.

There was a moment of awkwardness when he reached us. He leaned across to give me a kiss but stepped back away from my mum. Then my mum broke the ice by asking him how Gemma was and they both walked ahead of me talking about the coming baby. We went through the security gates and then on to reception. We were told to go to the Witness Waiting Area on the first floor. Once inside we sat down away from three other groups of people, all dressed formally, all looking nervous, huddled together, talking quietly to each other. In the far corner was a television showing a news channel. There was no sound coming from it and no one seemed to be looking at it.

'Our barrister will come and get us when she's ready,' I said, remembering what Annie had told me about the procedure, 'and Mr Parvez will be here as well.'

Mr Parvez was my solicitor. He worked for the Crown Prosecution Service and it was his job to provide the barrister with the information she needed in order to present the case to court. He was young, in his twenties, and was always taking swigs of water from a bottle he kept in his briefcase. I thought he seemed very serious. Annie said he was really good and I took her word for it.

Dad walked across the room to the window. I followed him and we were overlooking a large car park at the side of the building.

'You all ready for this?' he said, quietly.

'I think so.'

He put his arm around my shoulder and gave me a hug.

'How's Gemma? Has she stopped being sick?'

He took a great breath like a sigh and then smiled. 'Not really.'

'She'll get through it,' I said.

'Yeah. But we've got this to worry about now. The baby is still months away.'

Some voices were raised from one of the other groups; a young man and two older women were arguing, one of the women putting her hand on the other woman's arm as if to shush her. The young man stood up abruptly and walked away towards another seat, his face like thunder. He sat down with his back to the women.

We sat down again. Dad was on the end seat and I was in the middle beside Mum. There was no conversation between them. The few words spoken about the new baby was all they could manage. Dad pulled a wad of papers out of his bag and began to read them. I saw that it was some of the court papers we'd been sent weeks before. Sections of text shone out from under a neon pink highlighter. The bundle looked creased and well thumbed. I imagined my dad poring over the words.

My mum took my hand and held it.

She needed the physical contact. During the past few weeks she'd been very tactile with me; hugging me for no reason, kissing me on the cheek, grabbing my fingers to make a point about something. Usually she was like that with Jodie and, of course, Tyler. The lead-up to the trial was hard for her because she had found it difficult to talk to me *at all* about what happened. My dad was much more vocal, wanting to go over and over the two days, trying to find a point when I could perhaps have avoided the assault. He was analysing it as if it was a road traffic accident that could have been prevented; if only I had looked right before turning I could have avoided the collision. My mum couldn't work anything out; she just wanted to make it better.

I grabbed Dad's hand and pulled it away from his papers.

'It'll be all right,' I said.

'We're here for you, Stace,' my mum said.

'One hundred per cent, solid,' my dad said.

I nodded, silently. I knew they were on my side – they always had been; right from the day when I first told them both what happened.

Some days after I went to the Rape Crisis Centre I had asked my dad to come over one evening when Tyler had gone to bed. I knew my sister was going to be out at a friend's so I could speak to Mum and Dad alone. I had been nervous, afraid of what they would think of me. I got changed a couple of times as if clothes might make a difference. When I heard the front doorbell I stood on the landing for a few moments and watched my mum walk along the hallway with a tea towel in her hand. When she opened the door she was surprised.

'Joe! What are you doing here?'

'Stacey asked me round. She said she wanted to talk to me and you about something.'

'Really? She didn't say anything to me. At least I don't think she did . . .'

'Hi!' I called from upstairs.

I walked down quickly, ignoring my mum's quizzical look, her eyebrows raised from behind my dad's back.

'You want a cup of tea?' Mum said.

'No, I'm actually on my way out. I'm meeting Gemma at the cinema at eight.'

I shooed them both into the living room. My dad sat on one end of the sofa and my mum on the other. I was on the armchair by the fire where Jodie usually sat. I edged out a packet of baby wipes that had got stuck down the side of the cushion and put them on the mantelpiece.

'What's up, Stacey? Is this about uni?' my dad said, all businesslike.

My mum was looking puzzled, then a frown came onto her face.

'Oh my God, you're going to tell us you're pregnant.'

'Mum, no . . .'

'You're pregnant. Like Jodie was. You've got yourself pregnant!'

'No, Mum, I'm not. I'm not. I took a pregnancy test this morning. I'm not pregnant.'

They both looked straight at me. My dad sat forward with a frown on his face.

'You *thought* you were pregnant? When we had that talk last week I asked you then if you were and you said . . .'

'She talked to you last week?' my mum said.

'She did. What's wrong with that?'

'You talked to your dad before you talked to me?'

My dad was stiffening, shifting his shoulders about.

'I'm her *mum*. I'm here with her all the time. She can talk to me about anything.'

'Look,' I said, trying to get a word into the conversation.

But my dad was annoyed and was facing my mum, his finger in the air. 'You're so worn down by Jodie and the baby, Stacey never gets any notice. That's why she comes to me!'

'She *can* talk to me . . .'

'Mum, Dad . . . Listen, I'm not pregnant. Can you just let me speak?'

They both looked warily at me. My dad was leaning on the arm of the sofa, his shoulder turned away from my mum. My mum was staring down at the carpet. It was like looking at a broken picture. My throat felt lumpy.

'What is it?' my mum said. 'Are you involved with some boy? Some man?'

'Stacey, what's going on?' my dad said.

He was going to see a film with Gemma. He didn't have time for all this stuff.

I took a deep breath. 'I was raped.'

My dad's face tightened. My mum looked horrified. I kept talking.

'Two weeks ago I was raped by a man in an apartment.'

My dad stared at me. My mum sat back on the seat, her shoulders dropping. I had their attention. I carried on, forcing my words out, keen to get it all said before either of them started talking again.

'I met this boy called Harry. It was just after the night I stayed at your place, Dad, when you and Gemma were in Corfu. I was a bit down and I got drawn along with him. Anyway, his

58

brother looked after this apartment for a friend and he said I could stay there the night, so I did and all the time I was attracted to this boy. This boy called Harry.'

I stopped for a moment and let the words settle. This was the lynchpin of it all. I'd been charmed, unable to stop myself. My chest ached at the memory.

'So I stayed the night . . .'

My dad had his hand over his mouth but his eyes were steely. My mum was holding a scatter cushion in front of her. Neither of them spoke or tried to interrupt me. I knew I had to go on, tell them the whole story.

'. . . And the next day, as I was getting ready to come home, I started to get closer to this boy, to Harry. We were in the bedroom and I have to say that I wanted to . . .'

It was hard to tell the absolute truth but it would come out later. My dad's eyebrows seemed to knit together and my mum was picking bits from the corner of the cushion. I looked at the carpet. There was a red ball by the leg of the coffee table, one of Tyler's toys, and I focused on it until my eyes blurred.

'I wanted to have sex with him and I got undressed and we started messing about on the bed when the door opened . . . the bedroom door opened and his brother stood there.'

'Brother?' my mum said, almost whispering.

'He came across to the bed and Harry sort of got out of the way and this man, his name was Marty, he raped me.'

'A man?'

'Yes.'

'How old?' my dad said.

'I don't know, maybe thirty, early thirties . . .'

'He forced you?'

'Yes.'

'Did he hurt you?' my mum said, taking a great sniff, wiping her nose on her sleeve, tears in her eyes.

'No. He didn't physically hurt me. At least, it did hurt . . . But there were no bruises. He didn't *hit* me, if that's what you mean.'

'Was this the man who came round here? To the house, last Sunday?'

I nodded.

My dad's eyes were dark, flicking from side to side. I tried hard to make him look at me, wanting him to say something. To say it was all right; to say it *would* be all right, but he stood up suddenly and I could see his fists were clenched. He was wound up, ready to go off.

'What's his name? Where does he live?' he said sharply.

'I've reported him to the police. He's been charged. You can't go near him.'

He took a deep breath, then swore over and over. He walked to the far wall and then back again.

'He'll go to prison,' I said, my voice falling to a whisper.

My dad sat back down with a thump. My mum put her arm out towards me. I stepped around the coffee table and sat beside her.

'I'm sorry,' I said.

'You have nothing to be sorry about.'

'I was an idiot. I put myself in a dangerous position. I know that now. I was a fool.'

My mum put her arm round my neck and I rested my head on her shoulder.

'That bastard came round here. To the house. You were rude to him and I told you off. I wish I'd known. I wish I'd known.'

I reached out to my dad. I wanted to feel his big warm hand grasping mine, like he did when he went to help rescue someone from a smashed-up car. He didn't take it though. I thought he was angry with me, ashamed of me. He didn't like his little girl any more. I lifted my head up and looked at him, expecting to see disapproval or anger. All I saw were his shoulders shaking as he cried silently into his hands.

'Oh, Dad,' I said. 'Oh, Dad, I'm sorry.'

He shook his head and put his hand out and grabbed my arm.

'No, it's my job to protect *you*. I'm the one who should be sorry.'

Nine months later we'd all stopped crying. My mum, dad and me sat together in the Witness Waiting Area ready for what was to come. After what seemed like a long while the door opened and I saw Annie Mulligan standing next to a figure in a white wig and a long black gown. It was Ms Gardner, my barrister. By the side of her was Mr Parvez. We were to have our pre-trial meeting and then the case would start.

'Right,' my dad said, standing up, gathering his papers together.

My mum brushed herself down and kept her glasses on her nose, ready for any emergency reading she had to do. I stood up and walked towards them, steeling myself for what was to come.

Nine

Our barrister led us along a wide corridor. Her gown flowed out behind her and her heels clacked along the floor. Annie and Mr Parvez were just behind her. We were shown into a small room with a table and half a dozen chairs around it. The chairs were splayed out as though someone else had already sat in them. It was hot, the window was shut and there was a lingering smell of air freshener. Ms Gardner swept in first, laying a laptop on the table and placing a briefcase on a chair. She indicated to us that we should sit. Annie and Mr Parvez stood by the wall. Ms Gardner stayed standing while she spoke.

She was older than I'd first thought. Underneath the black gown and white wig she was thin, her cheekbones showing through, her hands bony, the veins in clumps. She had bright blue eyes, though, and a no-nonsense way of talking. I felt her strength as she spoke and she got straight to the point.

'Now, Mr Woods and Miss . . . Rawlings?' she said.

My dad nodded, smoothing out the batch of documents he had been looking at. I hoped he hadn't written a list of questions to ask the barrister. My mum shifted around on her seat looking awkward. She'd only recently reverted to using her maiden name.

'The first thing to say is that there is a delay to the start of the case. This is unfortunate. Our judge has some last-minute business regarding another case that has overrun. There are some unforeseen complications that need to be dealt with. We hope to select the jury this morning but realistically the opening statements and first witnesses will not start until after lunch. It means a bit of waiting around, I'm afraid. I'm sorry for the inconvenience.'

I closed my eyes with irritation. I just wanted to get it over with. Now there was hours to go before it even started.

'Nonetheless, I wanted to talk to you all together to go through some basic things. In the next couple of days you will hear some very unpleasant testimony. You will hear your daughter tell her story, which will be upsetting enough, I should think.'

My mum was nodding, my dad absolutely still.

'But it will get worse, because Stacey will be cross-examined and then you will hear what amounts to the attempted slander of your daughter. Martin Connaught's defence barrister is Mrs Helen Barnaby, a very experienced woman who will not shirk from her role. She will try to paint Stacey as a "sexually experienced" young lady . . .'

Ms Gardner made exclamation marks in the air.

'Mrs Barnaby will say that Stacey agreed to what happened, that she wanted to have sex with this man. They will probably say that she initiated this situation and try to suggest that she is a liar and that she wishes to destroy an innocent man's life.'

My dad's eyes flicked from the barrister to me. I could see that he was annoyed. My mum looked as if she might burst into tears.

'You will be upset by this. You might feel enraged by it. But you must not, on any account, show your anger or make any outburst in court. You must not indicate any animosity towards the defendant. You must not stare at him or make any gestures towards him or any of his family. Any disturbance in court brought about by you or your ex-wife will garner sympathy for the defendant. You must sit quietly and not react. I know this will be hard but this is your way of supporting your daughter. Is that understood?'

'Yes,' my dad said, his voice flat.

'What we want is the jury to decide on what is said in court.'

'I get it,' my dad said.

'Good! Now, Stacey . . .'

She turned her blue eyes onto me.

'The evidence is the problem. There is none. This is a case where it's your word against the defendant's. So we're going to present the jury with a narrative,' she said. 'The first witness will be . . .'

Bending over her laptop, she scrolled down a page on the screen.

'Patrice Randall. This is your friend, I understand?'

I nodded.

'Her testimony will start about an hour after lunch. It will establish the fact that you told her you were raped on the day after the offence took place. She will be cross-examined by the defence barrister. I don't expect that to take very long. After that you will take the stand and I will draw you through the events of the afternoon of 24th June 2015. I expect that to take the rest of today and possibly some of tomorrow. Then Mrs Barnaby will question you. I expect that to take most of tomorrow and possibly some of the next day.'

'Two days?' I said, alarmed.

'Give or take. Your S.O.I.T. has gone through this with you? You know what to expect?'

She glanced over at Annie, who was nodding rapidly.

'The key point in this trial is that the jury must decide which of you is telling the truth. The brother will give witness on behalf of Marty Connaught but their relationship makes this evidence a little unsafe. A brother will always support his brother. Furthermore, this young man had left the room before the actual crime had taken place. So although he is a witness to what led up to this situation he cannot say he was there at the moment of penetration.'

I gave a silent gasp at this.

Penetration.

It was such an ugly word. A forcing in; a breaking through; an incursion; a violent thrust. I had a memory then like a whisper in my ear: *Come on, Stacey, it's not like you're a virgin.* Was it Harry who had said that?

Ms Gardner looked sympathetically at me.

'My dear,' she said, 'rape is penetration. A man forces his penis into a woman, or, in this instance, a girl. The case depends on this. You have said clearly that this happened and that is why we are here. What you must not forget is that *this was done against your will*. This is what we will be asking the jury

66

to believe. Mrs Barnaby will be asking them to believe the opposite. And remember, we have truth on our side and we will do everything we can to get justice.'

'I know,' I said.

'Good. Now I will leave you all, but Mr Parvez will perhaps spend some time with Mr Woods and Miss Rawlings. I will go and further prepare for our time in court.'

I went back to the Witness Waiting Room. It was only ten and there was hours to go before anything important started. I sat over by the window and Annie sat beside me. There were some new people in there, an elderly couple. They were sitting on the edge of their seats looking round the room in a bewildered way. I half smiled at them but they didn't seem to notice. Annie was looking towards the television. Her eyes were narrowed as if she was trying to work out the words scrolling across the bottom of the screen.

'Did Ms Gardner have to be so blunt? In front of my mum and dad?' I said.

'You have to be ready for this kind of talk. So do your parents.'

'What about the newspapers? Is this the kind of stuff that will be written about?'

'Maybe. But your name won't be there.'

I would be *Girl X*.

'Where are the reporters?'

'There'll be a couple of local freelancers wandering the courts for something juicy. I'm sure one of them will pick up on your case. Question is whether he or she does any research into it. Whether they focus on the Poole Place address. It might go by unnoticed and just be reported in the local press.'

'The free newspaper that's given out at the shopping centres? Not many people read that,' I said.

'But there's an online version. Stories get picked up, yeah? Syndicated to other areas. The nationals keep an eye on them. You never know what might catch their interest.'

'Oh.'

'And it might get leaked by the civil service. Someone who doesn't like the minister. We just won't know until it happens.'

'You're cheering me up.'

'Sorry. But we must be ready.'

It was a mantra. *We must be ready for anything they will throw at us.*

'Anyhow, I have to go now. It's a drag but you should stay around here. You are the centre of all this and we need to know where you are. There are loos just along the corridor.'

Annie stood up. She was wearing a dark green dress under a three-quarter black cardigan. She still had on long earrings but she looked more *respectable* than usual. I realised then that she hadn't got any colour on the front of her hair. It was brown and tidy.

'This is my court persona,' she said when she noticed me looking.

'Very convincing,' I said.

She put her hand in the pocket of the cardigan and pulled out a crinkly bag of sweets. She tossed them to me. They were squashy jellies in the shape of animals. As she walked away I tore them open and munched my way through them.

For a few moments I was calm. The time would pass and we would get started. Then it was Marty's Connaught's word against mine. I wondered who the jury would believe.

Ten

Over the next half-hour the waiting area emptied out. Only two of the young men were left behind. They were about the same age and not sitting too far apart but they studiously ignored each other, staring down at their mobile phones, casually flicking across the screens as if it was just any other day. One of them was wearing a suit but the other had on dark trousers and a zip-up jacket. The suited one looked up at me but without any expression. I felt odd, disconnected to them. We were all victims or witnesses of something but they seemed from a different world to me.

I got a text from Mum.

Talked with Mr Parvez, all is well. Dad needs to go to the bank. I'll go and get sandwiches for lunch. Will buy magazines. See you later xxx

Everyone had gone and I felt deserted. I wondered when Patrice would turn up. I took my phone out of my bag to check the time, then did it again two minutes later. When I replaced it I saw the purple notebook that Patrice had bought for me. I

71

pulled it out and opened it. I grabbed hold of my pen and sat for a few moments, the first page of the book open. I wanted to write something but I couldn't think what. The paper was creamy with faint lines. I pictured the date at the top and then the words – *Trial – Day One* – which would be followed by line after line of neat handwriting. I could start by saying there was a delay. I positioned the pen but found that I couldn't write a word, so I shut it and put it away.

What was going to happen? I felt jittery, my stomach gnawing at me as if I was hungry. I'd waited for this for almost nine months and here it was and I had no idea whether it was going to go well.

It was Marty Connaught's word against mine. Ms Gardner had said it in a light way, as if it was no problem, no contest. But I began to feel an invisible weight leaning against me. *His word against mine*; a line of capitals beside a few lower-case letters. He was grown up, in a respectable job. He was from a well-to-do family. He'd been educated at great expense and he spoke proper English. Would his *words* carry more weight than mine?

I began to feel upset and walked to the furthest corner of the room and sat down, crossing my legs so that I took up as little space as I could. Honestly, I didn't know what to do with myself. I felt as if I was in some kind of time freeze. I wanted the next few days to be over but I had to wait it out. Each minute seemed stretched out, the seconds slowing down like a train coming to a standstill between stations. I thought of school going on even though I wasn't there, kids in the common room chatting about their weekends and the teachers gathering their papers together, opening their laptops. Ms Harper would be getting ready for Monday morning assembly except she called it a *Sixth Form Targets Session*. Budgens would have been open for hours already and only the full-timers would be there. The two Sues would be at college and Dan would be with his mates, perhaps showing them his latest photos of Woody, his dog.

My sister, Jodie, was taking Tyler to the doctor's because he had been crying and rubbing his ear. Before I left she gave me a hug and told me to *Give Marty-the-rapist some grief*. She'd smelled of hair shampoo and her skin was creamy; for the first time in a while she looked her age, her youth shining through the weariness of being a mother. *Marty-the-rapist* was how she always referred to Marty Connaught.

She knew that it would be my word against his. Two swords parrying, steel clashing with steel; each player holding on for dear life. He would say that I had agreed to have sex with him and I would say he forced himself on me.

I must have made a sound because both of the young men looked up suddenly. Neither of them made eye contact though, so I dropped my gaze down to my hands. My fingers were twisting together.

I thought of Harry. What would he say when he was in the witness box?

He wouldn't testify about the moment of rape.

Those moments gave me a sense of shame. Harry and I had been together on the bed when his brother walked into the room. I had sat up, bewildered, embarrassed at being caught half-naked by a grown man. I had tried to cover myself up, to get off the bed and grab my clothes. But Harry had his leg

73

across mine and was kissing my face as his brother began to undress. The memory of it gave me a sickly feeling. I'd said, *No, Harry, I don't want this*, but he had drunk too much that day and smoked dope and his reply had been distant. *He's my brother, Stacey. He does everything for me.* As if that explained it; as if it was an obvious fact and I should have realised the deal the moment I fell for him. He had left me there and afterwards had acted as if it was what I had wanted. *I thought you were cool about it*, he'd said, days later, outside my school, where he'd come to see me. As if it had been a game of tennis doubles and Marty had stepped in and taken over Harry's service.

Had Harry done all this knowingly or had he been pressured by his brother? Was Harry innocent in *any* way or was I just trying to find excuses for him, still – now, on the morning of the trial? He had done the same thing with Bella. She'd been his girlfriend and he'd left her alone with his brother. Was it possible that Harry was so besotted by his brother that he didn't know right from wrong?

I bit my lip. I *so* wished I could believe this.

I felt weak all of a sudden. I wasn't up to the battle ahead. I stood. I couldn't just hang around there. I needed some air. I wanted to get out of the waiting room, away from the sullen boys in their smart clothes. I walked across to the door and pushed it open and felt the cool of the corridor hit my face. I stepped outside, remembering that Annie had told me to stay put. But it felt like I was in a prison, that I was locked up, that *I* had done something wrong.

I turned towards the staircase and paused to look over the banister. The ground-floor reception area was mostly empty.

Security staff members were searching the bags of two women, one of whom was remonstrating at the inconvenience. There was no sign of Annie or Mr Parvez. I pulled out my phone and saw that it was ten past eleven. I went down the stairs, slowly at first, then gathering speed. I slowed down when I got to the bottom, not wanting to look like someone who was trying to make an escape. I made myself walk in a measured way, passing by a couple of women who had just come through a swing door and who were talking to each other and laughing about some family party.

I swept past them and headed for the heavy doors. Then I was outside on the stone steps that led down to the drive. A couple of barristers were standing looking at the same folder, their black robes mingling together. I walked down to the driveway where I'd been waiting with my mum earlier. There were people standing outside in twos and threes, smoking. Nobody looked at me, no one took a bit of notice; they were all deep in conversation.

It felt better to be outside. I started to walk on the path that led round the back of the building. I passed a sign that said *Car Park A* with an arrow pointing to *Car Park B*. Most of the spaces were taken but there were a couple of cars driving up and down each lane, the drivers peering from side to side, looking for a space. Behind the car park I saw a newer building and people milling round outside it. There was a sign that said *Courts 7–15*. I put my head down and walked on and I began to relax. I counted the paces in my head; twelve, thirteen . . . twenty-two, twenty-three. In a few hours I would be on the stand. It wasn't going to be hard. All I had to do was tell the truth. I had to describe the events of an afternoon that I had thought about, pored over, analysed every day since. Then when today was over there was tomorrow to face. *One day at a time, yeah?* Annie had said. *And if you're worried by that, then one hour at a time.*

My phone beeped and I slid it out of my pocket. It was a text from Patrice.

Delay on the Tube but we'll be there soon. Mum and me are walking up to court now XXXX

I felt immediately revived. At least I would have some company now and Patrice wouldn't mind the waiting around. She would be blown away by being part of a real-life trial. I turned to walk back to the entrance of the main court building and my mood lifted. I went quickly and felt my shoulders squaring as if she'd given me a pep talk already. I remembered what she'd said about being on the stand. *Bring it on!* She had the guts and the intelligence to face him down.

I turned the corner of the building, looking down the long driveway to see if I could pick her and her mum out. After a few moments I could see them in the distance behind a group of women who appeared to be walking abreast with linked arms. I raised my hand to wave but mustn't have been watching where I was going because I bumped into a group of smokers.

'Sorry,' I said, and went to walk around them.

A man stared at me. At first I didn't register who it was.

'Hello, Stacey,' he said.

Marty Connaught.

I was shocked to see him. I'd thought he would be in a room somewhere, hunched over with worry. I had a vague notion that he might be handcuffed. But he was here, large as life, smoking a cigarette.

'Hardly recognised you with the red hair. Looking good though . . .'

He was wearing a dark suit and white open-neck shirt. His face looked shiny and clean and I saw that he had a pin on his lapel, like a daffodil; a charity pin, raising funds for some kind of cancer.

'At least say *hello*!'

'Why are you here?' I said.

'The case is not starting until later. Not meant to be out here, but just grabbing a last-minute smoke. Given me a chance to see you . . .'

I felt my face twist up and stepped back away from him, but he moved towards me. He had a cigarette in his fingers and he held his other hand out as if he might touch me. He didn't though, but the hand was there, in the air, in my space, and I edged further away.

'Sweet Stacey . . .' he said, his face breaking into a smile.

My mouth was frozen and my throat dry. The group behind him all had their backs to us and were talking loudly about something, a couple of them breaking into a laugh.

'Stacey . . .' he started, 'there was no need for all this . . .'

He waved his hand in the direction of the court building.

'Don't talk to me,' I said.

'You bumped into me,' he said.

'Marty!'

A woman's voice called from the car park. Marty looked over his shoulder and then turned back to me. His expression was flat. He inhaled his cigarette for what seemed like a long time, then tossed the butt sideways onto the grass.

'MARTY.'

The voice was louder and the woman was getting closer. I recognised her. It was Mary Potter, Marty's old girlfriend. She worked in Selfridges. Harry had introduced me to her and I'd spent half an hour in her office, where she'd told me some stuff about the fashion industry. She was half walking, half running towards him. They were *together*?

I started to back away but he put out his hand and his fingers brushed my arm.

'Stacey,' he whispered, 'you were so much better than *her*.'

I was stunned, sickened. Mary Potter was just a few metres away.

'Marty, I'm here now. Sorry I'm a bit late . . .' she called.

'You better get off, little Stacey. It won't look very good if anyone finds out that you came to talk to me.'

'I did not. You're the *last* person in the world I want to talk to,' I said, my voice cracking.

Mary Potter was behind Marty. He didn't turn round to greet her and she looked puzzled, glancing from him to me and back again. He had his eyes firmly on me as he pursed his lips together and blew a kiss. I flinched at it, as if it had been a sharp stone he had thrown at me. I walked away as quickly as I could, looking down at my feet, my cheeks hot with rage. When I got to the corner of the building I leaned on the bricks, my insides scrunched up. I wanted to look back but I stopped myself. *Sweet Stacey*, he'd said. The very words he'd used when he pushed himself inside me. I leaned forward, thinking that I was going to be sick. I put the flat of my hand across my mouth and steadied myself, swallowing back bile. What was I doing? Walking around the building allowing myself to come into contact with him? What would it look like if anyone knew? If anyone found out?

I walked quickly towards the entrance. I could see Patrice coming along, her mum a few steps behind. She smiled delightedly and ran over to me. Her face dropped when she got close.

'Are you OK?' she said.

I nodded.

'You're not. What's wrong?'

I pushed her towards the entrance. I wanted to get as far away from Marty as I could.

'Just some last-minute nerves,' I said.

'Hello, Stacey,' Patrice's mum said.

'Hi.'

Patrice flung one arm round my shoulder and we walked up the steps together.

'You're bound to be nervous. Let's go and nail that posh stockbroker, shall we?'

I nodded, my hands still trembling with the upset of seeing him.

Eleven

I started to give my evidence in the afternoon just before three. I was shown into the courtroom by a clerk who had picked me up from the waiting area. I stood at the back for a few moments while the barristers were talking. I glanced around and saw the jury sitting to the right of the judge. To the left were the public benches; Mum and Dad and Annie were sitting in a group. Then there was a gap and several other well-dressed people were sitting in two rows, and I guessed it would be Marty Connaught's family. In the rear bench was a blonde woman holding a tablet and I thought immediately that she might be a reporter. The door opened behind me and an older man came in wearing a long leather coat and carrying a briefcase. He went and sat on the end-of-row seat in the benches. Maybe another reporter, I thought, and felt a tickle of fear in my stomach.

There was a gentle murmur of quiet conversation, whispers and some louder voices. I stood in a recess by the door. The clerk told me that proceedings would get started any minute. I could see the rear of the dock from where I was. Marty was sitting on a chair. His back looked straight and stiff.

I wasn't upset about him any more. In the hours since coming face to face with him I'd hardened up and become angry. I'd spent a lot of time with Patrice and her mum. When my mum and dad returned we'd all eaten lunch together; balancing sandwich packets on our knees, holding plastic bottles of drink. When the case finally started and Patrice was called I was on my own again. I'd ignored the other people in the waiting room, the same boys as before and a couple of new groups. I hadn't told Patrice that I'd seen Marty. I'd pushed it down inside and when she left I let it come to the surface and thought over what he'd said to me, how his comments had veered between being dismissive and mocking. And at the same time, underpinning it all, was that suggestive leer. *You were so much better than her . . .*

Then the kiss.

I felt my lips tighten with distaste. Marty Connaught was not stricken with remorse or even sorry, it seemed. He was still making light of it. *It was just a bit of fun, Stacey . . .*

The clerk came up to me and touched my elbow, so I walked down the aisle towards the witness box. I was shown into it by a different clerk and I stood as straight and tall as I could. I looked round the court. From the door it had just seemed like a place of work for some people, a public space where people were allowed to come and watch the business of the court. It was no big deal. But now, on the stand, I had a whole different perspective. I was the centre of it and everyone was looking at me. It was like a theatre and I was the main act. I looked round at the jury, their faces a blur. The judge had a serious expression, his white wig making him, for a second, look like a dame in a pantomime.

I glanced at Marty Connaught. My eyes were only on him for a few seconds but I saw immediately that he'd put on a tie and that the charity pin on his lapel had gone. Also gone was the smirk I'd seen earlier. His face was drawn down, his skin pale.

I saw Ms Gardner and Mr Parvez were at desks in front of the dock. Along from them was another female barrister, a young woman whose long dark hair hung below the sausage curls of her white wig. I assumed it was Mrs Barnaby. Beside her sat a grey-haired woman with heavy black-framed glasses. Further back were a couple of younger smartly dressed men. Everyone seemed to have a pile of papers in front of them that they were sorting through. Looking back up to the public area I saw the woman with the tablet, her fingers swiping across it. People were getting organised for what was to come.

The clerk was speaking to me.

'Please make ready to take the oath, Miss Woods. Do you wish to swear on the Bible or some other holy book?'

'I will affirm,' I said.

Both Annie and Patrice had explained this to me. I wasn't religious so I wasn't promising my honesty to a god. I was given a card with words printed on it and I read them out loud.

'I solemnly and sincerely declare and affirm that the evidence I shall give will be the truth, the whole truth and nothing but the truth.'

'Thank you.'

Ms Gardner stood up and waited for the clerk to return to her seat.

'Good afternoon, Stacey. I'm going to ask you some questions about the events of Wednesday 24th June 2015. First, though, I'd like to establish a bit about you.'

I could see Ms Gardner's blue eyes twinkling from where I stood.

'And when you answer my questions, Stacey, I want you to address the judge and the jury. Not me. These are the people who are here to hear your testimony.'

I nodded and gave the jury a good look and then the judge.

'Now, Stacey, tell us a little bit about yourself.'

For the next ten minutes or so, prompted from time to time by Ms Gardner, I gave some basic information about my life. Annie had explained to me that this was to give the jury some background but also to allow me to speak freely about things that were not contentious. It would establish facts about me and help me to relax on the stand. Ms Gardner kept using my name and she smiled a lot at my answers. For that period the court seemed like an easy place. As I spoke in the direction of the jurors I noticed a woman on the front row taking notes and the man beside her looking discreetly at what she was writing. Another juror caught my eye and seemed to smile. They all appeared very human.

It was all right. *It was going to be all right.*

'Now, Stacey, can you tell the court how you came to be in the apartment, 132 Poole Place, on 23rd June 2015?'

'Well,' I said, clearing my throat, 'I had some trouble at home, I'd rowed with my sister and I spent a night at my dad's apartment in Shoreditch. The next day – the Tuesday – I went into a cafe and that's where I met Harry Connaught.'

'To confirm, Harry Connaught is the defendant's younger brother.'

'Yes. We chatted and got on well and he gave me his phone number. I liked him and I rang him later in the day and we went to Selfridges to see a friend of his . . .'

I glanced across the courtroom and saw Mary Potter sitting beside an older woman who had a green silk scarf wrapped round and round her neck. Mary Potter was leaning forward to hear and looking intently at what was going on.

'Harry was really nice to me. He kissed me and then we had a drink in a pub off Oxford Street. That was when I told him I'd run away from home.'

'Had you run away from home?'

'No. Not really.'

'Why did you tell him that?'

'I suppose I was just being dramatic, I think. I wanted to impress him in some way. He was really nice about it and asked me if I wanted to stay in this apartment that his brother looked after for a friend. At first I said no but then it seemed like a good idea.'

'What happened next?'

'We took a taxi and went to where . . . Harry's brother worked.'

I couldn't bring myself to name Marty Connaught. The jurors seemed to perk up here and a couple of them leaned forward as if they couldn't quite hear. I raised my voice and tried to sound confident.

'When we got there I stayed in the taxi and Harry went out and spoke to his brother. He came back with the key to the apartment.'

'Did you speak to his brother?'

'No. Actually, before the rape, I never spoke to his brother at all!' I said with sudden indignation.

'Objection!'

Mrs Barnaby stood up suddenly, startling me. She looked affronted, as if I'd just insulted her. The judge mumbled something soothing and she sat down again. Ms Gardner frowned at me. It was only for a split second but I knew then that I'd said too much. Annie had explained, *Don't run ahead with your story, yeah? Give the barrister time to build it up. They know what they're doing.*

'Please confine your answers to the question,' the judge said, giving me a kindly smile.

'I did not speak to him. I stayed in the taxi,' I said, my voice a little lower.

'And then what did you do?'

'We stayed in the taxi and went back to Oxford Street. We got some food and then headed to the apartment. Harry had arranged that his friends were coming round so we bought some pizzas.'

'What were the sleeping arrangements in this apartment?'

'I stayed in the en-suite bedroom and Harry stayed in the other room.'

'Can you tell the jury what happened before you went to bed that evening, Tuesday 23rd June?'

'Yes. I went into his bedroom. I wanted . . . I wanted . . .'

I stopped. It was hard to get the words out. It wasn't because my mum and dad were there. It was because of *him*. I didn't want to describe my feelings for Harry with *him* there. It was

86

as if by saying it in front of Marty Connaught it made it all seedy and bad. In my mind he tainted everything.

'I wanted to have sex with Harry. I liked him, I liked him a lot.'

'Could you explain how you had these feelings when you'd only known this young man for a day?'

'He was so interested in me. I was depressed and he lifted me out of it. We talked a lot and I felt like I'd known him for ages. When we were on our own in the apartment it seemed like the natural thing to do. To show him how I felt about him.'

'What happened?'

'He stopped me. He didn't want to. He said it would be taking advantage. I tried to persuade him. I told him I wasn't a virgin in case he was worried, you know, about me not having done it before. I even told him that I had condoms in my bag . . .'

I looked down at the floor. I dreaded to imagine what the members of the jury would think of a girl who carried condoms around in her bag. Would they see her as sensible? Keen to prevent unwanted pregnancy and sexually transmitted diseases? Or that she was a slag, always ready for sex with anyone who wanted it?

'But he . . . Harry said we didn't have to rush it. So I went to bed.'

I shrugged my shoulders and looked up, noticing frowns flicker across the faces of a couple of the female jurors. Some of the men looked down as if they were embarrassed.

'How did that make you feel?'

'I liked him more for it. He could have had sex with me but he didn't and it made me think he really liked me. That maybe he saw a future for . . . him and me.'

Ms Gardner sorted through her papers and left a moment's quiet. I looked down at the wooden frame in front of me. I could feel Marty Connaught's eyes on me, but I wouldn't look up.

Ms Gardner moved on to talk about the next day. She asked me some questions about the morning and I answered as fully as I could. I was speaking easily, feeling on solid ground again, and then we got to the afternoon when I was getting ready to leave the apartment and go home.

'Did you intend to have sex with Harry Connaught that afternoon?' Ms Gardner said.

'It wasn't as planned as that. We were kissing and it just felt as though we were going to go further. It felt right.'

'How were you dressed?'

I felt agitated by this question because I knew it would make me look bad, brazen in some way.

'I'd just had a shower. I had my pants and bra on and a towel around me but the towel came off. After we started kissing the bra came off, so I just had my pants on.'

'And explain to the jury where you were in the room.'

'We were on the bed. Lying down.'

'Did you have sex with Harry Connaught?'

'No. I think we would have but the door opened. His brother interrupted us.'

'What happened then?'

'I was embarrassed. I thought his brother would be angry . . .'

Mrs Barnaby stood up to object, but before she could say anything Ms Gardner spoke.

'Please, Stacey, just stick to what actually happened. We want to know what you *did*, not what you thought about someone else.'

'OK,' I said, feeling that I had been gently reprimanded again. 'I sat up. I tried to pull up the sheet to cover myself but it was caught beneath us, so I used my arms to hide my body. Harry's brother just stood there looking at me.'

'What did Harry do?'

'He stayed where he was. Beside me.'

'Tell the jury what Marty Connaught did next.'

'He came into the room. He smiled and walked towards the bed. He said, *You are sweet, Stacey.* I was confused.'

'What was Harry doing?'

'He was kissing my arm. He said, *It's OK. This is my brother.* I didn't know what was going on. It took a few moments until I realised that something bad was happening. Harry's brother said, *You don't need to hide your breasts.* And then he began to take off his tie and I knew. At that moment I *knew* what was going to happen. I told him he should go. I told him I had to get dressed. It was all very quick. I spoke to Harry but he seemed out of it. He seemed stoned. I tried to move my legs, but Harry's weight was holding them there . . .'

My voice was cracking.

'What did you do?'

'I said no. I said it over and over. Harry's brother . . .' I started. 'His brother . . . *He*,' I said, looking at Marty Connaught. '*He* took his trousers off and left his shirt on. He sat on the bed and then he grabbed my ankles and pulled me down so that I was lying on my back.'

'What happened next?'

'He pulled my pants down and he got on top of me.'

'Now, Stacey, we have to be very careful here. I want you to tell the jury exactly what happened next. I know this will embarrass you but it's very important to use the right words here when you say what took place.'

I took a deep breath. I looked over at my mum and dad. and then my eyes settled on Marty Connaught. His face was a picture of innocence, his forehead in a frown, his mouth pulled back as if the words I was saying were giving him actual pain. If I hadn't seen him outside some hours earlier I might have believed that he was sincere.

'Stacey?'

Ms Gardner looked expectantly at me.

'Marty Connaught put his penis into me and moved back and forward until he'd finished. Then he rolled off so I was able to get away from him and lock myself in the en-suite.'

'Did you say anything to him while this was going on?'

'I said *no*.'

'You're quite sure of that?'

'Yes. I am certain.'

'Did he say anything?'

'He told me to relax.'

'I just want to ask this again, Stacey, so that all of us in court here can be absolutely positive of what took place. Did Martin Connaught put his penis into your vagina?'

I felt myself shrivel with shame at this detail, this description being spoken out loud in front of all these people. I'd been forced into nakedness with Marty once. Now it felt as though I was standing with no clothes on in front of strangers, my most private places talked about in a courtroom.

'Stacey?' Ms Gardner prompted.

'He did. He pushed his penis into me.'

'And what did you say when he did this?'

'I said *no*.'

Ms Gardner nodded.

'Thank you, Stacey. You've been very strong. That completes my questions for now.'

She looked at the judge and I let my head drop, a squirming feeling in my chest. I heard him saying that the time was late and that we would commence the cross-examination in the morning. I had my tissue tightly in a ball in my hand. I wanted to get out of there. Mrs Barnaby stood up then and I heard her agreeing, saying *Your Honour* several times in a row. I looked up at the jury. A couple of them were stretching their arms out as if they were stiff and uncomfortable. One man was staring at me, his expression unreadable. What did he think of me? I couldn't know.

'You may get down from the stand, Miss Woods,' the judge said.

The clerk opened the side latch for me and I stepped out and walked through the courtroom, my feet speeding up. As I passed the public benches I saw my mum and dad edging along the row. Behind them the woman with the tablet was making some notes on a pad. She glanced up at me and then looked down again and carried on writing at a feverish pace.

Twelve

I was in Patrice's bedroom. It was just after seven and I could smell food cooking downstairs. I was dog tired. The afternoon session at court had finished just before five. I'd gone home with a ringing headache and my arms and legs stiff from having sat around all day. Patrice's mum had asked me to eat with them and I'd agreed. I wasn't very hungry but it was a relief to get away from home, where Mum was describing the day second by second to Jodie. I'd got round there ten minutes before and I was standing by the window. Patrice was telling me about her time in court.

'I wasn't there for long. Your barrister asked me what you had said and I told her that you came round to my house on the night you were raped. The defence barrister objected about me saying you were *raped*. I was to tell them what you actually said to me – nothing else. Anyway, I told them I'd fallen out with you and didn't actually talk to you until the next afternoon, when I waited for you outside Costa Coffee. So then she asked me, *What did she say?* And I said, looking confidently at the defence barrister – daring her to object – I said, *She said, I was raped.* Then it was the cross-examination.'

Patrice was talking about it in a thrilled way, as if it had been a really exciting moment for her. Her ambition to be a barrister was charging this experience and I'm sure she was picturing herself in a black gown and wig, saying, *Objection!*

She began to talk about the cross-examination. She was gesticulating with her hands but I was only half listening. I looked out of the window at her back garden. The grass was green, except for a large patch in the corner which was bare and stubby. Patrice's trampoline used to sit on it. It had been there for years and in the summer she and I had used it as a late-night place to talk and look up at the stars. We'd often smuggled out a bottle of freezing-cold white wine and drunk it from tumblers and put the world to rights.

'You're miles away!' Patrice said.

'Sorry.'

I turned back to her.

'And the fact that Marty Connaught has got a woman to represent him is a real plus for him.'

Annie had told me about this already but I let Patrice go on.

'And she's a special type of woman. She's young, I mean compared to your barrister who is practically *ancient*. Anyway, she's young and attractive so the jury will warm to her. Also they will think – because she's a woman – she must *believe* Marty Connaught when he says he's innocent. After all, why would a woman defend someone she thought was guilty of a crime that is mainly against women?'

I nodded.

'If they had had a man as a barrister and he had to cross-examine you it might look as though you were being bullied by him and that would give you the jury's sympathy. This way it's this nice woman who'll be asking you questions.'

Patrice had stopped and was looking at me for a response.

'Is this meant to make me feel better?'

Patrice frowned.

'No, I just want you to know what's going on. However sweet and nice his barrister is, be prepared for sharp questions. Don't be lulled into a false sense of security.'

I nodded.

'Have I upset you?'

'No, really. I'm just grateful that you went and testified for me. It means a lot that you believed me.'

'In a heartbeat. I never for one second, for one tenth of a second, thought you might be making it up. No way. No way.'

I could hear Patrice's mum calling her.

'You all right? I'll have to help with the food.'

'Sure.'

Patrice went out and I felt annoyed with myself. She hadn't meant any harm; she'd thought she was forewarning me. After today, though, being examined by my own barrister and having to explain such intimate things, I dreaded what tomorrow would bring. Describing what took place was hard when the questioner believed me, was on my side. What would it be like when they weren't?

I looked back out to the garden. The trampoline had been gone since just after Christmas. I came round one day to do homework and stood in that very spot for a while before I noticed that it wasn't there. *Where's the trampoline?* I'd said, shocked. Patrice's mum wanted rid of it. Patrice had agreed

95

to a new upgrade of her phone if she allowed it to be broken up and dumped. My friend gave her trampoline up for a more up-to-date phone. I looked at the bare patch of grass and felt that something had been taken from me; a sense of loss even though it hadn't been mine. I had thought that our times on the trampoline were precious and it seemed that Patrice thought they were less important than a new phone.

I missed it though. Whenever I went to her window I'd be surprised all over again that it wasn't there.

'Stacey! Food's ready.'

I heard Patrice call.

'Coming,' I said, and headed off downstairs.

Later I walked home alone. Patrice insisted she would be at court the next afternoon when she had no classes. She said she'd be there for me, taking her own notes, making sure that everything had been covered. A part of me wanted to tell her not to come. I was afraid that the cross-examination would shame me further and I didn't want that in front of her. On the other hand, I thought it might be good to see her face on the public benches; maybe gain some strength from her being there. I didn't know *what* I wanted.

I walked along slowly, in no hurry to get home. I paused at the window of a charity shop. There was an unusual dress displayed at the centre of the window and I studied it. It was some kind of silk fabric with a diamond pattern. What was really nice about it was a gather at the side across the stomach. It had a V-neck and was ankle length. It was obviously an expensive make that someone had got tired of; now it was the star of the window display.

I didn't wear dresses. There was a time when I had liked designing them and fancied that I might do that for a job. I'd looked into fashion design courses at the London School of Fashion and thought that I might apply. But those ambitions came from a time before the rape. I was a different person then. Now I was more realistic about my life. People like me didn't move in that world. What was for me? University? Working in Budgens? I didn't know. I couldn't see myself, the person I would be, beyond the trial.

The window I was standing in front of was an Oxfam charity shop and I thought of Bella, who had worked in one in Shoreditch. I wished, not for the first time, that she had gone to the police when I had. How much better our case would have been if there had been two of us. My story sounded flimsy, even I could see that. But if Bella had stood up in court and said that Marty Connaught had raped her under similar circumstances, then no one would have disbelieved us.

I had promised Bella that I wouldn't tell anyone about her. Even though she wasn't a close friend and I owed her nothing, I had kept my word. There were a number of times when Annie had taken me for a drive and she'd said, *I bet my year's salary that Marty's done this before!* He had. I knew it and Bella knew it but no one else could. I pictured her yesterday, standing in her red velvet coat at the edge of Spitalfields Market sending me a text that was a lie. It still hurt me to think of it. I didn't expect to see Bella again.

'Stacey!'

I heard a voice from behind and I turned round to look.

'Stacey!'

Across the road was Dan from Budgens. He looked both ways, wove through the traffic and came across to me.

'Hiya,' he said, puffing a little. 'Still got the red hair!'

It was only a couple of days since I'd seen him in the supermarket.

'Er . . . Yeah!' I said. 'What you doing round here?'

'Seeing a mate. He lives near the Olympic Park. What you up to?'

'I've just been round my friend's. I'm heading off home now.'

'Fancy a coffee?' he said, pointing at a cafe further along.

I felt a moment's panic. I shook my head.

'I can't. Anyway, what about your mate?'

'It's a fluid arrangement. I can be late.'

He smiled at me and I realised that I was smiling too.

'I can't. I said I'd be home.'

He pretended a sad face. 'Just for half an hour? So I can show you more pictures of my dog?'

'No, really, I think I've seen enough pictures of Woody.'

'I could show you pictures of other dogs. Cats, even.'

'I said I'd look after my sister's baby,' I lied, 'so that she can go out.'

'Right, OK,' he said, frowning a little.

'But another time,' I said, 'definitely another time.'

'Depends,' he said, his face breaking into a smile.

'On what?'

'I might have something I have to do.'

'OK.'

'Bye, miss redhead.'

He walked off and I felt a moment's indecision. I should call him back, go for a coffee. He was a *friend*, that was all. A coffee with a friend was a good thing, nothing to be worried about. But I didn't. I stood on the pavement and watched him head off up the road towards the Olympic Park and I felt relieved to be on my own again. Better to get the trial out of the way before I made any new *friends*.

Thirteen

The cross-examination was worse, much worse than I could have imagined. Patrice had said that the female barrister would be soft and warm with me at first but it wasn't like that. From the moment Mrs Barnaby started, she was cold and stern. She took a while to stand, picking up different bits of paper. She smiled at the jury and came out from behind her table. She was tall, wearing high heels, and she used her free hand to pull her hair back over her shoulder. The gown hung heavily on her and she straightened her shoulders. I wished she'd get on and start. There were a few murmurs and people were clearing their throats. There was a feeling of anticipation. Eventually she spoke.

'Miss Woods, you've stated that you were undressed when Mr Connaught came into the bedroom of the apartment at Poole Place?'

'Yes, mostly.'

'Well, Miss Woods, you were? Or you weren't?'

'I had my pants on.'

'And nothing else?'

'No.'

'And you were lying on the bed?'

'I was . . . but . . .'

'Please, just answer the question, Miss Woods.'

'Yes,' I said dully.

'And Mr Connaught saw you like this?'

'Yes.'

'At this time who was in the sitting room?'

'Er . . . Harry and Dom.'

'That being Harry Connaught, the defendant's young brother, and Dominic Blake, his friend.'

'Yes.'

'And after this *alleged* rape had taken place, did you run out of the bedroom to tell these two young men what had happened?'

'No.'

'Why was that? Was the door of the bedroom locked?'

'No.'

'So why didn't you leave the room and tell them, ask them for help?'

'I was frightened and confused. The en-suite was closer, so I went in there and locked the door.'

'Was Mr Connaught chasing after you?'

'No, I just felt safer that way.'

'Was he banging on the door?'

'No.'

'Oh.'

Mrs Barnaby scratched the side of her face as if perplexed. She looked at the jury then turned slowly back to me.

'During this act had Mr Connaught threatened you with violence?'

'No. Not physical violence but he forced me . . .'

'Just answer the question, please.'

'No.'

'Did Mr Connaught strike you?'

'No.'

'Did Mr Connaught threaten to strike you?'

'No.'

She nodded her head as if agreeing with herself.

'What did Mr Connaught do, after you came out of the en-suite?'

'He was lying on the bed. He sat up when I came out.'

'Did he say anything to you?'

'He asked me if I was all right . . . and he said, *It was just a bit of fun* . . .'

'Then what happened?'

'He pulled some money out of his pocket and tried to give it to me. He said, *Get a taxi home.*'

'Mr Connaught offered you money for a taxi?'

'He did.'

'Did you take it?'

'Not exactly.'

'Did you take it or not?'

'He insisted.'

'How did you get home from Oxford Street on that day?'

'I got a taxi.'

'How did you pay for it?'

'With the money he gave me.'

She faced the jury. Then she turned back to the table, where her colleague passed her a note. She read it through, turning it over to see what was on the other side. I sneaked a look at two of the women on the jury. Neither of them met my eyes. I glanced over at my mum and dad, who were both stony-faced. From beside me I could hear the judge sighing and fidgeting.

'Mrs Barnaby, will you speed things up. We do not want any theatrics here. The jury have heard your line of questioning and now they, we, *all of us*, would like you to move on.'

'I do beg your pardon, Your Honour. Now, Miss Woods, if I could just take you back to the morning of the 24th of June last year. After waking up in the bedroom of the Poole Street apartment, what did you do?'

I answered her questions as clearly as I could. I described going to Selfridges for breakfast and then I told her about the dress that Harry had bought for me. She asked me about my feelings for Harry and after a while I began to relax a little. All the time, though, I was aware of the questioning to come about the rape itself. Me wanting to have sex with a boy I liked and being passed over to his brother. I dreaded how Mrs Barnaby would handle that, cringed at the thought of her going over each tiny detail.

But Mrs Barnaby was in no rush to get to the rape.

'Who paid for the breakfast in Selfridges?'

'Harry . . . Well, Harry paid but I think he used his brother's store card. He said he had an allowance.'

'So Harry used his brother's card? In fact, Mr Connaught paid for your breakfast?'

'Yes.'

'And what about the dress?'

'He used his brother's store card,' I said, my voice a little lower.

'So Mr Connaught paid for the dress as well.'

'Yes.'

'Miss Woods, what did you think when Harry told you that it was Mr Connaught paying for these things?'

'I didn't think . . . I thought that Harry . . . I mean it was money that Harry said was his allowance.'

She was trying to make me look as though I was the kind of person who took money wherever I could get it. I was thoughtless and greedy. I wasn't a nice person.

'I thought *Harry* was spending money on me. I was there for Harry. He said his brother gave him an allowance . . .'

'Do you like men spending money on you, Miss Woods?'

'NO, no, no . . . I don't. It was just the way it happened.'

'Thank you. Now we will move to the afternoon itself . . .'

She said it cheerfully, as if we were good friends chatting over a cup of tea. I glanced up at the clock at the back of the courtroom. It was only eleven; there was hours of this to go. I found myself gripping the edge of the witness box and wishing I could sit down, on an armchair, far away from where I was.

And then I thought of Bella, who hadn't put herself through this.

Had she been right?

'Where did you go after you purchased the dress?'

I answered, my voice sounding clipped and haughty. Now the jury would think I was being off and perhaps I would go down another notch in their estimation. After I'd answered a lot more questions all designed to show me as a loser, exploiting the generosity of the Connaught family, the judge interrupted

105

and said we should break for lunch and that he would see the barrister in his rooms at one thirty and we would start again at two.

'You may get down from the stand,' the clerk said.

My legs were shaky as I walked out of the box. Because of the direction I was taking I found myself making a moment's eye contact with Marty Connaught. His face was dour and serious but his eyes were smiling, mocking me.

His word against mine. If Bella was here her testimony would give my words some added weight. Then he wouldn't be so confident. But she wasn't there and I was alone. I walked on towards the exit and found myself in the middle of my mum and dad, both of whom had an arm around my shoulder.

Fourteen

At lunch we sat in the witnesses' waiting room and ate our sandwiches. We were in the corner by the television because the room was pretty full. The conversations around us were louder, heated in places; people reporting back from the trials they'd been involved in. My mum and dad in contrast were saying soothing things and I was nodding in agreement, but my mouth was dry and my throat was creaky. When my dad was getting a coffee I pulled at Mum's sleeve and said, *The jury don't believe me. I can tell. I can feel their disapproval.* But she shook her head, dismissing it, and gave me a hug.

Annie came in while we were eating our food. She was businesslike, pulling a chair over from the other side of the room.

'This is just the rough and tumble of the courtroom. Whatever Mrs Barnaby says to you will be gone over when Ms Gardner re-examines. Then there are the closing speeches. Ms Gardner is a powerful advocate. She'll see you get justice.'

She stood up to go, but I followed her to the door. I put my hand on her arm.

'It's not going well, is it?'

'Yes, it is. Just wait until *he* goes on the stand. Wait until Ms Gardner questions *him*. Then we'll see the truth come out.'

I watched her go out of the swing doors just as some other people were coming in. She seemed confident, and yet was there just a tinge of uncertainty in her voice, a hint that she wasn't sure? That my testimony was not going to be strong enough, so we had to wait until Marty was on the stand in the hope that he would trip himself up.

The trial was a heavy burden to carry by myself and I felt angry all of a sudden. If only Bella had come forward. I pictured her, in her red velvet coat in Costa, showing it off to me as if she hadn't a care in the world. How had she managed to put it behind her? She was as small a girl as I was. Like me, her size had helped make it easy for Marty Connaught to overpower her. She'd been wearing a skirt on the day he raped her and I recalled her wishing she'd been wearing jeans. *I didn't have much of a chance* . . . she'd said sadly. How could she forget that? Live with it? If only she'd come with me to the Rape Crisis Centre. Two of us in court would have been enough to convict Marty. My story, by itself, wouldn't do it; I suddenly knew this and it made me feel as if I was hauling a rock up a mountain with the full knowledge that it was going to tumble back down again.

It was long after lunch that we eventually started again. The judge was still involved in some discussions on the case that had overrun. At just after two thirty I went back on the stand. Patrice was in the public gallery beside my mum and dad. I saw that she had a pad with her and was making notes before things had even got going. Possibly she was writing a title. *Rape Case; Cross-examination of Complainant.* Maybe these notes would form part of a project that she would do in her Law degree. I felt the tiniest bit of resentment towards her and then hated myself for it.

Mrs Barnaby walked out to the centre of the courtroom. She stood in one place, referring to her notes, flicking through one page after another. She frowned a little as though she couldn't find something. I could see some members of the jury tensing up. One of them looked concerned, as if afraid that the barrister had lost her place. In the public gallery my mum and dad had their eyes on her all the time.

When she finally spoke her words were like a carefully aimed arrow.

'Miss Woods, do you always carry condoms around in your bag?'

'No . . . No . . . not now.'

'But you had some with you on Tuesday 23rd June when you propositioned Harry Connaught in the apartment at Poole Place?'

'I didn't *proposition* him. It didn't happen quite like that . . .'

'But you did have condoms in your bag. That's what you told him?'

'Yes.'

'Why was that? Why did you carry condoms with you?'

'I thought it was a good idea to be prepared. To avoid problems . . .'

'*To be prepared* . . . Prepared for what?'

She repeated my words with relish.

'To avoid pregnancy and STDs.'

'But step back a bit, Miss Woods. You said, to be *prepared*. Do you mean that you wanted to be prepared to have *sex?*'

'I . . . just thought it was better to . . .'

I found myself holding the pendant that Patrice had bought for me, my smallest finger threading through it. I waited with trepidation for what she would say next.

'You've told the jury here, in this court, that you met Harry Connaught quite by chance and that you developed sudden feelings for him. How lucky it was that you had condoms handy.'

I stared at Mrs Barnaby. There was no question as such so I didn't answer.

'Did you carry condoms around with you when you were in school or at your part-time job? Just in case the opportunity arose for sex?'

'Objection! The question has been asked and answered. My learned friend is simply trying to demean the witness.'

Ms Gardner looked angry.

'Please move on, Mrs Barnaby,' the judge said tersely.

I glanced up and met Marty Connaught's eyes. He was still and calm and didn't seem to blink at all. I looked away, towards Mr Parvez, who took a long drink from a bottle of water, then whispered something to Annie. I wondered what it was.

Mrs Barnaby smiled at the jury as if she was making a fresh start. Then she began to question me about the events of that afternoon. I described meeting Dom and then going to the pub in New Bond Street. She asked me about the taxi ride to Marty Connaught's workplace and I told her that Harry had been upset because his brother told him that their mother was angry with him for not working hard enough. She nodded her head in agreement with the things I said and looked friendly. Then, when we seemed to have finished talking about that afternoon, she took a different tack.

'What time was it when you met Harry Connaught in the cafe in Shoreditch?'

I had to think for a moment.

'It was just after eight. I think just after eight fifteen. I think . . .'

'Who started talking?'

'He did. He came and sat at my table and asked me what I was sketching. We started talking.'

'What time did he leave?'

'About eight thirty. He had to be at school at nine.'

'So you talked to him for, what, fifteen minutes?'

'Yes.'

'You said you rang him. What time was that?'

'About eleven, I think.'

'And you arranged to meet?'

'He said to meet at two.'

'And what did you do?'

'We went into Selfridges for a while and then to a pub.'

'How long did you stay in the pub?'

'I'm not sure, maybe forty-five minutes? An hour?'

'How long do you estimate that you were in Harry Connaught's company before you agreed to stay in the apartment? Adding up the cafe, Selfridges and the pub.'

'About an hour, two hours maybe?'

'And the rest of that afternoon and evening. How long were you alone with him? Roughly?'

'I don't know. His friends came round to the apartment, so we weren't alone very long.'

'But a rough estimate?'

'Maybe four hours.'

'So in all, Miss Woods, you spent four hours *alone* with Harry Connaught that day, the day before the alleged rape?'

'Maybe. Possibly. We were doing other things; shopping, I had a shower. I think he did too.'

'And that gave you enough time to get to know this young man so that before going to bed that night you asked him to have sex with you?'

'I thought it did . . .'

'Really, Miss Woods?'

'You can sometimes know people very quickly. Some people you can know for years without really getting to the bottom of them.'

I thought of Benji Ashe, who had been my boyfriend for a few weeks. I had hardly got to know him at all, even though we spent a lot of time together.

'I liked Harry. I thought he liked me. That's why I asked him . . .'

'And luckily, Miss Woods, when you did proposition him, you had a packet of condoms in your bag.'

'Objection! Mrs Barnaby is harassing the witness.'

Ms Gardner stood up so quickly her table rattled. Mrs Barnaby didn't seem to notice. She continued looking at me and then at the jury.

'Yes, yes,' the judge said, 'I think we've all had enough of this for today. I suggest we use this as a good time to adjourn until tomorrow morning.'

That was it. I got off the stand and walked through the court, aware of everyone's eyes on me. I didn't wait for anyone. I went straight towards the door and out into the corridor. I was supposed to go back to the witness waiting area and have a meeting with Ms Gardner to review the day's proceedings but I couldn't bear to do it. I headed from the exit and went out through the heavy doors and walked off down the long drive towards the gates.

It was just before four o'clock. I'd had enough of being questioned, poked and prodded, ridiculed and insulted, for that day.

Fifteen

I stayed in my bedroom. Mum came in and told me about the meeting with Ms Gardner and Mr Parvez. Dad sent his love but had gone home because Gemma wasn't feeling well. Jodie left Tyler with me while she had a bath. I had several texts from Patrice telling me to keep a clear head. She couldn't make it to court the next day but sent me her love. I was glad. I didn't want her to see me looking any more ridiculous.

On the bed in front of me was the purple notebook. I'd covered six or seven sheets with angry handwriting. It sloped and hurried towards the side of the page, some words linked up to the next. No paragraphs, no gaps, just line upon line of writing that tried to explain what was happening. When I could write no more I closed it up, making sure the marker was in the right page.

Annie called by. She didn't stay long but told me that things would look different after Marty Connaught had been on the stand. *Just wait and see how Ms Gardner questions him. There's everything still to play for.* She talked about other things too. She'd had a coffee with Patrice and my mum and dad and said how great they all were and how they were there for me.

After she left I lay back on my bed. I felt as though something was absent, missing. I hated the idea of Annie chatting to Patrice and I imagined that she'd seen Patrice as a strong girl, someone who would look after herself and not fall for the first guy who tells her he likes her. Patrice would never have got herself into this situation. She wouldn't have been bowled over by Harry, willing to do anything to make an impression on him.

I realised then that there had been no tiny bag of Haribos. Annie hadn't left any sweets for me because I hadn't been a good girl. I'd let her down with my stupid answers.

I sat up and thought for the hundredth time that Bella had been right not to go to court. While I was going through this misery she was swanning around baking bread in the artisan bakery and writing songs, unfazed by what had happened to her. I remembered she'd said, *I just have to accept that I made a stupid mistake and forget it*. Maybe she actually had forgotten it.

I reached over to my bedside drawer and pulled out a tiny cosmetic bag. I unzipped it and took a card from inside. The edges were curled and it looked a bit grubby from frequent handling. On it was the name *Harry Connaught* and underneath was a phone number and an email address. Drawn across the print was a rough pen sketch of a heart. It was misshapen and the lines didn't meet. I stared at it for a while and felt my own heart beating. Harry had given it to me with a flourish. Like having a gold star on a piece of work. I had taken it to mean that I had passed some kind of test; that I was special, one of the best in the class. But Harry had given one to Bella as well and maybe many other girls too. I had lost my way for a scribbled heart on a scrap of card.

Where was Harry now? In his parents' house in Fulham waiting for the time when he was due to be a witness? Or was he sitting alone in his bedroom, thinking of those days last year and wishing he had never brought me to the apartment. Was he regretting what he'd taken part in? Did he ever think of me? Of the girl he had met in Katie's Kitchen? I sighed deeply. There was something deep down wrong with me. Even now, after having been ripped apart by Marty's barrister, I wanted to see something good in Harry, something soft and remorseful. I wanted to feel that he had been led along by his brother in the same way that I had been led along by *him*.

And what about Marty Connaught? Was he at home with his family or out with his on/off girlfriend, Mary Potter? Was he out celebrating, toasting his barrister's performance with champagne? If only Bella could see what was going on in court. If she could hear what was being said about me. It might make her stand up and shout, *Stop! Stop! He raped me too*.

I could hear Jodie playing with Tyler in the next room and I walked along and knocked on her door.

'Hi!' she said.

Jodie's face was pink and shiny and her hair was wrapped up in a towel. Tyler was standing by Jodie's bed and when he saw me he made a shaky turn and began to walk towards me. He seemed to sway from side to side until he careered into my knees. I picked him up and held him close. He smelled of talcum powder and baby lotion. He was making mumbling noises.

'I'm sorry you're going through a bad time,' Jodie said, pulling the towel off her hair and letting her wet tresses fall onto her shoulders.

117

'I know,' I said.

I felt Tyler squirming in my arms so I placed him back on the floor.

'I know you don't think much of me,' Jodie said, 'but if I was on the jury I wouldn't believe Marty-the-rapist.'

'I do think a lot of you! I do!' I said, feeling dismayed.

'Come on. Fourteen? Pregnant? Stupid or what?'

I walked across to Jodie and sat down on the bed beside her.

'You made a mistake. But look at you now. Back at college in September. Getting your life on the road again.'

'Always have him though . . .' Jodie said, nodding at Tyler, 'Not that I don't, you know . . . *love* him.'

'He'll always be your number-one boy. And it'll get easier. You'll see.'

Jodie grabbed my hand. 'I'd come to court if I could but I think I might make things worse. I might shout a few choice things at that bastard.'

'Actually, I wish no one was in court. I don't like people seeing me carved up like that.'

Tyler had made his way over and was holding a red plastic car. He offered it to me.

'I hope he gets five years in prison!'

I smiled at Jodie and then got down on my knees and began to run the tiny car along the carpet.

Later, in my room, I couldn't stop thinking about Bella. The image I had had earlier about her sitting in the public gallery stayed in my head. I began to picture Marty Connaught in the dock, ready for another day in court, when his eyes settled on her. It might take him a few moments to place her, to remember who she was, but when he did he would feel a frisson of fear that she was there for a reason, that maybe she was going to be a witness, or worse still she had come forward to say that the same thing had happened to her.

His eyes wouldn't be smiling then.

He might ask for a sudden meeting with his barrister. It happened all the time, Annie had told me. Defendants pleaded *not guilty* to see how the evidence was stacking up. When it looked as though they may end up with a *guilty* verdict they change their plea to *guilty*. That way they got a lighter sentence.

All Bella had to do was come to court and sit in full view of everyone. She didn't have to go to the police or reveal what had happened to her, she just had to be there so that Marty Connaught could see her and be afraid of what she might do.

I felt an odd feeling, a sense of excitement.

What if I asked Bella to come to court? What if I went to her house, right that minute, and asked her to help me? Not to tell anyone what had *happened* to her but just to spook Marty Connaught. Her presence would give my words some extra weight even if she never had to open her mouth and speak.

Would she do it?

I stood up, picked up my phone and money. It was nine twenty; not too late. It would take me half an hour to get to her place and then I could ask her. I had nothing to lose and everything to gain.

I got out of the Tube at Dalston Junction Station and wove my way through people and traffic towards Bella's mum's place.

119

I'd only been there once before but it was a straight route with a right turn at a Turkish restaurant. Her street was full of old Victorian houses that had been turned into flats, and I remembered her flat was opposite a row of three small shops, one of which was a dry cleaner's. I felt a little bit of apprehension as I turned the corner. I was remembering that she had arranged to meet me the previous Sunday but had let me down and lied about it in a text. I had no idea why but I didn't want to dwell on it. I *had* to ask her this favour. If she said *no*, then so be it. If she said *yes*, then it might change everything.

Her road curved away from me and there were cars parked tightly at each side. There were humps along it to slow the traffic and I watched a pizza delivery bike see-saw along, followed by a van that was flashing its lights in an irritated way. Close to the corner there were groups of kids heading off somewhere. They took no notice of me as I passed. I walked along and saw, further up, the sign for Splendid Dry Cleaner's opposite where Bella lived.

I had to ready myself because she wasn't expecting me and the thing I was going to ask her to do was huge. I found myself slowing down a bit as I went along. Then, when I was about ten houses away, I heard laughter and I saw a young girl step out onto the street. I knew straight away who it was. I could see her clearly in the streetlights. Behind her was a boy in a hoodie. I slowed right up and then stopped by a large shrub that was spilling out of a front garden. She was talking loudly to the boy in a jokey way. He came out onto the pavement and stood with his side to me. She put her arms round his neck and I could see they were kissing.

Bella had really moved on. She had a boyfriend now and maybe that was the reason she hadn't come to see me on Sunday; she wanted to leave the past properly behind. I couldn't blame her for that. The boy was giving her a kiss and she lifted her arms up to reach for his hoodie and began to push it back off his face.

I heard the sound of a car engine coming from behind and several bumps as it went swiftly across the speed humps. I glanced round and saw that it was a black taxi, the yellow sign shining out in the dark road.

'Bye-bye . . .'

Bella's voice was calling out in a playful way and I turned back towards her as the taxi swept past me. By now the boy's hood was down and he was smiling at her. My breath caught in my throat as I saw who it was. The taxi halted alongside them, its brakes squealing. He pulled the back door of the taxi wide open and went to get in.

'Wait . . .' Bella called playfully, 'don't go yet.'

'I've got to. I'm on a meter . . .' he said, but gave her a hug.

It was Harry Connaught.

I stepped out from behind the shrub and saw him get into the taxi. The door slammed and it moved off. Bella watched it go for a moment. She stood on tiptoes and waved. She had her back to me but I could tell her body was taut and buzzing with happiness.

Harry and Bella. I couldn't believe it.

The taxi had disappeared into the darkness and Bella turned to go back into her house. She glanced at me and then, taking a second look, she seemed to start and gasp.

'Hi, Bella,' I said.

'Stacey!' she said. 'What are you doing here?'

'Never mind me. What's *he* doing here?'

She slumped a little and used her hands to pull her hair back off her face.

'You better come in and we can talk.'

I followed her.

Sixteen

'Do you want some tea? Or a cold drink?'

We were in Bella's kitchen. There was no sign of her mother, so I assumed she was at work. The room was tidy and there was the hum of a dishwasher. The only other time I'd been there we'd sat either side of the table and had coffee and a slice of chocolate cake which Bella had made.

On the way up the stairs Bella had talked nervously but I hadn't joined in. When we finally stood on either side of the kitchen table looking at each other she went to say something but stopped. I still didn't speak. I was still reeling with the unexpected sight of Harry Connaught.

'I'm sorry about not making it to Costa Coffee last Sunday . . .'

'I don't care about that. That's not important any more. What was *he* doing here? With you? After everything that's happened?'

'You don't understand . . .'

'I've been in court for the last couple of days trying to describe how his brother raped me and how he was a part of it. I think I do understand . . .'

'No, he's changed. He's different. He doesn't even speak to his brother now. He knows that those things his brother did

123

with you and . . . and me . . . That was wrong. He knows that. And let's be clear here, it was *Marty* . . .'

She lowered her voice when saying his name.

'It was *Marty* who raped you and me. Not Harry. He was young. He was under the influence of his brother. He loved him. He would do anything for him. He sees that now. He knows it was wrong . . .'

She pulled out a chair from the table.

'If you won't have a drink, at least sit down. I'll tell you what happened and then you might understand why I'm with him.'

Why I'm with him. So it wasn't just a recent thing. It was serious. Harry had changed. It was what I'd hoped for, what I'd fantasised about. When I'd seen him outside his school I'd known there was something different about him and I'd been right. And yet the confirmation of this wasn't giving me any pleasure. It was Bella who had experienced this transformation. Not me.

'Sit down, please.'

I pulled a chair out and sat down, my shoulder angled towards the door.

'The reason I didn't turn up on Sunday was because I didn't want to lie to you about Harry. It's why I haven't seen you for a long time. I'm really fond of you and I wanted to see you and wish you luck for the trial but I didn't want to have to pretend. I couldn't face having to keep all this buried inside me.'

She made tiny fists and pointed to her chest when she said it.

'Just after Christmas, he came round here. Not to my front door. He just stood across the road and I saw him when I was leaving for school. I ignored him of course, but he followed

124

me and when I stopped to tell him to get lost I could see he'd been beaten up. His eye was black and he had a bruise on his cheek and his lip was split. He said his brother had done it.'

I stared at her. She stuttered a little but continued.

'Harry said that over Christmas he and his brother had had a terrible row. His brother had accused him of not supporting him, of turning his back on him in a time of trouble. Harry said he tried to keep out of Marty's way but his brother seemed intent on picking a fight. And it wasn't just once. After a week or so he came to me. I couldn't help but feel sorry for him. I know that you said he was there when . . . when Marty raped you, but when it happened to me he'd gone out. He told me that he'd known nothing about it, that Marty had said I led him on.'

'You believed him *again*?'

'I could see the state he was in.'

'You helped him?'

'I did. I found it difficult to turn away from him. I had liked him a lot . . . I *do* like him a lot.'

We sat looking at each other. I noticed then that she'd had her hair trimmed so that it wasn't as wispy as it had once been. It looked tidy. And she was wearing a white shirt and looked like an office girl. I was suddenly glad that I'd seen her in the red velvet coat; the kind of thing she'd worn when I first knew her. She hadn't completely changed.

'I think he just got dragged along with it. He admired his brother and would have done anything to stay in with him.'

These words echoed the thoughts I had been having. Why now, when I found out I had been right, did I feel so wretched?

It should have been me he came to; it should have been me who cleaned up his injuries and gave him some comfort. Instead it had been Bella.

'If he's changed so much why is testifying on behalf of his brother?'

'He has no choice. He's been called as a witness.'

'What is he going to say?'

'He's going to tell the truth.'

'But what? Exactly what will he say?'

'He says he'll tell the truth no matter what his brother says or does. Look, you going to the police brought it all into the open. He had to admit that he'd gone along with Marty, buried his head in the sand. Your actions changed him.'

I felt heavy on the chair. I'd gone to the police and it had made Harry face up to the reality of what he'd been involved in. Then he'd gone to find Bella and cried on her shoulder. There was the tiniest flicker of anger in me.

'Does Marty know about you and Harry?'

'He does. Harry told him.'

'I thought they weren't speaking.'

'It was during a row. That's one of the reasons why Marty has cut Harry out of his life. Harry's glad. Harry doesn't want anything to do with him. It's difficult at home . . . with his family, but he stays out a lot. With Dominic. And he stays here . . .'

'Maybe you should have gone to the police as well,' I said, quietly. 'Then Marty would be out of the way for a good few years.'

'Maybe I should have . . . But now . . .'

'So you and him are serious?'

126

'He says he loves me.'

He loves me. The words were like little needles in my throat. And then I remembered another girl in Harry's life – *I thought I was in love with this girl . . . I just had to see her.* He'd stolen a teacher's car and driven to Oxford to be with this girl. I'd admired him for his passion and his willingness to do anything for love. He'd got himself into a lot of trouble and it had been his brother who had sorted it out. The brother he now disowned.

'I should go,' I said, standing up.

'You're angry with me. I'm sorry, I should have told you when it first happened, but after everything we'd talked about I knew you'd be upset.'

I would have been angry with her. But what right did I have to feel like that when I had spent the last few weeks trying to convince myself that Harry wasn't a bad boy any more. I stood up and I walked out of the kitchen and headed down to the front door. I could hear Bella's soft footsteps on the stairs behind me. Just as I opened it she put her hand on my arm.

'Why did you come to see me?'

I remembered then that I'd wanted to persuade her to come to court and sit in the public gallery so that her presence would upset Marty Connaught. What a stupid idea. He knew full well that she was with his brother.

'It doesn't matter now.'

She gripped my arm. 'Good luck with the trial.'

I didn't answer her.

I got home just after eleven. I was weary and hoping I could go straight up to my room. Mum was up but Jodie and Tyler had gone to bed. Mum looked worried. She was wringing her hands, her lips pursed tightly

'Annie Mulligan was here, about an hour ago.'

I felt a heaviness on my chest. Something bad had happened.

'Oh? Why?'

'She said to let you know that some of the press have found out who owned the apartment in Poole Place and that there might be stuff about the case in the national papers tomorrow.'

Newspaper reporters; I remembered the blonde woman with the laptop in the public gallery in court, and then there was the man who had come in late wearing the leather coat. Had one or other of them fished among the background details of the case, hoping for a tasty morsel? Will *Girl X* be on the front page of a daily newspaper?

'It'll be all right though, won't it?' my mum said.

'Course it will.'

I sat down on the sofa and let my head loll back against the soft fabric. Tomorrow I had to return to the stand for any last questions that Mrs Barnaby wanted to ask and then be re-examined by my own barrister. Meanwhile the newspapers would be poring over the details of my testimony.

Could things get any worse?

Seventeen

The third day of the trial brought the press. When I walked into court I could see that the public gallery was full. I was due to go on the stand to allow Mrs Barnaby to finish my cross-examination. The same blonde woman was there with her tablet and notepad as well as the man in the leather coat. There were also half a dozen other people who had not been at the trial in the first two days. Most of them were looking at phones but one of them, a woman with tight curly hair, stared at me as I stood waiting to be called. Then she began to tap a message out on her phone.

I swore to tell the truth, the whole truth and nothing but the truth. Mrs Barnaby got up from her seat and straightened her wig and smiled sadly at the jury as if apologising for the fact that we all had to be there at all.

'On the 23rd June, the day before the alleged rape, we have established that you wanted to have sex with Harry Connaught.'

I took a deep breath.

'Yes,' I said.

'What did you do?'

Mrs Barnaby looked round the entire courtroom while I squirmed.

'What do you mean?'

'How did you initiate this act?'

'I . . . I went into his bedroom and I started to kiss him. I liked him. I liked him a lot.'

'After you kissed him, what did you do?'

'He started to kiss me back and we sort of lay down on the bed . . .'

'What was he wearing?'

'He had boxer shorts on.'

'And you? What were you wearing?'

'I was dressed. I had jeans and a top . . .'

'What did Harry Connaught say at this time?'

'He said we shouldn't. That I was a guest and he said it was too soon.'

'And what did you do?'

'I argued back. I said it wasn't too soon. That was when I told him I had condoms in my bag.'

'What happened then?'

'I told him I wasn't a virgin. I thought . . . he might have been worried that I hadn't had the experience before . . . But I wanted him to know that I had, so he didn't have to worry about being the first boy to . . .'

I'd known all of this was going to come out. I knew that Harry was to be a witness for the defence later in the trial. There was no point in me leaving anything out or trying to soften the things I'd said and done.

'What did he say?'

'He said he liked me but it was too soon.'

'And what did you do?'

'I went to bed.'

'How did you feel, having been rejected by this boy you liked?'

'Objection! Leading the witness.' Ms Gardner was on her feet.

'I apologise, Your Honour. How did you feel?'

'I did actually . . . feel rejected, for a few moments, but then I thought, perhaps, it meant he liked me, that he was going to save this for the future. I thought there might be a future for him and me.'

'And when you were on the bed with Harry the next afternoon, the afternoon of the alleged rape, did he reject you again?'

'No.'

'You said he left the room.'

'Because his brother was there.'

'Were you upset that he left the room?'

'Yes, because his brother . . .'

'Please just answer the question, Miss Woods.'

'Yes.'

'Did you feel rejected again?'

'No, no . . .'

'This boy, who you liked a lot, left you on the bed with his brother. How did that make you feel?'

'I was confused.'

'Is that why you had sex with his brother, Marty?'

'NO, NO. I did not have sex with Marty Connaught. He raped me. He forced me. He raped me!'

'I put it to you that when Harry Connaught left the room you felt rejected for a second time and you had consensual sex with Mr Martin Connaught to make some kind of point. To show Harry that you didn't care.'

'No. Absolutely not . . .'

'And afterwards you felt bad about it and decided to make the claim that you had been raped.'

'No. I *was* raped. Marty Connaught forced himself inside me. He had sex with me against my will.'

She stopped and smiled down at her notes. I was stiff and tense, waiting to see what she would ask next.

'When you got home did you tell your mother?'

'No.'

'Your sister?'

'No.'

'Why not?'

'I was too upset.'

'Just to recap so that the jury are clear. You didn't tell the boys in the living room of the Poole Place apartment immediately after it happened. And when you walked into your house you didn't tell either your mother or your sister about this crime that had been committed against you.'

'No, no, no.'

I was tired of being asked the same question over and over.

'When was it, exactly, that you told your friend about this incident?'

I sighed, irritated, on the edge of being angry. I swallowed a couple of times and remembered what Annie said, *Don't get riled. Be calm, yeah? Show that you're a nicer person than the barrister.* Then I heard the judge speaking.

'Would you like a glass of water?'

Mrs Barnaby stood back and fiddled with the strands of her hair that were hanging below the wig. She twisted one of them round her finger. The judge must have nodded towards one of the clerks because a glass of cold water appeared in front of me. I drank from it, feeling the iciness on my tongue. I continued speaking.

'I tried to tell Patrice that night, when I got home. In the end I told her the next day.'

'Why did you have to wait?'

'She was angry with me,' I said. 'She was annoyed at me and didn't want to talk.'

'Right. And what other time did you try to talk to her?'

'The next day in school. On the corridor, in the dining hall. She was angry with me.'

'So you must have been quite desperate to be friends with her again?'

'Yes.'

'So when you saw her later in the day, what did you do?'

'I told her what had happened to me.'

'You told her a story that would make her feel sorry for you?'

'I didn't tell her *a story*. I told her the truth. Marty Connaught raped me.'

'I suggest to you, Miss Woods, that you didn't tell the boys in the apartment, or your mother, or your sister, because the assault didn't happen. When your best friend wouldn't talk to you, you decided to gain her sympathy by accusing an innocent man of raping you.'

'I did not. No, no. No, no.'

'After a fight with your sister you made a half-hearted gesture by running away from home. You hitched yourself up to this boy you had met and took advantage of his generosity. You allowed him to pay for you and you took an expensive gift from him. You tried to have sex with him on two occasions and when he turned you down you had sex with his brother. You left the apartment with money for a taxi. You told no one. When you got back to your normal life you found your best friend ignoring you and you needed a big drama to get back into her good books.'

I shook my head vehemently as she said these things. I did not look at the jury, or Marty Connaught, or my parents. My eyes sought out Annie, who was sitting by Mr Parvez. She had a pained expression on her face. I felt light-headed as if I might topple over. Then I let my eyes drop and gripped the edge of the witness box.

'No further questions, Your Honour.'

I don't remember how long it was before Ms Gardner stepped forward to re-examine me. I wasn't looking at anybody but I could hear murmuring and papers shuffling, footsteps and people clearing their throats. I closed my eyes for a second as if I was in a dark room. The door was locked and no one could come in and I was sitting in the corner curled up, hugging myself.

Then I realised that the noise had stopped and I could hear someone from the public gallery saying shush and I knew we were about to start again.

'Are you OK, Stacey?'

I opened my eyes and Ms Gardner was standing in front of me.

'Stacey, I'm going to go over a couple of things so that the jury can be clear about what happened to you on Wednesday 24th June, last year. Is that all right or would you like a break?'

I shook my head. I had to get through it. I had to finish what I'd started.

'Stacey, on Wednesday 24th June 2016 did you willingly have sex with Martin Connaught, the defendant?'

'No. He raped me.'

'Might Martin Connaught have mistakenly thought that you wanted to have sex with him?'

'No. he could not have thought that because when he was holding me down on the bed I said *no*.'

'Might Martin Connaught not have heard you?'

'I said it clearly. I said it more than once. I said *no*.'

'Thank you, Stacey. I have no further questions, Your Honour. That concludes the case for the prosecution.'

It was over.

Eighteen

The next morning I got up earlier than anyone else and went down to the kitchen and had breakfast. Then I had a shower and went back to my room to get ready to go to school. I packed my bag and sorted out clothes to wear. It was Wednesday and I had Art first thing then English. The afternoon was study time but I could do that in the school library. I could stay in school all day and while I was there I could pretend to myself that there wasn't a trial going on elsewhere with me at its centre.

Ms Gardner told me that I had the right to sit in the public gallery and watch the defence present their case. I could have been there when Harry gave his testimony. I could have heard the lies of Marty Connaught. I had decided that I had had enough though, and the trial would have to go on without me. My mum and dad would be in court, and Mr Parvez and possibly Annie. I would no doubt find out what was going on from them.

I could hear my mum in her bedroom and the sound of her hairdryer going. Next door, Tyler was making noises and Jodie was talking to him. I went onto Google and typed in *Poole Place Rape* and clicked on search. I felt my stomach drop as a list of headlines came up, one after the other. So many, so soon; it seemed as though the press had swooped upon the story, eaten it up and spat it back out again. I clicked on one of the national newspapers. The *Daily Mail: Minister's Stepson's Apartment Used for Rape*. Annie had been absolutely right in her prediction. I held my breath as I read the article. *An act of rape was said to have taken place in an apartment in London's West End, a stone's throw from Selfridges. A stockbroker, Martin John Connaught, has been accused of rape by a seventeen-year-old student, Girl X. The alleged offence took place in June last year.* I read it with great speed, dreading that at any moment my name would pop up somewhere by accident. *Stacey Woods, seventeen-year-old student from Stratford, East London, accuses . . .* But my name was not in it and never would be. I was to be a faceless accuser.

I read some of the others and they all focused on the apartment and the stockbroker. One of them gave more details; *. . . the seventeen-year-old girl was allegedly raped in a bedroom while other teenagers were playing computer games in the next room.* Another account gave me an unfortunate name: *Taxi Girl.*

After a while of looking through the reports I closed the laptop. Maybe that would be it. Once the press realised that the government minister had nothing to do with it, the story would quietly die a death.

My mum knocked on the door.

'Are you going to school?' she said, taken aback, looking at my clothes draped over the chair.

'Yes, most definitely. I need to get back to normal.'

138

At school I could spend time with Patrice and the others. Have a few laughs and jokes about the teachers and kids in the lower sixth. At lunch maybe Patrice and I could walk up to the Italian cafe and get paninis. We wouldn't talk about the trial because it would just be like any other Wednesday. I would make sure of that.

'Will you be all right?'

'Yes. The day will pass quickly for me.'

'Well, I'll send you texts then. Let you know what's happening.'

I shook my head. 'Please, don't. I don't want to know. I want to get away from it.'

'*We* have to go, you know that, don't you?' Mum said. 'Me and your dad have to be there so that this guy knows that you've got family. Plus we want to stare him out while he's up in the stand lying his face off.'

'I know. And I'm grateful.'

I called in on Jodie and Tyler before I left for school.

'I can look after Tyler when I get home this afternoon. Why don't you go out somewhere?'

'Are you sure? What about the trial?'

'I'm not going.'

'Really? I'd want to be there every minute to watch him squirm.'

'I can't stand to see him any more,' I said.

I walked the long route to school, going into a newsagent's that I didn't usually use. I bought a bottle of water and browsed the daily papers. I picked up the tabloids and scanned the front pages. There was nothing about the trial or the government minister on any of them. The story that had looked so widespread on the internet was probably a short column on an inside page. Maybe it hadn't made the papers at all but was just on the internet.

I was relieved and walked on to school.

The first person I saw when I got to the common room was Ms Harper. She was putting notices on a board using a staple gun to fix the edges and glanced round as I walked through the door.

'Stacey,' she said, stepping back from the wall, turning round to look at me. Her hands were full and she looked, for once, a little dishevelled, 'is it over?'

I shook my head. 'My bit of it is. I didn't want to go any more so I've come to school. That's all right, isn't it?'

'Of course it is. Do you need to talk? I'm free now . . .'

'No, I just need to get on with stuff . . .'

'But if it's not over . . .'

'It is for me.'

'Well, if you change your mind you know where I am.'

'I won't. I've got plenty to do. Must keep up the *momentum* for the exams,' I said, smiling, referring to our previous conversation, attempting a little joke.

Ms Harper frowned, then turned back to the wall and continued putting up her notices. She was clearly still put out about my deferring university for this year.

Patrice and Shelley came in soon after and we sat in a threesome talking about the stuff that happened at Roxanne's party. I was listening and yet not listening at the same time. I was glad that there was lots of gossip because it meant I

140

could pretend to be focused and ignore Patrice's quizzical looks. She wanted to know why I was there and not in court, but I didn't feel like telling her. Then Shelley started talking about Donny Martin, the boy from the lower sixth who had a passion for Patrice, and Patrice went red and started to roll her eyes. After a while Shelley went over to her locker to get some of her law books.

'Why are you here?' Patrice said, in a half-whisper.

'I can't talk about it. See you after Art?' I said.

She looked concerned.

'Go for a panini?' I said, as Shelley came back towards us. She nodded.

In Art I was beginning to feel a little shaky. Up to then my decision not to go to court, to head off to school, to act as if it was a normal day, meant that I was feeling emboldened. I was no longer the wimp in the witness box, the tiny teenager wilting in front of the wily Marty Connaught. Today I was travelling on adrenalin, in school, while the trial was going on five miles down the road. It meant that I was in control.

But then I started to think about Harry in the witness box. He would be answering questions about that afternoon of the rape. Part of me wanted to *know* what he would say but another part of me couldn't bear to hear it. I pictured him with Bella, outside her house, the taxi pulling up to take him back to Fulham or wherever he was staying. I had once thought that he could be mine; a modern Romeo and Juliet story. I should have known it would end badly.

I tried to carry on with my schoolwork. I got angry with myself because I'd forgotten some Art preparation I'd done. I set up my easel in a clumsy way and caught my finger in one of the joins. It gave me a painful pinch and I had to hold it for ages until the pain dulled. I stared at the still life in front of me; a cracked vase beside an antique clock. I had no idea how I was going to set it up or what angle I was going to sketch it from. I found myself standing by the window, my arms folded, looking around the room feeling dislocated from it all as if I shouldn't be there. My fingers found the heart pendant hanging round my neck and I gripped it.

'Everything OK, Stacey?' Miss Previn said.

She was smiling at me, unaware of the tiny hurricane going on inside my head.

'Sorry, I'm not feeling great.'

'Oh!' she said, cutting across my words. 'I thought of you the other day. Wait, let me get my laptop . . .'

She came back a few moments later with her laptop, opened it and put it on the bench beside me.

'I have a neighbour who was talking to me about her daughter. She's in the lower sixth – obviously in a different school – and she's thinking about where she wants to apply to next year. She's interested in fashion design. I immediately remembered that you had been keen on that at one time and you and I had talked about the London College of Fashion. Her daughter wants to move away from London though, and my neighbour told me that the London College of Fashion oversee a course at Brighton called Fashion Design and Technology. It's an outreach course for them; some of their tutors run it and the accreditation is by the London College of Fashion!'

142

I looked at Miss Previn and wondered why she was telling me this.

'Only,' she continued, 'I know that in the end you changed your mind about that course and have offers from Reading and Birmingham. I wondered if that was because you wanted to move away from home. Most eighteen-year-olds do. Well, here.'

She turned her laptop round to show me the screen. On it was the University of Sussex website and the page showed a BA Fashion Design and Technology.

'There's a course in Brighton. So you could move away from home and still do the course you wanted.'

She smiled, pleased with herself. I felt a moment's sadness; for the course, for my ambitions, for the fact that she knew nothing about what was going on in my life.

'Thanks so much,' I said. 'I'll have a look at it.'

'It's not too late to apply for another course. Not too late at all.'

She obviously knew nothing about me deferring for a year.

'I'm a bit under the weather. I'll just go and see Ms Harper and get a note to leave early.'

'Of course. I hope you feel better, Stacey.'

I packed up my stuff. I sent a text to Patrice to say I'd gone home. I went past Ms Harper's door but didn't knock on it. I left school and headed home, walking at a pace. I kept my head down, loathe to see anyone or to have to talk. I felt as though I'd failed. All I had to do was stay at school all day, then it would have proved how unaffected I was by the trial, how easily I could shake it off. Instead, it had proved the opposite. It had followed me to school.

Turning into my street, I slowed down. It was eleven thirty and the rest of the day spread out before me. What was I going to do? How would I get through the hours until this *thing* was over.

The street was empty except for a woman standing on the pavement a few doors away from my house. She was talking on a mobile and seemed to turn away as I approached. I put my hand into my bag and felt around to get my keys. I hoped that Jodie and Tyler were still out because I wasn't in any mood to be sociable. I wanted to go inside, to head upstairs, close my room door and sit curled up, by myself, in the quiet of the house.

As I got to my gate the woman finished her phone call and turned towards me. She pushed the phone into a shoulder bag and I recognised her immediately. It was the newspaper reporter from the court, the blonde one with the tablet. I stopped for a second, shocked to see her there, in my street, outside my house. She walked towards me and I stepped round my garden gate and stood behind it.

'Stacey . . .' she started.

Her face looked different outside court, less firm and determined. She had very pale skin and her blonde hair was almost white. She wore no make-up and had a low voice.

'You're not supposed to be here,' I said, loudly. 'You're not allowed to know where I live. This is against the law. I have anonymity. You know that.'

'Stacey, I'm not . . .'

'I won't speak to reporters. I'm not allowed to. You're not allowed to speak to me. How did you know where I live? Did you follow me here?'

She looked perplexed, glanced up and down the street as though she was worried who might hear. She went to put her hand out towards me and I was reminded of Marty Connaught round the back of the courtroom. He had wanted to touch me as well. Why did everyone want to take hold of me?

'I'll report you to the court authorities. Now, you go away and leave me alone.'

I went into my house and slammed the door hard. I stood against it for a few moments, my mouth twisted up. Whatever I did, I couldn't get away; from the reporters, from Marty Connaught and Harry, from the barristers in their funereal robes. The case threw long arms around me, holding me tight, making it hard to breathe.

Nineteen

At lunchtime there was a loud knocking on my door and I went into the living room to look out of the window in case it was the newspaper reporter again. It was Patrice. As soon as I pulled the door back she demanded to know why I had gone off. My answer was to burst into tears on the doorstep and she let her bag drop to the floor and gave me a bear hug. She'd brought paninis and we sat and ate them in the kitchen. I told her about the newspaper reporter and she was shocked. She said I should tell my solicitor and have her disqualified from reporting in court. I nodded but I had no idea what I was going to do about it.

She went back to school and I stayed in my room.

About two, I heard the key in the lock and saw my sister and Tyler come in. Jodie took a look at me and knew that I was upset. She gave me Tyler to look after and I was grateful for the distraction. I took him into my room and played with him until he was ready for his afternoon nap. When he dropped off to sleep Jodie came in with two cups of hot chocolate and I sipped mine slowly while we talked about other stuff: her time at the mother and baby group and her friend, Lizzie, whose mum's house she and Tyler went back to for lunch. We didn't talk about the court case at all.

My mum got home just after five. She looked tired and said she wanted to have a shower. I warmed up some lasagne for her and she came down in jogging pants and a big T-shirt. I considered telling her about the newspaper reporter but she looked stressed, so I didn't.

'How was it?' I said, forcing my voice to be upbeat, hoping she might say something to make me feel batter.

'Not great. Sitting listening to that vile man and his brother. It made me feel grubby. I've written some notes on what was said. They're in my bag in the hall if you want to read them.'

I shook my head.

'How about Dad?'

'He had to get off just before the end. Some problem with Gemma. I actually think it was good that he went. He was sitting like a coiled spring all day long. Every time that Marty opened his mouth to speak I thought he was going to leap out of his seat and throttle him.'

My heart sunk. They'd had to listen to lies about me while I had run away, thinking I could pretend it hadn't happened.

'Probably just as well that you weren't there,' she said.

My mum was pushing the lasagne round the plate. I gave her a kiss on the head and left her to it.

Later when Jodie was upstairs bathing Tyler I went into the living room and sat beside Mum on the sofa. The television was on but Mum was just flicking through the channels. I took the remote from her and muted the sound. From upstairs I could hear Jodie's voice and Tyler making splashing sounds from the bathroom.

'What did they say about me?' I said.

'The notes are in there,' she said, pointing to her bag which was now sitting down by the sofa. I glanced at it but couldn't bear to read anything in black and white. Not after looking at the press reports on the internet that morning.

'No, just tell me what you remember.'

'I remember it all,' she said quietly, 'every word that was said.'

'What about Harry?'

'Oh, Harry Connaught. Very smart. Schoolboy in a grown-up suit, looking fresh and clean like some bank trainee. He went through a long story about how he'd had some troubles that year, some difficulties at school and when he met you he thought you both had something in common. He thought you had troubles too and when you said you'd run away from home he wanted to help you. He sounded very plausible.'

He'd sounded plausible to me at the time.

'He said he'd arranged for you to stay in the apartment and offered to stay with you in case you felt strange on your own.'

That was true. I remembered him saying it when we were drinking in the pub in New Bond Street.

'He said you'd kissed a few times but he had no intention of taking advantage of you.'

We had kissed; on the escalator in Selfridges, in the taxi going to see his brother, in the apartment while his friends were coming up in the lift. These had been signs that he'd felt something more than friendship for me.

149

'He said that on the afternoon it had happened he had left the bedroom to play a computer game. He said you had seemed happy that his brother was there. He had no idea what went on. Afterwards he said he'd sent you texts. He hadn't known that you were upset until he saw you at your school.'

How clever of him to send those texts and pretend that nothing had happened. I wondered what Bella would think if she'd been in the courtroom listening to her boyfriend. No doubt she would have believed him, thinking perhaps that I had exaggerated his part in it.

'He said he was very sad about what happened because he liked you.'

I pictured him in a suit and tie, his face serious, shrugging his shoulders perhaps. A picture of innocence.

'What about Marty Connaught. Did he go on the stand today?'

'Oh yes. He's been questioned by both the barristers, his and yours. Tomorrow he'll be re-examined by his barrister.'

'What did he say?'

'Actually, there wasn't much for him to say. He said he went to the apartment to make sure all was well – as he looks after it – when he saw the other boy playing computer games, then he went into the bedroom. He'd been surprised to see you there. He was embarrassed to see you undressed and was going to leave but Harry said *he* was going. Marty then said he was afraid that you were upset, that perhaps some tiff had taken place. He said that you thanked him for the dress he had bought you. He hadn't known about it, he said, and apparently

150

you said, *If you come and sit on the bed I can give you a thank you kiss* or something like that.'

'Lies.'

'He said you put out your hand and pulled him over. Then you began to kiss him. He says he regrets it, but he simply did what any other man would do and . . . what was the phrase he used? I know . . . *responded to the invitation*.'

How polite Marty was. As if I'd issued an RSVP. *We are pleased to invite you to the* . . .

My mum was quiet.

'You didn't believe him, did you?'

'Stacey, we believe *you*. Everything you said, your dad and I believe it. He's a liar. Now I know you said you couldn't face coming to court today, but maybe if you had been there he might not have been able to lie so smoothly. Maybe your presence might have unsettled him.'

It was exactly what I had thought about Bella being in court. Her presence might have rattled him. Maybe Mum was right. Is it harder to tell a barefaced lie when the person you are telling it about is there in front of you?

'That's it, really. Ms Gardner in her cross-examination made him look grubby. *A grown man having sex with a seventeen-year-old girl who he's just met? A girl who, as far as he knows, has run away from home and is in a vulnerable place?* He just kept agreeing with her. *You're right. I regret it deeply but I didn't rape her.* I could feel your dad tensing up, ready to explode.'

We sat there for a while without speaking. The television played on silently and there was no noise coming from the bathroom upstairs. My head was full of Marty's words, as if I'd been there in the court when he'd been saying them.

'I'll make some tea,' Mum said eventually.

She went out to the kitchen just as there was a knock on the front door. I got up and walked out. All the while I was remembering Marty in the court car park two days before. *You were better than her* . . . he said as his girlfriend Mary Potter walked up behind him. If only the jury had heard that. If only they'd seen him as I had seen him.

I pulled the door back without thinking.

The newspaper reporter was standing there. I was startled. I tried to close it quickly but she used her hand to hold it open. I was about to shout out for my mum when she handed me something.

'I don't work for newspapers. I'm not a reporter,' she said rapidly, hardly catching a breath, 'and you'll never see me again, Stacey. But I would just ask you to read my letter. That's all.'

She'd given me an envelope. I looked at it, then back at her, confused. She'd been in court taking notes, looking at her tablet, both days when I was on the stand. She'd followed every word I'd said and I'd thought she was a reporter.

'Please read my letter. I won't bother you again.'

She stepped back and allowed the door to close. I was left in the hall holding a brown envelope. I pulled the door open again, angry now, still sure there was something going on; newspaper reporters used all sorts of tactics to get people to give them their stories.

'Wait,' I called, walking out along the path to the gate, 'Wait, you can't just . . .'

But she was further down the street. Without looking back she stopped at a car and got into the passenger side. Within seconds the car drove off.

I looked at the envelope. Across it in neat handwriting were the words:

Stacey Woods, please read my story.

Twenty

I went to my room and closed the door. Then I opened the envelope. My eyes swept over two A4 pages of tightly written prose. I took in the first few lines and felt myself stiffen.

Dear Stacey,
I hope you don't mind me writing to you like this. My name is Laura but I don't want to identify myself any further. I want to tell you my story. When you've read it you will understand why.
I was raped by Marty Connaught when I was fifteen years old.

I pictured the woman as she was in court, as she looked when she approached me in the street. She was tall with almost white hair and pale skin. She was certainly in her twenties, maybe twenty-five. I read on, my chest tightening.

My father was the manager of a coffee shop near to Belsize Park Station and sometimes, in the holidays, I helped out. It wasn't official, I was too young to do paid

155

work, but I'd help tidy up the tables and take some orders to nearby offices. Dad used to slip me a few quid and I felt very grown up doing it.

I was a bright student at school and expected to do well, take A levels and go to university. My big love was drama. I'd acted in school plays and I was a member of a local youth drama group. The summer before year eleven I spent a fair amount of time in the shop. Marty Connaught used to come in sometimes, round about eleven, and get some take-out coffees for people at his work. I remember he always had a little list of items he was to buy and it meant he carried a cardboard tray of drinks and paper bag of pastries back with him. One day he took his order but left a Danish behind and I followed him up the road and gave it to him. After that he was very friendly. He used to chat to my dad and to me. He asked me about my school and what I was studying and said he could arrange work experience in his company for me if I wanted, or even some kind of intern role. When I told him I loved drama he was very interested. He came in a couple of times with programmes of plays he'd been to see and once he popped in and gave me two tickets for a play at the National Theatre that someone he knew couldn't use. I went with my friend and we were amazed that seats had cost so much. Dad thought Marty was great. He said he could tell that Marty was from MONEY and that I should pay attention to the way Marty spoke because it was proper English.

I liked him. He was a pleasant, friendly man.

One day I was walking home from school. It was raining hard and I'd just left my friends at their bus stop. I had the hood of my coat up but I was still getting wet and I heard a beeping sound as a car pulled up beside me. It was Marty. He shouted out for me to get in and said he would give me a lift home. I didn't give it a second thought. I got in and told him where I lived. I felt bad because it was probably going to take him out of his way, but he said that was fine. He was delivering a statement to one of their clients and didn't have to rush back. Then he asked me if I minded if he delivered the statement first as it was an easier route. I said yes, no problem.

I was young. How was I to know that nobody delivered statements by hand? I just didn't think. When we got to this client's address I thought I'd stay in the car but he said, Why not come up? *This lady had been an actress for years. She was in repertory, never famous, but she was in Shakespeare a lot.* She's retired now, *he said,* and she gets quite lonely, I think. That's why I bring her statements by hand. She likes to chat. She'd be very interested in you.

So I went with him.

I can't believe I was so naive. I got out of the car and went into this old mansion block. He had to tap in a security number and then we went up in a lift. I expected us to knock on a door and wait for someone to answer it but he had a key. The client is not very mobile, *he said.* I always let myself in.

It might have been then that I started to feel a bit odd. Like it wasn't quite right. He opened the door and went in and I followed. He called out a name, Mary or something like that. Perhaps she's in the bedroom, *he said. I stood by the door. I didn't go any further into the flat but I could hear him walking through the rooms, his shoes tapping on the wooden floors.*

Then he called me. Give me a hand, *he shouted.* Can you come and give me a hand? *I thought something was wrong, that the old lady was ill, so I walked through the living room. It was only then that I realised that the flat was almost empty of furniture, just a sofa in the room and nothing else.* Can you help me? *I could hear him calling, so I headed for the bedroom. He was standing by the door and as I stepped into the room he closed it behind me.*

She must have gone out, *he said,* but we could have a chat.

I knew something was wrong. I said I had to go but he took my hand and led me across to a bed. It was the only piece of furniture in the room. I said, I want to go home. *He just kept talking in an ordinary voice as if nothing unusual was happening. He spoke about the actress and some of the roles she had played. He'd seen her once, he said, at Stratford-Upon-Avon when she played Cleopatra. As he was doing this he was touching my breasts and undoing the buttons of my shirt.*

I should have got up and run out, but I felt overwhelmed by him.

I don't want this, *I said*. You only think you don't want it, *he said*. You'll enjoy it. I'll be careful with you. I know you're a virgin. I'll look after you, it won't hurt. I am experienced. *And all the while he was pushing his hands under my clothes, pulling at them. And then he lay on top of me and he raped me.*

Afterwards he drove me to the end of my street and gave me two twenty-pound notes to buy something nice. He told me not to tell anyone.

When I got in I went straight up to the bathroom and took my clothes off. My pants were ripped down the side and my tights had great holes at the top where he'd pushed his fingers in. I stayed in the bath for a long time. I didn't tell my parents and I stopped going to work in my dad's shop. I went back to school in September and realised soon after that that something was wrong, that I was pregnant.

For months I hid it. I didn't know what to do. In the end my mum came into my room and asked me if I had anything to tell her.

I should have told them when I first got home the day of the rape but I didn't.

I should have told them in the next few weeks but I didn't.

When I first knew I was pregnant I should have told them.

I was four months gone when I began to show and I made up a story about a boy I had met at a party. My parents were upset but they stood by me, and in the following March I gave birth to a little boy. I still did my A levels and I went to university because my

159

*parents helped me raise my son. This little boy is the
centre of my life. He is ten years old now.*

*How can I tell him that he only exists because I was
raped? That his father is a rapist? How can I tell him that?*

*I didn't do drama. Just the thought of going to see a
play or act in a play is enough to make me feel sick.*

*I work as a clerk in a legal firm and it was by chance
that I saw Marty Connaught's name in the court
schedules. That's why I came along to see what had
happened. When I saw you on the stand I felt like I was
watching myself struggling to explain how something like
that had happened. I so admire you, I wanted to leap up
and shout out –* I know she is telling the truth because
it happened to me! *For the first time since it happened
to me I wanted to come forward to tell my story in the
way that you had. But how can I do it? It would mean
telling my son the truth and I don't want him to know
what kind of man his father was.*

*Please forgive me for not coming forward, for not
supporting you. I won't come to court again but I'll be
thinking about you, hoping that Marty Connaught is
found guilty.*

Xxxx

I put the letter down on my bed. I felt like I was on the brink
of tears.

Now I was carrying the burden for *two* other women as
well as myself.

Twenty-One

I went to the trial the next day.

Annie, who had texted me the previous evening, told me it would probably be the last day before the jury retired. She was pleased to know that I was going to come. *You've got to keep strong, yeah?* she'd said and I told her I would. I avoided going on any news websites that night or the next morning. I couldn't read what was being written about the case. I had to just see it through until the end.

We arrived in plenty of time and I sat beside my mum and dad in the middle of the front row of the public gallery. I sneaked a look around to see if Marty's family was there, in particular whether *Harry* was there. None of them were. I wondered whether they had had enough or were waiting outside somewhere; or possibly they were back in their house in Fulham. Had the press coverage scared them away?

There was a buzz from people coming in after us, the courtroom doors swinging open and shut, letting in members of the public and journalists, one or two of whom looked surprised to see me there. The seats quickly filled up. I avoided making eye contact with anyone. I *did* want Marty Connaught to see me there and I was going to sit up straight and hear every word that came out of his mouth.

I didn't tell anyone about the letter I'd got from Laura, the drama student. There was a ten-year-old boy who didn't know what sort of man his biological father was and I understood that she wanted it to stay that way.

Marty Connaught wasn't on the stand for very long. I focused on him as he held the Bible and said *I swear by Almighty God that the evidence I shall give shall be the truth, the whole truth and nothing but the truth*. He stared ahead, looking at some point towards the back of the courtroom. His shoulders were square and his back straight as if he was standing to attention. A couple of the jurors kept looking across at me and then back to him.

Mrs Barnaby welcomed the jury back and asked her questions in a very upbeat voice as if she was a television presenter on a daytime show. She'd plaited her long hair and it hung out the back of her white wig. She took a while looking at some papers again and I could see the judge getting impatient.

'Are we ever going to commence proceedings, Mrs Barnaby?'

'Most certainly, Your Honour.'

She turned to Marty.

'Why did you have sex with Miss Woods?'

He hesitated, startled perhaps by the directness of her question. He seemed to swallow and take a moment before answering.

'I was attracted to her.'

'But you didn't know her. You'd never met her until that time in the bedroom at Poole Place.'

'I was attracted to her physically.'

162

'In what way?'

'She was wearing almost nothing. But it wasn't just that. She was interested in me. She asked me to sit beside her on the bed. I was flattered . . .'

He shrugged as he lied.

'Do you regret it?'

'I do. It was a moment of madness. It's not the way I am with women. I'm happier when in a relationship. At that time I was alone.'

'Did you rape this girl, Mr Connaught?'

'I did not. She wanted to have sex. I would not. I am not that kind of man.'

He glanced in my direction. I wished for a moment I could stand up in court in a dramatic way, like on a TV drama, and shout out, *What about Bella? What about Laura, the drama student?* I didn't though. I tried to catch his eye, to pull him into my gaze, to show him I wasn't fazed by his protestations of innocence. He was a liar and a rapist. I wanted him to see that written all over my face. His eyes slid away though, back towards the jury.

The barristers went on to give their closing statements. Ms Gardner faced the jury and gave a long speech about a vulnerable girl taken advantage of by a man who had a privileged lifestyle. She said that I was a naive teenager, my head full of romance. I had been drawn into a situation that I wasn't able to get myself out of. *Be clear though*, she said to the jury, *the responsibility for this lies with the defendant, a thirty-four-year-old man, who took the opportunity to force a girl of seventeen – who he had never met before – to have sex. This*

163

was a premeditated act. The defendant knew this girl would be in the apartment and he had connived with his brother to have her ready for when he came. It was a despicable act.

Mrs Barnaby repeated the things she'd said to me when I was on the stand.

This girl latched on to the brother of the defendant. She allowed him to pay for her, to let her sleep in a borrowed apartment. She took gifts and tried to persuade the defendant's brother to have sex with her. When that failed a second time she had sex with his brother and then tried to say that it was rape. I suggest to you that this is not a bad girl; just a confused one. It is up to you, the jury, to decide whether or not her confusion should lead to the ruination of a man's life.

Several of the jury seemed transfixed by her words. Their eyes followed her as she walked up and down. One woman looked directly at me, her forehead slightly pinched. Then Mrs Barnaby sat down.

The judge summed the case up. He went over all the points of evidence, one after the other. He was painstaking, pointing out this and that side of the argument. When he finished it was almost one and the people in the public gallery were becoming restless. My legs felt stiff and I could feel my mum shifting about on her chair. My dad hadn't moved though; he seemed frozen in his position. Finally, with what seemed like a deep breath, the judge made his last statement.

In the end, members of the jury, it will be up to you to decide which of the accounts you believe. There is no forensic evidence; as in most rape cases there are no witnesses. It is simply Miss Woods's word against that of Mr Connaught. You have heard

them both speak and now you have – what I consider – a difficult
task. That is to unravel the truth from these differing accounts.

And the jury was sent to deliberate.

We sat in the witness rooms. My dad got sandwiches and cans of drink. The place was full of people and the sounds of various conversations were all around us. Just before two o'clock people started to drift off and we were left sitting there, completely alone. The silence seemed heavy and full of tension.

We just had to wait. The jury would be talking about me, about what happened to me, and there was nothing else for us to do but to hold our nerve and see what decision they reached.

In the corner the television news was on. There was no sound but I watched it and noticed, with dismay, footage of Marty Connaught walking up the driveway of Snaresbrook Court, shaking his head and looking down at his feet as he was asked questions by a number of reporters. Behind him were what looked like members of his family, who shied away from the cameras, turning their faces in the opposite direction. It must have been filmed that very morning. Underneath, the text on the running news bar explained: *Jury retires on Poole Place Rape Case.*

'It's on the telly!' I said, looking over to my mum and dad.

'It'll be over soon. And don't forget they can't show *your* face or identify you in any way,' my dad said.

'They can show *him*, though. That's one good thing,' my mum said, looking pleased for once.

I turned my back on the television and walked across to the far window that overlooked the car park where I'd bumped into Marty a couple of days before. Now there was no one around, not even a group of smokers. The afternoon schedules were underway and everyone had somewhere they had to be.

Except for us.

I went back to Mum and Dad and sat down. None of us spoke. We stayed like that for a while, and I tried to think things through. Annie had told me that juries sometimes came to a quick verdict. The quickest she'd seen had been an hour and that was because it was clear that the defendant was guilty. On the other hand, it could take days if they didn't agree and sometimes juries were sent to hotels to stay overnight so that they didn't talk to anyone else about the case. I wondered which it would be.

'How's Gemma?'

I heard Mum talking to Dad.

'Still sick all the time. She's worried that it will affect the baby. I try to reassure her but . . .'

'It's her first. She'll worry about everything. This whole business is probably a bit of a strain for her as well.'

'It is . . .'

My dad went quiet. *This whole business*. The words seemed like a slap in the face. I was causing everybody difficulties. Even Gemma and her unborn baby were feeling the stress. For a second, I wanted to shout out, *What about me? What about how I feel?* I felt like I wanted to argue with someone, to walk out in a huff. But when I looked at Mum and Dad's faces I couldn't help but feel ashamed. Both of them looked grey with worry; my dad chewing at the side of his nails, my mum's mouth permanently turned down at the sides. I noticed then that my dad's papers had been put away and my mum's reading glasses were no longer hanging round her neck. Their jobs were done.

Now they just had to wait.

'I'm going to the toilet,' I said.

I walked out into the cool corridor. In the toilets I splashed water on my face and used the paper towels to dry my skin. I felt myself calming down a bit. I looked at my phone and saw some missed texts from Patrice. I sent an answer telling her that the jury had retired and saying I would let her know about any developments.

I headed back towards the waiting area and saw Annie in the corridor coming towards me. I stopped until she got to me.

'The jury are coming back into court.'

'What?'

I pulled my phone out. It was only three twenty.

'But they've not been out very long.'

'I know, but they're coming back in. Get your parents. They've reached a verdict.'

Annie went off and I pushed open the door. My mum and dad looked up expectantly. The jury had made a quick decision. Had they believed me? Was that why they hadn't taken very long?

'We have to go back into court,' I said. 'The jury have decided.'

My mum and dad were both startled by my words. They glanced at each other and then gathered their things and followed me out.

Twenty-Two

The courtroom was packed and silent as the judge came in. Marty's family were back in their seats but I couldn't see Harry anywhere. The older woman who I thought was probably Marty's mother was wearing a bright blue silk scarf wound round and round her neck so that the edge of it came up to her chin. Next to her was Mary Potter. The clerk spoke and everyone stood up while the judge made his way to his seat, then the whole courtroom sat down again. After a few minutes the jury were led in. I looked at each of them as they emerged from a door at the side of the courtroom, trying to work out what kind of expression they wore, their body language, how the women were holding their bags and the men were fiddling with their jackets. They all avoided looking at me or Marty Connaught. There was some coughing and they took a few moments getting their seats, making themselves comfortable. They'd only been out for a couple of hours and yet it seemed as though they'd been away for days.

The short time they had taken made me hopeful. I grabbed my mum's hand and squeezed it. The jury had accepted my story. They'd believed me and had discounted Mrs Barnaby's theories. They hadn't even taken the time to discuss them.

The barristers were sitting up, looking expectant. Mr Parvez was staring at the jurors and Annie was beside him. I caught her eye but she looked distracted and didn't smile. When it was over I wanted to go and thank her for all the things she'd done for me, all the evenings she'd sat in her car and explained the procedures. How she'd kept my spirits up. The bags of Haribo sweets.

The court became quiet. My dad leaned sideways and whispered in my ear, *Here we go. Fingers crossed.* Inside my chest was a feeling of excitement. I looked over at Annie again but she was doggedly looking down at something on her lap, flicking through a book or a file. I focused on Ms Gardner and saw that she had turned round and was speaking quietly to Mr Parvez. He was nodding at what she was saying and his eyes flicked up towards me, then away.

The clerk was standing up. He spoke directly to Marty.

'Will the defendant please rise?'

Marty Connaught stood up. His hands were on the edge of the dock, loosely clasped. He looked still but tense. He stared straight ahead, his mouth slightly open.

The clerk then turned to the juror on the end of the box.

'Chairperson of the jury, have you reached a verdict on which you all agree?'

The man stood up. He was grey-haired and wore rimless glasses and I'd not noticed him before. He was wearing an open-necked shirt underneath a suit jacket.

'We have,' he said loudly.

'Do you find the defendant Martin John Connaught guilty or not guilty of the crime of rape?'

Everyone in the courtroom seemed to hold their breath. I felt my mum's hand grasping mine. I turned and saw Annie looking at me. Her face was stern, her expression gloomy.

'We find the defendant not guilty of rape.'

Not guilty.

I heard my mum gasp. My dad seemed to slump back. Then the courtroom exploded with noise. There were yelps coming from further back where Marty's family were. All around us people were talking in loud *surprised* voices. I noticed a number of people getting out of their seats and exiting the courtroom and others tapping into laptops furiously.

Not guilty.

The judge was standing up, ready to leave, and banged on his desk with a gavel. I wasn't really taking a lot of notice of what was being said but I could see his lips moving as he directed his comments to Marty Connaught, who was waving at his family. The security man beside him tapped him on the shoulder and pointed towards the door and Marty nodded and turned back once more to the courtroom. His eyes met mine and he gave the tiniest shake of his head. I closed my eyes. I felt my dad's arm go round my shoulder and my mum leaned in towards me as if they were both trying to shield me from the tumult that had erupted.

Then Annie was squatting in front of me.

'Stay here, until everyone has gone. We can talk it through.'

I couldn't hear my dad's answer but I felt Annie's hand squeeze my arm and she stood up and seemed swept away by the people moving past, trying to get outside the courtroom. I felt overwhelmed by the noise and the movement around me, like I was a tiny island in the middle of a gushing river.

Then it was gone and the courtroom was calm. The commotion had moved out into the corridor. The atmosphere was hushed, the low voices of the barristers and solicitors talking to each other. A door opened on the far side, where the jurors had previously come in and out, and a young woman in an overall entered, holding a black plastic bag. She had headphones on and a nose ring. She pulled on some rubber gloves and paused, looking around the empty courtroom. It was her job to tidy up, to pick up the detritus left by the people who had been here.

'I've got to get out of here,' I said, standing up, shaking off my mum and dad.

'Annie said it might be better to wait . . .' my mum said.

I couldn't stay there another second so I headed out into the corridor. The area in front of the courtroom doors was empty but further up were a knot of people standing around. In the middle was Marty Connaught. His mother and his barrister and solicitor were by him. A couple of men walked up and patted Marty on the shoulder. I could hear *Congratulations*, as if he'd just won a medal.

'Come on, Stacey, let's get out of here.'

My mum was behind me, I could feel her pulling my arm in the opposite direction to where the celebrations were going on.

He *had* won. They had believed him and not me. I felt my legs begin to weaken and turned to follow Mum when I saw Harry striding past me on the way to where his brother and his family were. He didn't pause when he saw me, he merely looked straight ahead. My eyes followed him as he gathered speed, walking up to the group of people around Marty.

'Come on, love,' my dad said.

But I couldn't turn away. My gaze was fixed on Harry as he reached his family and held his arms out in a gesture of delight. Marty saw him and pulled him to him and the two brothers hugged while members of their family and friends clapped and said *Ah* and *Well done*.

Bella had said that Harry was estranged from his brother. They were no longer close. Harry had come to understand that what Marty had done was wrong. She was positive that Harry was a different person than that boy I had known the previous June.

It didn't look that way now.

PART TWO

Twenty-Three

On the evening of the *not guilty* verdict Annie came round. I was in my bedroom. I'd been there since getting home that afternoon. I hadn't eaten, I hadn't changed my clothes, I hadn't spoken to anyone. My mum must have told Annie where I was because she knocked gently on my bedroom door and opened it without waiting for me to call out. I was instantly embarrassed because she'd not been in my room before. I felt exposed; my old clothes lying across a chair, my bed rucked up, my schoolbooks and papers abandoned from days before. It was stuffy and dark in there too, over-warm, the windows closed, the blinds half drawn. She found me in a twilight world, moody as hell; as if I'd been sent to my room because I'd not been raped after all.

'Hiya,' she said, coming in and perching herself on the end of my bed.

I nodded and sat up straight, feeling awkward.

'This verdict was always a possibility,' she said.

'You didn't say that before,' I said sulkily.

I noticed that she was still wearing her courtroom clothes – a loose dress with a jacket over it. Her hair was pulled back. She looked like a school teacher.

'I think I did. There was always a chance that he might be believed, but it doesn't undermine what you did.'

'I lost.'

'You stood up. You grabbed the courage from somewhere and you made a stand for every woman or girl who's ever been raped by some cocky bloke who thought he could break the rules.'

'But I *lost*. How does that help anyone?'

'Because every time a woman goes to court for rape it makes every potential rapist out there think a little more before he does anything. We've lost a battle but we've not lost the war.'

My throat felt as though it had been tied in a double knot.

'Marty Connaught is happy tonight but his life will have to change. Everyone knows what he was accused of. He won't be raping anyone else in a hurry. At least you have achieved that.'

My bedroom door swung open suddenly. It was Jodie. She looked startled to see Annie.

'Oh, sorry,' she said breathlessly, 'but he's just been on telly. Marty-the-rapist. He was answering questions. It's over now, but get it on your laptop. ITV local news.'

'On telly?'

'Someone must have doorstepped him,' Annie said.

I picked up my laptop and took a few moments finding my way onto the news channel. I was all fingers and thumbs.

'I can't seem to access it . . .' I said, frustrated.

'Here . . .'

Annie took it off me and clicked a few times and then held the screen between us. Jodie was looking over my shoulder. Marty Connaught was walking along, smiling at the reporters.

The camera was shaky and I could hear on the soundtrack several questions being shouted at him, some louder than others.

Mr Connaught, how does it feel to be acquitted?

Do you feel any resentment towards the girl, Martin?

Do you think the case should have been brought to court?

I saw that Marty had the charity pin in his lapel again and he'd taken his tie off. He looked like someone's nice uncle. He was dismissing all the questions in a genial way, his hand up in mid-air as if fending off the reporters and the cameraman. But then his expression changed as if something had just come into his head. He stopped walking and turned to the camera.

Jodie let out a splutter.

'Look at his big face. He thinks he's a celebrity now!'

I held my breath to see what he was going to say.

I would like to thank the jury for their verdict.

'He thinks he's won an Oscar!' Jodie said.

I would just like to comment on one thing. The girl who accused me of rape has had her identity protected. My identity has been all over the press. It's my view that the law should be changed so that defendants have the right of anonymity. It's supposed to be "innocent until proven guilty" after all. Thank you.

He was staring straight into the camera and his voice was firm and reasonable. The older woman with the blue scarf came up behind him and pulled him away. The clip ended.

I sighed. Annie sighed, Jodie swore under her breath. We all sat for a few moments saying nothing. Then Annie stood up and smoothed down her dress.

'I have to go,' she said. 'You look after yourself, yeah? I'll be in touch.'

I was surprised at her sudden exit. I'd expected her to stay a while, to talk soothingly to me; to try and make it better. But she was a policewoman and she had other cases. Jodie followed her out and I could hear them talking as they went down the stairs. I pressed the replay button and watched the clip again and again. Marty's face there in my bedroom making me shiver with discomfort.

I want to thank the jury.

I thought of those men and women; just everyday people. In their real lives they were mums and dads, aunts and uncles, next-door neighbours and friends. Why hadn't they believed me?

I stayed in my house and my room for five days. I lay on the bed, looking at my laptop for a lot of the time. I wrote in my purple notebook. I lay my heart out on every page, the quality of the handwriting a gauge of my feelings. Sometimes it was neat and tidy, resting on the lines, uniform gaps between each word. Other times the words flew across the page, sliding off the lines, bumping into each other, some scribbled through, some tailing off, the last letters just a sloping line. The book had once been pristine but now the corners were curly. I was supposed to use it for notes and then write my story on a laptop, but that wasn't going to happen. Typed script was too tidy, too uniform. It didn't suit the way I felt.

I didn't want to speak to anyone. I told my mum I wasn't going to school or to any revision lessons. I had no intention of going into Budgens. When Dad phoned to ask me round I shook my head and refused to take the receiver and speak to him. I got texts from Patrice and answered saying that I'd see her soon. I couldn't face anyone.

I scoured the internet for the press reports. It was all there.

Stockbroker Not Guilty of Rape

Rape in Gov Minister's Apartment Didn't Happen

Jury Acquit Stockbroker of Rape

No Rape in Luxury Oxford Street Apartment

The stories gave as much salacious detail as they could.

The unnamed student 'Girl X' who was seventeen at the time of the incident was almost naked when the defendant arrived. She wanted to give me a thank-you kiss, she was a willing participant, the stockbroker told a packed court. Afterwards she took money for a taxi home.

Another paper made much of the young people in the apartment.

The apartment, owned by a junior government minister, was used by the teenagers for drink, drugs, computer games and sex. The seventeen-year-old student claimed that she'd run away from home and took money and hospitality from the other teenagers. After sexual foreplay with the defendant's brother she initiated sex with the stockbroker. The jury found the man, Martin John Connaught, not guilty of rape. I gave her money for a taxi home, he'd said. I had no idea she was upset.

Commentators on the internet said what they thought. It was easy to find stuff. I put *Taxi Girl* into the search. I read each of them with grim determination and felt my irritation bubble up. *Taxi Girl Case Raises Issue of Consent.* It was a long article from a serious newspaper. A few lines underneath was a tabloid: *Sixth-Form Student Must Take Some of the Blame.* I felt annoyed at the words and wanted to rub my thumb on the screen as if to remove them. The last one was the final straw: *Brainless Girls Who Give Feminism a Bad Name.* I shut the lid, holding it tight for a few moments.

How dare they talk about me like that?

It was all right to be enraged. Annie had told me so months before. *Don't hurt yourself and don't throw things around the room, yeah? When you get angry, use the emotion to galvanise yourself, harden up.*

But the anger never stayed long enough for me to turn it into something positive. It was like an assailant waiting for me in a dark alley. It pounced, made me double up in pain, and then it fled. Even as I sat on the edge of my mattress, I felt it skulking away, leaving me beaten and bruised again.

From time to time I played the clip of Marty on the news. By then I knew the words off by heart. I wondered if Bella had seen it. I hadn't heard anything from her, not a call, text, nothing. I kept picturing her and Harry when I'd seen them together that night in her street. *He doesn't speak to his brother*, she'd said afterwards. But Harry had been embracing his brother when I saw him.

Maybe he had never fallen out with him at all.

The idea began to take hold of me. Marty had encouraged Harry to stay in his relationship with Bella. He had realised, just as I had, that the presence of Bella in the courtroom would not be a good thing. Perhaps he thought that the press interest in the story would alert Bella to the trial and possibly she would turn up, maybe even go to the police herself. He couldn't have known that she had already told me that she wouldn't, that she had asked me to keep her secret.

So Harry turned up outside Bella's house. He'd fallen out with his brother. He was at odds with his family. He thought his brother was a bad influence on him. He needed saving and Bella was the one to do it for him.

Had Marty put him up to that? Or had Marty just been happy that it had happened? If Harry was in a relationship with Bella, then Marty would know that she wasn't going to suddenly turn up in court. Why would she put Harry through any more grief? Harry and Bella as a couple meant that there would only ever be one accuser. The more I thought about this, the more it took root in my mind.

I got a letter. It was addressed to Miss Woods and it had been delivered by hand, pushed through the letter box so that Mum picked it up when she came home. She was concerned about it in case it was some kind of hate mail, she said, but I recognised the neat writing and the envelope. I knew who had sent it. My mum then looked around my room at the mess. She walked straight across to the window and pushed it open. The sudden breeze made the net curtain billow. When she left I opened the letter. It was from Laura, the drama student. It was short.

Dear Stacey,
You have had a terrible time. I'm so sorry that the
verdict was not a true one. What you did was really
important. You can hold your head up.
   There is no shame for you. You did your best.
   xxxx Laura

No shame for me. I did my best. Why did it not feel like that?

Twenty-Four

'Do you want me to do your hair?' Patrice said.

I shook my head. It was the end of the first week of the Easter holidays and we were in her bedroom. On her dressing table was the purple notebook. Patrice had been reading through the notes I had made. There was a lot there and it had taken her a few days.

'Come on. I can talk better when I'm doing hair. You know that.'

'I can't.'

The thought of having Patrice parting, combing, plaiting or pinning was too much. I could hardly bear to wash my face or brush my teeth. It meant looking in a mirror and I hated the sight of myself.

'OK. Let's go get a panini. We can talk in the cafe,' she said.

We walked for about fifteen minutes to a cafe near our school called Tony's Gelato. It was where some of the sixth form went for lunch. We didn't talk about it en route. Patrice was listening to something on her headphones, pulling one off her ear from time to time to tell me about the music or some gossip about some other kid that we knew. When we got there it was pretty full but I managed to get a table near the window. I cleared off the bits and pieces that the previous occupants had left and waited for Patrice to bring over the toasted paninis.

It was two weeks since the verdict and I was still bruised. I'd been feverishly writing my story, getting the words down on the page, going over everything that had happened.

Patrice had insisted on reading it.

She plonked a tray on the table with the food and drinks and sat down. I started eating straight away. It gave me something to do while I waited for her to start talking to me about my scrappy notes.

'So . . .'

I waited to see what she would say.

'Are you definitely starting back at school after the holidays?'

'Yes.'

She'd asked me this a dozen times.

'No more time off?'

'I'm *coming back*.'

She was quiet, holding up her panini in mid-air, looking at each end of it as if not quite sure where to start. Her headphones were round her neck.

'Your notes made me want to cry,' she said, placing the book on the table between us. 'I knew you were going through a bad time, I just didn't know how bad.'

She was looking straight at me. It felt odd. We did a lot of our *serious* talking looking at each other through a mirror. Either she was doing my hair or I was doing hers. We used to talk about important things lying on the trampoline in her back garden but that had gone. Her eyes were dark and sad. I put my hand across the table and grabbed the sleeve of her shirt and held onto it for a few moments.

'But going to court was the right thing to do,' she said. 'If people didn't take their grievances to the police, to court, what kind of society would we live in? I know I'm biased because it's what I want to study. It's what I want to do with my life, but honestly, you had to *try* and get justice. The fact that you haven't is something you're going to have to find a way to live with. You've had a bad deal. You've been let down. His barrister was able to make a more convincing case than yours.'

'What about the *truth*?'

'The truth is always there. *We* know what happened to you.'

It wasn't enough. I'd wanted more people to see Marty Connaught for what he was.

'What does your policewoman say? She must have spoken to you about it?'

I shrugged my shoulders. I thought about Annie and felt a twinge of hurt. Since the evening of the verdict I hadn't seen her. I'd sent her a couple of texts which she'd replied to with smiley faces or thumbs up but no words, nothing personal. It seemed as though her job with me was over and I wasn't to have any contact with her again.

Patrice had been chewing a mouthful and had swallowed.

'You could have told me about Bella. I wouldn't have said a word to anyone.'

'I told Bella that I wouldn't tell anyone.'

'But I thought we told each other everything.'

'Not always,' I said.

I didn't want to go into detail. Patrice had big chunks of her life that I wasn't part of. There was a time when I would have minded, but not now.

'Anyway, I gave her a promise. We weren't close friends or anything but we had this big thing that linked us. I had to be loyal to her.'

'Even if it cost you the trial?'

'Yes. Even that.'

'That's the annoying thing about you, Stacey. You're so loyal. It's also the really *good* thing about you.'

I continued eating, but she placed her panini back on the plate. Then she put her hand in the pocket of her coat and rummaged. She produced a sheet of paper folded up a few times.

'I've written a list,' she said, 'and I'm going to read it to you.'

I suddenly thought of the lists I used to write. Divide a page in half; write *Good* on one side and *Bad* on the other. Then note down all the things that were going on in my life; make a tally of how happy or sad I should be. I was sure Patrice's list would be different.

'I have some things here I think you should do.'

'A to-do list!'

I raised my eyebrows in a half-jokey way. Just then the cafe door opened and a group of lads bustled in. They were loud and a couple of them were messing around with a baseball cap. One of them was ignoring the melee, staring down at his phone. It was Donny Martin, the boy from the lower sixth who liked Patrice. She turned round and saw him. She didn't say anything, just swivelled back to me and held up the piece of paper. I tried to focus on it. I could see the lines where it had been folded. The type showed through. There was a numbered list.

'Don't you want to say hello to Donny?'

'I do not!'

'He's looking over at you.'

'Can we get on with this?'

I nodded. I put my elbows on the table. My panini was half eaten, so was hers.

'I think you have to go forward and I know that sounds like a cliché. I also know, given the stuff you've written in your story, that emotionally you might not be able to move on. So for a while you're going to be split up the middle.'

'That sounds uncomfortable,' I said, smiling.

'Do you want my advice?'

'Yes,' I said.

'I knew I should have done this while I was doing your hair. Maybe I should leave it at that.'

She folded the paper back in half.

'No, no, no. Go on, please. That's why I asked you to read my stuff. I need your advice.'

She unfolded the paper, laid it on the table and smoothed it out.

'In your heart you're going to be stuck in the past. But it's in your head that you're going to have to move forward. Think about it like this. Marty Connaught has ruined this last nine months for you. If you don't move away from it, then he will ruin your future.'

189

Ms Harper had said something very similar to me before the trial. I remembered sitting drinking tea from her china cups, watching her face drop as I told her I wouldn't be going to university after all.

'So, here's my list. Shall I read it out? Or do you just want to read it?'

'Read it out.'

'OK. One: go back to school, work for, like, twenty-five hours a day and get the best results. Two: do not on any account defer university for a year. Three: go down to the University of Sussex for an open day and find out about their fashion course. Four: go for a coffee with that boy Woody who works in Budgens. Five: come to Donny's birthday party on Saturday week.'

'What?' I spluttered. '*Woody?* His name's not Woody. That's his dog's name! His name's Dan!'

'OK, so go for a coffee with Dan.'

I plucked the piece of paper from her and stared at the list.

'Why Sussex? I've already got offers from two unis,' I said.

She took the list back.

'Do it, Stacey. It was what you wanted to do before this all happened. Be a designer of clothes. It was your ambition. Don't let that Marty take that away as well as everything else.'

She was speaking with such certainty. I could see why she wanted to be a barrister. I thought about the barristers at Snaresbrook Crown Court; draped in their gowns and wigs, looking alien. I wanted to say to her, *Don't be like Mrs Barnaby.*

'Number six . . .'

'More?' I said.

'Only joking. No more. That's enough to be going on with . . .'

'Wait a minute,' I said, remembering something, glancing across the cafe at the group of boys who'd come in, 'Did you say Donny Martin's *birthday party*? Are you going to his party?'

'I am.'

'Are you and him . . . ?'

'Maybe. Now and then.'

'How come you didn't say hello to him?'

'I can't be seen out with him in public. He's too young. Maybe after his birthday . . . We'll see. Anyway, enough about me. Are you all right? With that list, I mean. You seriously need to do all those things because I've got another list of things – on hold – that need doing to your hair!'

That made me smile. Everything, in Patrice's world, came back to hair.

We finished our paninis. She'd left the sheet of paper on the table, so I took it, folded it up and put it into my notebook. I didn't know whether I'd follow her instructions but I wanted to have the list. Just as we were getting ready to go, Patrice seemed to remember something.

'Oh, one last thing.'

I steeled myself. I didn't think I could take any more advice.

'I'm sorry about the trampoline. We had some great times on it. But it was part of my past. It had to go. I'd grown out of it and, actually, so had you.'

She was right. I'd grown out of a lot of things lately.

Twenty-Five

I finally went to work for the first time in a couple of weeks. The supervisor, Mrs Bakhtar, was sweet about me having had time off. She made me a cup of coffee and brought it out to the till and told me not to stress myself about anything. I wondered exactly how my mum had embroidered our story to explain my absence. The two Sues from Plaistow chatted for a while and told me they'd missed me. Dan was stacking shelves and he waved when he saw me. Later he came over.

'You OK?'

'Yeah, I am now,' I said.

'Too much revision to do?' he said.

'Something like that.'

'Sounds a bit secretive.'

'It's not. I just don't want to . . .'

'No problem. I'm just being nosy. See you at break?'

'Sure.'

I was busy on the till, then I spent a while trying to sort out one of the self-service tills. An elderly lady asked me where cat food was and I showed her. While I was doing it she told me about her son who lived in Edinburgh (who was thirty-five in

June – where do the years go?). He couldn't get to see her very often because he was a dentist and had lots of appointments all the time. His name was Martin and he lived with another young man called Gerry (whose parents owned a fish shop in Glasgow – very nice people). She missed him, she said, but she had her cat, Mr Darcy. I found the right product for her and she told me I was a very nice young lady, not like some others who lived in her street. I walked her to the door of the shop and waved as she went. I felt emotional all of a sudden but, for once, it wasn't about me. I noticed that she walked in a sprightly way and it made me sad that she didn't see her dentist son very often.

A while later I had my break. I expected to see Dan in the staff area but he wasn't around, so I sat on my own and drank from a bottle of water. I looked at my phone and saw that I had no new messages.

I felt very flat.

The end of the trial and the drama it had brought had subsided. The press had moved on to something else, although there were still some new postings from day to day on the internet. I had stopped looking, mostly. Everyone had gone back to their everyday lives. Mum was at work and Dad and Gemma were talking about the new baby while looking at property websites. Jodie had become a little stroppy again. A few days ago she'd barged into my room while I was getting dressed and asked if she could borrow a T-shirt. In the past I would have been enraged but this time I just waved her in the direction of my chest of drawers.

It was over for everyone else. It was even over for me. I had to move on, Patrice said. I saw myself as a broken-down car on the road, other vehicles moving round me. Somehow I had to ignite the engine and get going. I had Patrice's list to help me; all I had to do was get started.

The door opened and Dan came in. He had his phone in his hand. It looked as though he was going to show me something on the screen.

'I don't want to see any more photographs of Woody,' I said, loudly.

He covered his phone in a shocked way.

'I had no intention of showing you any. I wanted you to look at this on Facebook. It's something my brother is organising.'

'Oh, sorry.'

He sat down beside me and I looked at his screen. There was a promotion for a Charity Football Match in Victoria Park.

'It's on Sunday at twelve. Then afterwards there's a picnic. At the park if it's dry; at our house if it's not. He's raising funds for Cancer Research – his girlfriend's dad died recently.'

'It sounds good. A good cause.'

'Will you come? The two Sues are coming. And Woody's coming, of course.'

'On Sunday? Oh, I don't know . . .'

'You could bring your sister and her baby along. I mean, if you're worried about there being no one to babysit.'

I couldn't help but smile at his reference to my previous excuse.

'Or you could come by yourself.'

He was looking straight at me, his eyes on mine, making it difficult to look away.

'Do you mean you want me to come as a *friend*?'

There, I'd said it.

'What else would I want you to come as? An enemy?'

'No, I mean . . . Well . . .'

'I know what you mean. Look, I could never ask you to come as a *girlfriend*. I couldn't have a girlfriend with hair that colour . . .'

'What?' I said, touching my hair. 'Now I'm offended.'

'But you'll still come? On Sunday. Victoria Park. A hundred metres up from the cafe.'

'I might.'

'So why were you off? Is it OK to ask?'

'It was . . . It was . . .'

I shrugged my shoulders.

'OK, don't worry,' he said.

'I don't want to make up a story for *you*. I've done that with lots of people.'

I thought of the kids in school, people I liked who I wouldn't normally lie to.

'I can't tell you *why* I was off. It's really personal. It's actually been a real bad time one way and another. But I wasn't sick or revising. Will that do?'

He nodded slowly. My break was over, so I got up and put my empty bottle in the bin.

'So, I might see you on Sunday then,' he said, grabbing a newspaper someone else had left behind.

'You might.'

When my shift was over I went into the staff area to get my coat. Dan had left a while before but the two Sues were standing at the back door with cigarettes held out into the dark. It wasn't allowed but they did it all the time. I was getting my jacket on when the shop-floor door opened and Mrs Bakhtar appeared. The two girls dashed outside and I pushed the back door shut. The smell of cigarettes was still in the room but Mrs Bakhtar didn't seem to notice.

'A friend of yours, Stacey. She seems a bit upset, so I brought her back here.'

Behind her was Bella. I was surprised. She looked terrible.

'Go in, my dear,' Mrs Bakhtar said, closing the door behind her.

'Hi,' I said

She hadn't come to commiserate. That much was clear. She began to cry; great sobs shook her shoulders and she kept trying to speak but couldn't.

'What's wrong? What's wrong?'

'He's left me. Harry's left me.'

She grabbed my arm and held it fiercely.

'What can I do?'

'Sit down, here, sit down.'

She sat down, a wad of tissues in one of her hands held up to her mouth. Her hair was tied back and she was wearing a baggy shirt over leggings. Her nails had been painted scarlet but some of the varnish had chipped off.

'I know I should have got in touch after the trial was over. I meant to a number of times. I can't make any excuses. I've been selfish. I've had things on my mind . . .'

I inhaled deeply. She *had* been selfish. But now she was in trouble.

'What happened with Harry?' I said.

'You knew he would leave me, didn't you? When you were round my house that night, you *knew*.'

I didn't answer. I glanced out of the back door and saw the lights from the girls' cigarettes. I couldn't make out either of the Sues but I imagined they were looking in, wondering who it was who was crying and why.

'He seemed to change as soon as the trial was over. I didn't see him for a few days and I didn't know why. I mean, I knew his brother had been cleared but I didn't think it would affect him.'

Of course it would. Marty was his big brother who he idolised.

'He'd talked about you. He'd said how sorry he was about what happened. When his brother was acquitted I expected him to come round to me. But I didn't see him for three days. I phoned him, I sent texts. He answered but in a cold way saying there was stuff going on in his family. Eventually he came to see me. We went out, we spent some time together, but as he was leaving he said that he'd moved back in at home for good and that he was making a last effort with his exams. His mum had hired some tutors to help him cram. He never mentioned his brother.'

Bella's face had reddened and she was looking at her nails, scraping away at the polish, pulling strips of red off.

'I never saw him for a week then, until he came round this afternoon. He said it's finished. He doesn't feel the same any more.'

I felt sorry for her. She'd been taken in by Harry more than once and he had finally made her believe that he loved her. It

198

was a heartless thing to do, but then Harry's emotions were all about him.

'Why do you think he broke up with me?'

Her eyes were glittering with tears. I could have told her the truth. I could have said, *Why do you think he stayed with you? So that his brother was sure you wouldn't come to court. He was using you.* I could have been brutally honest with her and told her what I thought. But she was hurting enough.

'Harry followed his heart. Honestly, Bella, he fell in and out of love very quickly. I'm sure he did care for you but he's not someone who holds those strong feelings for a long time. Perhaps all this stuff with his family, with his brother, has made him an unstable sort of character. He doesn't really understand his own feelings.'

'Do you think he might come back? In the future?'

'I don't know. But if you've got any pride or any sense you'll have nothing to do with him. He's hurt you. Let him go.'

'I don't know if I'm strong enough. If I look out my window one day and see him there I know I'll just go to him. It's crazy, I know.'

I sat there, unable to think of anything helpful to say. How could I give advice? I was the girl who had fallen for Harry over a conversation in a cafe. He had sprinkled stardust into my day and when his taxi turned the corner I stood watching it go with my heart on fire. Before the trial I went to his school just to *see* him. I persuaded myself that he was a changed boy, that he was remorseful and a better person than he had been. It was Marty who was the pervert. Harry had been drawn along by brotherly love. I'd been wrong though. There was something bad in Harry, his good looks and sociable ways just sweetened it. I couldn't blame Bella for her feelings, because I'd been just as much a fool myself.

I felt her hand grab mine. I didn't pull it away. Just then the door opened and the two Sues came in, one after the other.

'Sorry to disturb,' one of them said.

'No problem,' I said. 'We were just going.'

After I got my things I walked along to the Tube station with Bella. She'd stopped crying.

'How's the singing going?' I said.

'Oh, I dropped out of it for a while.'

'Start it up again,' I said, 'get your life back. Leave Harry to his life. With a brother like his, it won't be good. Don't let him take your voice away.'

I was giving her the kind of advice that Patrice had given me.

'Shall I text you?' she said.

'No.'

She looked crestfallen.

'Whenever I get a text from you I'll immediately think about Harry, Marty, the rape, the trial, and I don't want that any more. So, don't take this as a rejection, I just think it would be better for me – and in the long run for you – if you don't.'

She nodded.

'I get it,' she said.

I gave her a hug. I knew I wouldn't see her again.

Twenty-Six

There were no students in school because of the holidays. I saw a couple of teachers who I knew as I walked through the building. They said hello but I didn't stop to talk to them. I was heading for Ms Harper's office, hoping she would be there. I knew there were revision classes as well as anxious sixth-form students for her to deal with. In any case, I had this unfair idea that school was Ms Harper's life and that she haunted the place, even in the holidays.

I was right. When I knocked on her door she called out for me to enter.

'Hello, Stacey,' she said, standing up as soon I walked in. 'How are you?'

'So-so,' I said.

'Right, let's put the kettle on.'

I sat in the low chair and watched as she made herself busy. I was surprised to see two white mugs and raised my eyebrows as she put a tea bag in each and then filled them with water. She placed them on the table with an opened carton of milk and a Tupperware container of sugar. I wondered what had happened to the china.

'Obviously I read about the trial,' she said, making herself comfortable, 'and I was extremely unhappy to hear the verdict. This man has got away with it, and it's a very sad day for you and for any other woman he gets involved with. I imagine that you feel cheated . . .'

'Ms Harper, do you mind if we don't talk about it?'

She flinched and looked a bit hurt.

'Don't be offended. It's just that I've thought about it constantly since the verdict, I've talked to people about it – my family and Patrice. I've written about it. My head's just full to bursting. I need to get it out of my mind. That's why I've come to see you.'

'I see.'

That seemed to please her, because there with a hint of a smile on her lips. I noticed then that she was wearing dark jeans and a loose blouse. The jeans had been ironed with a crease but still it was a departure from her usual style. And then I got it. It was the holidays; no china cups or smart suits. This was Ms Harper in a *relaxed mode*.

She was waiting patiently for me to talk.

'I remember when we spoke and how I told you I wanted to defer uni and you asked me to put off any decision until after the trial. I was annoyed at the time but I see now you were right.'

'You *will* go to university this year? Is that what you are telling me?'

'I will go if I can get a place on the Fashion and Design course at the University of Sussex. It was always what I wanted to do, but after everything happened I sort of lost my way. I realise that I'd have to go through clearing and that I've got two other offers, but Miss Previn suggested it might not be too late.'

'It is pretty late . . . I suppose it might be quite a popular course, but you are predicted high grades. Theoretically, they could make you an offer . . .'

'I know the open days are probably all over but I thought I might go down there myself and look around. Just to see what the campus is like. I want to see if I can *picture* myself there.'

'We can contact the uni now. You have special circumstances; we can make a case for your being given some latitude. The head and I can make a plea . . .'

'No, no, I don't want that. I want to be like everybody else. I want to apply and if they don't make me an offer, then I'll apply again next year. I've decided that it's what I want to do, but I want to go through the proper channels.'

'I see. Do you mind me asking why you are so certain about this?'

'I'm taking a step back a year and trying to reclaim some of the things that I lost because of the rape.'

She sat forward in her chair and gave me a beaming smile.

'I'm overwhelmed by this change of heart. I think it's the absolute best thing that could happen. Do you mind waiting here for a few moments while I see if Carol Gregory, Head of History, is still here? There's something I need to ask her which is relevant to you. You'll wait?'

'Sure.'

'Drink your tea and I'll be as quick as I can.'

I sat where I was as she left. I took a mouthful of tea but the mug felt enormous and the tea tasted different. I glanced

203

down at my bag. I'd been shopping before I came and I'd bought two things; one from a charity shop and one from the chemist's. I unzipped the top of the bag and looked in. I was pleased with both purchases.

I was telling Ms Harper the truth about my decisions, but there was a bit more to it than I had said. That morning I had gone onto the internet and found some more posts about Taxi Girl. *She should stop asking men to shag her, then accusing them of rape!* It had riled me and I'd been tempted to make a comment but I knew that was pointless and was only giving these people what they wanted – attention. I'd sunk into a mood, all the positive stuff of the last few days collapsing in the face of this unjust judgement of me. Then I *made* myself close up my laptop and decided to clear out the drawers of my desk. I knew that I had to get organised, with the exams only weeks away. I took each drawer out and upended it and made piles of stuff: things to keep, things to file and things to throw away.

When I reached the middle drawer of the second side I had trouble opening it and I realised that there was a book in there. It was a large book and had been wedged in so that it was difficult to get the drawer out. I had pulled and pulled and eventually it came, bending the cover of the book.

I smoothed it out with my fingers. It was a hardback book about fashion – *Twentieth Century Style*. Patrice had bought it for me on my last birthday. It had been second-hand then and I had loved it and pored over the pages, looking at fashions throughout the twentieth century.

I sat down on the floor and did the same thing again, flicking through page after page, looking at photographs and diagrams.

After a few moments I found the pattern. It slipped out, a small white paper pocket in which there was a tissue pattern for a wedding dress. At the time I had been delighted to discover it; whoever had owned the book had left it there and it had fallen out like a bit of treasure from the past. I turned it over yet again and looked hard at the diagram; a woman in a long white dress with sleeves which almost covered her fingers. The dress had a pleat all the way up the back. It was lovely; old-fashioned and elegant. I looked at the drawing and thought of some of my own sketches; dresses, suits, tops, coats. I'd taken care with them, often thinking of the fabrics and trims. It had been amateur stuff, I knew that, but once I had thought I might do something with it.

I'd closed the book and felt a tiny flame flickering in my chest.

Why not do what I wanted to do before the rape?

Now the door swung open and Ms Harper came back into her office. She was smiling widely. It was a side of Ms Harper students rarely saw. She sat down opposite me.

'Good news,' she said. 'Carol Gregory's daughter Rhiannon has just finished her second year at the University of Sussex. Carol has just rung her and she's said that she'd happily show you round the campus one day after Easter. You can go there and back in a day and she'll give you a good idea of what the university life is like. She'll even find some fashion students to introduce you to!'

'Oh!' I said. 'That's really nice of her. You didn't say anything to Mrs Gregory about . . . me . . . ?'

'About what, Stacey? There's nothing *to say* about you. You're just one of my students who's had a last-minute change

205

of heart and I'm asking some help from a colleague. She knows I'd do the same for any of hers.'

'Thank you. I'm so grateful.'

'So we'll see you next Monday back in the sixth-form block? Cracking on with the work?'

I stood up, nodding. I felt choked up at her kindness.

'Oh,' I said, 'I got this for you. I just saw it in a charity shop. I thought you might like it.'

I took the small wrapped item from my bag. The woman in the shop had covered it with newspaper and finished it with a skin of bubble wrap. I put it on the coffee table beside the giant mugs.

'What's this?' she said, looking awkward.

She unwrapped it. Then she took it out of the paper. A tiny cup and saucer sat on the table. It was light pink with deep blue flowers. The handle was angular and barely big enough to slip a finger through. It hadn't cost much but it had taken visits to a few shops to get the right one.

'I'm touched, Stacey. It's lovely. It shall have pride of place on my dresser.'

When I left she was still looking at it, holding the cup upside down to look for markings. I walked out of school with a lightness in my step that I hadn't felt for a long time.

Twenty-Seven

On Sunday morning, I found a text from Annie. She'd sent it late the previous evening.

**Need to see you. Free about
eleven thirty?**

I was surprised because I'd not heard from her since her answers to the texts I'd sent. Her lack of contact had upset me because I'd got really fond of her and leaned on her a lot. For some silly reason I'd thought we were *friends*. I'd quite forgotten that in seeing me she was simply doing her job. Once the court case had finished, her role with me was over. I now understood that but I couldn't say that it didn't hurt a bit.

I was too reliant on friends. I'd learned that about myself. I was no longer so possessive of Patrice, but it seemed I had just transferred my neediness onto Annie. Maybe that was why I had been such an easy target for Harry. He'd made himself sweet and shown interest in me, so I latched onto him. I had to stand on my own two feet.

I replied to her text.

207

11:30 is good. I have to be
somewhere at 12.

I decided to do my own hair. I took out the bag from the chemist's and let the sachet drop out and read the instructions. It seemed simple enough. The colour was chestnut brown and it would last six to eight washes. If it didn't come out right I could wash it feverishly until it faded. I waited until Jodie and Tyler were out of the bathroom and I took my towel in and closed and locked the door. I picked up the scissors and snipped off the corner of the sachet. Then I squeezed it onto my hair and began to massage it through. Afterwards, I showered, then went into my room to use the hair dryer. When it was done I combed it round my face; no plaits, no curling, no ties. Just plain Stacey Woods staring back at me. It was a little lighter than before and there was maybe a hint of red still coming through, but I liked it. I got dressed quickly, jeans and a shirt and a long woolly cardigan in case it got chilly at the park.

I was ready to go but it had only just gone eleven. I had a little time on my hands, so I went onto the internet. I looked up the website for the University of Sussex again. I went to the page for the BA in Fashion Design and Technology. Underneath, it had the words *Accreditation by the London College of Fashion*. I read it over. Then I looked at the Student Facilities section and information about Halls. Each student had their own room and shared kitchen and shower facilities with others.

I clicked on Google maps and saw Brighton, by the sea. In the map the sea was a vivid blue like something coloured in by a child. I knew it wasn't that colour but it didn't matter. It was somewhere different than east London. It was a place where I could start again. I could leave the bad bits of my life behind and be a new person. I would still be Stacey Woods but a bit harder, a bit less needy; someone who wouldn't fall for the first boy who could spin a good story.

It was twenty past eleven and I looked out of the window and saw that Annie's car was already there. I picked up my bag and my phone and went out, calling goodbye to Mum and Jodie, glad that they weren't close by to make any comments about my hair.

'Hi!' Annie said, when I got into her car, 'Where are you off to for twelve? I could give you a lift.'

'Victoria Park, actually.'

'OK. It's not as if I don't know the way!' she said.

She was upbeat. I wondered if she was putting it on for me. Maybe there was a bit of her job that focused on post-trial blues. Or maybe I was reading too much into it and she was just in a good mood. She drove and as usual we sat silently. The music was playing quietly for once and I glanced over and saw that she had sprayed the front of her hair pink. It was nice to see her back to normal instead of being dressed seriously for court.

When we got nearer the park she turned the music off.

'How have you been, Stacey? I've been worried about you.'

I was surprised. It seemed as though she'd forgotten all about me.

'OK. Last few days I've been feeling a bit better, making plans for the future.'

'Good. It will still hurt for a while but in the end it will recede. The memories, I mean. No one ever forgets but it will get easier, yeah?'

I didn't answer. I felt, for a moment, as though she was reading something from a pre-prepared script. She was winding down her involvement with me and wanted to leave it on a good note. *It will get easier*. Would it? I would never forget that day, I thought. When Marty Connaught's face was pushed up close to me, his body squashing me down on the bed, pushing himself inside me. I could go to university and live in Brighton and have new friends and maybe even a career of some sort in fashion but I would never be able to exorcise that memory.

The car came to a stop. We were close to one of the park entrances that we had used in the past. I took my seat belt off and turned to say goodbye. It was nice of Annie to come but really she was part of that past as well.

'Look after yourself,' I said, touching the door handle.

'Wait a minute. I haven't told you why I wanted to see you.'

I sat back. I'd thought we were done.

'I shouldn't really be here and maybe I shouldn't be telling you this. Oh, you'll hear about it in the future, you'll be kept in the loop, even though, legally speaking, it's nothing to do with you any more.'

'What?'

'It's one of the reasons I haven't been to see you. There's been this stuff happening, and until things were settled I didn't want to have to pretend nothing was going on.'

'Annie, what?' I said impatiently.

'Well, you know how the press got hold of the story about the trial? That was bad for you, even though they weren't allowed to print your name. The thing is, they *were* allowed to print Marty Connaught's name, yeah? Plus the fact that he did that bit for the TV news outside the court. That was an unbelievable mistake on his part. Well, to cut a long story short . . .'

'What?' I said, exasperated.

'Three other women have come forward and said that he raped them.'

I didn't speak. I couldn't speak.

'On the day after the verdict, a woman in her twenties walked into a police station in west London and told her story. Two days later another woman, also in her twenties, rang up a Rape Crisis Centre in west London. I've been informed that both these woman have been taken seriously and that the ways in which they were raped bear similarities to your story.'

'I don't know what to say . . .'

'But that's not all. Two days ago a teenager from Essex came forward and she has also claimed that Marty raped her.'

'A teenager?'

I thought of Bella; but it wasn't her. She would never come forward.

'I can't say anything about them. These women have anonymity, just as you did. What I can say is that the case has been built up and, as we speak, police officers are going to Marty Connaught's home to charge him with rape.'

'Now? This minute?'

'Yes. That's why I've waited all this time to come and see you.'

'I thought you'd forgotten me!'

211

'No. I had this news inside me. I didn't know whether I'd be able to keep it in.'

'He's being *arrested*. I can't believe it.'

'Yes, and this time, because there are *three* women, he won't get bail. He'll spend months in prison waiting for his trial. And because it has been in the news recently it'll be reported widely. The press will make a meal of it, especially because the last verdict was not guilty. It'll be all over the papers again.'

'Oh.'

I felt myself slump back into the seat. I was smiling, I was sure I was, but there were tears coming as well. I put my hand over my mouth and felt my chin shaking. Annie produced a box of tissues and pulled three out. She pushed them into my hand and I held them against my nose and mouth. Annie let me cry. She sat beside me and didn't speak. When I was done I took a few deep breaths. *Three women* had come forward.

'Hey, this is a good day, isn't it?' Annie finally said.

'It is. It's a good day. Will I hear any more about it . . .'

'Maybe. You won't ever hear anything about the women, but you might get a courtesy visit from one of the detectives.'

'Can I tell my family?'

'Course. It'll be a huge weight off their minds.'

'I really don't know what I would have done without you.'

'You didn't get justice this time. But when this trial goes through and he gets found guilty, then people will look back at your case and they will know that a mistake has been made. Course they won't know it's *you* but –'

Her phone rang and she snatched it up. She made an apologetic gesture towards me and started to talk rapidly. I stared out of the car window while she spoke and thought of Marty opening his front door and seeing two police officers waiting there, arresting him, taking him to the station to be charged. There would be no smiling then, no smirk, no feigned innocent look. And Harry would be broken up when his adored brother was sitting in a prison cell waiting for his day in court.

I pictured Laura, the drama student, looking at a newspaper and seeing Marty's name and the charges against him. Or maybe it would be on the news and they would play the clip of him outside Snaresbrook Crown Court looking straight at the camera and saying, *I want to thank the jury*. Possibly her son would be there watching television or playing a game on his computer. She would look fondly at him and feel elated and certain that this time justice would be done.

I wanted to conjure up a similar image of Bella but I couldn't. Instead, I saw her coming out of her front door and looking sadly across the street, hoping to see Harry there. Maybe, when his brother was out of the way, he would creep back to Bella. I hoped for her sake that he didn't.

'Sorry, Stacey,' Annie said, finishing her call. 'I know you've got to be somewhere for twelve.'

'I'll go then . . .'

I didn't know quite what to do, how to get out of the car, whether to give her a thank-you peck on the cheek.

'Yeah,' she said.

I got out of the car and began to walk towards the park entrance. I turned to wave and saw that she had put the driver's window down.

'What's wrong with your hair?' she called. 'Where's the red?'

213

I shrugged my shoulders and went to walk on. I heard her call again though, so I stopped. This time she was out of the car and walking towards me.

'Here,' she said, handing me a packet of Haribos. 'Where you off to, anyway?'

'I'm going to meet someone. And a dog.'

'A boyfriend?'

'Just a friend.'

She put one arm around me and pulled me into a hug. It was awkward but nice at the same time.

'Look after yourself.'

'See you sometime?' I said.

'Not if I see you first.'

I opened the bag of sweets while she headed back to the car. I chewed through the jellies as she started the engine and drove off. Then I pushed my brown hair behind my ears and headed for the cafe and the charity football match.

USEFUL ORGANISATIONS

Rape Crisis England/Wales

The UK's leading national rape crisis charity.

National rape crisis helpline – 0808 802 9999

Locate your local centre – rapecrisis.org.uk/centres.php

Safeline

National advice and counselling service for survivors of rape and those effected. One of the few rape charities to provide online counselling.

General helpline – 0808 800 5008

Young people's helpline – 0808 800 5007

Male helpline – 0808 800 5005

Text message support line – 07860 027573

Email support line – support@safeline.org.uk

Find more information on https://www.safeline.org.uk/

Specialist information for young people on slyp.org.uk

Women Against Rape

National charity providing support, legal information and advocacy for victims of rape.

Access to their self-help guide detailed legal procedures and everything reporting a rape entails – womenagainstrape.net/resource/self-help-guide-survivors-rape-and-sexual-assault

Survivors UK (male specific charity)

Offers individual counselling, group work and helpline services to anyone affected by male sexual violation.

https://www.survivorsuk.org/

Chat via SMS – 020 3322 1860, via WhatsApp – 07491 816064

Anne Cassidy

Anne Cassidy was born in London in 1952. She was an awkward teenager who spent the Swinging Sixties stuck in a convent school trying, dismally, to learn Latin. She was always falling in love and having her heart broken. She worked in a bank for five years until she finally grew up. She then went to college before becoming a teacher for many years. In 2000 Anne became a full-time writer, specialising in crime stories and thrillers for teenagers. In 2004 LOOKING FOR JJ was published to great acclaim, going on to be shortlisted for the 2004 Whitbread Prize and the 2005 Carnegie Medal. MOTH GIRLS, published in 2016, was nominated for the 2017 CILIP Carnegie Medal and shortlisted for the 2017 Sheffield Children's Book Award. Follow Anne at www.annecassidy.com or on Twitter: @annecassidy6

Thank you for choosing a Hot Key book.

If you want to know more about our authors and what we publish, you can find us online.

You can start at our website

www.hotkeybooks.com

And you can also find us on:

We hope to see you soon!

Contents

Part Four: Scale

Part Five: Measure and Refine

Foreword

I recently found an old YouTube clip online from 2012, a fresh-faced 22-year-old version of me is talking about The Reasons You Need to Grow a Personal Brand. I am tripping over my words slightly, I'm not experienced in the slightest, but there is an unwavering conviction in my eyes. I don't know who or where or why I felt so strongly about this 'personal' element of growing an online presence, but I delivered a talk to over 100 people onboard the ship, HMS *President*, moored on the Thames. 'Start to lay the foundations, now', I said to a crowd of all ages, 'because the foundations you set now will only carry on cementing throughout your career.' Platforms may change, trends may switch, social media channels change in popularity (RIP Vine), but your personal brand will stand the test of time. I don't know where this mission came from. When I came across Natasha's work, I felt that I'd discovered a kindred spirit.

No one is above personal branding. Even Michelle Obama has featured on an episode of 'Carpool Karaoke' with James Corden. Anyone can be famous now: a reality star from the Bronx called Cardi B has 22 million followers on Instagram (at the time of writing) and has carved out her own online narrative and new empowering career. Yes, personal branding is important for connection, growth and longevity, but also: it's a serious money maker.

One of the other main positives of having a personal brand is the connections I have made. Natasha's brilliant portfolio, brand and ability to connect with anyone made me instantly happy to write this foreword. She shines online and instantly stands out among a sea of emails.

Initially, no one told me to build a personal brand, and I certainly didn't learn it at school, so where did my dogged motivation to build one come from? Looking back, the reason for me was simple: if I was going to combat career obstacles in an effective way (the recession I faced on graduating from university, or the subtle discrimination women still face in the workplace), I told myself that I not only needed to be shit-hot at my job, but I also needed people to *know* about my work, too. I needed to craft an online brand that got people's attention. It's a noisy world out there. That way, I thought, I would get new, exciting job offers; I would get more eyeballs on my writing; and I would be in a better position if I wanted to dip out of work and one day have a baby. That was my logic, anyway. I needed a way to empower myself.

Fast-forward to now. All of my biggest opportunities have something to do with the fact that I've built an online portfolio of work that aligns with one 'brand': me. It's evolved, sure. I'm not the same person I was when I was 22. I even wrote a book called *The Multi-Hyphen Method* because I refuse to be pigeonholed into one industry. But there is a consistency in my voice, my ideas and the themes of my work. And that enables you to leapfrog and pitch yourself higher and higher, because you have a wealth of evidence at your fingertips, at the click of a button.

I love that the playing field has been levelled for *everyone*. Anyone can attract a mass audience now. Anyone can be listened to. The old gatekeepers have gone. The Internet has many negative threads to it, but the fact that we all have a way to spread our messages now is an exciting one. When it comes to amplifying diverse voices, or creating new media outlets, or climbing our way up a ladder in a non-linear way, it's all up for grabs. There's room for us – and for you, reading this.

Knowing you need to work on your personal brand and *actively* growing it are two different things, however. I believe we are in a time when we are overwhelmed with tools, tech and opportunity, and yet, we are also in the midst of a confidence crisis. *Where do we start? What if it goes wrong? What if I don't have a passion? What if I fail? What if people see it? What if it's not perfect? What if I change my mind?* These are all understandable and common fears, because building a personal brand also means putting yourself out there, publicly. And for most of us, that's a horrifying thought.

Building a personal brand isn't just about becoming the next online celebrity, but it *is* about growing your business and owning your message. And then, just when we need her, here comes Natasha and her incredible book, *#StandOutOnline*. In this book, Natasha tells it how it is – there is a real honesty and raw insight in the pages you're about to read. Reading this book is a confidence-boosting experience, too. As she points out, you already have a personal brand. You don't need to build one from scratch – you already have one – and Natasha is here to help you grow it. The practical steps and interactive parts of the book are brilliant too. This is a thorough, well-researched guide and your own personal journal all in one.

I love the way Natasha describes building a brand as having your own micro-niche. It's a call to arms to do it *your* way, to build *your* thing and not to try to blend it or copy the crowd. All the practical, wise nuggets of advice you need to get started and dig in deep are in the pages of *#StandOutOnline*. Buy one for yourself, and for your friends who feel stuck.

If you feel lost, confused or overwhelmed right now, this book is the one for you.

Emma Gannon, award-winning blogger and author of *Ctrl Alt Delete* and *The Multi-Hyphen Method*

Prelude

In the United States, a new phenomenon is sweeping the most determined and driven of start-up founders, visionaries, change-makers, CEOs, celebrities and ambitious employees. It involves digital self-promotion to a new extreme – and the employment of a full-time video-content crew. In the same way that reality TV stars have used their daily lives to capture the attention of millions of television viewers, these individuals are using their own regular working routines and their voices to entertain, educate, inspire and build their own audiences via the Internet. The most successful of these people are said to have full-time editorial crews of up to 12 people trailing their daily lives and publishing the content in a mix of formats ranging from text through to videos and audio – and, no doubt in the future, as virtual reality – across social media platforms, blogs, vlogs and websites.

The goal? To build themselves the most visible of personal brands online and to turn themselves into the stars and leaders of their own micro-niche. And it's working, with these digital pioneers becoming household names in their own right.

I have a question for you. Have you ever felt that someone has come out of nowhere and now they seem to be everywhere? They're being interviewed on podcasts, they're on your Facebook feeds, they're giving talks, they're writing books and they're even appearing in the mainstream media? Which means that their business is growing faster, their message is spreading further, their influence is more powerful, and opportunities are landing at their feet. Although they might not necessarily be at the extreme end of the spectrum with the 24/7 trailing film crew, the chances are that the Internet is a key driver in their success – and it can be in yours too.

PART ONE

Strategy

Right now, you probably have a burning desire to build your personal brand, reputation and influence in whatever it is you do. That's why you've picked up this book. And that's great, because that's where everyone starts. The first part of this book is all about working on your vision, mission, goals and strategy, so that you have clarity and direction. You have the desire, and this section of the book will show you how to devise a plan of action that will help you achieve your long-term goals and deliver real results.

Welcome to the Dawning of Stand Out Online

There's nothing new about the concept of personal branding, of course. Irrespective of your background, you know that the personal brand of Cleopatra is synonymous with Ancient Egypt and for Julius Caesar it is Rome. For millennia, personal brands have supported organisational brands, and individuals have become known for their talents, passions, knowledge and for what they do – and then they have used that positioning to attract more opportunity and to exert more influence. More recent examples include Richard Branson and Virgin, Bill Gates and Microsoft, Steve Jobs and Apple, and J.K. Rowling and Harry Potter.

Against this backdrop, however, there have always been plenty of other people who are just as talented and just as ambitious, yet they never become well known, they never acquire memorable personal-brand status and they are left thinking what could have been if only they'd been given their time in the spotlight. And that's because a powerful personal brand requires two things: ability and visibility.

You need to be good at what you do – but you also need other people to see you doing it. And in the past, yes, that was often a matter of chance, luck or even connections. The issue was that for most of us, achieving the same degree of fame as these big names in terms of our personal profile just wasn't an option, unless some sort of miracle occurred. Until now . . .

Technology is changing everything

We are right at the start of a wave of opportunity that will soon become our new reality. Everyone now has the power to publish and create micro-fame and recognition through putting out content and to do it word-by-word, post-by-post, video-by-video. Smartphones have changed the world forever: the average person spends 3 hours a day on their phone and checks it 80 times a day, according to research from Facebook, and hundreds of millions of everyday people, just like you and me, have been schooled by Instagram, Facebook and YouTube – and they understand not only the power of creating beautiful, magazine-style, billboard-size content, but also how to do it. And if you don't know the 'how' yet, the chances are, if you're reading this book, you have the inclination to learn.

This pace of change is not slowing down, but speeding up. This means that a consciously created and shaped personal brand is an asset and no longer a choice, but a necessity.

You already have a personal brand

I'd go as far as saying that regardless of how tight your privacy settings (in fact, really you should forget the notion of absolute privacy right now), you already *have* a personal brand, whether you like it not. If you've ever commented on a blog, or set up a profile on a social network, or sent a tweet, or you have been featured on your employer's website, your personal brand is already out there.

The CV will soon be relegated to history: why bother reading a CV when you can usually find out everything you need to know from Google and social networks? And if you're reading this thinking: *Things just aren't how they were,* no they are not – and thank goodness! You should be happy about this, because in today's world, people trust and listen to other people, not corporate brands or faceless organisations – and this offers tremendous opportunity for you. Just look at some of these stats on the fragmentation of the media and the changes in our behaviour. They'll make your eyes water! And we're only hurtling – as a society – further in this direction!

- Facebook predicts that by 2020, more people will have mobile phones than running water or electricity at home.
- Ninety-seven per cent of consumers search for products and services online (US Small Business Administration).
- One-third of the entire world uses social networks regularly (HubSpot).
- Three-quarters of people aged under 35 want to see a business owner's photo with their story on a company's website (2016 Small Business Marketing Trends Report).
- Feeling the urge to pick up your phone? You're not alone. Researcher Dscout found that the heaviest smartphone users click, tap or swipe on their phone 5,427 times a day.
- Our society is obsessed with screens. Google discovered that 85 per cent of adults consume content on multiple devices at the same time, while three-quarters of the British population go online on a different device while watching TV.
- If Facebook were a country, it would be the largest country in the world. It has more users than the populations of China, the United States and Brazil combined.
- While Facebook is experiencing over 1 billion mobile visitors a day, 24 of the 25 largest newspapers are seeing record declines in circulation. This is further proof that we're getting all our news online, and most likely via our mobile phones.

Are you a social media ghost?

Let's look at what this means. If you haven't got your online profiles set up, you are actually doing yourself more harm than good.
If someone can't find you online, they're actually going to think
there's something very strange about that and *not* trust you. In
the digital sense, not having great profiles online is the same as
not turning up to a meeting.

In fact, I'd go further. Without working on your personal
brand, you risk finding yourself in the slow lane for evermore,
left behind and overlooked. Whatever industry you are in, there
will be others coming up, or even in existence already, who have
embraced the power of the Internet, and they will overtake you
if they build their personal brands and you don't.

Likewise, neglected online profiles are also damaging. If people
look at your Twitter and see no posts since 2014, they will probably
presume that you must have died. You have a personal brand online
in the same way that you make an impression in the real world.

You wouldn't go to your next meeting with food on your jacket,
messy hair and having not washed for five days (I hope). But if
people visit your LinkedIn profile and see no photo, very out-of-date
information and no recommendations, you'll have the same impact
on them as would a scruffy tramp turning up for a job interview.
Although this might sound bad, not actually having a profile at all
on some of the key social media platforms is considered to be even
worse. That's the real-world equivalent of turning up to a meeting
to find that not only has the other person not turned up, but they
have sent you no communication before or afterwards. Imagine
that. This is what many millennials refer to as a social media ghost.
If you cannot be found online, you simply cannot be trusted.

Now think of it in reverse.

Think about how it works in the real world

Imagine a guy or gal who turns up in an Aston Martin wearing a perfectly tailored on-trend outfit with a PA who not only confirms the meeting beforehand but sends a handwritten thank-you note from the boss afterwards. You're going to trust them more, assume they do a better job and you are likely to be willing to pay above market rates to work with them. That's in the real world, now bring it online: the people who put out the right impressions digitally, who communicate using interesting and relevant content, who are reaching and influencing thousands of people with ease – it's same deal. They're the ones who are charging more, getting more opportunities and moving towards their ever-more ambitious goals.

A leader in this space is the American entrepreneur Gary Vaynerchuk, who has pioneered a 'document, don't create' movement when it comes to content production. Rather than focusing on sitting down and creating blog or podcast content from scratch (although he does do that, too) he has a team of eight (currently) who follow him everywhere and document his travels, talks, conversations, meetings and interviews.

He has created his own set of shows across platforms and media formats – in video, audio and written form – featuring himself at the heart of it. One of the products offered by his digital agency VaynerMedia is VaynerTalent, which costs $25,000 per month and now builds the personal brands of other people in the same way Vaynerchuk has built his own. Their clients are the most successful of entrepreneurs for whom a video crew is put in place to follow them around and capture raw footage, which is then repurposed into YouTube shows, podcasts and social content.

OK, so what we are talking about here are the dizzy heights of personal-brand success and determination, and you certainly don't have to spend $25,000 a month. At my agency, Bolt Digital, we offer a similar talent product (Bolt Talent) at a lower price, but for most of us, employing a full-time content crew is not going to be a possibility. The reality is that plenty of people have successfully launched their personal brands at no cost at all (bar the cost of their own time) and done everything themselves. But for the sake of inspiration, let's hear from one of VaynerMedia's Talent clients right now to show us what happens when you do go large on your personal brand.

MY STORY Cy Wakeman 'Our revenues have doubled, thanks to my full-time video crew'
Cy Wakeman is a CEO, speaker and author. The American-based founder of Reality-Based Leadership, she began investing $25,000 per month in January 2017 as one of VaynerTalent's first clients. As a result of building her personal brand, her seven-figure revenues have doubled. The content Cy creates includes a YouTube show called 'No Ego' and a podcast with the same title, as well as social content across Twitter, Facebook and Instagram.

Where were you in terms of your personal brand before enlisting the help of a full-time content crew?
I'd been in business for 20 years and was already a New York Times bestselling author. I had a new book coming out, and it seemed that the traditional methods so many people were working with (salespeople, publicists and print magazines) were just not working for me. Historically, if I had a book coming out, I would have worked to get on all the cable shows, all the news shows, and in all the print media. Meanwhile, I employed a

full-time salesperson to develop relationships and business with HR people. It felt like nothing had the power it once did. We were getting media coverage, but the sales were still coming from word of mouth, friends of friends who'd heard me speak, and people who'd loved my book.

You wanted to do things differently?
I'm the mother of eight sons, and not one of my kids consumed information in traditional ways. They were all consuming content online. And people couldn't get to me personally, as although I had Twitter and Facebook, I wasn't using these in a thoughtful way to engage with people.

So, yes, we decided that if people are going to be distracted by content online, then *we* should be their distraction. We should be the YouTube show your boss allows you to watch. Our first step was to hire our own videographer to work inhouse. We realised pretty quickly, though, that this was not about video but about a philosophy, consistency and building pillars of content across platforms. In 2017, we became one of Gary Vaynerchuk's first clients on his VaynerTalent programme.

Any traditional branding agency will tell you to build your company brand, not your personal brand. But the new thinking is to build your personal brand and then you can put anything through it, whether it's your company or any other initiative that you like. It is really hard to build a company brand and to differentiate yourself, but to build a personal brand isn't that hard if you're authentic and have the right motives.

What's been the cost?
The monthly fee for the VaynerTalent Programme is $25,000 plus around $30,000 in paid media over the course of a year. I'm a pretty gutsy and intuitive person, and I went all in. We pulled out

of all other forms of marketing – we used to spend $20,000 multiple times each year to go to large trade shows and stand there for three days trying to talk to people in HR. I felt the money was better spent on new media.

What was the reaction in your industry?

Shock! My peers all said, 'If you're giving it all away, why would people hire you?' and I was like, 'That is not how the world works, people who play music give it away knowing that more people will come to their concert.' Everyone was sceptical in the beginning, and now I probably get three calls a week from people asking, 'How are you doing this?' and they want me to teach them social media.

It's a different approach, and I think some people in my industry think I must be very egotistical to have someone follow me around with a camera, but it's not ego. It's actually a pretty selfless act, as you are more vulnerable when someone is following you around with a camera, but I just want more and more people to be helped by our work.

What's been the return on investment (ROI)?

We have so much evidence of ROI. Our revenues have doubled, our business is exploding, and on every call, people say, 'I heard about you, and then I went and checked you out' – and they've called with the feeling that I am the real deal. We've won clients such as Facebook, I've been on bigger stages and with bigger audiences, and our voice has been amplified. What has happened, too, is that people will hear about me, check me out, then automatically choose us over competitors. The last time I launched a book, I spent $60,000 on paid media and PR. This year we spent half that amount and I sold three times the number of books. Two months into 2018, we had nearly booked our entire revenue for the previous year.

You're across all platforms, how does that work tactically?
Yes, we're on YouTube, Facebook, SoundCloud, LinkedIn, Instagram, I have a blog, a Facebook Watch show, YouTube show, a podcast. A lot of people go nuts trying to serve all these. What we do is we create a pillar of content, and then serving all the different platforms is just the execution. We film for about four days per month, and this is our 'pillar content'. I also have an inhouse social media person who films me ad hoc, and we send the content over to Vayner for editing. Most entrepreneurs are overwhelmed by the thought of creating all this content, but we document a lot of what I do rather than creating it from scratch. I'm just doing my business and happen to have a team filming, who then create the content for the different platforms with very little effort from me.

Has there been any downside?
At first I put pressure on myself for everything to be perfect. I wanted to review everything before it was published, but I had to let that go.

Also, I would think, *Oh I should stay up tonight and engage with more people on Facebook*, when really I didn't want to, I just wanted to go to bed. It is about being OK with good enough. The hardest thing for women on social media is that there are some trolls, so when I first started putting things out there, guys would write, 'Hey, you would be pretty if you lost some weight.' Personal trainers would write, 'I could help you be happier with your body.' It wasn't a big deal because I am in HR and handle this stuff all the time. I would just not let my ego get in the way and would thank them for their offer.

Is content a way of life for you now?

Yes, and it will be a way of life for us all. In my presentations, when they introduce me they always say, 'Everyone put away your cell phones and pay attention', and I say, 'Everyone get your cell phones out. I have worked hard on all these graphics so that they will work perfectly as images for Instagram and Twitter, so please take a photo of every single slide. Here is my hashtag.'

My husband (and business partner) was a bit worried about the amount of money I was spending, and he said we could employ a team at less cost. But then I'd have to manage that team and have the vision, and we don't have expertise in that space. It makes absolute sense to me to outsource it to experts. We've leapfrogged over the traditional system, and this is absolutely the future for me.

From mainstream media to *you are* the media

When you hear the word 'media', do you automatically think of daily newspapers, magazines and TV shows? Does your mind flit to the *Sun*, the *Daily Mail*, *This Morning* and *ITV News*? If it does, you're not alone.

But the media has changed, and the power to publish has shifted into the hands of everyone and anyone. At a precise level, what I'm talking about is the power for individuals to become media companies in their own right, and this is down to three things: the rise of the smartphone and lowering barriers of entry for content/video production; the systematic dismantling of the media; and the empowerment of us all as individuals to distribute content through websites and social platforms. You can be a publisher now, you can be a TV network, you can be a radio station, just like those who have previously been responsible for distributing the media we consume.

Because I am a former national newspaper journalist, these major societal shifts are my favourite topics! Over the past 20 years, I've seen the world in which I spent the first two decades of my career shattered into a thousand different pieces and fragmented beyond belief, and I still don't believe most people working in that (rapidly shrinking) industry have any idea what the future will bring them.

This doesn't upset me, partly because I'm no longer in this industry – in fact, I love it! Of course, there will always be those candle manufacturers who felt utter despair at the invention of the light bulb, and the knocker-uppers who cried real tears at the invention of the alarm clock. But industries can and do die, and, generally, when seismic evolutionary changes happen in society, the best thing to do is roll with it and work out how to use them to your advantage.

To take it personally, or to think it is about the now anyway, is just plain stupid. If we remove the past five years or so from our thinking, we're actually living through a 90-year stretch of general media evolution which began in 1928 – not that long ago really – with the world's first television broadcast, and which will end with, well, only time will tell, but probably us beaming into each other's worlds through virtual and augmented reality.

Think of the Queen: she gave her first televised broadcast in 1957, and in 2017 – just 60 years later – she broadcast live via Facebook for the first time. It took Facebook just three and a half years to reach 50 million users. Compare that to how long it took television (13 years), radio (38 years) and the telephone (75 years).

The media as we know it is being totally dismantled

The further we head down this route, though, the more anyone and everyone is empowered to publish, not just those with money or luck on their side. And this can only be a good thing – and it's no good keeping your head in the sand.

I remember back in the early 2000s, when I was working on one of the UK's largest newspapers. People like me were the gatekeepers through which anyone – from ordinary folk to celebrities – could be heard. The phone would ring and whoever was on the end of it, whether they were royalty, a celebrity, a celebrity PR or just a regular person with a mission or experience to share, would have to convince someone like me that their story was worthy of attention. And even then, we might well put our own spin on it.

The ability to publish was owned purely by the traditional media – television, newspapers, magazines and radio – and ordinary people weren't empowered. I remember a guy phoning in to a national newspaper where I was overseeing the health pages – he'd invented a cream that had cured his wife's psoriasis. He had a really sweet story of putting all the ingredients into a barrel and rolling the barrel up and down his driveway to mix it. It had worked, and now all his neighbours were asking him for jars of his cream. I thought it was a great story and wanted to feature it, but my editor disagreed and, as such, this man had a door slammed right in his face. If he had developed the same product today, he wouldn't have to depend on jumping through all the hoops of journalists and editors, he could just get on and share his story on a blog and social networks and via influencers.

MY STORY BBC Presenter Jeremy Vine: 'Is a journalist anyone with a smartphone?'
BBC presenter and broadcaster (and Bolt Digital client), Jeremy

Vine is an avid user of Twitter and Facebook. His daily programme, *The Jeremy Vine Show* on Radio 2 is now the most listened-to radio current-affairs programme in the UK, having overtaken Radio 4's flagship *Today*. He also presents *Eggheads*, a teatime staple, which is now one of the longest-running quiz shows in British TV history.

Jeremy, as a well-known figure, how do you use social media and digital?

I have a website and I use Twitter and Facebook. With my social media, I am filling in a bit of background behind my daily work in a way that is (hopefully!) compliant with the BBC.

I also use social media as a way to allow people to get in touch with me. People are now pinging on my phone and then they get a reply straight away. The joy of social media is that you don't need a stamp – a quick reply could just be, 'Thank-you so much.' Another great thing is this: it's rather like being able to eavesdrop on every conversation that is going on about you in every pub in the country. Even to the point when two people are saying in a pub in Bradford, 'Jeremy Vine's show is shit!' and it's as though I can tap them on the shoulder and say, 'Oh, can you tell me why? Because I am just having a pint over here and I heard you talking.' It's useful for feedback.

How do you get the balance right between the BBC and you as a person?

I think this is something that will resonate with people who work in big corporations. There is a constant tension between a person posting, in other words me saying, 'I have this amazing woman in my studio right now', and the organisation itself. I recently had a guest on my show, Sarah Ezekiel, who is an artist but has motor neurone disease and paints using her gaze onto a special laptop. The question is this: is that for me to post as the person in a room with another interesting person; or is it for the show to post? By nature, social media is not very corporate, and that is why there is this tension. It's all a work in progress.

Are there any downsides to social media for people like you who are in the spotlight?

Anyone is only a tweet away from sudden death, so there's a huge amount of responsibility. I had a friend who went to the cinema and she realised she had gone into the film with the subtitles on and just before she turned off her phone she tweeted something about 'Why can't they turn these ridiculous subtitles off?' When she emerged from the film two hours later, she was trending, because, understandably, people who are deaf around the world did not like what she had said. It was a genuine mistake, but the thing is you do need to monitor the immediate response so that you can see if things are starting to mushroom out of control. It's important that it's handled like petrol and matches. The only thing I would say in defence of people like me, who broadcast, is that we are quite used to the peril of the open microphone. We are not going to think: *Wait, this tweet is only going to be seen by ten people.* That applies to all people – we used to have an old-fashioned megaphone where 20 people could hear you, and now you have this monster-sized speaker system that reaches the entire world. That is progress, but it is also lethal.

As a journalist what do you think about the way the media is changing?

Well, I can only just go back to my time on the Coventry *Evening Telegraph*. In 1986 I was a trainee there. I was one of three people they took on every year, and there were 85 editorial staff. Now there are, I think, only seven. I honestly thought, *This place has got a thousand years more to come; it is the biggest building in Coventry, full of journalists reporting the news to the people in Coventry* – it was so strong! It sold 90,000 copies every day. Now look at it. It is humbling. One of the advantages we have at Radio 2 over print media is that we have an audience in their sixties who may live into their nineties and, therefore, you have got fantastic loyalty, but the challenge is getting young people in. The culture changes. Now, I wonder, is a journalist simply someone who owns a smartphone? Why did we ever think it was a profession? I still believe in it, and I still believe in the truth of reporting, but it's amazing now that every person has their own platform and they will put it on Facebook and other people can judge whether it is important. The audience decides, and if it's important, it will be seen by a million people. It makes you wonder why journalists ever thought we were special.

My parents always told me that a job is something someone gives you, and now I am telling my children a job is something you create for yourself. That is the change.

It's not just the media – the Internet itself is fragmenting

Even the Internet itself is undergoing seismic shifts. Ten years ago, when I had my first online business, there was really only one door to online visibility: Google and the other search engines and browsers. It was very simple. You googled a name, a service or an idea; the results listed a whole load of website links; you selected one and, bingo! you reached someone's website. That was it.

Today, that 'Internet' encompasses multiple types of social media platforms, each with its own way to find, reach, connect to and communicate with other people. Each social network represents a door to visibility or a channel in its own right, and the number of networks is continuing to grow. Then there are all the new opportunities as each media form – from video through to audio – becomes easier and more within reach to learn how to create and master. When those in the future look back at today, the age of the traditional media (television and newspapers) will be a small part of a communications shift that happened in fewer than 100 years but ultimately gave everyone on this planet the ability to have a voice.

Now, the question is: what will you do with yours?

Prepare for your five-star rating, Charlie Brooker-style

'Nosedive' is an episode of Charlie Brooker's fictional dark-satire series *Black Mirror* that takes social media to a new extreme. If you haven't seen it, you must (Netflix or YouTube should have it).

In the episode, a single platform connects everyone to each other, and everyone carries a handheld device and wears a futuristic version of Google Glass. This technology allows everyone instantly to see the ratings of whoever they are looking at, and simultaneously to rate that person.

Rude waiter? Give him one star. Don't like someone's dress sense? Mark them down as a two. The result is that the most highly rated are virtual celebrities, living five-star lives (the best houses, jobs, holidays and lifestyles), whereas everyone else hovers around a four-star rating, while dedicating their whole life to improving their ratings. Those who dip below three, well, they become total outsiders and outcasts in society.

Of course, this is pure fiction (although most certainly food for thought), but how far off that are we now, truly? Certainly, from the point of view of corporations, especially places to visit, we are already there. Most of us would be concerned about going to a hotel or restaurant with a three-star or lower rating on TripAdvisor, for example. And as soon as we're unhappy with customer service, we take to Twitter or Facebook to complain.

For now, though, such a ratings system isn't in place for individuals, but are the beginnings of it already in our world? Look at the way we can rate Uber drivers, for example. Would you allow yourself to be picked up by a driver with a poor rating? Or would you wait for the next one? And most who operate in the online space have to prepare themselves on occasions for a 'thumbs down' or hits of the 'don't like' button.

Just as in this episode of *Black Mirror*, the upside of visibility is so great that the occasional bruise from negative feedback is massively outweighed by the upside potential of increased trust, visibility, influence and profits that will follow when you get it right.

But what about you?

How can you – wherever you are now – take the same principles outlined above and benefit from all the media creation and distribution that is now open to you, and use content to build your own profile in a way that is achievable, sustainable and affordable to you? Generally, the people who can benefit from this book fit into four main categories:

1. **Start-up entrepreneur/self-employed professional expert** *#StandOutOnline* will help you understand how to use your personal brand to promote your business and build a profile in an area that you are passionate about.
2. **Employees who want to become a recognised freelance expert or attract new job opportunities** You've nailed it as an employee. *#StandOutOnline* will help you to learn how to use your personal brand to further rise through the ranks and/or to start and grow a sideline so that you can escape the rat race.
3. **Influencer/celebrities** *#StandOutOnline* will help you understand how regular people become influencers, and how celebrities are taking their mainstream media profiles into the social space.
4. **CEO/founder** *#StandOutOnline* will show you how to further build your personal profile for the benefit of your company. Increased trust, influence and profits can come with very little time invested.

How this book works

Our personal brand and digital footprints are made up of dozens of individual strands created by a collection of ordinary daily activities and online behaviour. This book is all about how to pull together these separate strands, take control of them, fine tune them and power them up to transform your passive accidental brand into a powerful and competitive proactive personal brand that stands out.

In this book, I'll be covering everything from the strategy, mindset and tactics that you'll need, to how you can use your personal brand for greater trust, influence and commercial gain.

We'll also be hearing from others about their own experiences of building their personal brands and where it has taken them.

I'll also be presenting the systems and processes that we use at Bolt Digital, the London-based digital marketing agency of which I am a co-founder, to build our clients' personal brands. These proprietary processes are the result of years working in the mass mainstream media and now digital media. If you're new to these concepts, this book will really help you to understand what to put into your own personal brand.

I'll also be offering my best tips in bite-sized chunks – don't miss them!

Tash's Takeaways

- You have a personal brand online, whether you like it or not.
- The new world trust paradigm is: 'If I can't find you online – I don't trust you.'
- The dismantling of the media and the rise of the smart-phone means that *you* have the power to be a publisher, to be a TV network and/or to be a radio station, and you can use this for the benefit of your personal brand and your business. All of this is possible at a fraction of the cost that it was just a decade ago.
- What we are seeing is part of a wider shift in communication that has been happening for the past century.
- Now is the time for you to find your voice and work out what to do with it. Because if you don't, I assure you that your competition will.

2

Personal Branding:
Accidental or by Design?

If you didn't know before, you now understand that you are already leaving digital footprints all over the Internet and, as such, you have a personal brand online. Let me ask you a question right now: what does that brand look like? If I were to search for your name in Google, seek out all your social media profiles and find you online, what would I see? Here is an exercise for you. I suggest you stop reading and do these activities if you haven't done them all before and/or don't do them regularly:

> **EXERCISE: find yourself online**
>
> 1. Google-search your name and click on all the first-page links.
> 2. Do a Google image search of your name.
> 3. What about a Bing or other search-engine search?
> 4. Now try a YouTube search of your name.
> 5. And then do a search of your name on all the social media sites.
> 6. Finally, do all of the above again, but with your name combined with where you live or your name and your employer and/or business name.

Are you impossible to find? Do you have half-baked or outdated profiles that don't truly reflect who you are? Or are there some old threads on Twitter or other profiles where you were obviously included for a cause or a sport, hobby or a location for a period of time, but then it just falls off a cliff?

If you want to really understand where you score and what people are likely to think of your online brand, I have created a free and short quiz that will provide you with some great and valuable insights and answers: www.boltdigital.media/standoutonline

You really need to understand that the more you present, nurture and grow your personal brand, the more you will build your reputation as a leader in your field – and the more you will stand out online. That's crucial because it brings with it influence, and the more influence you have, the more you will be sought out for expertise, talents and products and/or services. The monetisation opportunities are endless and ever growing, whether that means more clients, jobs, bookings, donations to causes you are passionate about, or any other opportunities you might want to capitalise on, now and/or in the future.

One thing my team and I hear almost every day at Bolt Digital is someone saying: 'I need to build my personal brand', or 'How do I get myself out there?' Sometimes they know what it is and understand what they need to do, but at other times they want the 'personal brand switch' to be flicked (if only it was that easy). Others know they want to 'be' a 'someone', but don't really know where to start.

Before we go any further, take a look at the benefits and risks chart on page 30, which outlines why this is so important.

Benefits of a strong personal brand	Risks of not having a personal brand
More sales	No, or low, trust
Higher profile	Bad first and lasting impression
More influence	Less leverage and influence
Greater trust	Lower sales/profits/influence
More connections	Less memorable
Greater ability to connect to other influential people	Harder to differentiate from the competition
Ability to create change/promote good causes	Being considered as plain, boring and unremarkable
	Being the only tramp at the party

Accidental personal brands

For many people, any personal branding that does exist has happened more by accident than by design. We don't set up our profiles properly, or we do and then we forget to update them for the next three years. We have the best intentions to write blog posts or record videos, and then put that to the bottom of our to-do list. We end up busy with our 'work', and our own profiles get forgotten about.

Everyone has a platform

In online personal branding, you'll often hear the word 'platform' being spoken of. People will talk about building their platform, using their platform or wishing they had a bigger platform. Within the media landscape, the word 'platform' is not the raised surface on which people can stand, although the concept is similar. Audiences have always been able to consume media in different formats through a range of platforms, although until recently that would have mainly been old media, such as newspapers, radio, television, adverts and computer games. Celebrities have long talked about having their particular show as their platform.

Today, in the world of new media and on-demand content, the word 'platform' refers to the websites, blogs, vlogs, podcasts, apps, email lists – and anything else through which one person is able to communicate directly with the masses.

Because the barriers to entering these platforms are so much lower compared to landing a slot on TV, and so much cheaper than taking out an advert in a newspaper, it's now the case that everyone has a platform. The concept of distributing media to an audience to consume is the same, it's just that your platform will be centred on your online profiles and social network.

Tash's tips

There will always be some people who stumble unintentionally into fame and celebrity. And there will always be those who take conventional routes, such as starting off as a studio runner and rising steadily to the rank of presenter for a major television programme. But, equally, there's a growing number of those who deliberately create, present and nurture their personal brands to achieve the same kind of outcome. Make sure you take this opportunity now!

I'm soon going to share with you the systems and processes that my team and I have developed to build personal brands and platforms online, but first I'd like to share with you my own story of how I became a leader within a very specific micro-niche.

Building trust where there is none

In 2007, having been working at national newspapers and magazines, I started my first online business, Talk to the Press – www.
talktothepress.co.uk – which I later went on to sell successfully
for a significant profit in 2014.

Making this a success meant that I had to understand the new
digital landscape and opportunities created by the Internet. This
was in the days well before social media was all the rage. It's hard
to remember that time, but trust me, back then it was all about
Google and SEO (search-engine optimisation). But I faced one
particular issue in my former chosen niche of buying news and
feature stories and supplying them to major news outlets. None
of them really liked journalists! How, then, would I overcome
this problem and build a company that had integrity, honesty
and trust at its core?

Many of my competitors were, for some reason, hiding behind
an anonymous generic corporate business identity. Although
their websites looked professional, with smart logos and nice
sensible colour schemes, they were not about people and featured
no names of anyone who actually owned the companies or who
worked there. I instinctively felt that people connect to people,
and therefore what potential customers wanted to see was the
people behind the business. I realised that the way to stand out in
this niche – as well as building the trust – was through developing
my personal brand.

How did I do it? I used a lot of the same techniques back then
that are now part of the processes you'll be learning about soon:

- I commissioned a professional photoshoot and put the
  photos all over the website.

- I wrote regular blog posts for my own website and other websites demonstrating my knowledge and expertise in that field.
- I had professional videos made of me talking about the business.
- I published a book.
- I hired a PR agent who got me on *BBC Breakfast* and secured me a regular slot on ITV's *Lorraine* show reviewing the daily newspapers.
- I wrote and published free guides about how to handle press attention.
- I appeared on a Channel 4 documentary and on radio discussing the media and our work.
- We regularly published photos of my team and myself escorting our clients on to television programmes such as *This Morning* and *Good Morning Britain*.

Let's be clear, I'm not talking about becoming a mega celebrity (although if that's what you aspire to, or are already, then there is always value in increasing your brand online). I'm talking about becoming a big fish in small pond – being the most visible and memorable person in the micro-niche in which I then operated.

If anyone back then was considering which story-brokering agency to use, would it be the one with not a single actual person featured on the website, or the one whose owner they had just seen on *Lorraine* that morning and with a friendly people-focused website? You guessed it!

And that's why my company became the UK market leader in our space. I had a great run for six years, before I decided to cash in my chips by selling the company to the UK's largest news agency group.

I had to do this too

As the CEO and co-founder of Bolt Digital, I've developed my personal brand alongside our business brand. The list below highlights a cross-section of some of the many doors that I've been able to open, and its diversity shows you how your brand-driven reach can expand exponentially. Here are just a few of the results I achieved in 2016 from regular content production, distribution via social media channels, building an email list and sending regular opinion and educational content out through my distribution channels using text, audio and video:

- A commission by a major UK publisher to write two expert books, including this one, #*StandOutOnline*.
- Receiving national mainstream-media attention, including being interviewed by Radio 2, Radio 4 and the *Observer*.
- I was approached to be a TedX speaker and delivered a Ted keynote address.
- I was selected to advise the government and invited to 10 Downing Street to take part in a round table regarding the pace and potential impact of digital transformation.
- Facebook identified and trained me as an independent brand ambassador (and one of only eight accredited trainers) as part of their She Means Business initiative, which has now reached more than 10,000 female entrepreneurs.
- I have attracted clients, including celebrities, CEOs and aristocrats, who have been reassured by my personal brand and the trust, authority and positioning that it gives me.

All of the above came about because I have more genuine expertise and experience than the vast majority of other people who run digital agencies, but without putting my brand out there, and making sure it would stand out from the crowd, I am certain that not one of these opportunities would have landed in my lap. There is an old saying that goes, 'If you build a better mousetrap, people will beat a path to your door.' I disagree. You might have the best mousetrap, but if no one knows you have it, or where to find it, you will never be successful.

How to deliberately build a personal brand online

Over the next few pages, I'm going to share with you a number of proprietary processes that we have developed at Bolt Digital that enable us to build the personal brands of our clients systematically, *but* which will also be helpful to you as you build your own personal brand. I am going to be detailing the how-to elements of these processes as the book progresses, but let's look at it all in a nutshell right now.

The Bolt Star

This is a useful way of summarising what goes into a personal brand.

The elements inside the star are all about you. They are the key components that will magnify your personal brand. The more clarity you have, and the more of these elements you have locked down with clarity, the more powerful your brand will be; however, you also need to project and publish your brand, products, services, or whatever else is important to you, to the outside world. And the elements outside the star contain a range of distribution and marketing activities that you can utilise. Below the line is everything that goes into a personal brand that people can't always immediately see (the strategy, planning, tools and so on), whereas above the line is what people can see (your output).

The elements needed to build your personal brand

The Bolt Wheel of Opportunity

The Wheel of Opportunity on page 37 highlights the actions you need to take to build or further expand your personal brand. I have used this model as the framework for the rest of this book. The following chapters will walk you around the wheel in a logical and practical manner. Right now, we are in Part One of the book, which is the Strategy section of the wheel.

On the outside of the wheel, you will see the growing opportunities coming your way as your brand develops. Let's continue with the Strategy section, and you can look forward to working your way around the wheel as the book unfolds, with opportunities popping up again and again at any stage along the way.

How are personal brands created?

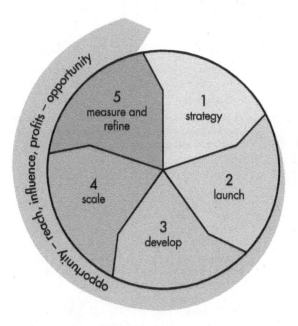

The Stand Out Online performance matrix

I love the following model because it neatly summarises the mistakes I see most people and most marketing agencies making day in and day out. To be effective, your personal brand and your marketing must serve your personal and organisational goals and objectives. In short, it *must* drive results. That's the commercial aspect of the horizontal axis. The key focus and measure here is ROI (return on investment); however, if you only focus on the commercial aspect and neglect the more creative angles, you won't optimise your results.

Which animal represents your online approach?

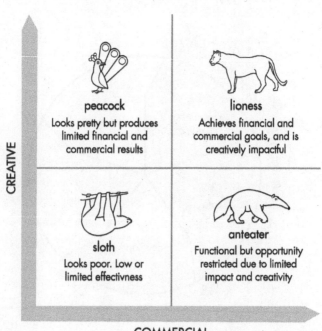

peacock
Looks pretty but produces limited financial and commercial results

lioness
Achieves financial and commercial goals, and is creatively impactful

sloth
Looks poor. Low or limited effectivness

anteater
Functional but opportunity restricted due to limited impact and creativity

CREATIVE

COMMERCIAL

Sloth This is the worst of all the quadrants. People and organisations in this space have old-fashioned websites, out-of-date blogs, amateurish graphic design, and business models that don't make money. Whatever you do, *don't* be a sloth. Follow the instructions in this book and work with capable professionals, and you will never have to spend any time in the bottom corner.

Peacock Highly creative types tend to be peacocks: their brands look great but they have weak business models that either don't make money or they produce low rewards for the time and effort invested. You'd be astonished by how many influencers, for example, are struggling to make a decent living from their huge followings online. They simply lack the commercial knowledge, skill and expertise, and they are either destined to fail or need help to adapt and grow. My hope is that this book and my experience and expertise will help turn many thousands of peacocks into lions and lionesses before it's too late.

Anteater Picture an anteater for a moment in your mind. Hard, grey and with a long and ugly snout: very practical for attacking ant mounds and getting a decent meal (if you are an ant connoisseur, I guess). They are definitely fit for their evolutionary purpose, but would you like to stroke or admire them, or want one as a pet? Probably not! Personal and organisational brands can be anteaters. They usually achieve commercial results, but they are at risk of being overtaken by the competition. Brand loyalty is also usually very low, which in turn depresses their potential to build trust, to reach their market, to influence, to make profits and to increase in value. Anteater brands usually come across as unprofessional, uninteresting and, frankly, boring.

Lioness I'm using the female term lioness, as opposed to lion, for two reasons. Firstly, I'm a woman, so I'm biased, and secondly, because it better portrays the point I want to make, which is that lioness brands consist of the very best of both female and male talents and energy. They are beautiful, creative, interesting and charismatic, as well as being focused, commercial, structured and driven by measurable results. The best personal brands are lionesses, so that's what I want you to become. (OK, I'll let you use term 'lion' if you are a proud guy who just can't get past aspiring to be a lioness!)

Social action

You can connect with me on social media. Please use the hashtag #standoutonline to get my attention!

- Instagram.com/tashcourtenay
- Facebook.com/natashacourtenaysmith
- Twitter.com/tash_courtenay

Does it need to be all about my online brand?

It's a good question – and one I am often asked by audiences that I speak to when I am representing Facebook and my own business, Bolt Digital. The question is usually asked by older clients who are feeling left behind by the massive digital disruption that we are experiencing. The accurate answer to the question is no. But it would be naïve to believe that you can make your brand stand out without serious investment in online activity. The fact is you can't.

Perhaps the best way to look at it is this: you will be promoting your personal brand to various groups of people, many of whom are actually people in your 'real' world. *But*, you'll still be reaching and influencing these people – and many, many more – online. You will almost always get far greater exposure at a much lower cost online than offline. In an ideal world, you'll be doing both in an integrated manner. But remember the example of Cy Wakeman in Chapter 1? She went all-in online and doubled her revenue as a result, in super-fast time. And remember, that was done in a business-to-business and historically traditional and staid sector of human resources services for large companies.

Finally, although you will launch and/or grow your personal brand online, you can also feed and nourish it through plenty of offline real-world activities, such as exhibitions, public speaking, referrals, networking at events, traditional media and so on. The real world and online world work together. Consider the difference like this, the engine and propulsion of all of this (if you are not a celebrity and you don't have a regular slot on television) is online, but cementing relationships over the long term often happens in the real world.

MY STORY Phanella Mayall Fine: 'We built our brand online and in the real world'
Phanella Mayall Fine is a career coach and co-founder of the Step Up Club, an online learning community and platform that supports women in work, success and confidence through books, events, online learning and brand collaborations.

Phanella, how did you get where you are today?
My background is that I did French and German at Oxford University. I was very academic and perhaps as a result of that I was very much funnelled into law. Personally, I have always been quite financially motivated, and as a child I had a vision that I'd be the President of the United States (where I lived until I was eight) or the CEO of Coca-Cola. Law seemed to fit with these big corporate career dreams. I thought I'd be like Ally McBeal, spending my time having meetings in beautifully cut suits, but the reality wasn't quite the same, so I ended up leaving. The process I went through then has been what has defined my career ever since. I had a scattergun approach to career

change, in which I tried lots of things, even taking four days to shadow my friend who was a teacher, in a bid to find out what I wanted to do. I moved into fund management at a big bank. It was a fascinating job, but it was difficult to make it work in terms of flexibility when I had children. I then experimented with blogging and went to see a careers coach. It was through seeing the careers coach that I realised I was very interested in career choice, and decided to become a coach myself.

What's your advice for people who are thinking of changing career?

Changing career is challenging because you can't go to a recruitment consultant, as they tend to only want to recruit people who are already experienced within roles. The way I've always done it is to strategically network with people and always open up conversations about how I am looking to do something different. All the opportunities I've had to change career have come via that approach. I always advise people to build on what they have done before rather than start afresh, and to see a change of career as a series of stepping stones. Going from fund management straight to Step Up Club would have been impossible, so what I did was use my prior experience and network to get work with a firm that coached women in law firms and banks. I also did a master's in organisational behaviour. I've been a practising coach in these kinds of firms ever since, doing maternity coaching, executive development and working on female leadership programmes.

How did Step Up Club come about?

It's always been an ambition of mine to be seen as a true expert at what I do. I'd look at food influencers online, such as Hemsley

& Hemsley, and wonder why no one was doing the same thing for careers.

I decided to write a book on career change and partnered with an old friend, journalist Alice Olins, to do this. We put a book proposal together quickly and pitched it to agents, but we were told we'd never get a book published as we had no platform – no email list, no social followers and we weren't famous. We decided to host a women's career event to prove the appetite for our fresh take on careers. We were confident we could get 50 people through our own networks, and our agent invited commissioning editors from publishing houses. In the end, we had 75 people at our event, and Random House commissioned the book. It was published in September 2016.

How does Step Up Club operate today?

We've used real-world activities such as events, speaking and media coverage to build awareness at the same time as building our brands online via our website, newsletter and social media. We're told all the time that we have a unique combination of real expertise that works across industries, coupled with a stylish and engaging take on everything we do. We now have two streams of income. Firstly, we are influencers within the careers space – we've worked with huge brands such as Karen Millen on campaigns centred on women's careers. Our photos were in the window of every Karen Millen store around the globe, and our videos got over a million views. Secondly, we've launched the Step Up School, which is a real-world learning programme: a year-long course to change women's careers (and lives) for the better. And next, we're launching our online school. Step Up School has had two cohorts of students through it and both sold out within 24 hours.

What's the big vision for Step Up School?

The vision is a big global membership club for women who want to create change in their career, whether they want to change career, change the way they are working, start a new business, or go from a junior to a senior level. What we get pleasure from is having an impact on individuals. The thing about achievement is that if you are achieving for achievement's sake, then goalposts always move forward; for example, early on I used to get excited when I saw myself in magazines, but gradually you become more used to that. But when you change your goal to helping other people change their lives, the joy you get from seeing your impact never diminishes. To be able to expand that from a small group of women in London to potentially around the world is really motivating.

Tash's tips

One mistake many people make is to think that being successful online means that they can live in their pyjamas and never leave the house. There isn't an influencer I know who doesn't work hard in the real world. That's because they understand the different types of people they are trying to reach and the value of each one.

Your tiers to influence

Another way to consider the interaction between what you do online and in the real world is to think in terms of tiers to influence. This concerns the sizes of the audiences you should be thinking about reaching and influencing, and where you will find them. Think of it as an upside-down triangle with tier 1 at the bottom. As you move up each tier the number of people you reach/ influence should increase markedly, and you will most likely take a different approach with each tier.

Tier 1: Existing clients and those who already know you professionally We often forget the people we've already worked with. Our job is done and we move on. Yet content and value will keep us in their mind and put us out in front of the competition. They're a very valuable group, because your existing clients know that you've done a good job. They know you walk the talk. Certainly, word of mouth is a valuable driver for many businesses.

Tier 2: Your extended network This group of people – your friends, your family, your old colleagues, your old school and college friends – may not be a huge audience, and you might feel kind of awkward promoting yourself in front of them, but they're such a valuable audience because they actually know you in real life. Many of them, whether they're from school or college, know the real you, as in the you that you were before you were a professional at anything. They'd love to be able to recommend you for what you do. The question is, do they actually know what you do?

Tier 3: Your own audiences on social media and on your email list It doesn't matter how many or how few of these people there are. These are the people who do not necessarily know you in real life, but they followed you or opted into your list and have some sort of interest in who you are and what you might say. Treat them well. They're there. They've raised their hand and said, 'Hey, I like the look of what you do. I'm following you.' They might share, recommend or become volunteers or donors themselves.

Tier 4: Local and niche media Most people I work with want national media coverage. I've lost count of the number of times I've heard, 'Can you get me in the *Daily Mail*?', 'Can you get me on *This Morning*?' We're coming to that, but it's not all about the *Daily Mail* or the *Telegraph* or *This Morning* or the *Sunday Times* or *Style* magazine or *Grazia*, or any of those publications.

Don't overlook the power of your local media. They are content-hungry. They're most likely crying out for decent content, and most local publications are relatively easy to get into. In this tier you can reach a larger group of people who don't know you, as well as gain the credibility of being featured by an official news outlet, who will appreciate the local angle to your story or business.

Tier 5: Mainstream media National media is, of course, brilliant for reaching new audiences, and many mainstream media outlets (daily newspapers and television programmes) still have hundreds of thousands, if not millions, of readers, viewers and listeners. They bring traffic to your website, people to your physical business and, most importantly, it's fantastic for your brand and positioning, and for giving you credibility. If a news organisation decides that you're the teacher or lawyer or doctor or hairdresser or musician, or whatever, that they're going to ask for a comment, or bring into a debate, that gives you a ton of credibility. Even better, you can then take their logo and put it all over your website with the tagline, 'As seen in . . .'.

Tier 6: Online media and social media The largest audiences you can ever potentially reach are the global ones found online and accessed through online media and social media. Online media with a link to your website can really drive traffic and attract new clients, and can improve your SEO, which in turn helps you get yourself out there – and it can improve your online visibility. Online media churn through more content than print outlets, and as such there's more opportunity for you to raise your profile in them. Online media are chewing through content like crazy, so it is comparatively quick and easy to find these opportunities, because they are constantly on the lookout for more.

Tash's Takeaways

- Most people's online personal brands have been created accidentally, despite the fact that everyone now has a platform from which to speak and build their personal brand.
- When looking at deliberately building a personal brand, Bolt's Star model, Wheel of Opportunity and Stand Out Online matrix sum up the processes involved at a glance.
- Although the Stand Out Online process is about online, real-world activity is important, too.
- Every individual should stop worrying about overnight success and reaching millions of people instantly, but instead look at their own personal 'tiers to influence' and focus on those.
- And remember to be a lioness and share your journey and progress with me and others on social media #standoutonline

Your Values, Vision
and Mission Statement

So far, we've been talking about personal branding on a macro level. You know it can help you in all sorts of ways, from making more money, winning more customers, creating change or raising money for charities. But let's come down to the micro. Why do you want to do this? What's the strategy behind your desire to build your personal brand? What are you passionate about? What are your business organisations or personal objectives? What is the personal vision, mission and values statement empowering your personal branding process?

For most people, it's not just about the money and opportunities but also other factors, such as recognition, reach and the influence that comes with having a strong, visible personal brand. It's about being heard and effecting change.

That's why the first step to building a personal brand for any of our clients at Bolt Digital is a strategy session. It helps people to clarify and simplify the foundations of their personal brand, including their vision, mission and values, as well as their short-, medium- and long-term objectives. Most people have a few doubts and objections over whether or not building a personal brand is right for them (it is) or will work for them (it will), but these concerns should also be considered.

Without doing this, there's no point in getting started with any content creation at all, because you won't know what to say or the purpose of what you are doing, and you won't be able to maintain momentum. In the same way that a big corporation uses a mission, vision and values statement as a part of its strategic planning, so is the case with a personal brand.

Prepare your statement

A mission statement explains your big reason why, and your over-all intention; your vision statement is your vision for the future you; and your values statement encompasses what you believe and how you will behave.

Let's take a closer look. Please take the time to review each question below and make notes on the answer, and at the end, you'll be able to complete your vision, mission and values statement for your personal brand.

What are your core values?

People who live by their values find it easier to know what to say, and they feel empowered to keep up the effort of building their personal brand for the long term. When you know your values, they also provide a barometer and guidance for your behaviour and decisions. It's not always easy, though, to unravel what your values are, and most of us value what we are told to value by society and the media without giving much thought to what our own values are.

Taking some time now, in a notebook, write down as many of your values as you can think of. Here are some examples of values to give you inspiration:

Accountability	Individuality
Achievement	Justice
Balance	Kindness
Boldness	Love
Challenge	Optimism
Courage	Patience
Dedication	Persistence
Efficiency	Recognition
Energy	Security
Fairness	Significance
Family	Teamwork
Gratitude	Trust
Growth	Understanding
Happiness	Wealth
Health	Wisdom
Independence	

Now, can you narrow your list down to seven of the most important values to you? You might find that some values on your long
list are similar and you can narrow down by categorising them;
for example, values like drive, dedication, optimism, persistence
and recognition can (depending on what they mean to you) all be
contained within one master value, which is achievement. Write
these master values in your notebook.

What are your personal or organisational objectives?

Your objectives describe what you or your company expects to
accomplish through developing your Stand Out Online process.
Summarise these in a list in your notebook.

What are you really good at and/or passionate about?

What are you all about? What are you interested in? What are you passionate about? What do you talk about most often? What do you do in your spare time? What things do you enjoy buying and get really excited about? If money were no object, how would you spend your time? Start writing down your thoughts.

The most respected personal brands often tend to be experts in their field. They may be conventional experts, such as doctors and lawyers, who studied the subject at university and have a degree in it – but don't forget everything is different in this new online world. Online, people make millions out of topics such as crafting that don't come with university degrees. Ask yourself what people talk to you about and ask for your advice on, and write these down.

What is your USP?

In your notebook, describe your unique selling point (USP). How are you different from others in your sphere or industry?

Who are you trying to reach?

This is about your audience. Who are you trying to reach and connect with? What are they looking for? What do they want to know about? Write this down as well.

What is your vision?

Work out what success at standing out online looks like for you. Write down five key measurable goals that you'd like to achieve. Examples might be:

- Having my own online show watched by X number of people.
- Being commissioned to write a book on my subject.
- Having social media audiences of X thousand.
- Appearing on TV.
- Being invited to advise government.
- Being nominated for a Queen's honour.
- Increasing my income by X amount.

The potential list is endless and entirely yours.

Write your statement

Now copy the table below into your notebook and complete it.

My draft values are	My draft mission is	My draft vision is

Using what you've uncovered from your values and objectives above, complete the following statement in your notebook:

I am a [*describe how you see yourself professionally*] who *describe your unique talents and passions, and how you use them*] for [*describe who your target audience is*] so that they can [*describe the desired experience or results you want to give to your audience*] and so that I can [*describe your long-term vision/ purpose/mission*].

You don't necessarily need to publish this anywhere; it's just for your own reference – a personal brand statement that is distinctive to you and you alone. If you think about the strapline or catchphrase that famous household products have, this is your own personal equivalent.

MY STORY Carl Reader: 'Building my brand online has been a game changer professionally and personally'

From starting his career as a Youth Training Scheme hairdresser at 16, serial entrepreneur and author Carl Reader heads up d&t, a multi-award-winning, mid-tier accountancy firm. Established in the 1990s, the firm now supports thousands of businesses across a wide range of sectors. Under Carl's guidance, the firm won a British Accountancy Award in 2013 and a 2020 Innovations Award in 2014. Today, Carl is often featured in the media and widely recognised as a leading voice in the business world.

Carl, you were very strategic when it came to building your personal brand, tell us about it.

As the CEO of d&t, I was giving a lot of speeches about business and the future of business, and one phrase I would often say was that business is not just B2B or B2C, it's H2H (human to human). But I wasn't really living that within my own businesses at the time, where I felt we'd lost the human touch. It was actually a video by the American entrepreneur Gary Vaynerchuk that inspired me, in which he said that an audience of one is better than an audience of none. So, in January 2016, I started building my personal brand.

I treated the project as business in the way that I structured my approach. I wanted to be clear about my core values and key drivers and have a clear strategy. One of the exercises I did early on was to define my key values, which included credibility, plain speaking and integrity. I wanted to be sure that I would really live up to those values within every interview I gave and within every action that I performed personally.

What about how you would make money from your brand?
I also reviewed all my key drivers for developing a personal brand from a financial perspective. I didn't plan to monetise it per se, although I knew it would bring money through the trickle-down effect of it positively impacting everything I do and my businesses. The key drivers from my perspective were to give the business a visible figurehead and human face. I had some personal motivations as well: one was that when my kids were older, they'd be able to look at press articles and online content featuring me and think: *Our dad is an alright bloke.* Another driver was around my frustrations that there are so many people in the business space overcomplicating business. The reality is that business is really simple, and if I can do it, anyone can – and success to me meant getting that message across.

I also asked myself if I prepared for what it would entail – the whole exercise takes time and can turn your job into an evening and weekend job, too. Journalists, for example, can't wait, so if they wanted an interview at 11pm, would I be prepared to do it? Once I'd mapped all this out, the content just seemed to unfold naturally. Although my main business is my accountancy firm, from a personal-brand perspective my whole message is around business rather than numbers.

Where did you start?
With Twitter. I searched the #journorequest hashtag and con- nected with journalists who were looking for particular stories

around topics such as business, finance or even mindset. Within the first month, I had five pieces of national media coverage. I gave myself the target of doing one interview each day, whether it was with a blog, a newspaper or TV, it didn't matter who the audience was, I just wanted to get my name out there. I put my voice forward and tried to add value or to offer a unique perspective. I just had a few really simple rules and they were to make the journalists' job as easy as possible and to be the first responder. I also contributed to trade journals and wrote a blog.

Did it work?

I'll be very honest – it was really hard to quantify the business benefit of all the effort initially. It is not like devoting an amount of time into walking around streets and dropping leaflets through doors, where – as long as you know your numbers – in theory you know what the results will be. With building a personal brand, it was great insofar as showing off on Facebook, but it was hard to see the business benefit in those early days. Down the line, if I were to look in retrospect, my businesses have grown massively: we had a record year last year, and are up around 30 per cent on the year before; we're up on revenue, up on staff numbers, but, perhaps more importantly, it has brought up a load of opportunities both personally and for new business.

You're across all platforms now, aren't you?

What I noticed is that when you focus on one area, you neglect others. Yet true personal branding is very multifaceted, and you need to be aware of every angle. We're always thinking about how we are going to push forward in radio, how are we going to push forward in the papers, how are we going to push forward

In TV, how we are going to push forward online and *where* we are going to push forward online. There are a lot of people who focus on being Facebook celebrities or Twitter celebrities or Instagram celebrities. They are completely disregarding the outside world beyond that one platform. My opinion, for a strong personal brand, is that you need to have a view that encompasses them all.

Does the mainstream media coverage have a positive impact?
The reality of it is that the quality of work my team provides to my clients is actually completely unrelated to the level of exposure I get. If I have a quote in the *Telegraph*, that has no impact whatsoever on the ability of one of my team members to produce a tax return and calculate the numbers correctly! But yes, it's had a huge positive impact. A lot of the mainstream coverage is online, so it has an SEO impact; it makes it easier for businesses to find us, it makes it easier for us to convert because it gives us credibility and it helps us retain customers because being sought after for opinion brings huge implied credibility.

Are you seen as pioneering in terms of personal branding within your industry?
Well, the stereotypical accountant is grey haired, in their forties or fifties, probably wearing glasses, probably sat behind a desk with a quill and an atlas. When I kicked this off I was in my mid-thirties, with a shaved head, tattooed arms and looking like I belonged on a building site or as a bouncer for a nightclub rather than as an accountant, and I also had quite a strong local accent rather than the Queen's English.

Across accountants, there's a general view that marketing and promotion are bad, and accountants tend to be introverted and couldn't think of anything worse than putting themselves up for publicity, having an opinion and potentially alienating some of the prospective client base. I travelled to California to speak to a theatre of accountants about personal branding and the reality is I think it would be phenomenal if even one of those in the room actually does take action and do anything. But, without doubt, it's worth the effort. It's defined my businesses and undoubtedly been a game changer for me personally and professionally.

———————————

How will you monetise your personal brand?

In the next chapter, we're going to be looking at the most commonly used ways to monetise a personal brand and the business models that power personal brands. You may already have some ideas though, so if you do, write them down in your notebook.

What will be the positives – and the negatives?

The positives are obvious: that's you becoming an online leader in whatever micro-niche you are in, and getting all the benefits that you are dreaming about. Just list some of them in your notebook. That said, it's important to be clear about what the negatives might be, too, so that you have a chance to plan around them and are not taken by surprise when they arise. This is the moment to gather together your worst fears and pour them out on paper.

What is your image?

This is all about your visual/physical/in-the-flesh image – what people see and/or experience of you and what logs deep in their minds as a representation of you. Yes, it is all about being the real you on the Internet and being authentic, but first impressions count. I also want you to start thinking about the practicalities. If you are going to be doing video, where are you going to do it? What will your backdrop be? Do you have a location you can access that is suitable for filming?

I realise that some people are uncomfortable with the concept – arguing that looks and backdrops are not relevant to their profile as a thought leader or an entrepreneur. But people will always form impressions, even if at the subconscious level, based on how we present ourselves. Studies show that we reach conclusions about other people in less than a second, based on things like attractiveness, likeability and capability.

Tash's tips

Backdrops really matter too. We form so many judgements about people based on their backdrops. In particular, I get very tetchy about interiors, and I think this is from the years I spent working on national newspapers. Pictures are hugely important to the way a story is perceived, and I've known many interviewees who have had to be rephotographed because of things like their sofas instantly giving an impression of the person that doesn't fit with the impression given by the article. Look – good people sometimes have terrible sofas, but the last thing anyone wants is to destroy the way a story lands because of their dodgy sofa. If you were working with my team at Bolt Digital, for example, unless your house is very contemporary, we don't want to see anything of your domestic interiors in the background, because we know people will judge you on it.

Can you keep your head above the parapet?

Do you have the courage to form opinions and use them? There are people I've met in life who talk like this: 'Oh it's nice when it's nice; that was nice and isn't it a nice day?' They're very pleasant, but they're not dynamic or memorable, and it doesn't work for personal brands. Opinions help to project your personal brand and keep it dynamic, engaging and even challenging. Opinions are just that: opinions. They're not fact, so people can disagree with them; but when relevant and well expressed, they command respect and attention.

Using your opinion to build your personal brand is a sure way to become a thought leader in your niche. But you've got to be bold enough to have opinions in the first place. Are you?

What are going to be your short-, medium- and long-term measurable KPIs (key performance indicators)?

When we are working with clients on YouTube shows and channels, or social media, we always say to them, 'Right, we are going to do this for at least a *year* before we even *think* about whether it is working or not.' Of course, most people see results far sooner, but the bottom line is that it takes time to build a personal brand. On a recent podcast, the American entrepreneur Gary Vaynerchuk spoke about how he advises people not to even consider whether things are working or not until they have been publishing content regularly for 18 months to two years. His own personal brand may seem to have exploded from nowhere, but the reality is he's been publishing content regularly for 11 years. He is no overnight success and you shouldn't expect to be either.

With that in mind, you need to have clear short-, medium- and long-term KPIs.

Tash's tips

A realistic short-term goal is to commit to content creation and distribution (publishing), and make it into a habit without considering whether it is working or not. A medium-term goal (that is, 18 months from now) might be that by now you will have seen five benefits from your publishing strategy. And your long-term goal will involve a key milestone that shows you are moving towards your long-term purpose. You're going to be investing a lot of time, and even money, into this process, so having these key markers planned out will help you feel confident that you know the direction you're going in.

Write down your KPIs in your notebook:

Short-term KPI:
Medium-term KPI:
Long-term KPI:

'What if I'm not good enough?'

I'm occasionally asked this by clients who are really sold on the concept of personal branding but still feel inadequate or unready, or have imposter syndrome (more on that in Chapter 8). It's a very natural concern to have. And the answer is that we're all growing our expertise all of the time. Remember that personal branding is not a final destination but a continual journey, and in many ways the sooner you start, the better. One of the things you'll always be focusing on is growing your personal brand and gathering your credibility indicators as you go. (I'll be talking about this later in the book.) One thing you can do is to start small and practise. Repetition is the mother of skill. But don't make the mistake of falling into 'analysis paralysis'. You won't know what works and what doesn't until you put it out there. And remember, you are only ever one finger away from being able to press delete. Do you remember what you were reading or watching last month online? Probably not, and neither does anyone else. Mistakes can easily be deleted.

Yes – by all means be inspired by the very successful people who have already branded themselves online and have thousands of video views and podcast listeners. But don't be overawed by them. You can achieve the same – and in the same slow, methodical, consistent and focused way that they did. They all have one thing in common: they all started somewhere.

Tash's tips

Your actual level of expertise and experience in your niche will certainly influence the level at which you pitch your new personal brand, and to some extent the rate at which you grow your audience. But the process is the same for everyone. It starts at the beginning. If you are starting out, aim to become the person best known for what you do in your local area. If you are already successful, then national or international expansion might be part of your ambition.

Think about it as you would your real-world work: whatever it is that you've already been doing and/or intend to do more of as a result of your personal brand impact. That doesn't reach a point and then stop, does it? Nor does it catapult you to a senior level without you having to climb your way up the ladder rung by rung first. To succeed in the Stand Out Online process you will simply be doing what you've always been doing in your professional life. You will continue to strive to be an expert in whatever you do, and to grow your experience and impact in parallel with your personal brand.

Whatever your style of brand, you can find your starting point right now. There is no need to wait, no requirement for you to become 'good enough' – you are already.

MY STORY Sarah Akwisombe: 'All of this is a shortcut to reinvention and opportunity, wherever you are now'
Sarah Akwisombe is an award-winning interiors blogger, stylist

and influencer. Since building her personal brand, her interior work has included designing interiors for commercial buildings, she's collaborated with brands such as eBay and featured in their Christmas television advert, and she's launched her No Bull Business School, which runs online courses on start-up businesses and blogging.

When did online personal branding start for you?

About 15 years ago when I was starting out in music. I performed on Myspace and learned what to do and what not to do on there. I discovered that you show yourself and take people on the journey, then they start to understand you and become engaged. Within a couple of months of publishing on Myspace, I'd found a manager and been offered a publishing deal. I also made mistakes. I was inconsistent, I kept changing the style of music I was publishing and the style of clothes I wore. Every time I did that, I'd lose my initial audience. But overall I learned that the Internet is a shortcut to everything.

By the time I launched my interiors styling blog http://www.sarahakwisombe.com and social media channels, I'd left music and had been working in tech start-ups, and I had had a baby. I'd realised I naturally can't be employed. I'm too rebellious. Everything that anyone puts forward I always think I can improve on. After getting fired from my boring office job, I decided to follow my gut, take the plunge and try to get into interiors, and I did it via blogging and social media. I am a good reinventor, and there wasn't a big plan as to what exactly would happen. I just knew that if I built up my personal brand, it would happen. When we bought our first flat a few years ago, my passion for interiors reached dizzy heights – I'd become obsessed, and that's what I posted about.

Did you feel you were good enough?

Whatever I decide to do, the first voice I hear is, 'That's going to be amazing! That's awesome! Everyone is going to love it!' I'm just that kind of person. There is none of this, 'Oh, it might not work.'

The reality was, however, that I had no qualifications. I am an obsessive learner, though, and felt that I needed to study, so alongside my blog I took an interior design course; however, I found it slow and boring. People were starting to ask me to help them with their interiors, and I thought: *I don't need the qualification then, I'm already getting work.* I just told myself, 'I am an interior design person now. I know what I am doing.'

The reinvention worked – what opportunities started coming to you?

One of the first opportunities was a competition in which I won £200! I thought: *OK – at least someone thinks I'm doing a good job.* I then won a Best Newcomer blog award and brands started wanting to work with me. I also had clients who wanted to work with me on their houses. What's interesting is that you almost have to take *all* the opportunities to work out which route will truly be best for you, what you're going to enjoy and what your personal goals are. I found that what I loved was commercial design. Commercial property owners want interiors that are 'Instagrammable'. They want their spaces to be amazing and memorable but not like something you'd have at home. That fits in more naturally with what I do.

I'm also an influencer, which means that my personal brand and my personality can work with other brands. I don't just do things that are interior design any more, because brands can see how my personality and following can fit with other niches, such as lifestyle and technology.

And I have an online school called the No Bull Blog School, which teaches people how to do what I've done through online courses. Over 2,000 students have been through it so far. The power of social media is such that I just went on Instagram and said, 'This is a course I am doing, and it opens tomorrow', and hundreds of people signed up.

What's the biggest mistake people make?
They give up too soon. A friend of mine was complaining she's only got 4,000 followers on Instagram. She's only been on it for a year or two. It took me four years to get to 5,000 people, and obviously it grows faster from there. People also worry too much about what people will think or what their peers will think. I used to do that with music, and then I realised that the only people I should have cared about were those who were buying the music and turning up to the gigs. And it is the same now: the only people I care about are the ones who enjoy my content or buy my courses or turn up to the events I am doing. Worrying about what other people think is the biggest block to getting where you want to go.

Tash's Takeaways

- Working out things such as your vision, mission and goals as part of your strategy before launching your personal brand will help you to have clarity and direction.
- Other strategic considerations prior to launch include understanding potential revenue streams, and what will be your short-, medium- and long-term KPIs.
- You don't have to have reached your final 'success' destination before embarking on your Stand Out Online project. As with any career, you will develop as you go.

What's in it for You?

Many of us are thinking right now about our own brand – brand 'Me'. What is it? Where will it end up? What are the possibilities? Remember how we said that, typically, the groups of people who can most benefit from the Stand Out Online process are:

1. Start-up entrepreneur/self-employed professional expert
2. Employees who want to become a recognised freelance expert, attract new job opportunities or start or grow a sideline business
3. Influencer/celebrity
4. CEO/founder/business owner

There are, however, different ways and financial/opportunity models through which these people can benefit. If you're asking the question, 'Where will the money come from?', the answers are coming up.

The Bolt Opportunity Vortex

The model on page 67 outlines just some of the many ways in which a personal brand can lead to value and profit, as well as the fact that the different ways of extracting value tend to overlap. It's not usually a case of one or the other. You can think of this as similar to a wheel of fortune, with all kinds of great things available to you for your future.

Ways of boosting income and influence

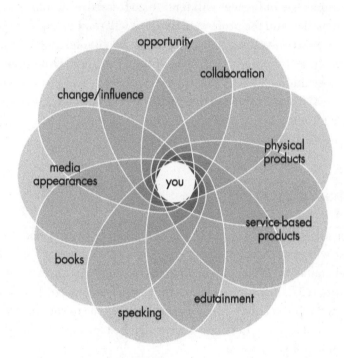

The most common ways successful, visible brands boost income and become even more successful and/or achieve their goals are:

Opportunity	Speaking
Collaboration	Books
Physical products	Media appearances
Service-based products	Change/influence
Edutainment	

Ironically, doing any one of these also serves to strengthen the personal brand and open up other opportunities.

Technically, although each of the groups listed on page 66 may generally sway towards particular opportunities (for example, the influencer will tend to go towards the collaboration model, and the professional expert will tend to go towards the opportunity model), crossover is inevitable. But at the same time, in order to truly benefit from the Stand Out Online process and be able to measure your success and refine your process, it's advisable not to try to do all of this at once. Brands aren't built in a day, and no one launches with all of this 'stuff' going on at the same time.

Where do we start?

The answer is that if you can get one or two of these nailed, the rest will start to open up for you – as long as you are focused and confident. If you pull in all kinds of directions, attracted or distracted by anything and everything, you'll end up nowhere. By contrast, if you stick to what you know to be true to you, you can grow and achieve. Let's take a more detailed look at what might open up for you now.

Greater opportunity

Since writing *The Million Dollar Blog* several years ago, I've given many talks in packed lecture halls. And I always ask two questions: 'Who here wants to be a blog star or influencer?' and 'Who here is more interested in becoming a visible expert?' I always assume that, given the glamour associated with being a blogger and the rush into that industry (a recent survey revealed that 25 per cent of under-25s in the UK regard blogging as their career of choice), that most hands would shoot up at the first question, but no, it's the second that gets the biggest response.

Although this puzzled me at first, coming from the London media world where a desire for fame seems to be the chief goal for so many, I've come to understand that our desire for recognition and opportunity in our professional lives and careers is the main driver when it comes to personal branding online. Many people don't want to have visible personal brands just for the sake of it or to work with brands. They want to be the most visible in their own particular space, with future opportunity – including everything from writing books, to speaking, to being on TV as an expert in their niche, to raising prices, to winning awards – being their chief goal. And that's true whether you are a solopreneur or a CEO.

Many professionals won't even have a particular single opportunity in mind. Their desires will encompass things from charging higher prices to being the person chosen once a new and exciting opportunity opens up.

The benefits will be focused on income and opportunity within your sector, because that is where you are already known. And it doesn't matter if the sector you are in is law or medicine, dog walking or beauty therapy, the goal is the same. The best rise to the top, and the top is where the best opportunities are.

A nation of high achievers: how does it work?

Why does this revenue stream and desired outcome offer so much appeal to professional people? Firstly, many of us have had a fairly traditional education and come from traditional backgrounds (traditional in that they reflect the world before the digital revolution changed everything). With this traditional inheritance comes an instinct to be good at what we do professionally. And although the British way is generally not to push oneself forward into the limelight, we are usually more comfortable, or even keen, to present our professional self publicly. I guess that we're a nation of high achievers who place a lot of value on being good at what we do, and many of us feel best about ourselves and our lives when we are achieving at work. I'm not saying work success is the only determinant of happiness, but it is surely a contributor.

Secondly, the field is relatively empty – there's lots of space in which to build your expert personal brand. Let me illustrate by referring once again to bloggers. Here in the UK we have a lot – and I mean *a lot* – of bloggers and vloggers, especially in the more popular niches of fashion, beauty, parenting and lifestyle. It is a hugely competitive field, but the really successful ones grow into blog and vlog stars, people who have become famous as personal brands *and* are able to make great incomes from it. By contrast, the professional expert sector is underpopulated, at least for now. It's much easier to gain traction when professional opportunity is your goal, and you'll be likely to see results faster.

Collaboration

Blogging or vlogging are tools that you will need to use, no matter what type of personal brand you develop; however, a blogger or a vlogger is the name of a particular genre of personal brand who tend to focus on brand collaborations as their monetisation route. Usually, collaboration is the financial aim of bloggers/vloggers/social media stars, who are focused on being influencers within a niche.

Basically, in its simplest terms, the blogger/vlogger/social media star (I'll just refer to them collectively as bloggers from here on) creates an audience and becomes a conduit for reaching that audience. Once they can define their audience, they can sell access to that audience just as ITV can sell ad space to brands between programmes.

Whereas the professional expert or CEO is generally looking for new business opportunities and an ability to raise prices and establish their positioning as the best, the blogger is generally selling advertising space in the form of sponsored posts and brand collaborations (in other words, working with brands to help promote a new product). The greater the blogger's influence and reach, the higher their rates.

Brands are always looking for subtle but effective ways of getting in front of an audience and promoting their products. Partnering with a blogger or influencer who is then paid to write a piece reviewing or discussing their product works because audiences trust the blogger or influencer more than they trust the brand or traditional advertising (note that this is *not* the same as writing your own impartial reviews as part of your mainstream independent content). Most influencers refuse to just publish what the brand asks them to, and instead look for creative ways to cover the brand's topic in a way that works for their audience, feels natural, and doesn't sound like a hard sell.

Influencers are selling more than just the opportunity to reach their audience; they are also selling their own endorsement and personal take on the matter, which is more than any mainstream outlet is ever able to do. Instead, the mainstream media can only ever publish content made by the brands themselves. Bloggers also earn money from affiliate links by taking a commission when someone buys a product they have recommended.

How to collaborate with the world's largest brands when you're new

The Tribe app (www.tribe.co) is a new tool to allow all micro influencers to collaborate with the world's biggest brands.

The world of securing brand collaborations can be messy. Once you reach about 10,000 followers and have a clearly crafted message, you might find brands start approaching you. Another option is to take on a manager whose job it is to secure collaborations with brands for a share of the revenue. Or you can network at industry events in order to meet the digital managers at the brands responsible for the influencer budgets.

Tribe removes the middlemen and allows smaller influencers (those with audiences of 3,000–100,000) to communicate and pitch directly to brands.

How Tribe works

Every day, dozens of brands use Tribe to publish briefs for the influencer content they are looking for, both to have influencers publish on their own platforms and for the brands to use on their own platforms and in advertising campaigns. Influencers can view briefs every day and decide which ones they want to submit content for. The brands only pay for the influencer content if they decide to go ahead and purchase it for use.

Bec Gawthorne, an early adopter of Tribe, says: 'I've made over $100K on Tribe since its launch in November 2015. Every day there are dozens of new campaigns, so if you're

OK with not getting approved for every submission, then you control how much you want to earn. You're only limited by your creativity.'

Brands that use Tribe to work with influencers include Bacardi, L'Oreal, Kleenex, Westfield, Adobe, Red Bull and Ikea, plus many more.

Who can be an influencer?

The blog star/vlog star/influencer is first and foremost an ordinary person, and their personal brand is typically based on passion rather than qualifications. Blogging is open to everyone – from children through to adults through to animals. As a blog star you are not a professional, or even an acknowledged expert, although it's quite likely that you do have expert knowledge and a passionate love of something – fashion, beauty, cars, film, parenting – even if you lack recognised qualifications.

Nearly all bloggers are actually entertainers, even if their content is serious, just as a heavyweight documentary about, say, drug abuse or murder on television is actually a form of entertainment. Bloggers are effectively publishing their own digital magazine – which features themselves. They write about their topic or niche, but in a way that makes their own personality an important part of the end-user's enjoyment.

The opportunities from being a blogger are multifold but often not as directly or quickly beneficial financially or career-wise as the professional expert. But it's not all about money, especially in blogging. All bloggers blog for passion, many blog for change, and others blog for lifestyle reasons. In one of the most famous and talked-about niches – that of the mum blogger – most make very little money at all. But they love their craft because it brings all sorts of other benefits, such as being invited to events, getting to test out new toys and being invited on different experiences, all of which help them as parents and make for happy kids.

MY STORY Naomi Isted: 'The best thing is I have the freedom to be creatively free'

Fashion influencer Naomi Isted is ranked in the top 5 per cent of fashion influencers globally, the top 100 London Fashion Week influencers and is a respected voice on fashion for many national and global print and broadcast titles. Social media has become a family affair with Naomi, her two children Fleur, eight and Rocco, two, all having their own social channels and regularly attending premiers and red-carpet events.

Naomi, fashion influencing is one of the most competitive niches there is, where did you start?

I studied broadcast journalism and did some TV in Scotland, where I was brought up. After moving to London in 2008, I created a beauty show called *Harley Street Beauty*, which aired on Wedding TV. I am a creator and always have been – whether that's written or video content. So at the same time, I launched my blog ultimatelifestylist.com. I didn't really know what I was doing at all, but I started writing my thoughts on filming that day. It helped that the programme was on air – even now, that show airs to 27 million people in North Africa and the Middle East – because that catapulted my reach.

I then joined Twitter and really went to town learning how to use it. Next, I joined Instagram and learned how to use that. Some people will be a blogger or an Instagrammer or a YouTuber. I am over all platforms, and I still do TV stuff. The three things I do in all my content are educate, inform and entertain.

Everyone is fascinated by brand collaborations – how do they work?

Brands started approaching me early on and, for me personally, I won't be told what to do and I won't just be an advert for a brand, as I'm looking for longevity and authenticity. When I work with a brand, I want to know their plans for the entire year, and I want to brainstorm with them. I don't think I'm working *for* them; it's a collaboration, and we're going to work together and create amazing content together. A one-off post is not of interest to me at all, although I did do those early on.

What have been some of the best collaborations you've worked on?

My career high was for my latest birthday when I was featured in *Vogue* magazine for the brand Jayne Pierson, a talented designer whom I've supported for years. She asked me to model for the *Vogue* shoot, as she felt I was a great representation of her brand. I'm thinking: *I'm 39 years old, a mum and not a model!* Through the growth of my career, things like presenting red-carpet fashion at the Oscars and BAFTAs has also been a high, which might not have happened without my blog.

Tell us about your directory at ultimatelifestylist.com

I get asked so many questions all the time from my community all over the world about where to shop, where to eat, where to stay, what are the best salons, which massage I'd recommend. My directory is turning answering these questions into another revenue stream, in which brands I genuinely love pay to be listed. It's all about quality not quantity for me. I am not interested in being Yellow Pages with thousands of companies featured, I'm interested in listing the one hair salon that I would personally go to in New York.

You had a career in conventional media – have you reached more people online?
Absolutely. I love being freelance and having the scope to work across broadcast, print and online, but also the brand collaborations are really fun and exciting. I love being able to work with different brands that are really fitting for my family and myself. I love the freedom I have now.

I use gratitude every day that I am in this position and that I get to be creatively free. I have the choice and opportunities to be creative. I could not sit behind a desk every day and do the same thing. I get to live my dream every day and I feel very blessed, I don't ever take it for granted.

Find out more about Naomi at https://www.ultimatelifestylist. com and on social media @naomikisted.

Physical products

From influencers such as the beauty vloggers who have developed beauty brands (think Zoella, Samantha and Nicki Chapman of Pixiwoo, Huda Kattan of Huda Beauty) through to foodie influencers who've developed food ranges, the world of products and merchandise is appealing to many.

Even cats can do it: Tardar Sauce, commonly known as

Grumpy Cat, is an American Internet celebrity known for her permanently grumpy facial appearance caused by an underbite and feline dwarfism. Grumpy Cat merchandise includes T-shirts, mugs, soft toys, drinks, key rings, calendars and computer games, giving the business a value of $1 million.

Although not every Stand Out Online project will lead to an extensive range of merchandise, a visible face can be used to support any form of products-based business.

MY STORY Steph Douglas: 'My company wouldn't have succeeded without the platform I'd built with my personal brand' Steph Douglas is the founder of the gift company Don't Buy Her Flowers, an online store that sells gift packages for women. The idea for Don't Buy Her Flowers came after Steph had her first baby and was inundated with bouquets of flowers and realised that there must be more useful and practical gifts for new mothers.

Steph, when did you start building your personal brand, and how did it develop into your products-based business, Don't Buy Her Flowers?
In 2012, I started writing a blog about motherhood. I wanted to start my own business, but I knew that was a massive step, so I set myself the challenge of a blog first: could I set up a website, could I engage people, could I get a following? I began writing honestly about motherhood and relationships. The blog was called Sisterhood and All That, which now sits on Don't Buy Her Flowers. I was posting weekly and built up to 20,000 views monthly without putting any money behind it, as people were sharing my posts.

At the same time, I had the idea for Don't Buy Her Flowers when I had my first baby and was sent lots of flowers – it seemed like a bonkers gift to me. It's the go-to gift, but it's not helpful for a new mum in a state of exhaustion to have to deal with lots of flowers; two bunches is possibly OK, but then you run out of vases and the flowers start dying.

When friends had babies, I'd then send them a magazine or chocolate – something for the mum. After maternity leave, I went back to work but I couldn't shake the idea that there was a business in *not* sending someone flowers. I set up the business two years later, in 2014, and initially it was a website for gifts for new mums, although now we have expanded into gifts for all sorts of occasions, such as get well and bereavement.

What impact did the profile you'd raised as a parenting blogger have on it?

Everything! I wouldn't have had an audience without it. It was on a Sunday night in November 2014 when I pressed go and the website crashed because my audience was sharing it. My personal brand gave me a massive launch pad that I could not have afforded – I didn't have any money beyond the basics of what I'd put into stock. And it was also a very genuine audience who knew me and liked and shared my business. I ran the business from my house for two years, but we've grown fast and now my brother runs it with me from Gloucestershire, which is where I'm originally from.

How has your personal brand developed?

I think people are interested in women – especially parents – starting businesses and they want to follow the journey and hear about the lessons learned and to get inspiration. People are interested in the juggling act of having a business and having kids. Part of me thinks, *Oh, are we still talking about that?* but actually it is still a really big deal, because women still have babies and we are not equal in the office or at home, so it is a massive challenge to add a business into the mix. I still share my story and experiences as we go. I have an agent who works with me on brand collaborations, but I'm different from most influencers in that my main focus is the business. Instead of doing anything that is off-piste, any brand collaborations I do have to work for Don't Buy Her Flowers overall. But, as a person, I'm always of interest; for example, I've just had my third baby, and I've done collaborations and media around that, and as the business is growing, I'm being asked to do more business profile pieces in the press as well, which is great. We always see, too, that the most popular posts on social media are the ones with a more personal angle – people are still interested in where the business came from, and me and the family.

How does your personal brand support the business now?

We can really see it in the messages we get. Our customers report back to us and to me personally about how their gift went down with the person they gave it to. They want to tell me how much that person loved and appreciated it. At the same time, they are really loyal, and we have a very high percentage of repeat customers. To some extent this is due to the fact that they know the business has come from a genuine place, they know our story and they feel as if they know me. We also get a lot of word-of-mouth referrals, and that's because our customers know of the passion behind the business.

I think big businesses want people to fall in love with their brand, and they want to create a personality for their brand, but it is harder to do if you are someone like John Lewis. Big companies spend hundreds of thousands of pounds trying to create a personality for their brand, because people like buying from people. Small businesses can use this as an advantage and power growth with it.

You've had quite a bit of mainstream media coverage – for the business and for yourself too – has that helped with your success?
Yes, we've been in the *Mirror*, the *Guardian* and on the BBC and it's all part of the puzzle. You want to be in these places because of credibility, and we've gained some great coverage without spending masses on PR. But online and being featured by influencers has really helped us, because nothing beats one click from an article and then people are on our website.

What would you say to someone else thinking about building a products-based business now?
Social media is very powerful and most probably you're thinking that you wish you could pay someone else to do it for you. But the best place to start is doing it yourself so that your customers can see your passion. That way, you are constantly engaging with your customers or potential customers. Just get stuck in, don't just say, 'Oh, I'm no good at that' – just learn how to do it.

Service-based businesses

In Chapter 3, we met Carl Reader, whose personal brand helps drive sales of the services his accountancy firm provides. And he is far from alone. In the UK, 79 per cent of gross domestic product (GDP) comes from the service sector, which has increased by 46 per cent since 1948. From solopreneurs and freelancers through to big businesses, many of us work in service-based business. Ninety-one per cent of London's economy is in the service sector (businesses providing services to other businesses or people, such as retail, housekeeping, nurses, transport, and even digital agencies, like mine), higher than all other areas of the UK.

Yet, providing services is competitive. There is always someone else who could be chosen, and usually there is someone else who is cheaper. Being seen as the best and being the 'most seen' in a niche is a route to being in demand and making that competition irrelevant.

MY STORY **Dr Leah Totton**: 'As a business owner you have a responsibility to yourself and your customers to promote yourself' After winning *The Apprentice* in 2013, Dr Leah Totton co-founded the Dr Leah chain of aesthetic clinics with her business partner, Lord Alan Sugar. She has continued to build her personal brand online and in the media, and now has three clinics. Her flagship London clinic has won Best Cosmetic Clinic at the prestigious MyFaceMyBody Awards for two consecutive years.

Leah, *The Apprentice* must have given you an amazing platform, tell us about it.

There were three main things to come out of winning *The Apprentice*. The first is the investment of £250,000, which is about what it costs to open one clinic; the second is the mentoring directly from Lord Alan Sugar; and the final thing is the profile. Looking back on it, the mentoring and the profile are the most valuable. What the profile allowed me to do is shine a light on the failings of the cosmetic industry (in particular the lack of regulation) and provide a medical alternative, setting a new gold standard for aesthetics.

As the owner of an aesthetic clinic, how important are your reputation and profile?

Hugely. You are only as good as your worst case, and safety is the main driver in choosing an aesthetic clinic. Customers go to the person whom they trust the most, and to be that person you have to be the best at what you do and have the least amount of complications. My time is dedicated to being truly expert and to ensuring my doctors are, too. There's a massive onus on all medical professionals to be the best, and I've dedicated the majority of my time to the medical aspect of the work, doing further NHS work and aesthetics training, getting a degree in dermatology, and I've become an international trainer for Silhouette Soft due to the volume of cases I've done.

How does it benefit a service business like yours to have a persona as a visible figurehead?

Our USP in this market is that we are a chain but still have a figurehead, unlike other chains. People want to know someone is accountable, and being a professional yet relatable expert has made me a trusted figurehead, which instils confidence in the brand. With a faceless brand you are always wondering who is ultimately responsible if things go wrong. Our customers know that there won't be a scenario where we just refuse to answer or there's no one to go back to if you have any issue with treatment.

The disadvantage, though, is the scalability of the brand, and we've scaled slower than we might otherwise have done. I'm quite obsessive with the level of expertise and skill that my doctors need, and the training and personal mentoring that I give them, and I've struggled to delegate. We now have a great team of doctors in place, trained and mentored by me, and we look forward to scaling more rapidly in the coming years.

Is it beneficial for doctors running private medical clinics to raise their profiles?

Aesthetics in particular is a very saturated market. Yes, demand has increased as the stigma around injectables has decreased, but the marketplace is more competitive than ever with more doctors wishing to leave the NHS and work in aesthetics. I think most doctors who are doing well are promoting themselves and building their profiles. I believe that, as a business owner, you have a responsibility to yourself and to the general public to help them make an informed choice about who is best to provide their treatment, and whether you are the best and most experienced. If no one knows how many cases you've done or about your experience, it's difficult for customers to make an informed choice to come to you.

What is your favourite social platform and why?

Instagram, because it's so visual and allows us to demonstrate the treatments and to showcase the results we get. It's a huge driver for clients – people get in touch with us via Instagram messenger. We now take more bookings through social media, as opposed to paid search or SEO.

Digital products – the edutainer

Welcome to the world of online training courses and membership websites – a world where education and entertainment sometimes overlap. The online educator, or edutainer, is a space in which professional expert meets blog star meets university professor. Your role is to entertain, motivate, inspire and educate.

Call them the teachers of 2018 and beyond, if you like. These are the people who develop their visible personal brands as someone who can teach you online, usually through a mixture of coaching, group coaching and online courses. A decade ago it would have been impossible to launch an online course, as the cost of development and hosting would have been too high. The digital world makes video, webinars and live lectures easy to set up and deliver.

Whereas the professional expert normally seeks to build something in the real world, such as a service-type business, the blog star or influencer is seeking to collaborate with brands, and the online edutainer is a visible expert who monetises their knowledge through online teaching and coaching. Of course, that's not to say that the professional expert doesn't do this as well, or that the online edutainer doesn't get real-world benefits (there's always overlap), but most people launch with the focus on one model and then the benefits from the other come in the future.

Are you qualified?

Online education is a trend that first caught my attention back in 2008, but my first thought was: *Surely only properly trained and qualified people can teach.* Wrong.

Today, online teaching is a large part of what we support at Bolt Digital. Many of our clients have existing online programmes that we help to develop, or whose profile makes them ideal for creating and offering an online programme. Others have developed online programmes but have no idea how to sell them. It's extremely

Tash's tips

Not having a school or university teaching qualification does not invalidate anyone's ability to teach. This is the dawn of a new era in which everyone can reach anyone. In fact, I have myself learned valuable new skills by taking courses with online educators who understand the world in a way that those within the current education system definitely do not!

common for people to get caught up in the hype of the idea of selling a shedload of digital courses – aka passive income – and putting a ton of time and money into developing one, only then to realise that the development of a digital product brings them right back to the beginning, and now they need to understand how to sell it.

There's a huge movement centred on online educators earning money from telling people how to become an online educator (yes, it is a little 'pop will eat itself' out there) but the reality is that online courses take time to create and then a complicated strategy to market and sell. If you're reading this and thinking that this is easy money or passive income, I would urge caution. For every success at the top of the pile earning millions from their digital programmes, there are hundreds who have never completed the course or created something incredible but not sold any.

Let's dive into how this model works.

Could you be an online teacher?

First of all, the online world is not regulated, so you do not need to acquire online educator qualifications; there is no such thing. If there is something you are good at, then you absolutely can teach others how to do it.

Please don't become one of those online teachers who teach people how to make money online, even though their only experience of making money online comes from the teaching itself. It's a bold strategy that gives the sector a bad name. I firmly believe that to be an honest online educator with integrity, you should already, and independently, have your own direct experience of what you plan to teach and not be guiding students without direct experience.

You do need to be able to demonstrate to the marketplace that you already have both knowledge and the skills to share it. And if you teach something, please let it be something that people can use in their own lives, not just by teaching other people the same thing! Your goal should be to take on a student who does not have your experience and help them progress to the next stage and the next.

MY STORY **Grant Baldwin**: 'Expertise is in the eye of the beholder' Grant Baldwin is a public speaker, entrepreneur, author and podcaster. He is a leading online educator teaching speakers to start, build and grow their business through his online programmes. His podcast, The Speaker Lab, teaches listeners how to get into the speaking business, sharing a mix of personal stories, interviews and Q&A with other professional speakers.

Grant, how did it all start for you?
My career actually started as a youth pastor. I was working in a local church and working with high-school students when I was in my early twenties. I was doing a lot of speaking and I felt like I was good at it, which made me want to do more of it. I met a couple of guys who were speakers and I basically ended up leaving the job that I was in and spent the next couple of years working on trying to build a speaking business. I have been a full-time speaker for about the past eight or nine years or so.

I think speaking is no different from a lot of other industries in the sense that it takes time. It took me several years to get to the point where I was doing it consistently on a full-time level and get to a point where I was making six figures.

Tell me how the world of online education works. Did you think to yourself, *OK, how do I scale what I know?* **and go from there?**
Speaking doesn't scale very well. The only way to make more is either to do more events or charge more, and at the time I was on the upper end of what I felt comfortable charging, but I didn't want to do any more gigs. I was already gone around 70–80 nights a year.

At the time, I started to see more things like web courses, training and podcasts emerge into the online landscape. I had done a lot of speaking about careers, so I started a podcast in 2013 called How Did You Get Into That?, where we interviewed unique people who had bizarre, interesting careers.

So many people were asking questions about speaking – things like, 'How do you do it full time?', and how to book gigs. I didn't really know anybody else who was teaching the business side of speaking, actually explaining things, such as, 'This is how you actually get a gig.' I created a course around that and it really took off.

You weren't necessarily known online at that point. What tools did you use? What did you do to grow these courses?

Webinars. That's basically what we started doing, and it's what we still do. We do a live one every three to four weeks right now, and then we have Evergreen ones that run every single day. On the webinars, we present our online training and sell people into it.

People in this space get really excited about the idea of 'passive income' but many don't realise how it works. Would you agree with that?

I would totally, totally agree with that. I think passive income is a huge misnomer and a misconception. So many people think: *Yeah, you just make a course, put it online, run some ads to it, do a webinar, and it's all set.* But it just doesn't work like that.

It's very much a momentum thing. We do a weekly pod-cast and I have a private Facebook group. I was in there for about an hour this morning answering questions. We do a once-a-month office-hours call, where I'm just on live answer-ing questions. There are so many moving pieces. Even now, we've been doing it for a couple of years and I still work 30–40 hours a week.

What about this notion of being an educator when you aren't officially qualified?

Expertise is in the eye of the beholder; for example, if I go to the local mechanic to get the oil in my car changed, I see the mechanic as the expert simply because they know more about cars than I do.

The mechanic might not consider themself an expert, because they might only know a few little things, and other people in the shop might know more about cars than they do. But I'm not looking at those people, I'm looking at that one mechanic fixing my car, and, to me, they are the expert, because they know more than I do.

That said, I don't like that people in the online space can pretend they're experts when they aren't. People can take one course and say they're an expert, even though they might never have actually worked or done what they're now telling other people to do. Any one of us could spend a couple of weeks reading about blog posts and doing a bunch of learning and all of a sudden claim we are an expert at Facebook ads. There are plenty of people who do that.

I think one of the things that has helped me is that I have a lot of experience. I was a full-time speaker for eight years, working at hundreds and hundreds of events. I think that practical real-world experience is a big thing that's really helped us and really differentiated us from others.

How does it work?

If you feel you have something valid to share as an online educator, you can create your personal brand as your passport to a large fee-paying classroom. But when it comes to making money, you will generally need to have in place a product staircase – a suite of products at different price points – which slots into a sales funnel too. Most online educators give a tremendous amount of education for free to attract students and then charge handsome fees for the more advanced/in-depth learning once their students are engaged and making progress.

As with any personal brand, you first need to create and project your identity and professional personality into the wider online world (or those parts of it where your potential students hang out). And you need to maintain this with plenty of related content – blogs, social media, videos, podcasts – to reinforce your credibility in your niche. This is the activity that leads many to talk of this sector as 'edutainment', but it is the essential first step, building your audience before converting them into fee-paying learners.

And you need to be a good edutainer. This sector is a very crowded space, and standing out takes persistence and determination.

Online membership clubs

Traditional online learning programmes involve selling a digital product once and continuing to have to sell that same product to new customers. But with a membership or subscription business the product is repeatedly sold with a lower monthly payment, which results in regular monthly income for a seemingly unlimited period of time.

It often feels easy to think of filling a membership club with 1,000 members paying £15 a month each *but* the reality is that there are pros and cons to membership clubs versus selling one-off courses.

To be successful, you need to remember that your ultimate goal is to make your customers happy and successful. If your customers aren't happy and successful, you lose members. Making sure that members stick around is about providing them with a good reason to stay, so you'll have to sell to them every single month. This means providing them with fresh content and support on a long-term basis. You'll have to build real relationships with the members, so make sure you're actually engaging and interacting with them consistently.

The pros and cons of membership clubs v selling one-off courses

Pros	Cons
Recurring revenue with high profit margins	Giving customers their money's worth on a regular basis
Continual traffic to your site	Retaining membership over long periods of time
Customer loyalty and ability to create a great email list instantly	Maintaining a good reputation with members and their referrals
Referrals that create additional members/revenue	Membership retention can be difficult

Have you got the X factor?

In the television series of the same name, the X factor refers to the undefinable something that makes for star quality. Having the X factor is going to be a key driver of your success in this space. Take one of the world leaders in the edutainer niche, Marie Forleo, who undoubtedly has the X factor. This is not just about having Marie's looks but also her ability to speak, to appear sincere and kind, to lead, to inspire, to basically make those who engage with her top-of-funnel content (more on this shortly) fall in love with every aspect of her and be willing to pay whatever it takes to get more of Marie – to enter the next step of the funnel.

Tash's tips

As an agency, we have worked with edutainers who want to sell huge quantities of digital products, but their audiences aren't engaged enough. And, boy, is it hard work!

None of this means you have to be a show-off or an extrovert, you just need people to like and connect with you. You may nail this immediately (although in fact you probably won't) but you need to always be considering whether *you* are part of the problem in terms of how well your digital products are shifting. Should you be smiling more, laughing more, engaging more? How can you develop that star quality in your presentations and content? It will always be as much about you as it is about what you teach – hence 'personal' and 'edutainment'. And projecting 'you' into the online digital arena is an ongoing job.

I've covered some of the opportunities that are available to you online and will be useful to you when planning your brand strategy. Later on in the book we will cover the opportunities for speaking, books and media appearances, which will be useful for later on in your brand development, once it's time to scale up.

Tash's Takeaways

- There are nine key ways online personal brands reach their financial or strategic goals: opportunity, collaboration, physical products, service-based products, edutainment, speaking, books, media appearances and change/influence making.
- There's nothing to stop you aiming for one or all of these, but it's generally more manageable to focus on one or two first and allow the others to come as your brand develops. Start by thinking about which routes to making money you should focus on first.
- Whichever you choose, it's important that you are likeable. Although you don't have to be a model, a presenter or an actor, you do have to have some degree of X factor.

PART TWO

Launch

You've reached the point in the book – and in your own journey – where it's no longer a question of *if* but *when and how* you're going to build your online personal brand so that you stand out online. But for now, the million-dollar question is:

How do you get started?

What exactly do you need in order to build a personal brand, and how do you get it all set up?

All Journeys Start with the First Step – But Make it a Strong One!

You're playing the long game here, with your sights set far down the line on increased visibility and new opportunities. But the stronger you start, the stronger you will grow. There are lots of choices, including:

- Personal brand website
- Social profiles on every platform that exists right now
- Weekly video shows on YouTube and Facebook
- Podcasts
- Guest articles on other websites
- National media coverage
- Local media coverage
- Online media coverage
- SEO to get top rankings on Google

Quality not quantity

It can be overwhelming. You'll certainly be bringing many of the above into play as your brand develops, but to launch, I want you to focus on quality, not quantity, and what we call the Bolt Triad of Assets:

1. A simple but modern website (with professional branding).
2. Two social media channels that you are absolutely committed to.
3. Commitment to manageable content output in a manageable media format.

Think of your website as your shop window, or the spine of your business. Social networks in general are the busy streets where you might want to site your shop. Your own social media channels are the doors from those busy streets into your website; some people will walk straight in, whereas others will loiter outside. Some may never come in but will still reserve their spot right beside your door so that they can get to know you a little better.

What about the content output? This is the dynamic component of your website that attracts powerful search traffic and gives you something to share on social platforms.

Together, this triad of assets will provide a launchpad that will enable you to reach out into the online world, attract those incoming searchers and begin nurturing a reputation and a following; however, this is not the only combination, and there is no right or wrong way of lining up your assets. You might decide to build a website first and then to launch your social channels. Or you might decide to build your social followings and then launch your website. Some people never launch websites; they do everything off social platforms.

If you already have these in place and you are looking to scale, you are probably at a point where you need professional input and support.

Tash's tips

What you need to focus on right now is the minimum you need to get you started with your personal brand, because everything else can come into place afterwards.

Let's take a closer look at the triad of assets.

Your website

When you launch your brand and start promoting yourself, people will begin to hear about you and your services. Perhaps they'll meet you or be impressed by what you're doing. They will be curious and want to know more; and the very first thing they will do is look you up online and do a bit of cyber-stalking.

Let's look at research from the Hinge Research Institute, which specialises in understanding how so-called 'visible experts' are created; in other words, those with the most powerful, potent and well-known personal brands. They found that when purchasers are looking for experts for a job, the first thing that 30.6 per cent of them do is turn to online, compared to just 19.1 per cent who ask for a recommendation and 18.8 per cent who look in publications. You can see how important it is to be discoverable online.

In terms of where exactly people look online to find an expert, again the majority of the looking is done via search engines, with 34 per cent turning to Google compared to 19 per cent visiting LinkedIn, 16 per cent attending webinars and just 2 per cent searching Facebook. These stats demonstrate that the majority of people looking for an expert rely on the Internet and primarily search engines. This will lead them to your website or, if you don't have a website, to those of your competitors.

Finally, once a searcher has pinned down that *you* might be someone for whatever job they have in mind, where do they check you out? It's a slam dunk for your website, with 80.8 per cent of people checking out a potential professional service provider's website, 59.9 per cent checking their social channels and just 0.7 per cent not checking someone out at all.

Need I say more! However, you don't just want your website to be found; you want it to amaze or impress and have a deep impact. Even if you've met your potential followers in the flesh and dazzled them, they're going to land on your website at some point and it, too, needs to have the wow factor.

Choosing the right type of website

You need your website to be the ultimate endorsement of who and what you are, the reference point that many potential followers will go to for confirmation of their interest in you and to find out your whole story. It's also where people go to check your full credentials in detail before offering you all those fantastic new opportunities.

The first step in your promotion is getting that website right (although, that said, websites are never finished and always works in progress). At Bolt, my team and I are often asked what sort of website is needed for a strong personal brand or for raising your profile. A quick survey of a cross-section of established personal brands' websites will reveal what appears to be a complete lack of uniformity in how they look at first glance. But the good news is that even when visually very different, structurally, personal-brand websites tend to fall into one of three main categories:

1. **A static showcase site** This is the simplest form of website, little more than a CV and autobiography, with interesting details of your more recent achievements and exploits, and perhaps some flattering comments from credible others. This is the lowest-maintenance type of website, needing small updates just once or twice a year. But it must look absolutely professional and convey total confidence.

2. **A showcase website with a blog/vlog** This is the same as category one, but with the all-important addition of a dynamic and regularly updated section: your blog. It's all of your latest articles, opinions, research and thoughts. It also helps your website to be found by Google, so having a blog on your website opens up that SEO door.

   The content you publish on your site (whatever format it is in) soon grows into a wealth of information demonstrating your personality, knowledge and expertise, with blogs grouped under their respective topics. Each new blog post can be titled and set up with behind-the-scenes tags that the search engines will find.

   Although no one (outside Google) completely understands how the Google algorithm works, what we do know is that it regards relevance and authority as key determinants of ranking. Writing regularly about your area of expertise makes your website more relevant and authoritative.

   This is why you need to avoid the mistake many people make of starting a blog and then letting it drop to the bottom of your to-do list. And the bottom line is that regularly added new content draws more traffic to your site.

3. **A showcase website with a blog *plus* additional functionality, such as e-commerce/email-list building/ online learning platform** Anything you want to add to a website usually falls under the remit of functionality: that is, I want a pop-up to collect visitors' email addresses – that's functionality; I want an e-
commerce shop – that's functionality; I want to sell digital products – that's functionality, too. What you are looking at here is a pretty standard website with additional functionality that fits with your long-term goals.

Certainly, I would advise, no matter what, that you collect email addresses. You can regard anyone who visits your website as a potential follower and a fan and promoter of your brand. Collecting their email details along with other relevant data (their areas of interest in what you do, what you sell and so on) creates an instant direct relationship between you. You can then develop and strengthen this relationship, and there are plenty of ways to do this, such as offering extra content only available to those on your list or simply keeping in touch personally via your email. You can also retarget them on platforms such as Facebook (more on that later). It's all about building brand loyalty and holding on to it.

The golden rules of website design

Good web design remains as much of a creative challenge as ever – and if you don't have a clear idea of what you want or need, then even the best designers will create something that isn't really fit for the job. What follows is my personal recipe for an effective Stand Out Online website that will make the right impact and will do the right things:

Professional branding This is your logo, colour scheme and the textural feel that the on-screen experience provides. It makes people think: *Wow, this person means business!* Today's sites have amazing visual and user/interface features that can transform how you experience them. And, of course, all design aspects need to be repeated consistently across your business card, letterhead and so on.

Professional photography This makes a huge difference, and you'll also need photos for your social profiles, plus for all the media attention you'll start to get as you grow your personal brand. No matter what type of website you choose, a professional, styled, art-directed photoshoot is essential, and, where appropriate, with hair and make-up done professionally. You must look as if you've stepped out of a magazine, not just done a quick selfie in the kitchen. And remember, no domestic backdrops please!

Real-world credibility indicators Your site must actively promote and share all the things that will help you to stand out and position you as the 'better than the others' prospect. It will promote any books you've written, the public speaking you've done and the logos of any media outlets you've appeared in.

Clear statements of purpose and vision You need to promote a clear understanding of the key messages and desired outcomes of you and your work: who you are, what you do, what you bring to the world, and why it's important and adds value to your audience.

Accessible products and services This refers to any way that your website promotes and/or sells your products and services. Your site must make it easy to understand what you offer, what options or service levels are available and, most of all, how convenient and positive it will be to work with you.

Clear calls to action Yes, yes, yes! It's nice to have people on the site, and all of that, but you need to start funnelling them into your offers with clear calls to action, which have clear purposes, such as 'Download a guide' (to get someone on to your email list), or 'Shop products' (to get them to your shop) or 'Book a discovery call' (to get them to make contact with you).

Bear in mind that people have very short attention spans, and even though they may be visiting your site to get real evidence of who you are, they will still speed-read and skim through your content. That's why you need the wow factor to make a great first impression, and it's also why you need to write and present your content in small and instantly comprehensible bites.

Social media channels – entering the public domain

Your website is sorted. The bad news is, it's not going to get any traffic. Well, not simply because you publish it, at least. We've launched so many websites at Bolt Digital, and one thing I see time and time again is people believing the launch of their website is the arrival at their destination (press the evil-cackle-sound button here). Joking aside, the launch of a website is just the beginning of a much, much, much bigger project.

You've now got to get traffic to your website. I often see clients stuck in trying to perfect their website, changing 'and' to 'but' and moving buttons two pixels to the left, when really, in my view, websites are never finished and, in fact at some point, you have to switch your attention to what is going to be your next *major* issue:

starting to generate traffic. One of the key routes in which to do this is through social media, content and building your followings on social platforms.

MY STORY **Niki Webster**: 'I had a tiny following for a long time'
Niki Webster is a raw chef, food blogger and the founder of Rebel Recipes, who has over 260K followers and growing daily. Her mission is to show how simple and beneficial it is to eat vegan recipes without any of the clichés. Her income comes from a mix of brand collaborations and services, including food consultancy, food photography, food styling and recipe development.

Niki, when, where and why did you decide to build your personal brand?
I've been obsessed with food for as long as I can remember, I had been a vegetarian for many years and was always spending my time creating recipes and finding new places to eat. I had it in my mind for a long time that I should start a blog to showcase my recipes, and three years ago I finally got myself into gear and launched my blog. My goal was to one day work for myself and challenge misconceptions over vegan food. At that point, I almost wouldn't have dared to dream it would be a business, but at the back of my mind I always wanted it to be.

What were the early days like?
Well, my lovely husband, a graphic designer, helped me with my website and, of course, I wasn't top of his priorities, because he has other clients, so that took much longer than I had wanted. And then, of course, I had no clue what I was doing – not in the slightest. I had recipes, but I had no photography, no writing skills

and no idea whether people would find my recipes interesting in the slightest. The only thing I had in my favour was that I had worked in food marketing, so I knew the channels I wanted to use to create a presence and promote my blog – primarily Instagram and Facebook, although it latterly became more about Instagram than Facebook. For the first year and a half I was still working in my job, getting up at 6am to create content for Instagram, and literally every single second of the day I wasn't working I was creating content and engaging, and all the things you need to do to make these platforms work.

Everything was just trial and error. I posted every day, which I still continue to do three years later, and I tried to create nice images. The more time I spent on Instagram, the more I understood it and that it is genuinely about being sociable, having conversations and liking and commenting on other people's photos.

How did you build your following to the size that it is?
For the first year or so, I had a tiny following, and I definitely wasn't getting any opportunities at all. The hardest period is when you have just a few hundred or thousand followers, but retrospectively I also think that's a good period. It gives you the time to try things and make mistakes, put other content out there, experiment with good and bad content, and find what works – learn from it.

Content creation is the most important thing. Whatever you do in whatever area, really try to create the best quality content you can. Ask yourself, 'Why is that piece of content a good piece of content? Is it shareable? Is it likeable?' If you were looking at it, would you engage with it? The second thing is just to be super-sociable, engage with people whose content you love, and say how much you love it; I am sure they will (they just might) return the favour. The third is to be consistent and authentic.

What I think really boosted my Instagram page was that I got a lovely shout-out from Nigella Lawson and got around 3,000 followers that day, and after that I saw faster growth. When I got to 10,000 followers I started to be approached by brands for tiny little collaborations, or I was sent free products and things like that, and then the momentum builds.

Right now, you straddle between being an influencer with being a consultant/service provider, how does that work?
The consultancy side feels very natural to me. I knew there was demand for the services that I offer, and I understand what food brands need, so I can talk to them very strategically. At the same time, I work with brands on collaborations, and there's the opportunity for Rebel Recipes to become a range, or a book, or a delivery service.

My weeks are very varied. I can be at a shoot one day, doing styling the next, then days at home doing recipe development. It's a real combination and great fun. I'd love to scale up the consultancy side and work more with brands. There's no right or wrong answer. And everything I do on my platforms keeps exposing me to more brands. I'm very ambitious, and all of it excites me.

Could any of this have happened without your blog and social platforms?
It would have been so much harder. Having a personal brand and social media audience opens up doors because people can really see what you do and what you've created right there in front of them. It's visible proof of your expertise in an easy-to-understand way.

———————————

Social networks versus Google: how do they work?

As mentioned previously, no one knows exactly how the algorithms for Google and social networks work, but what we do know is that they work in different ways, and both are important for your visibility and discoverability.

When you want to buy a new car and you start to google, the results will include websites, blogs and links to social media content relating to new cars. Essentially, unless you have visited one of these websites before, in which case you are more likely to be shown it again, Google decides which one is the most important and relevant, and what to show you, and it will show all searchers similar results (removing issues such as where searchers are located, as that also affects the results that they see).

When you go onto Facebook and other social networks, however, what you see is not the same as what someone else sees on their device. Social networks provide a more customised and personalised experience than search engines.

Instead, what appears on your screen is your own personal feed, a sequence of posts and content (and advertisements) that is selected by the technology because it relates to things you've previously looked up or tagged in some way (by 'liking', for example). The experience is ultimately a personalised one based on an individual's interactions with the platforms. This is a hugely important difference between the way you'll use social media to attract an audience and the way you'll use your website to promote your brand.

Both Google and social networks are doors to visibility, and I am talking about:

- **Search doors**, which enable searchers to find you through search engines and

- **Social doors**, which enable browsers to discover and follow you on social platforms (although, increasingly, people do use social networks as search engines too).

These personalised feeds rely on users interacting with (your) content. The more they do this, the more the systems can second-guess what they might like to see next time.

Tash's tips

From the point of view of your Stand Out Online journey, you want traffic from Google as well as engagement on, and traffic from, social platforms. You want Google to consider you authoritative and relevant so that it shows your website to more people who don't yet know you. Google will send you more traffic once you start creating content (more on this in the next chapter).

You want those on social media to interact and engage with you so that social networks automatically feed more of your content to your followers when they open up Facebook or Instagram.

There are other ways that the platforms decide whose content to promote the most. Length of engagement is one measure, so content that keeps someone's interest for longer – a video or a slideshow, for example – can be powerful.

'How do people first discover me on social media?'

Generally, people discover people, brands, companies and so on on social media by doing one of the following:

- They stumble across you either by happy accident or because someone they're linked to shared a feed to your content.
- They search for a hashtag that you are using on social media and find you.
- You can also follow brands or individuals, at which point (unless they have so many followers that they no longer care!) they will most likely check your profile and decide whether or not to follow you back.

A core aim of your online personal brand is to grow an audience. Some people (such as your mum) will be straight there, following everything you do and interacting in whatever way you enable; others will have spotted you as someone they may be interested in and will follow you.

Choosing your two primary channels

I've suggested that you can launch with two primary social media channels – but which ones? The list seems endless, but in reality there are seven main platforms to consider: Facebook, Instagram, Twitter, Pinterest, LinkedIn, YouTube and Snapchat. They each offer their own particular flavours, and different tools for creating a profile and presence, and for developing a network of followers. But for a simple and effective initial launch, you can't really do better than to focus on the twin powers of Facebook and Instagram. That recommendation does come with two caveats, however. Firstly you need to consider the sector in which you operate and where your target demographic spends their time online. And secondly, it's useful to know the various nuances, rules and operating principles that underpin the various platforms, as some will be better suited to your goals than others. The final point to consider is that the online world moves quickly, so you need to be flexible, because what works today might not work anywhere as well in the months and years ahead; for example, Facebook grew largely from a university and youth user base, but when their parents started joining in droves, many of the younger generation migrated onto Snapchat. You also need to be mindful of platform algorithm changes; for example, Facebook made changes in 2018 prioritising friend content over business content, thus limiting the organic reach of posts from businesses, which led to a number of super-users reconsidering LinkedIn as a platform because their content was going to be seen by many more people.

I should admit some bias to my recommendation, as I am one of only eight accredited UK trainers for Facebook's She Means Business campaign. As part of this, I teach people how to use these platforms for their businesses and personal brands, and as an agency we know these platforms inside out. But even without this bias, the stats bear out the reason why it's worth focusing on Facebook and Instagram in most instances at the time of publishing this book.

Two out of every five mobile minutes in the USA is spent on Facebook and Instagram. Worldwide, there are more than 2 billion active users of Facebook and 700 million using Instagram, and these numbers are still growing. There is no question about the sheer dominance of these two platforms right now. People talk of shifting trends, but loyalty to this pair seems pretty unshakeable. Other networks such as Twitter, LinkedIn and YouTube are certainly effective and powerful, but the combined impact and reach of Facebook plus Instagram is a great beginner-friendly combination.

What's the difference between Facebook and Instagram?

I often get asked, 'Do I have to use Facebook *and* Instagram?' or 'What is the difference between Facebook and Instagram?' Hopefully I can answer these questions here.

Although both are owned by Facebook, Facebook itself is the daddy and Instagram the newer kid on the block. But a simplistic distinction is that Instagram is primarily a channel for sharing photos and videos – imagery – while Facebook supports sharing of all kinds of material, from images to audio, documents and articles to text greetings.

Many people identify as 'Facebook' people or 'Instagram' people, and from the point of view of which to use for your business, I am primarily a Facebook person. Facebook dominates in terms of lead generation. But Instagram comes a close second, particularly for tribe building, glimpses behind the curtain and selling the dream, which personal brands need to do as part of their strategy.

In a recent study, 'A Tale of Two Feeds', carried out at Facebook HQ, marketing-science researchers explored how various groups of people relate to Facebook and Instagram, and explained what their research revealed about how people perceive and use these two social platforms on a weekly basis. The FB HQ research found that the two feeds have a lot in common: the key appeal of both feeds is to make a connection; people visit both platforms at similar times of day; people share content at a similar rate.

People have a different mindset on each platform, however. In particular, the research revealed that people are more likely to use Facebook to interact with close family and friends, whereas they use Instagram to share images with a broad range of people and to connect with businesses.

The popular social channels

All the stats below were correct at the time of going to print.

Facebook

What is it? I'm sure you know, but what began as a way for college students to connect has grown into one of the world's largest social networks.

Stats
- Over 2 billion active users and over 1 billion daily active users.
- 75 per cent of users are men and 83 per cent women.
- 90 per cent of views of content are from mobile phones.
- On average users spend 40 minutes a day on the channel.

Key features
- Advanced targeting functionality makes it a hugely popular platform for advertising.
- The ability to train the Facebook algorithm to put your brand in front of the right people.

LinkedIn

What is it? LinkedIn is a social network for professionals and is for anyone who wants to take their professional life seriously. It can be used by people across all professions. This is the natural habitat in which to talk about your professional goals and successes and to connect to people openly to discuss work.

Stats
- 500 million LinkedIn users.
- 40 per cent of members use LinkedIn daily.
- 40 million students and recent college graduates are on LinkedIn.
- 13 per cent of millennials use LinkedIn.
- 57 per cent male users and 44 per cent female users.

Key features
- You can see who has viewed your profile, such as the person's name, headline, location and industry, and how the people found you, the keywords they were using, their title and more.
- Make your profile and expertise stand out by linking it to visual examples of your work in your LinkedIn profile. Add documents, photos, links, videos or presentations. LinkedIn will link directly to where your work can be found online.

Instagram

What is it? Instagram is a visual sharing social media platform and everyone's main intention is to share and find the best photos and videos. It's owned by Facebook. If you're very arty and creative, use Instagram as a showcase of your visual abilities. If you're not, use it as a candid look into your life and to share your life on the move.

Stats

- Over 800 million monthly active users and experts think it could reach a billion in 2018.
- An estimated 71 per cent of US businesses use Instagram.
- 80 per cent of users follow a business on Instagram.
- 60 per cent of users hear about a product or service through the app.
- 30 per cent of Instagram users have purchased a product they discovered on Instagram.
- 59 per cent of 18 to 29-year-olds use Instagram.
- 80 per cent of Instagram users live outside the US.

Key features

- Instagram Stories, which are videos or photos that only last for 24 hours and which are only available through the app.
- Filters to improve your photography.

Snapchat

What is it? Snap and chat! Or just follow other snappers. Snapchat is good for sharing anything easily with your friends. You don't need to be as polished as you would be on a platform like Instagram. For personal brands, it is great for creating a relationship with your audience and engaging one-to-one with your customers.

Behind-the-scenes posts are helpful for showing people who you are and what you do, and they are good for building a positive association with your brand.

Stats

- 71 per cent of Snapchat users are under 34 years old.

- About 70 per cent of Snapchat users are female.
- 30 per cent of US millennial internet users use Snapchat regularly.
- 45 per cent of Snapchat users are aged between 18 and 24.

Key features
- Lenses, filters and effects; filters will ask you to open your mouth, raise your eyebrows or they will change your voice.
- You can add text, stickers and draw doodles onto your images.
- You select how long your friends will be able to see your images for.

Twitter

What is it? A feed of tweets that used to be just 140 characters long but now can be up to 280. Twitter is really useful for announcements, commentary, topical debate and talking to people one to one. It's also great for joining in debates that are already happening, whether that is a TV programme you're watching at that moment or a wider issue in the news. Just search the hashtag of whatever event you want to discuss and jump right in!

Stats
- Twitter has about 330 million monthly active users worldwide. Sixty-nine million of those 330 million users are located in the US.
- 81 per cent of millennials view a Twitter account on a daily basis.
- Tweets with images are 150 per cent more likely to get retweets than text-only tweets.

- 500 million tweets are posted every day.
- 23 per cent of adult Internet users use Twitter.

Key features
- A chronological collection of tweets made by Twitter users.
- Trending topics that are always big news events or viral posts.
- Very easy to share content by retweeting.
- Pin one of your tweets to the top of your profile so that it stays visible even as you post new tweets.

Tash's Takeaways

- In this chapter we have covered how to launch your personal brand. The minimum requirements for the launch or growth of your Stand Out Online project are:

  1. A simple but modern website.
  2. Two social media channels that you are committed to.
  3. A personal blog/vlog.

- The highest proportion of purchasers turn to the Internet to look for people like you, so they will find your website and social networks.
- Social networks and Google work in different ways, and ideally you want traffic and reach on both.
- If you're new to social media, it's best to start by committing to just two of many more possible channels.

→

Before you go on to the next chapter, you've taken in a lot of information. Just pause to reflect on how you are jumping into a joined-up, cross-platform, multimedia-formatted world and how, in time, you will learn to understand and master it all.

Getting Started with Content

Blogging, inbound marketing, vlogging, podcasting social updates, content strategy – what's the difference? Don't be confused by marketing lingo, when it comes to your Stand Out Online project, it's all effectively the same. The vital ingredient in your path to visibility, when coupled with distribution, will be *how* you reach and communicate with audiences.

Content creation is essential

We live in a world where we have several gods: Google and the large social platforms. All of them reward content creation and publishing with visibility. Each time you publish a blog post to your business website, traffic to your site spikes and it increases your chances of being found in the future. Each time you publish a social update, eyes turn to you. There is no alternative here but to create content – and to publish it.

Content plus distribution equals visibility and influence. Content creation, therefore, is a given. The only questions you will need to answer now are:

- What form of content can I realistically create and maintain for the long term (or can I afford to pay someone else to create and maintain it for the long term)?
- What am I going to say/talk about?

There is no doubt that different forms of content require different levels of talent, confidence, technical ability and different skills, as well as pushing you out of your comfort zone. The chart below gives some indicator of where content types typically fall, *but* it all comes down to the individual and how they operate; for example, if you come from a media background or you are naturally confident, you might find that even those videos that have been properly produced (edited with professional-level lighting) are low in skill and technical level for you, whereas you might find the written word harder.

Content form	Skill level required	Technical level required
Writing/blogs	Low	Low
Social updates	Low	Low
Produced videos	High	High
Live video	Medium	Low
Podcasts	Medium	High

It's also important to remember that everything is learnable and, in fact, in the online world, the skills required are getting easier, even as technology develops, thanks to the increasingly intuitive nature of software and SaaS (software as a service) solutions.

Speaking personally, the one thing I have forced myself to conquer that has made a difference is tech skills – both my *fear* of not understanding it and genuinely not understanding it! I strongly believe that out of all the things that hold us back, tech can be learned. If someone had said to me five years ago that I would be building and launching websites, I would have laughed. Yes, I was running an online business that was entirely SEO dependent then, so I knew a lot about websites, but when it came to building them from scratch, I would have thought that was beyond me. But I took myself down to the local college and learned how to build them alongside a bunch of 21-year-olds. And the same goes for video production and editing. I just learned how to do it. It wasn't easy, but it wasn't impossible either.

More recently, I needed to use the sound-editing software Audacity. I thought to myself: *It will be like iMovie – it will be easy* (note to self: two years ago I never would have described any video-editing software as 'easy'). Anyway, I downloaded Audacity. I opened it. And, argh! It wasn't like iMovie. I couldn't work it straight away. I hated it. Its layout looked stupid. There was nothing intuitive about it. It made me cross, really cross. I started googling other sound-editing alternatives. I was just about to delete Audacity from my laptop, when I thought: *Hang on, there are tons of people who use Audacity and they are not all brain surgeons. I must be able to understand it.* I went to YouTube to watch videos. Literally 15 minutes later I edited my first audio track, cutting out problems, adding music and even fading the music in and out! It was learnable.

Don't fall foul of the fear of technology

I see so many of my clients being held back by technology and not understanding how to do things, ranging from updating a website to resizing an image to editing a video. I'm passionate about demonstrating that it is all learnable, but you can't learn it without effort and discomfort, plus huge amounts of irritation, as I went through with Audacity. Of course, there is new vocabulary, and lots of buttons, plus data overload and moments when everything crashes and nothing makes sense. But none of it is life threatening, it's all fixable, and it's all learnable.

Don't let a fear of technology hold you back. I suggest, therefore, that having reviewed the table on page 120, you create your own (see below) and map out how producing the different types of media formats feels to you. Bear in mind when you do this the types of content you'd like to produce and how much you are prepared to learn.

Content form	How the skill level feels to you based on where you are now	How the technical level required feels to you based on where you are now
Writing/blogs		
Social updates		
Produced videos		
Live video		
Podcasts		

One of your long-term goals might be to publish outstanding pieces of content in every type of media form conceivable across multiple platforms, but this is unlikely to be where you start.

Content creation is a habit, and once you acquire the habit, it is much easier to do. Once you've chosen your media formats, it's a question of getting started.

MY STORY Sean Vigue: 'Work with real people, and then put all that knowledge into your content'
Sean Vigue is 'The Most Watched Online Yoga and Pilates Guy' and has reached around 20 million people with his workouts. He is a seven-times bestselling author and has been featured in

publications including the *Washington Post, Fox News* and *Ultra Running* magazine, and his assets include an online member-ship vault and several apps.

Sean, I have lots of questions for you, such as how did you get into this, how often do you create content, and how has it all changed your life?

These are things I think about all the time. When you have your own brand, you think about these things a lot. Before I was in fitness, I had trained as an opera singer and was in professional theatre for 13 years. Name a musical or show, and I'll have been in it. That gave me many of the tools I use now: how to use your body, how to work with people, how to communicate and, especially, how to enunciate. I always liked to work out, and I started training company members at the gym – you really suffer doing a lot of shows if you are out of shape. I ended up burned-out by theatre and all the travelling, so around 2003 I transitioned into teaching English, and then personal training and became a certified yoga and Pilates instructor. I then got really busy with classes, teaching about 20 classes a week, working all over the place in schools, businesses, homes and gyms, and it felt like being in theatre again.

If this was 2007/08, the possibilities of online personal branding were in their infancy then, right?

Yes, absolutely, YouTube had just started. I was thinking more about getting into DVDs and getting them published and sold in shops. My best friend, Stephan, who is a real tech nerd, told me to get a MacBook Pro and a flip camera and start filming. I went to Best Buy and bought a flip camera and filmed workouts on it. I then posted them onto YouTube. I started filming outdoors, because at the time I lived in Florida and there were loads of beautiful parks. In those early days, I actually did make DVDs, which I promoted on YouTube and on my website. I was posting out thousands of them to customers all over the world. One of my DVDs was named 'Workout of the Year' by *Pilates Style* magazine – I'd filmed it on my flip camera.

Where has your brand grown to today?

I have over 600 videos now and I publish new ones twice a week. I have a lot of revenue streams now: books, several apps, online training programmes, videos and live class collaborations. Highlights are reaching an international audience – you have people emailing you saying, 'By the way, I am in Portugal', 'I'm in India', 'I'm in Australia' – that's really awesome. Even a DVD distributed through a traditional publisher would never have reached that far. I still teach some classes in Denver, and people who are visiting the Denver area, who have been training with me for a long time sometimes take detours to come to a real class of mine, as though I'm a tourist attraction. It's very gratifying, and I always remind myself how amazing that is, because a few years ago I would not have been able to do any of this at all. They always say I am the same in real life as on the videos, which is how it should be.

So many people want to create video content – what is your advice?

Anyone with an iPhone or an Android can film, and you edit right there on the phone. It is amazing what you can do, and then you can put it out, this work of art, wherever you want to on YouTube, Instagram, Twitter or wherever. At first, it's nerve-racking as you don't know who is watching. I consider YouTube to be a really well-paying stock: it gives you dividends while you sleep, while you're eating, while you're off on a walk. It's constantly working and giving income. But YouTube is a big step. People ask me for help, and I notice a lot of apprehension about YouTube because you are so exposed and you are using longer videos, rather than just 20-second videos on Instagram. YouTube is set up so that people can comment and give feedback, which does make people a little nervous sometimes. A lot of people want a YouTube channel, and then they think about it and get nervous and decide against it.

How quickly can people expect to get views?

I am sure there are a lot of people out there who are thinking: *By my fifth video I want to be getting a ton of views and all these offers from brands and for people to pay me to advertise things.* That's not how it works. I cut my teeth doing theatre and taught thousands of fitness, yoga and Pilates classes. I then took my live class experience and put it into a video and a book and an app. What I do is based on having got out there and worked with people – and I still teach people today. I would recommend that you teach people, work one-to-one with people and do live classes – really interact with people on a personal level, and then put that into a video.

Any final words of wisdom for people who are looking at you and thinking: *How can I be like Sean Vigue*?

No one can be like me, just as no one can be like you. Never try to imitate somebody else. Don't overthink it, and be aware when you *are* overthinking it. Comparison is a thief of joy – I don't like a lot of platitudes, but that one really sticks with me.

———————————————

What shall I say?

It's a new day. You're sitting at your computer, all fired up. You begin to type today's blog post – and you freeze. The screen remains depressingly blank as you feel your anxiety levels rising. You've got to write something – but what? And it's not just today. Whatever the content forms you've committed to, you've got to produce something tomorrow, the next day and the next. But all you can do is sit there wondering how on earth the best visible personal brands continually come up with content ideas.

Don't worry – you are not alone. It's the same as the phenomenon that I remember from my days working at national newspapers. To keep the inspiration flowing we would have 'ideas' meetings – and they were the worst thing. As soon as someone asks you for ideas, your mind goes completely blank.

The solution involves two key tactics used by the mainstream media:

1. To be able to switch your thinking around ideas quickly so that you see new ideas everywhere or get a new idea from an existing idea.
2. Content forward planning.

There are also three other tactics that we have developed at Bolt Digital:

1. Key Category planning.
2. Key Topics and Themes planning.
3. Minimum Input, Maximum Output.

In Chapter 7 I'll give you the tools to implement these strategies yourself.

The value of commonly used content categories

Because it's a very noisy world out there and you need to stand out, you're going to need to keep what you say on track and, to a large extent, repeat content categories that fit with the personal brand you are trying to create. A content category is a repeatable format and style of content, like a regular page in a newspaper or magazine. What you actually say will vary each time. I used to see this all the time in the mainstream media where nearly every idea ultimately fits into a category that runs again and again. They just feature different takes on what is ultimately very similar content: for example, bikini bodies, rags to riches, triumph over tragedy, kiss and tell, and so on.

Tash's tips

It is much easier to produce content to category than it is to produce content for a blank page or a blank screen; for example, within the *Daily Mail*'s health pages, they have a regular category called 'Me and My Operation', which features a person and their surgeon talking about the operation. They get much faster results by saying to themselves, 'We need a few more "Me and My Operations"' than they do just looking at a blank page and saying 'We need something to go here.'

You can obviously generate your own categories depending on your own personal brand, but below are my 'commonly used content categories', with examples that will generally fit most Stand Out Online projects. You can either create your own content categories or use the ones below.

You can then give each category a more specific name that fits in with your own niche. If you are a finance CEO and producing content for your 'news hijacking' category, for example, you can rename that category 'money in the headlines'.

News hijacking

All niches have their own news and happenings, and you can use developments and events in your industry to inspire your content. Try to be one of the first to offer your comment or opinion on major industry developments or suggestions as to how the industry as a whole can improve. Over time your content may even become a resource for others in the industry, which will improve your profile as an industry leader. Set up Google alerts for keywords that relate to your industry and use these news stories for inspiration.

Customer/audience questions

Think about what your customers are asking you – and then produce the answer in your content. Remember you are creating content for your customers, audience and potential clients, not for your friends or peers, so think about your customers. Their questions are the best source of inspiration all the time, but especially when you are starting out.

Document, don't create/behind the scenes

Your world is interesting – it really is! It's just that when you're in the middle of it all every day, you don't see it that way. Showing a glimpse of your world also helps to build that all-important trust. Look at the things you routinely do, see and say in your business, and just record them or cover them using photos – document them. It's about *documenting* what is going on around you versus *creating* something new from scratch, an approach pioneered by Gary Vaynerchuk and called in brief 'document, don't create'. Although Vaynerchuk takes an almost 100 per cent 'document, don't create' angle, in the Stand Out Online process we use the technique at a lower level.

Whenever we work with business owners wanting to develop their personal brand, and we visit them at their premises, they only need to start talking and our brains will be firing: *There's a blog post in this. There's content in that.*

I recently worked with a luxury-worktop company and we filmed behind the scenes at their factory, showing worktops being made and the team in action. They thought this was mind-numbingly boring and looked awful, because their team were covered in dust from the production process. Almost immediately they received feedback from customers showing that this insight, rather than just videos of the finished article in situ, was what they appreciated most.

What you want to tell people

If you've chosen a niche that you are passionate about, you are going to have lots of ideas and knowledge in that area. You'll be thinking about your niche constantly, with all kinds of thoughts flitting through your head from: *Wouldn't it be great if... to I hate the way everyone thinks...*

I guarantee you that these can generate 20 great ideas every single day that could be developed into content titles. All you need is to learn to spot and capture these ideas as they flit through your brain, and not let them vanish as random thoughts often do. Use the notes app on your phone and observe what you think about and the ideas that you have. Using these topics, you can also extend your thinking to include what you would like your customers to know about your business or understand about the industry you operate in.

Competitor inspiration

It pays to keep on eye on what the competition is doing. And when you're stuck for ideas, it can serve one up on a plate! Go through other blogs and content in your niche and have a look at what is being said. Write down some of their headlines, content forms and regular articles that you love. Note any posts that have gone viral.

Now think about how you can reposition this for yourself. How can you talk about these topics in your own voice? Remember, you can take inspiration for your content from anywhere, and you might be inspired by your competitors, but ultimately your content needs to be unique for your followers (and to avoid falling foul of plagiarism!).

Google keyword analysis

Use Google's keyword planner to check search volumes of specific words in your niche. This will tell you what your potential audience is actually looking for. Research this using both short search terms (such as 'Chicken Soup') and long-tail ones (such as 'What is the best ingredient for a warming winter chicken soup?'). You can also use Google's Trend tool to find out if specific keywords such as 'chicken soup' are increasing or decreasing in popularity. Add all the popular terms to a spreadsheet. Go through the spreadsheet and use it to generate ideas based on keywords that must appear in your content.

Key theme planning

No matter which category of content you are producing, you also want to have key themes and topics. These are the subjects and more targeted messages that you'll talk about. You may repeat these messages again and again, albeit without saying exactly the same thing over and over again. This is because to build your reputation it's no good just saying something once and never saying it again. As part of your consistency you're going to have to discuss the same/related/similar topics in a number of different ways.

You may have up to two-dozen key topics or messages that you want to repeat. What they are depends on what you do and what you want to achieve. For a dog trainer this might be:

- A trained dog is a happy dog
- There's no such thing as a naughty dog
- Even untrainable dogs can be trained
- Dog training requires consistency
- Dog food
- Dog comfort

Now make a list of key content messages/themes/topics.

The audio opportunity

Podcasting is a growing trend, with some people comparing it to the golden age of radio. An Edison Research survey released in 2017 showed that over the previous year, the growth of podcasting has been steadily rising at 21–24 per cent year on year, and research by HubSpot found that 11 per cent of marketers plan to add podcasting to their efforts in the next 12 months. Why? In your mission to make yourself the stand-out or authority person in your industry, podcasting may well be a great medium, because:

- Content is intimate: it speaks directly into the ear of a client or prospect.
- Content is complementary: it can be consumed while the user is involved in another task, such as driving, cooking or working out.
- Podcast consumers are truly a captive audience, who tend to listen to most of the episodes they download. Weekly podcast listeners tend to consume five shows per week.
- Adoption is surging among younger adult audiences: 45 per cent of consumers aged 18–34 consume at least one podcast a month.
- A podcast allows you to reach a brand-new audience: those people who might otherwise never find or consume your content because they prefer the more portable audio format.
- Podcasts have a balanced demographic of listeners – equally male and female adults between the ages of 18 and 44.

With podcasting, you have two key options: produce a weekly podcast on an ongoing basis, or produce a small batch of limited-run podcasts that focus on a narrow theme and may have only 8, 12 or 16 episodes.

You also have to choose your podcast's topic and format. It may be obvious or you may need to get creative about it. And next is to make decisions on format. Will it be you interviewing other people, you talking by yourself, or with a co-host, or a combination?

MY STORY Manny Coats: 'My podcast was the basis for developing a leading global software platform'

Manny Coats is the founder of the software company Helium 10, which contains a dozen tools that help Amazon sellers to find high-ranking keywords, identify trends, spy on competitors, and fully optimise product listings to increase sales exponentially. He used podcasting to build his personal brand, which then formed the basis of his software and training businesses.

Manny, what came first, the idea of a personal brand or your e-commerce software company?

I've been doing e-commerce since 1999. I have been involved in various e-commerce businesses, mobile games, and lately the Amazon space. With selling on Amazon, I knew that there were a lot of people like me, who were starting out and had the same questions that I had. You only hear about successes and how easy everything is if you just follow steps A, B and C. But, in reality, it's not always that simple.

I decided that I wanted to chronicle my journey – the good and the bad. And I would do this via a podcast, because that was the medium I liked best for absorbing information. Unlike a video that requires your full focus, I could listen to a podcast while driving, working out, on a hike, in the gym, on the toilet, or even while showering (thanks to waterproof bluetooth speakers).

What was the format of your podcast?
I wanted to be 100 per cent transparent, so I showed my numbers to people. I talked about actual profit margins and not just how much I sold. It's easy to sell a million dollars in products and show no profit. Being profitable is another story altogether.

I think people really appreciated this fresh approach. From what people have told me, they liked that I told it how it was: that making a million dollars in sales doesn't mean you have that money in the bank – that, after expenses and taxes, hopefully you still have a quarter of that left over.

People don't like talking about failures – it kills the 'guru' status, right? I didn't care. My first product failed. I talked about how I turned that failure into something good.

When I interviewed people, I asked hard questions. I didn't sugar-coat it. I asked the questions I would want to have somebody ask as a listener. I didn't always go with the flow of what everybody was teaching. I didn't just regurgitate what was out there. I did my own research, and if it conflicted with what everybody was saying out there, so be it. Word got around, and people started to tune in. From there I decided to start the Facebook channel, which quickly grew to where it is now, approaching 40K Amazon sellers in our community. And from there, we launched helium10.com, which makes powerful tools that I use to help me in my Amazon business. Originally it was just for me, but eventually we released it to the public, and now it is one of the top SaaS platforms in the world for Amazon sellers.

Where did you start with the podcast?

I launched the podcast at about the same time that I started my Amazon private label business. One thing that people don't realise is that the podcast was partly created to keep me accountable to myself. By announcing goals and making it public, it was a challenge to myself to hit those goals – and if I missed them, I'd better have a very good reason for doing so. This would force me to really analyse everything I was doing and to keep notes of what I was doing. This was extremely helpful.

What about the tech side of podcasting?

Running a podcast is demanding. I think people underestimate the amount of work that goes into it. At the start, it was just myself and my business partner, Guillermo Puyol (Gui). I would record the audio podcasts, edit them, then hand them over to Gui, who would get them online. He set everything up. Making the podcast popular was a combination of telling it how it is, without sugar-coating things. We also experimented a lot with the show. We tried to be goofy and not always take things so seriously.

Today, we now do our podcasts in video format, so that we can be on iTunes as well as on YouTube. This increases the complexity a lot, because when you're doing an audio podcast, you're not sharing screens or anything like that. With video, we're often sharing screens, and since this gets ported over to the audio version for the podcast, you have to be careful about how you say things to ensure somebody listening knows what you are showing on screen.

The podcasts don't generate revenue directly, but indirectly they generate traffic and status as a figure in the space, which then leads into projects that are fulfilling and profitable.

What doors have opened up for you?

I've been at this for two years in this space. My current average day is not ideal. I found out that I am really good at saying yes to every idea, and now I am learning to say no. But at the moment, we have a *lot* of projects happening all at once, and our team has grown to two dozen people.

We now have the AMPM Podcast, our Amazon Private Label business, our Helium 10 software, Pixel Perfect Photography, Freedom Ticket, Illuminati Mastermind, managing our Facebook group, speaking at live events and several other projects, all ongoing. Eight hours goes by in the blink of an eye. I wish I could say that I work fewer than 40 hours a week and have three-day weekends, but that isn't the case at the moment.

All of this exposure has been a blessing and has opened up numerous opportunities. It's pretty awesome to speak to people who tell me that I was the reason they got started or that I somehow had a small part in them being successful Amazon sellers.

The podcast has certainly opened the doors to speaking at events, which has opened doors to incredible friendships from all the people I have met. Two years ago I would have paid $10,000 to sit in a room with specific guys in this industry, just to learn from them. Today, these same guys speak at my conference and are just a phone call away if I want to hang out. That's a pretty awesome feeling.

What would you say to someone thinking of developing their own personal brand?

Get out there. Find something you do better than others, and push that part of you. If you're not sure what that is, ask ten of your friends what they think you shine at. If they are good friends, they'll tell you. If you're thinking of starting a podcast or speaking on stage, or whatever it might be, just do it. There will always be a reason in your mind not to do it, to wait a little longer until it's perfect. Guess what? It will never be perfect. The time will never be right. Just implement and go for it, and you can tweak things the next time around.

Finding your voice

If your Saturday nights are as wild as mine, you may well find yourself 'enjoying' weekly instalments of *The X Factor* and *Strictly Come Dancing* every autumn. And during one of these Saturday nights I picked up a piece of wisdom from Simon Cowell, which directly relates to your Stand Out Online project. One week he talked about authenticity and finding your voice, both of which are huge buzzwords online and something that everyone who is trying to build their own brand – whether business or personal – wonders about. In the programme, Simon Cowell urged several contestants to stop watching YouTube and mimicking American singers, and instead to focus on developing their own unique way of singing and performing. He said that just because certain hand gestures and ways of performing work for whoever-it-is on YouTube doesn't mean that the same thing will work for Richard-from-Barnsley-currently-auditioning-for-*X Factor*, and he told them that they needed to develop more, and to perform more in front of more people until they started to find their own way.

When you live in a world like this one right now, it's only natural to start wondering and worrying about whether or not you sound 'right' and to draw inspiration from so-and-so person or business over there who you really admire and who seems to have the whole thing nailed. But if you're trying to be someone else, you definitely haven't found your voice.

The similarity for singers and content creators is that their work is public. What you do is judged by other people, and this can feel awkward while you're still learning. Actually finding your voice can't be done by planning and thinking; it can only be done by starting and publishing. At this point in your journey, you are not necessarily going to be 100 per cent certain of your voice. Just like the singer who needs to do more gigs in pubs and working men's clubs to truly hone their talent; however, it's all a process each time you publish and each time you post, and over time your voice develops.

When it's not just about you

For many people reading this book, your personal brand will be one part of a wider organisation. If you're the CEO or founder of a business with staff, for example, or a product-based business, or even a location-based business such as a tourist attraction, you (or your team) will be wondering how to get the right balance between talking about what your business does and bringing yourself into it as the face of the organisation. Many people take the view that their personal brand is separate from their business brand and will start an entirely new platform for themselves, knowing that its reach will trickle down into one or any number of the organisations they are involved with. Others will have their personal brand as one category within their businesses' content output, as is the case for Rebecca Hopkins whose story follows.

There's no right or wrong answer; they are just different approaches. Your route will depend entirely on what will work for your business/offering and what you feel most comfortable with.

MY STORY Rebecca Hopkins: 'Our customers love the trust that comes from seeing the people behind the business'

Rebecca Hopkins is the co-founder of Balance Me skincare along with her sister Claire. They are currently stocked in 900 stores, including John Lewis, Marks & Spencer, Sainsbury's and Wholefoods as well as online stores including Ocado and Feel Unique.

Rebecca, many beauty brands are anonymous, but you and Claire are very much the public faces of Balance Me. What's the thinking behind this?

Our business started over a chat at the kitchen table and, essentially, Claire and I create products for people like us. We are still self-funded, so we are very relevant and integral to the brand. Balance Me is what we do, and it's our passion, so our strategy is to give a glimpse into our lives and the products we create and to be the figureheads of the brand. We are part of what gives the brand a clear point of difference, that we are sisters, and so we feature on the website and in social media. Our customers love the trust that comes from seeing real people behind the business. It's not just us, though; we want it to be clear that we are not lab technicians wearing lab coats, and we work with a team of incredibly talented people.

How often do you feature yourselves in your content?

Well, we do see that we definitely get higher engagements and comments when we share photos of ourselves, and that's because people-based feeds are more personal and engaging than brand-based ones. There's always the question of 'Should we do more?' At the same time, though, we are a product-based beauty brand, so our social feeds are primarily about products. What we try to do is fuse our approach and find

a balance between posting personal things and product information. We want people to connect and make more informed
choices about what to buy.

How much personal detail do you share?
We definitely don't overshare! Because we know our customers
really well, we try to tap into their passion and points of interest.
We will have a select number of posts about things like nutrition or where to go on holiday, where one or both of us will be
offering our personal advice. We also post photos of ourselves
and our families to tie in with events such as Mother's Day or
Thanksgiving. Our goal is always to try to share relevant content
that will enhance the reader's mood in some way.

**How else do you develop your personal brand alongside the
business brand?**
Over the years, we've shared our story of building the brand on
lots of blogs and websites and through the media. We've been
featured in *Red* magazine, *Get the Gloss*, *The Lifestyle Edit*, the
Telegraph and more.

   We also do events and speaking. They are time-consuming,
but it's so powerful and relevant to get in front of people and
join in with real conversations. Typically, we'll be asked to speak
about our journey and female entrepreneurship. We both love
to help inspire other women to set up businesses and do things
that they never felt would be possible, such as juggling a career
with a family. But with anything we do, we are always focused
on being sure the audiences we are speaking to are relevant to
the brand and that what we are saying will resonate.

_____

What makes good content?

Coming from the traditional print media, I find the question of what makes good content, and the meaning of 'good', fascinating but also highly bemusing. You see the concept of 'good' is changing rapidly, and the baton of decision is being passed with increasing pace from the old school – the editors and the commissioners – to the new world, that of the actual – ahem – reader and consumer!

In the old world, there are various people of power (editors, commissioners, producers) who, through whatever reason, know what makes good content, and what their readers want. Their knowledge comes from experience, and talking with each other to decide how to put messages across, and what is best for the reader, and what the reader does or doesn't need to know. Really, though, who appointed any of these people the oracle?

In the old days, readers would write in by post to let editors and commissioners know their opinion, although their letters didn't always reach those on high. Even in the modern world, in which the readers are able to comment on articles and openly criticise them, many of the old-world chiefs don't really care or change direction based on feedback, because they believe that they know best. Which maybe they do. Or maybe they *did*.

Today, everyone and anyone is a publisher and a media company, as we know. Publish, understand your stats and you'll find out whether your content is good or not. Publish more of what your audience wants (you'll be able to tell through likes/comments/shares/engagement). In the new world, you publish, wait, assess and then do more of what your audience feeds back to you is good. It's not a one-way conversation.

What I've learned about the new world is that it actually doesn't matter what I think, or what you think, about what makes good content. It doesn't matter that your teacher at school might have told you that things have to be written in a certain way. Or that paragraphs must have more than four sentences in them. It doesn't matter if you think the world is being dumbed down because people communicate using emojis, or if you think that we need to get back to how things were. It doesn't matter if I think a piece of content is good or not. As an agency owner, I've given up spending that much time thinking about things like which video I personally think is the best one for use in a Facebook or Instagram campaign, because I'm often wrong! Just publish them all, and let the audience decide.

I love the democratisation of it, the slow but steady shift of who decides on what is good content or not, whether it's editors and other people in power or those who actually consume the content. It's the reversal of assessment of what is good from those who think they know, to those who actually consume.

Final thoughts on launching content

The most important thing is to get started and begin producing, but before you do that here are seven final considerations.

1. Take content seriously

Content writing is not a job that can be delegated to a part-time PA or landed on the plate of an already busy employee. It requires thought – and a schedule. Even if you only publish once each week, the week can quickly roll round with the next blog post still not written. Take it seriously – make it someone's primary job, if not your own.

2. Just hit the 'publish' button

Your content must be of a quality to reflect your professionalism, but nobody is expecting Pulitzer prize-

winning journalism.
Simply get writing/filming/recording and write/speak in the same way that you talk.

3. Forget what you learned at school

Lessons from the past can hold you back when you're trying to produce content – after all, you're not writing essays or formal letters. Content needs to be quick to read and easy to scan at a glance. This makes it simpler for you to devise and write content – just create one paragraph for each idea, and keep paragraphs short, three or four sentences at most. If you find you can't do this, you're probably trying to write a dissertation! And nobody is going to read that online.

4. Think about ease of content digestion rather than 'good' content

What makes good content? What indeed? Whether content is good is entirely subjective. There is plenty online that doesn't impress me, yet it has a huge readership, and vast followings – so really, who am I to judge?

In traditional newspaper journalism, good content is about eloquent turns of phrases and overarching themes that run throughout entire articles. It's about thought-provoking conclusions that reflect questions asked in the introduction. Your readers are likely to be sitting down, entirely focused on the paper and really interested in the subject of the day, and they are prepared to concentrate as they read. Online content is very different.

You see, having been a national newspaper journalist for some 15 years, I like to think that I can write. Yet I've learned that writing for the web is not at all like writing for print, because a new factor comes into play: scannability. That is why in online editions of newspapers we're seeing the style changing to follow that of good blogging. An example of this is the adoption of the 'listicle' (bullet-list articles) and 'clickbait' (provocative headlines that get articles opened) – genres that have successfully earned blogs readerships of millions.

5. Think about scannability for written content

Scannability is the vital component for getting readers' attention – and it's important for encouraging people to continue to delve into your blog on return visits. You want the blog post's general sense to be gleaned from the shortest of glances at an iPhone while hopping onto a bus, ordering a latte or scrolling through social media.

Headings midway through the post are great for breaking up the text and improving scannability. They also provide a map of your topic, helping the reader to appraise the content at a glance, and they then reinforce the story that is unfolding as they read.

Use space too – online readers don't have the patience to wade through it all and are often reading in challenging circumstances (walking, on a bus, squeezed in a café chair, using a screen in bright light, and so on). So, as well as keeping paragraphs and sentences short and to the point, insert big returns between paragraphs to create space on the page. This breaks up the text to make it easier to read, especially on the move.

Tash's tips

Another way to break down your text into digestible and readable portions is with bold and italic font – it draws attention to the really important words and phrases (great for the skim reader) and helps to keep the reader's eye moving forwards. You can also use devices such as 'drop quotes', where you repeat a key phrase from the main text and give it prominent formatting such as larger font and a different colour. This can really help to keep a reader's interest simply by making the page/screen look much more interesting and inviting.

---

6. Make your main points up top

Having 'graduated' from journalism to blogging, I'm very aware of one basic difference: newspaper features take the reader on a journey, slowly revealing the full story or argument and often withholding the final conclusion until the very end; online, though, content needs to get straight to the point. The main arguments should be made right away, clearly and be easy to find. Once again, it is because of the difference in reading behaviour: online readers and viewers pay far less attention and won't give you much time at all before deciding whether your piece is worth reading or not. They need to make their decision up top, the moment they see your headline. Think very carefully about your content title. Try to assess it without having the benefit of knowing what it's all about to see if it is compelling and engaging. Ask yourself if it clearly conveys the real value of the story or is it too cryptic? Think whether or not you are saying something that is of interest to them.

7. Use lists

It's no secret that some of the most successful websites in the world, from Buzzfeed to the *Huffington Post*, churn out list post after list post – and the reason is that readers love them. They are quick and easy to read and can still be very engaging. Use lists and bullet-points to break up text, but remember: with list posts you need a really tempting headline or title; with so many other list-based posts to choose from, you want your new readers to choose yours!

Remember, no idea is truly new

Don't get stuck with the thought, *But it's all been done before.* So what? Genuinely new content ideas will be few and far between and will probably revolve around being the first to hijack a current news topic in a particular way. It's about presenting your unique take on things, on your own unique website and in your own unique way.

Tash's Takeaways

- Creating content and publishing it is the only way you can create your own visibility online. You have no choice but to start.
- There are a variety of media formats that you can use to create content, the key question is to ask yourself what form of content you can realistically create and maintain for the long term.
- You will need to plan your content categories, a repeatable format and style of content, like a 'regular page' in a newspaper or magazine, as well as your key topics and themes, which are the more specific subjects you'll talk about.
- Accept that it will take time to find your voice, even if you complete every exercise laid out in this book.
- Don't make excuses, just hit 'publish'.

PART THREE

Develop

By now, the basic foundations of your Stand Out Online project are in place. The next section of this book is about developing them. How do you take what you've got already and up-level it again and again? How will you be able to produce enough content, and what systems can you put in place to make it all more manageable? How will you reach more and more people while continuing to engage with your existing audiences? The answers are coming up.

7

Advanced Content Creation and Management

What should be clear by now is that to see the full (or any) benefits of the Stand Out Online process you are going to have to commit to this for the long term. Once your categories and themes are decided, you'll need to put in place systems to create, manage and distribute content for the indefinite future. And how to do this is what we are going to cover now.

Standard, flagship and pillar content

Across the content-creation industry, you'll hear people talking about standard, flagship and pillar content.

Standard content is the material you post on a daily basis, providing simple updates, reflections of what's going on in your life or your topic, and news and information.

Flagship content works as the big draw to you. It's the principal feature that represents what you are all about, and the reason for your reputation. Perhaps it's a single post that explains your mission and ethos, or it could even be a great FAQ on your industry. Think of it as the content equivalent of the high-street flagship store, standing proudly on a busy corner.

Pillar content is solid, evergreen content that gives your readers, listeners or viewers value. This is content that has longevity without becoming out of date, and it is relevant each time a new reader discovers you.

Although this is certainly a helpful way of thinking of things, as an agency, we also tend to categorise content into two key categories:

1. Long-form content (which encompasses both pillar and flagship content).
2. Short-form content (which is primarily for social media).

The dilemma of what to post today

The question is, when there is a seemingly unlimited amount of content to produce, how can you do it without spending all your time producing content? How can you avoid that nightmarish, 'What am I going to post today?' moment? Step forward the concept of Minimum Input, Maximum Output.

You need to create a lot of content – and you need it to be good; but you don't want to spend your life doing it! One option is to use an agency like mine, but if you prefer to create your own, you can still use the efficiency model that we follow. It would be absolutely impossible for us to create the volume of content that we do if we didn't use this model (combined with the forward planner, which is coming up). The model is essentially about repurposing content until it can be repurposed no more.

The basic principle is that it takes far less time to sit down once and plan ten blogs or vlogs in a batch than to sit down ten times and create individual blogs each time you need them. If you can get as efficient as we are, you just need half a day to generate the basis of your content for a month or longer.

We'll begin by making six long-form videos for YouTube or Facebook, each lasting 2–3 minutes. The reason we start with video is because it's the most complicated to produce. Typically, this would involve filming and editing videos for a YouTube or Facebook weekly show, which might be either directly answering questions to camera or reportage-style and will take half to one day of time to capture. You must not leave this session until you have completed at least four (for the four weeks of the month), if not six, videos, as it's always nice to have a bit of a contingency built in!

The videos are then edited into individual episodes and transcribed (we use a service called Rev.com, which charges $1 per minute for transcription and returns the transcript within about 24 hours). The same content is then turned into text-based long-form pillar content; in other words, blog posts, newsletters, long-form articles for platforms such as Facebook and LinkedIn. And it doesn't stop there. Each of our long videos can be broken down into two to five shorter videos for social media – we call them 'social shorts'. These are deliberately designed for quick viewing, and act as tasters to draw people into the longer ones (and your other content).

A great benefit of video making is that you will also definitely make some funny mistakes during your filming. *Voila!* You have out-takes, at least one per video, giving you six more. People love out-takes and they're ideal for social media: quick, funny and with high sharing appeal.

But don't stop there!

People love images, so go to a nice free image site such as Unsplash.com and download some attractive and relevant photos.

Sit down for an hour, go back to your long-form articles and cut up the words to make captions. Take the most powerful messages and turn them into quoteables on which you add the quote to the image itself.

All that's left is to schedule the entire lot so that it will publish automatically, without any input from you. And you now have what I call base-level social/website and newsletter content all covered for the next four to six weeks. You must still do live or on-the-day social content and share updates on what you're up to – and, in fact, you *should* do this – but you can relax knowing that, at a base level, your content is largely done for the entire period.

MY STORY Neil Patel: 'As the Internet develops, there's more to do – accept it or move on and do something else'
Neil Patel is a co-founder of the software companies Crazy Egg, Hello Bar and KISSmetrics. He helps companies such as Amazon, NBC, GM, HP, and Viacom grow their revenue. The *Wall Street Journal* called him a 'Top Influencer on the Web'. *Entrepreneur* magazine credits Neil with creating one of the 100 'most brilliant' companies in the world. He was recently listed in Brand24's top five of the 100 leading digital marketers in the world.

Neil, when people look at all the content that you create around your personal brand, they might feel overwhelmed. Where should they start?
I blog daily, podcast daily, do videos weekly, and I speak at a lot of conferences. Over time, I've actually increased how much I'm doing to build my brand. But when you start, you have to take it one step at a time and pick one thing. It could be a blog, podcast or video. Once you've got that up and running

and gained traction you can expand to different mediums. It's a lot of work, time and money to do all of them at once, so start slowly and grow from there. For most people, the ideal thing to start with is a blog – or just participate on Twitter or Facebook, it doesn't have to be too hard.

Where did you start – and why?
I didn't really try to intentionally build a Neil Patel brand. I didn't have any expectations either. I was trying to generate business. Back in the very beginning, I couldn't afford ads, so I started blogging and creating content as a way to generate leads without spending money. If someone had said to me then what my brand would look as it does today, I would have thought they were crazy. I never believed things would work out this well – things have worked out way better than I expected.

What have been the benefits?
Everything: the business, the book deals – it's easier for me to grow my revenue in new channels. All are possibilities because of building a brand. A personal brand opens up doors and gets you into meetings. I've met with billionaires who've said, 'I read your content, I want to hire you.'

What's the one thing that's had the most impact?
There's not one thing in particular that has worked for me. Instead, it's a bit of everything; all the different content in all the different forms. The one thing that has worked for me, though, is consistency. It's because I've been consistent when others haven't: every single day, every year, I still am consistent. The way it works for me is that by being consistent you don't really see any *drastic* changes – it just gets better

over time. The one thing I've learned is that you won't build a strong personal brand unless you are consistent with whatever you are doing to market yourself. Consistency is what builds a personal brand.

How does this work from a practical point of view?
I do podcasting in batches. I record 15–20 episodes per time, so I only record twice a month. My co-presenter helps me to plan the episodes. I write blogs daily, and I'm used to it, so it doesn't take me more than a few hours, and I do email blasts whenever I like something or have something valuable to share. Update your online channels every day and continuously grow your online presence.

To be consistent, how often do you need to generate content?
Every day. The landscape is getting more competitive, so you have to put out better quality information and content. It's also changing because there are more mediums and channels. Over time you have to leverage multiple platforms and multiple media formats. As the internet develops, there's more to do – accept it, or move on and do something else. I'm prepared to commit more as platforms diversify. Start one step at a time and be consistent. Ideally, you need to be as consistent as me, and ideally from day one. The biggest thing to realise is that if you are not consistent it, won't work.

How to be a thought leader – know what is topical

Creating topical content for your website and social media feeds is really important, because it helps you to position yourself as being on the ball and on top of what is going on. Also, it helps you to attract journalists who are always looking for experts to comment on topical matters.

Tash's tips

If you want to get publicity by writing for online publications, or even print outlets, then it's much easier to get editors to agree to take a piece that is topical. The television is filled with experts having debates on this or that, and you want your chance to be one of those asked to join in.

All visible personal brands – bar those that aren't 'allowed' an opinion, such as the royals – are masters at this. And the easiest way to do it is to set up Google alerts for various keywords. We work with a number of beauty brands and other businesses whose target market is women over 50. With them in mind, we have Google alerts set up for all sorts of keywords relating to that age group, such as 'midlife', 'menopause', 'middle-age women'. That means every day Google sends us the latest news stories featuring these keywords. A quick skim through the articles and we can glean what is topical within our client's industry.

How to 'be' topical

Once you know what is topical in your industry, how do you then 'be' topical? In the last chapter, I mentioned borrowing a process from mainstream media, which involves a quick switch of your thinking around ideas so that you can create more ideas or get a new idea from an existing idea. Editors and commissioning editors use this quick-switch process all the time, otherwise it is impossible to generate ideas or remain topical. This is a process that is very helpful for thought leaders: those who want to use their opinions to stand out as visible online leaders.

News hijacking and the 60-second thought-leadership process

Whatever industry you're in, there is always industry news. Keep on top of all your industry publications and what they are talking about, and select a story that is already running. Then use the following process to create your own unique take on the industry story.

1. **Use the news cycle of your industry, and turn it on its head** As previously stated, whatever industry you are in, there is always industry news; so keep on top of all your industry publications and turn ideas on their heads. Let's take a fictional fashion consultant, for example, who wants to be a fresh voice in a luxury fashion industry that is currently full of doom and gloom. The news is all about how it's over for luxury fashion, with several high-profile fashion label closures. Now, if my client joins the fray talking about how it's all belt-tightening from here on for luxury fashion, her voice will get lost in the noise. Instead, she can turn the story on its head with ideas such as 'Why there has never been a better time than now to launch a luxury fashion line' (and obviously back this up with a load of credible and relevant reasons).

2. **Move an industry story on to its next chapter** A different way of launching on the back of what's hot and

current in your news sector is to develop the story further rather than challenge it. Stories don't really end – every story is linear, and there is always something else that can happen next. In the case of the closure of high-profile fashion brands, 'next chapter' content could take up the narrative in a number of ways: new up-and-coming labels have more space to come to market; fashion industry reaction; what's next for the designer; and so on.

3. **Offer an analysis of a topical situation** OK, so the industry news in fashion is about the closure of luxury brands. An analysis of the what/whys/hows/how did it come to this/where will it go next is another opportunity to be a thought leader.

4. **Offer a solution to an industry problem** Luxury brands are closing – what's the solution to this? Part of being a thought leader is to be the person who always seems to have the answer to a problem. You'll see this all the time in the national papers. But do these commentators who are called on to proffer solutions to problems really know best? Probably not. They just offer a solution in that moment and talk about it in an interesting and engaging way, promoting further discussion.

It doesn't have to be the best solution in the world, just something that provides food for thought, is well argued and gives a new voice or fresh take in that particular moment. Solutions are often subjective, and there might be hundreds of different solutions to any given problem. No one is going to hold a gun to your head if your hypothetical solution isn't right! Probably no one will act on it at all, but the net result is that simply offering up a solution helps to position you as an industry leader.

EXERCISE: generate thought-leadership ideas

Take a news item that is happening in your niche right now and work through the questions below to generate five thought-leadership ideas. Write them in your notebook. The important thing is to not dwell and agonise over it but to give yourself, say, 60 seconds to generate your ideas – then pick one to move forward with.

1.   Existing news story – what is it?

2.   What does this story look like if it's turned on its head?

3.   What does this story look like when you predict its next chapter?

4.   What does a topical analysis of this story look like?

5.   What is the solution to this industry problem?

Allow yourself to have an opinion

It's a dilemma I see often: people who find it scary to admit to and share their opinions, as if they have no validity. Someone recently asked me, 'Am I allowed to have an opinion on what is happening in my industry?' The answer is *yes, yes, YES!*

I think this insecurity comes from the way that blogging has completely reversed the way we have always expected things to happen. Traditionally, whether in our working corporate lives, at school, or even simply at home as young children, we were always asked for our opinions; we were not encouraged to offer them unsolicited. It's just like the way that we were selected for promotions and opportunities rather than being expected to go out seeking them. Generally, throughout our lives, and particularly for those of us who grew up in the world before the digital landscape of today, you kept schtum until someone else anointed you with the privilege of whatever it was you were looking for: they asked if you'd speak at an event, they'd invite you to write for their publication, they'd select you for promotion.

The Internet has turned all that on its head. What we see with blog stars and leaders now is that they take the decision to stand up and be counted, to have an opinion, to put it out there and to keep putting it out there – and their raised and enhanced personal brands and profiles follows from that initial confidence and mindset. They don't wait for someone else to ask them or to be granted permission. They just make a decision and use their own voice.

The Bolt Content Forward Planner

When it comes to using the Minimum Input, Maximum Output model, another part of its success revolves around being ahead. Although you might, and can, produce content today for today, or today for tomorrow, you generally want to have your base content produced well ahead. At Bolt, we aim to have content produced four weeks ahead for all our clients at any one point. As well as being efficient, it also results in minimum stress for our team and our clients.

With that in mind, we use simple Excel spreadsheets to forward plan our content and keep track of what we have done historically and what is coming next. We use the Excel tabs at the bottom to store content year by year so that we can easily access past content, too. The spreadsheet looks like this:

Week	Long-form title	Video/ Podcast URL	Post written	Post scheduled	Post URL	Newsletter written	Newsletter scheduled
1							
2							
3							

Viral content

Viral content is content that spreads just like a virus through social media – and often ends up reaching mainstream media, too. And it's all because something in the content made people feel compelled to share it. Having your content go viral is every content creator's dream, as it means that you reach new audiences and put your personal brand under the noses of thousands of new people.

The great book *Contagious* by Jonah Berger explains that virality isn't completely random or down to luck or magic. His studies reveal six key steps to drive people to talk about and share your content: social currency, triggers, ease for emotion, public, practical value and stories.

Social currency is all about posting content that makes others look in the know or feel good. People enjoy the kudos of discovering impressive and insightful content and sharing it. Triggers are those 'top of mind, tip of tongue' things we quickly relate to because of our environments. This is why topical content does well, as does content on big topics such as parenting – it's all about finding out what is at the front of the mind for most people. Likewise, content that triggers an emotional reaction, whether positive or negative, also spreads fast.

In his book, Berger explained how 'public' is to do with the fact that people look to others for guidance and have a fundamental curiosity. If they see others reading your content, therefore, they'll look too. Practical value rests on the fact that the more usable a piece of content is, and the more helpful information it contains, the more it spreads. Finally, good stories have never-ending virality and can survive.

Therefore, create content that tells a wider story and isn't just about promoting an object but also offers thought-provoking life lessons, a good story, practical value and triggers emotion. That's easy to do, *non*?

Tash's Takeaways

- If you don't want to be caught in a daily cycle of 'what shall I say today?', you should batch and create content at scale, repurposing it for use across platforms and time periods.
- The Bolt Minimum Input, Maximum Output model is one way of doing this.
- Becoming a thought leader really matters if you want to stand out in your industry. To be a thought leader you need to do two key things: (1) know what is topical in your industry; and (2) understand how to take what is topical and add your opinion to the debate.
- If you find coming up with topical opinions difficult, use my quick-switch thought-leadership process to train your brain to generate ideas and opinions.

Removing Your Own Self-Made Hurdles

The Stand Out Online process is just like any other entrepreneurial activity: it relies on your own energy and drive to make it happen. It's no good expecting the dynamism, vision and staying power to come from someone else. Therefore, not surprisingly, the biggest threat to your own success is yourself.

I want to share with you some of the hurdles that I know you will put in the way of your own progress. Believe me, you will. And because some of them may already be in place and holding you back, we need to sort this out right now. We're talking about growing a serious audience that truly wants to know and hear more from you, the person – you the real person. And that starts by acknowledging your own doubts, and it continues by addressing and resolving them.

When *you* get in the way of you

All personal brands hit problems early on – and later, too, but by then you're more experienced and may well be using an agency like mine to take the strain for you. These problems are almost always self-made. The only person who can really get in the way of your personal branding is you. Here are the eight most common hurdles people face; make sure you're equipped to sail right over them:

1. Forgetting the work you've done on your strategy
2. Ignoring your core values and giving up too early
3. Not living your passion
4. Feeling uncomfortable and worrying about what people think
5. Imposter syndrome
6. Fear of technology
7. Being too busy
8. Consistency

Hurdle 1: forgetting the work you've done on your strategy

There is an excellent book that I can recommend to you which goes into tremendous detail about the benefits of a single focus. Called *The ONE Thing* and written by Gary Keller and Jay Papasan, it explains the dangers of multi-tasking, of working to conflicting agendas and of the numerous ways that we can be deflected from our true course.

As you immerse yourself in the exciting process of Stand Out Online, you will feel yourself being drawn in multiple directions, and for most people this means that you'll be hopping around the Bolt Opportunity Vortex, chasing a million different opportunities at once, and the next thing you know you'll have burnout.

In my agency I often meet people who have already achieved online success in terms of followers, and typically these people will be in the influencer space: that is, they started from scratch and have built up a large following and reach. The issue is they are making no real money from it at all. You would be surprised by some of the big names that suffer from this.

Tash's tips

Don't get distracted by the 'shiny objects', forgetting which business model you are meant to be following and going for all opportunities at once, such as launching an online course, doing collaborations with brands and writing books. Further down the line, when you are established, it is fine to aim for multiple targets in this way. But focus is required at first.

In his book, Gary Keller talks about really successful people – and he identifies the one thing they have in common: a single focus, their ONE thing. Every person who has engineered their own success has done so by focusing consistently on one goal at a time. You need to pick your goal and stick with it – for now. That's why it's so important to complete the planning and clarity exercises detailed in Chapter 3. If you skipped those, go back to Chapter 3 now.

Hurdle 2: giving up too early

As with hurdle 1, this one exists only because of human nature. When you start something new and exciting, with ambitious expectations, you're so eager to get there. And that's why the early stages of this personal-brand journey are by far the most dangerous. The usual mistake people make is to go crazy creating content and then become disillusioned with the early results and quickly throw in the towel. There are so many blogs, vlogs and podcasts dying slow, painful deaths all over the Internet. You've got to learn to manage your own expectations. You're right at the beginning of your Stand Out Online process. You have a long, long, long road ahead.

My own agency, for example, works for Zita West Fertility Clinic. We created a strategy that included creating a show, *The Fertility Show*, on YouTube. We committed to this show for a year before even considering whether it was working or not. We know that the online revolution is happening and will continue to happen. We also know there is no such thing as overnight success. But we knew that Zita West would be the first fertility clinic to make this platform their major means of communication with their market place. We therefore committed to it properly rather than doing what so many people do: posting a flurry of videos for a month and then giving up.

Tash's tips

Within the modern world, it's not even a question of committing for one year and seeing where you end up – although that's a good place to start. You're going to need to commit for the long haul.

Hurdle 3: not living your passion

Personal branding is essentially about business and career success, but just make sure you actually *like* the career and field you are in! Michael Gerber, in his *E-Myth* book series, explains this very well when he talks about the 'seizure of entrepreneurship'. He is referring to when we make a rational plan that, due to a lack of true passion, grinds to a complete halt; for example, a baker working in a supermarket gets fed up with being an employee and decides to set up his own bakery. He knows how to bake, so there's plenty of rational thinking there. But he doesn't particularly enjoy baking bread; in fact he's completely bored by it. Now, with his own bakery, he is still baking bread – plus he's filling in all his spare hours running a business as well.

You must think carefully about your plan and make sure you actually want to be living and breathing your topic. You are going to need to create a lot of content, so you must be passionate about what you do.

Also, make sure you examine the authenticity of your passion: is it really your own, or is it something that you just think you should feel strongly about?

MY STORY Janey Lee Grace: 'My personal brand grew out of pure passion'
Presenter Janey Lee Grace is the co-host of Radio 2's *Steve Wright in the Afternoon* show. She has turned her passion for a holistic, eco-friendly way of life into her books, *Imperfectly Natural Woman* and *Imperfectly Natural Baby and Toddler*, and become an influencer and media consultant in the natural living space, running her own annual awards, training and directory for natural, eco and organic products and services.

Janey, you've developed your passion into a personal brand and business outside of broadcasting, tell us how that happened
It started 12 years ago. I was on air talking about the things I was passionate about: natural and eco living, and sustainable products, and a publisher approached me and asked if I'd ever thought of writing a book, which I hadn't. I wrote my first book, *Imperfectly Natural Woman*, and it was literally my bible: my life's work and passion poured into it. When it came out, I harnessed the power of my own determination and managed to get myself a radio interview, and the book went to number

one on the Amazon bestsellers rankings overnight. But back then it was pure passion, there was no business side to it at all.

Is passion a good place to start?
Absolutely! I always say to people that if you've got a message to share or anything you want to talk about, you've got to be passionate about your topic. Some people are scared of public speaking, but the bottom line is it's much easier if you are passionate.

What were the steps in terms of turning that book into a separate business for you alongside your work as a presenter?
Well, we are talking 12 years ago, which isn't that long ago, but it's a totally different digital landscape from how things are now. It all started with an online forum on which people asked me questions and I learned what people wanted, and I became an influencer in which brands paid to collaborate with me. The forum was very busy, but really it was just me phoning up businesses saying, 'I've featured you in my book, I've recommended you, can we work together and do some sort of collaboration,' and it all grew from there. I've never done affiliate links, as it felt inauthentic to me to be getting a direct margin kickback on sales. It's laughable, because everyone's an influencer now, but I was one of the first doing this sort of thing.

What other opportunities have come your way?
The interesting thing about a personal brand is the way different opportunities open up as your personal brand grows. Five years ago, I launched my Platinum Awards, which I run every year. I also morphed into training, consulting and helping the business owners I work with to get media coverage and exposure, although I do not call myself a PR agent. I started with therapists and practitioners, and I offered them some training

in the basics of how to get your message out there; for example, how to prepare for interview, how to get their pitch right and their press release right, and which aspects they should share.

Often, business owners will resist doing things, such as sending a headshot to the media, and they'll say, 'It's not about me; it's about reflexology,' and I'll say, 'It *is* about you, because there are millions of reflexologists, and millions of therapists, and millions of people who do exactly what you do, but there is only one you.' That has actually been very successful for me, and it is hugely fulfilling. I get to see people who otherwise would have literally kept themselves small and in darkness.

I could probably teach these principles to anyone, but I stick very much to my niche and holistic sector – which is where my passion is. This works because the language I use resonates with these business owners. I will suggest to people that they make a vision board for example, which will probably not resonate with everybody, but it does resonate with the therapists, authors, experts, practitioners, coaches and small business owners who offer holistic or natural products.

Was it easier because as a radio presenter you were already known and had a platform?
To some extent there's a profile there that can get you noticed. But because my presenting career and my passions are quite separate and not really connected, a lot of people follow my Imperfectly Natural brand and buy my books, and it's quite a long way down the line before they go, 'Oh, you're the person on Radio 2.' Where the two worlds come together is great; for example, I have some fabulous celebrity judges involved in the awards, such as Zoe Ball and Carry Grant, and it's wonderful for the brands to think these people are going to be trying and testing their products.

Hurdle 4: feeling uncomfortable and worrying about what people think

Brace yourself for a basic truth about Stand Out Online:

You will be pushed beyond your usual comfort zone.

What is genuinely difficult about using the Internet for personal branding is that you have to do it publicly. You have to go through a period where you feel like no one, or very few people, are reading you, watching you or engaging with you. But that's OK. That's good. You will be fine, because you already possess the one essential tool to cope with this, and by harnessing it you will have just put yourself one big step ahead of your competitors. That tool is your own resilience.

Anyone who has risen through the ranks to reach a position of even moderate success with their personal brand has relied to an extent on resilience to get there. And it's not any old resilience either; it's just the right mix of stubbornness, determination, curiosity and vision to get ideas on track and build their audience.

What I want you to do is turn it into a fully conscious strategy, to harness and exploit it in order to rise above the middle ground of 'good enough'.

When you start building your personal brand, you will encounter some pretty tough obstacles – but because I'm telling you this, you'll be ready. You will have times when no one is reading your content or watching your videos; your antennae will tell you that some people, including your friends, are talking disparagingly about you behind your back, unable to see what you're trying to achieve. You'll take a look back at the content you posted just six months ago and you will cringe, not wanting to believe that you were so naïve back then. And if you're using an agency, you might feel as if you're shelling out money for months without necessarily seeing enough concrete evidence of a positive outcome.

You will have to maintain your belief in the big picture, however. It can all begin to feel very uncomfortable indeed. And you will need to use every bit of your resilience to get through the worst times. But even just by acknowledging this, you have put yourself ahead of your closest competitor. You have dug strong foundations for success online. And while your rivals fall by the wayside, you will keep going – and your brand will keep growing.

What does this resilience look like? It is a mixture of the essential attitudes you need to become a success in anything, whether in sport or music, politics or business:

- **Vision** This is what you mapped out in Chapter 3: it's the goal and purpose that shape every decision you make, including the decision not to give in.
- **Curiosity** A detached way of reflecting on what's happening, whether good or bad. You need this drive to step back, understand what might be going wrong and to find the positive lesson in it.
- **Determination** The force that keeps you moving forward. You simply refuse to give up on your dream.

Hurdle 5: imposter syndrome

Recently, I hosted a discussion about the struggles for people embarking on the Stand Out Online process. I ran a quick poll, but I thought I already knew the top answer: it would be about the technology, the complex tech to set up and use in order to reach and manage all these media and platforms. But I was wrong.

It turns out that the biggest obstacle to gaining visibility, even among the many types of experts I help, is poor self-confidence and too many self-limiting beliefs – also known as imposter syndrome. It goes like this. If you're building your personal brand or a business around yourself, you know that you need to build your profile. But inside you there's a little voice saying, 'Who are you to think you can do this?' (Or whatever variation on this theme your little voice says.)

Apparently, imposter syndrome is particularly troublesome for women who have a desire to set up a business but fear a lack of credibility. I think this just shows how real the hurdle is, especially if women of the success and competence of, say, Nicola Mendelsohn (vice president of Europe, Middle East and Africa for Facebook), talk openly about their own experiences of imposter syndrome. Don't worry – you're in good company!

Hence, my best piece of advice is to take the next steps anyway, regardless of these feelings. One thing I have learned from writing both my books, and working with loads of fabulous (and famous) people who feel this way even though they seem to have the world at their feet, is that self-limiting beliefs must be some kind of default brain setting that once had a use for our ancestors squaring up to sabre-toothed tigers and woolly mammoths, but today it just isn't really relevant anymore.

Hurdle 6: fear of technology

There's no getting around it: if you want to build your personal brand online and you want to do it yourself without paying an agency, and if you want to be in complete 100 per cent control of your brand online, then you will need to learn tech skills. And that will involve overcoming a fear of genuinely not understanding, having to learn and enduring many hours of frustration.

Recently, I learned the software Infusionsoft. It made me feel irritated, frustrated and annoyed! I hate it when I'm on the technology learning curve. But there is a lot of déjà vu for me, because since starting my first online business in 2008, I've been down this route with lots of different software, processes and ways of thinking (because online you need to think a bit like a ball inside a pinball machine rather than in a straight line). I remember during my 'maternity leave' with my son, I'd just set up my online business Talk to the Press. (I put maternity leave in quotation marks, because obviously you don't really take maternity leave when you are self-employed, particularly if you have just started a business.)

Back then, you lived and died on SEO and I wanted my website to rank number one in Google for my main key terms. I didn't just *want* it to rank, I *needed* it to rank, otherwise I wouldn't get as many leads as I wanted. I bought a book called *Get into Bed with Google: Top Ranking Search Optimisation Techniques*. In between feeds, I read that book and tried to do every single thing in it over the course of about six months. Cue feeling hugely irritated, frustrated and overwhelmed. Some of those pages I read about 120 times in order to understand them. It didn't even work straight away! My website wasn't ranking. I was thinking: *Does this mumbo jumbo stuff even work?* And I wanted to give up. But by the end of my time off, there were only two things in that book that I hadn't managed to do myself and had to get someone else to do.

My website was now on page one of results. Over the next few months it went up to the top five positions for *all* our main keywords (reaching number one or two for most of them), and that website – no longer owned by me – has never lost its position since.

It's been the same with everything I've learned subsequently –
Google PPC (pay-per-click), WordPress, iMovie, Final Cut, Facebook
ads – reading, reading again, irritation, frustration and annoyance.

The most annoying and irritating thing is when I want to be able
to do something immediately and can't because I've got to learn
it. Argh! The frustration, the longing for a shortcut, to skip the
learning curve and to just 'know'. In the instance of Infusionsoft,
how I longed for someone to just insert the Infusionsoft disk into
my domain so that I could be an Infusionsoft ninja rather than
have to learn the blasted thing.

The good thing is that I now recognise it as just a process – and
an extremely necessary process! Unfortunately, I can't tell you
(sorry!) that you don't need to go through a tech learning curve.
Even if you are good at tech, there will be more software coming
along that you'll need to learn. But it is doable. It can be learned.

Hurdle 7: being too busy

I hear this excuse a lot! And to be fair, it is not an excuse but a
truth. People *are* busy, especially ambitious and successful people.
But creating content, building social followings and learning
takes time. How can anyone do it all? The only motivation here is
to think of the benefits of doing this and the risks of *not* doing this.
With that in mind, I'm showing you again the risks and benefits
table that we first encountered in Chapter 2.

Stand Out Online benefits and risks

Benefits of a strong personal brand	Risks of *not* having a personal brand
More sales	No, or low, trust
Higher profile	Bad first and lasting impression
More influence	Less leverage and influence
Greater trust	Lower sales/profits/influence
More connections	Less memorable
Greater ability to connect to other influential people	Harder to differentiate from the competition
Ability to create change/promote good causes	Being considered as plain, boring and unremarkable
	Being the only tramp at the party

Hurdle 8: consistency

Let's think for a moment about the world of big corporations. They rely on the brand awareness that they create – it is fundamental to growing market loyalty. And the instantly recognisable, visible aspect of this branding is paramount. Recognition breeds confidence, and confidence breeds loyalty. Once we have decided what our preferred brand means to us, we look for that brand on the high street and we continue to choose that brand.

In personal branding, though, consistency is not entirely wrapped up in logos and colour schemes. It goes on to include the things that you say, share and do, *and* it is also about consistency of publishing.

If you launch a (great) website here, you can get more bookings or sell more products there. You get some media coverage here, you have more credibility for your social media followers there. You consistently blog and create content here, you get more following there. You build your social media following here, you get a book deal there. You get a book deal here, you are asked to appear in a brand video there. And all of this gets you more website traffic there. But you've got to keep at it! You've got to be consistent. Keep creating, keep posting, keep sharing, keep talking.

What I witness is that there is no straight line or overnight path to standing out, being more visible, getting more opportunities or whatever it is that you want, *but* results do come from sustained, consistent effort and putting yourself or your business out there across numerous platforms.

MY STORY Dr Buck Parker: 'I committed to vlogging for one year and saw the benefits much sooner'

Dr Buck Parker is a general and trauma surgeon at St Mark's Hospital in Salt Lake City in Utah. He sees patients with hernias, appendicitis, gallbladder disease, skin and soft-tissue infections, bowel obstructions and colon disease as well as traumatic injuries. He is also a public speaker, and a medical expert for the media after building up his profile online following a 2015 appearance as a castaway and medical expert on NBC and Bear Grylls' reality TV series *The Island*.

Dr Parker, you're a working doctor, but about a year ago, you started vlogging and building a social media presence – what was the plan?

I've always been interested in the internet since building a website and selling some products back in 2007. For the past few years, I've just been working in my regular salaried job, and I wanted to do something different. I decided to commit to building my personal brand via video and social media for one year and see what happened. At this moment I'm around seven months in and I've built my Instagram to over 50,000 followers and my YouTube to over 20,000 subscribers. The one season I was on *The Island* on television helped to boost the following, because as the programme airs in places such as India, Africa and the Philippines, I get more followers.

What do you talk about?
Well, at first I didn't know what I would talk about, so I just talked about the things I saw in the hospital (I have a schedule based on a 12-hour working day, 7am to 7pm, and I do 7 or 10 days in a row and then have days off). Then people started asking me questions about becoming a doctor, and my focus shifted to helping medical students and people interested in becoming doctors. I'm no perfect student myself – I ended up at a Caribbean medical school instead of a US one because I messed around in college too much and I didn't really have direction until I was a bit older. I didn't know how to study in high school and college. I did poorly and I thought I was dumb, but I wasn't dumb, I just didn't know how to study.

My message has become about helping others to realise that you can get to where I am, even if you sometimes go off track. After I was on *The Island*, people told me that I'd inspired them, and I felt that I'd made an impact. I would have loved to do more TV, but as a doctor I can't just get onto a load of reality shows – that wouldn't feel right. So I decided, this is who I am, this is my message and I chose myself, and now I help and positively impact people via social media.

How does it change your day-to-day life as a doctor?
I'll just be doing my job in the intensive-care unit and people will say that they found me on Instagram and are following me. That's cool. But I also get negative feedback. I have nurses

telling me that other doctors don't really like what I am doing. Doctors can be quite old-fashioned and don't get social media. One cardiac surgeon told me, 'Doctors shouldn't be on the Internet.' But at this point I have thousands of positive messages sent to me, which I could show my CEO and say, 'How is this a bad idea?'

How do you fit this in with your job?

I publish about four videos a week. I've got more efficient and faster at recording as time has gone on. I have some guys I found via Upwork who edit the footage for me. I just record it and send it to them. It used to take me a while to come up with ideas, but now I get ideas from my followers, who ask things like, 'How do you study?' or 'How do you stay motivated?' and I just answer their questions.

The main thing about Instagram and YouTube is about being consistent, which can be a difficult thing to do for anything. I have to schedule it in and give it time; I have to think about what posts I need for the week ahead and plan what I am going to do.

What's the hardest part?

It's when you are starting out and creating content – and then taking the ridicule for a while. People snigger and say, 'You're on Instagram. I see you posting on Instagram about this,' or 'You're the YouTube guy.' So they snigger and laugh a bit, and then when you hit 50,000 followers, they are like, 'Oh, *you're* the Instagram guy!' and their tone is completely different and they want to know how you do it.

There is a window during which it sucks and you are by yourself. But I think that is the same with any business, because you have this vision and nobody can really see your vision. You can try to explain it, and some people will get it, but most people won't. Some will even think: *That will never work.* I don't have great advice apart from saying that the fastest way to build it is to be super-authentic – whatever that means to you.

What's the long-term plan?
I have a few. My biggest aspiration would be to create a free online medical school for students in developing countries. I'd also like to create an online academy or programme for the people I am helping now. There's also a massive opportunity for doctors who understand how this can work for us. People think that doctors shouldn't be marketing, but all doctors have competition. And it's not necessarily about getting patients either. Here in the US, the government hires rock stars to tell people in adverts not to drink and smoke – why can't doctors be influencers and spread this message too? We have credibility behind us.

Tash's Takeaways

- Personal branding relies on your own energy and drive to make it happen.
- Self-made hurdles can be a threat to your success.
- Common hurdles include chasing shiny objects, giving up too early, not living your passion, being scared of technology and worrying about what other people think.
- Try listing three of your own hurdles and planning how to overcome them.
- Consistency and determination are the keys to overcoming all these hurdles.

PART FOUR

Scale

Do you remember back in Chapter 2 we talked about your tiers to influence? This was about all the different groups of people you can reach as you move from one tier to the next. In this section of the book we're going to be talking about getting the most out of tiers 5 and 6 – mainstream media and reaching more people online with paid traffic.

Media Coverage – The Media
as it Stands Today

It's through combining online visibility with traditional and online media coverage in magazines, newspapers, websites, podcasts, video, radio and TV that your customers and clients consume that you are truly able to turbo-charge your visibility and increase your credibility and positioning.

The question is: how can you get yourself into mainstream media publications and outlets?

Securing media coverage isn't always easy, which is why, ever since the advent of mass media, there has been an accompanying and thriving PR industry to help people and businesses work out the right angles for their products and offerings, and to pitch them accordingly. Of course, times have changed, and looking back – and not necessarily with rose-tinted glasses – it was all much simpler then.

For a long time, there have been more publications and media outlets in existence than one can ever hope to be in, but now the routes to coverage are limitless. Not only do we have the traditional media but also the expanding world of online media and influencers too. Even within a single geographical region, the limited forms of print media are being replaced by unlimited online media, ranging from blogs (some of which have more readers than traditional print media) to news websites. And now the potential reach is global. Yet, at the same time, everything is still as it was. Just because there are now hundreds of thousands of media outlets, instead of a few hundred, it doesn't mean that you have to be on all of them. Remember, it's quality over quantity, and the match between outlet and audience, that counts.

Much of what we've covered so far in terms of the Stand Out Online process has the dual-pronged benefit of making you more attractive to journalists. And if you get your digital exposure right and master topical thought leadership, the chances are you will find journalists coming to you. But what I am covering now is how you can go to journalists and pitch to them.

The three key reasons why you should want press coverage

1. **To get yourself in front of a new group of people** who aren't reading your social media posts, who haven't yet found you by themselves. In other words, to jump into a pool where there is a huge audience and give yourself a chance to be seen.
2. **To draw traffic to your website** and reap the SEO benefits. With pretty much every mainstream media outlet having an online version, links to your website/social channels from trusted media channels have powerful SEO benefits.
3. **To feed back to your existing audiences.** Yes, press coverage is all about getting yourself and your messages out there in front of people by being featured in newspapers and on radio and television. And it definitely works. If you get press coverage and then you add it right on the front of your website with a stamp saying, 'As seen in ...', then old press coverage will continue to have a positive effect on your positioning and personal brand, even years

after the original article has been forgotten. Do you remember how, back in Chapter 3, the serial entrepreneur Carl Reader spoke about how press coverage helped him to retain clients as well as attract new ones? This is because of the implied credibility and status that come from being featured in the mainstream media.

MY STORY Vicki Psarias: 'Journalists and researchers need you to make their lives easy'

Vicki Psarias, aka Honest Mum, is a leading British lifestyle and parenting influencer in the UK. A former filmmaker, she worked as a TV and film director before setting up her blog while on maternity leave in November 2010. She is the author of *Mumboss* and has done collaborations with brands including Jet2.com, and Jamie Oliver, among others. Vicki often appears in magazines, newspapers and on TV programmes, such as *Good Morning Britain* and *Sky News*, debating topical issues around motherhood, tech and work–life balance.

How does mainstream media help your personal brand?
All influencers have to build their brand from dot. You start as an unknown. The only way to build is to constantly and consistently share your voice, improving the way you write, film and photograph as you go and grow, and to market yourself. You could be the most talented person in the world, but without PR, no one will know who you are! Success requires tenacity and a thick skin too. When people say no to you, you must never let that stop you. You must keep going until you receive a yes. The media is desperate for new voices, so it's about finding a way to stand out. I know people who start blogs and weeks later are discovered by researchers and producers for mainstream TV. Talent will always

rise to the top. It might take a few months or several years, but opportunity favours the bold and those who don't quit!

How does being topical help you get media?

The media loves topical debate, and I've always written honest opinion pieces – I even have a category on my blog called 'Opinion', and although the posts are not always tied into the news per se, they do reflect my own experiences, some of which are naturally newsworthy; for example, I wrote a piece about how, despite my obsession with the online world, my most meaningful connections exist thanks to regular phone calls or in real-life meet-ups. I asserted that the virtual world will never replace reading emotion face-to-face and friendships/business relationships formed in person. It resonated with many.

This is because I *am* my audience. I'm a thirty-something working mother sharing my world, which naturally mirrors that of my readers, so it has a natural resonance with them. As a blogger, you can create your own media platform by writing about the things that matter to you, whatever they might be. You are your niche. You. Let your passion lead you.

For example, I'll write about the juggle of motherhood, and I'll honestly share how I work and raise a family – the down-sides and the good – and I'm staggered by the response: the retweets, the views, the commentary and debate. I only write about subjects I feel strongly about. Blogging is a form of therapy and/or a means to offer insight and advice to others after much trial and error experienced myself or to start up a conversation. This honesty has led to me being regarded as pioneering and influential. It's the integrity of my content and my character, as well as the way I share with abandon, that has created trust with my audience and that of even bigger platforms when my work is shared on television and so on.

I appeared on *Sky News* after writing a piece about imposter syndrome, which had been inspired by Sheryl Sandberg's book *Lean In*, which was out at the time. We don't live in a vacuum, so I reflect and respond to the media, arts, the economy, etc. and how they affect my world directly, which also connects with my readers.

Any advice on speaking and pitching to journalists?
It helps to have an archive of content for the media to see so that when you speak to them you can show them examples of your work. The same applies when you work with brands. Remember, these researchers and journalists need you to make their lives easy, they need to cast you on the news, they need to ask you for quotes, they need experts for their programmes, so be searchable, embrace SEO and optimise your site, be active on social media and ensure you have a contact form on your blog so that the gatekeepers can find and email you. Crucially, make a commitment to developing a strong argument in your work and a substantiated opinion so that when opportunity knocks (or you go knocking yourself), you're ready with the gold they want.

The two simple truths

Two simple premises are the basis of what I do for my clients and they should be at the heart of your media promotion strategy, too. They are based on what I know from having spent almost two decades in journalism, from securing dozens of front-page stories, thousands of print articles and hours of TV coverage for my clients. And they are:

1. Journalists are very simple creatures. The more you can make their life easy, the more success you'll have. As this chapter goes on, you are going to learn how simply journalists see things. But to give you a flavour, all they are thinking is: *Is this a good story?* and *Are there any good pictures?*
2. People (journalists and readers) are attracted by things that look good and that engage them (emotionally, intellectually, visually) and that are topical.

As an agency, we don't even consider taking on any clients for PR unless they have addressed the issues that we have already covered in this book to do with positioning, having a mission and purpose, and having a great website and photography. And that is because journalists only give the matter limited attention, and if you haven't got these things right, the chances of you catching a journalist's eye are radically reduced. I am telling you from years and years of pitching stories to newspapers and securing front-page deals that journalists want an easy life.

Tash's tips

It takes longer and is more effort to convince a journalist through words. It's easier to show them via a great site with good pictures. This is where your online forward-facing appearance really matters. If they land on your website and see professional photography of you, that's a tick in their box. You've even saved them money on a photoshoot, as they can just use your photos. Remember, the journalist is always thinking: *Is this a good story, is it relevant, appealing? Does it have good pictures?*

How to secure coverage in local and niche media

I can't even begin to tell you how much I love local media. Think about local newspapers, local radio, regional television and local magazines – and the good news is that it's easier to secure coverage in local and niche, and to do it repeatedly, than it is to do the same with national media. It also works well.

Tash's tips

We recently handled the publicity for the BBC presenter Cerys Matthews, who has her own festival, The Good Life Experience, in North Wales. We secured her a ton of coverage. A lot of it was mainstream national papers, but do you know what worked best? The local stuff. Small local newspapers in North Wales, the *Liverpool Echo* and interviews on BBC Radio Herefordshire. All these outlets were thrilled to either have content that we had created for them or to be able to interview Cerys, and to be able to use our beautiful imagery, which we provided for free.

We were obviously thrilled to have them promote our local event to the people actually living where it would be happening. It's all very well to think: *I want to be in national papers or I want to be in Grazia.* You know, *Grazia* is really read by an urban crowd, many of whom are in London and the south-east, and, realistically, how many people from London are going to travel to north Wales to attend such an event? Not that many, but how many people from the *Daily Post* are going to think: *Oh, actually this event is on Saturday, I'll head down there*? A lot more. You can really see the power of how it converts.

Wherever you live, you'll have local media. And whatever you do, you'll have niche media. Let's look at both more closely.

Your local media

Local media will most likely comprise free magazines, news-papers, radio stations and websites. Start diligently collecting them, listing them and looking at what they do. Don't just rely on looking them up online. Actually get them, and get to know them. Familiarity is the key. We're going to be coming to pitching shortly, but you need to start understanding your local media and the sorts of features they run. They are pretty much always looking for stories featuring people from the local area.

You can target local media in the area you grew up in, the areas you studied in and the areas in which you now live. Look out for regular pages that might suit your needs. Do they profile local individuals doing interesting things each Tuesday? Do they have a 'what's on' section that you could be in? Grab a pen and list your local media, and include publications from where you studied and where you grew up as well.

Niche media

This is media centred more closely on a specific topic; for example, using Cerys Matthews again: I can get her national media and I can get her local media, but equally powerful is niche media. Her festival is all about the great outdoors and craft, so the niche media in this field is publications such as *BBC Gardeners' World* magazine, festival guides and *BBC Countryfile* magazine, which are more targeted on the area of interest. Niche media is also easier to get into than mainstream media, but it still has the large audiences and prestigious feel.

Make a note of the industry/niche media that you'd love to be featured in.

Online media brands

An online media brand is an organisation that considers itself a bona fide media outlet but has never had a print edition. There are many online magazines that usually started as one man in his bedroom but have become large global media brands with large teams working on them. Many online brands have far more readers than traditional print publications (the difference is, their readers aren't necessarily as focused as they are often surfing/reading on the move). Still, online coverage can really drive traffic, interest, improve your SEO and raise awareness.

Online media can also be relatively easy to get, because online media brands really, really need content, and lots of it. In that sense, if you provide them with content, all the journalists are thinking is: *Fantastic! Job done. I can relax for one minute before I have to create my next bit of content.* They churn through more content than print outlets, so there is more opportunity there.

Online media is always looking for interesting, diverse, fairly short, bright and breezy content, and particularly pieces that are photo-led and that might go viral. Make a note of the online media brands that you would like to be featured by.

Influencer media

We've already talked in this book about becoming an influencer. But there's also the potential to be featured by other influencers, whether that's on their blog, podcast, YouTube show or social posts. Influencers, particularly those with thousands of followers, *are* the media too. An influencer in your sector might have many more readers than your local newspaper, for example. Top bloggers sit firmly among traditional media in the hierarchy.

There is a huge trust benefit to being featured by an already trusted blogger. Just as brands love the endorsement of being featured by a trusted influencer, so should you, as a personal brand. Your strategy and approach should be different; because most influencers don't have editors, you'll be dealing with the influencer directly. They are also not driven by the news, per se, but by the niche of their blog or message.

Although you can work with influencers as a collaboration (where you pay them), just like in newspapers, you have paid adverts and free editorial coverage, you *can* get free coverage from bloggers if you approach them in the right way with the right pitch. Another way to do this is to network with influencers online and build 'virtual' friendships so that they invite you to be featured by them. Parenting influencers have whole online communities where they all support and encourage each other, and many end up meeting and becoming friends in the real world, too.

Bearing in mind that I'm going to show you in the next chapter exactly how to pitch, make a note of which influencers you would love to feature you or interview you. In the case of online networking, you start by liking and commenting on the posts of those you want to build friendships with.

National media

It's time to get into the *Daily Mail*, *Telegraph*, or to get invited to *Sky News* or the *This Morning* sofa and into glossy magazines.

National media is, of course, brilliant for reaching new audiences, particularly big audiences. It brings traffic to your website, it brings people to your physical business (if there is one) and, most importantly, it's fantastic for your brand and positioning and for giving you credibility. National media journalists are looking for strong stories, topical stories, great photos and stories that tick every single box. They have a much higher bar with regard to what makes a story for them, so they will want great photos, strong angles, a topical point and a strong headline.

Surprisingly, national publicity won't always result in a flurry of traffic or sales – although, of course, it can. I had the experience of appearing on *BBC Breakfast* to talk about my previous business and, as a result, so many new enquiries flooded in that I had to hire two people whose sole role was to sort through them. But, generally, if you were to get coverage in a magazine, newspaper, TV or radio, a potential customer will have to remember your name or business name, go to their computer, google your business name and find your website. As you can see, it is a much longer process for people to actually find you than it is if you appear in online media.

Which national media outlets do you feel would be perfect for you? Write them down on your wish list.

Tash's Takeaways

- The media as it stands today is divided into local media, niche media, online media, influencer media and national media, and it includes magazines, newspapers, websites, podcasts, video, online platforms, radio and TV.
- A comprehensive strategy would be to secure coverage across a range of media types and formats, although some are easier to get into than others.
- Remember, the true list of where you can be featured will be endless, so start by narrowing it down to a list of those you would most like to be featured in and those that will be the most beneficial for your own goals.

Pitching *You* to the Media
Step-by-Step

When you're thinking about publicity, it's common to believe that your own story about what you or your business does is enough to capture the media's interest. The bad news is: it probably isn't. And even if it is, you need to present it in a certain way to capture a journalist's (or even an influencer's) attention.

When I was running my online business, Talk to the Press, I secured acres of coverage for some of the most (at first glance) non-stories ever. We were working for ordinary members of the public, so we really had to dig deep and work on angles and ride topical themes to prepare pitches to take something from ordinary to placeable. Let's find out more.

Seven ways to turn a non-story into a story

I'm not suggesting that what you have to say or do isn't helpful or impactful, but you need to understand how to pitch yourself in a way that will capture a journalist's attention.

1. Make it topical

I've stressed the importance of topicality several times in this book, and pitching to media is another reason to nail how to be topical. Whatever you pitch needs to have a hook or a peg, or a reason. Typically a hook ties into a new development, or take, on a topic, or something topical that fits in with what is being promoted. This happened when I finished my last book *The Million Dollar Blog*. I was working with the publisher to promote it when suddenly a new piece of research came into the news saying that blogging and vlogging was now the career of choice for under twenty-fives in the UK. This 'peg' was a gift from the gods, as it allowed me to secure coverage on Radio 2 (twice), the *Daily Mail*, *Grazia*, *Closer* and *British Airways High Life* magazines, and numerous other media outlets. The book hit the Amazon bestsellers lists straight away – and really it was all thanks to looking out for a topical peg and using one when it arose.

2. If there is no hook or peg, add a sense of timeliness

There needs to be some sense of timeliness to the idea you're pitching to the press. Why do they need to feature you and your business right now? Does your idea tie into something timely like a holiday or national event?

3. Make it more visual

This comes back to being prepared with photos/angles/text that journalists can see instantly. This is where having great photos of yourself matters so much. I've had not very good stories make it into print on the basis that the pictures are good and the subject looks glamorous. You need that great set of photos in which you look the part, and you're not wearing sunglasses or a dodgy coat or hat. You might think this sounds odd, but you'd be amazed how many people send photos of themselves wearing sunglasses.

A photo of you with sunglasses is not going to make it into print! Mainstream media has a no-sunglasses rule and a no-hats rule. Send a great-quality photograph that can be published straight-away and that makes them think: *Yes, this person looks the part.*

4. Make the journalists' lives easy

I don't want to give you the impression that journalists are lazy, but the more copy you can write for them, the more quotes you can provide for them to copy and paste into their pieces, and the more you can send them in the direction of the relevant topical studies that are the peg for your pitch, the better.

5. Make it free

Continuing from the above, all mainstream media budgets are declining. This means that they want stories at very low cost and more preparation done before it is pitched. Of course, publications still do photoshoots and send reporters out and about, but the more you can provide a good story that they don't have to invest resources in, the more they will consider it.

6. Make it stronger

In the media, we talk about how strong a story is – it's a word that we all understand, but the media definition probably doesn't appear in any dictionary. It's the feeling a story gives you, whether that is shock, surprise, a raised eyebrow, the thought, *Wow this is interesting or incredible,* or how emotive it is. A story can be heartbreaking, but if it is strong, a journalist will feel excited and enthusiastic about covering it.

Sometimes, strong stories just can't be placed for no clear

reason at all, but generally, if you can't place a pitch, it's because the subject matter just isn't strong enough for the outlet in question. Don't take it personally; instead, work on strengthening the angle and becoming more topical, more interesting and more research based.

7. Make it specific

Every publication is different. Over the years, I've blasted out press releases to thousands of journalists, and I've pitched hundreds and hundreds of stories to journalists one by one. You *always* get the best results by pitching a specific story and angle to a specific journalist, and by making them feel that not only have you brought a specific story just to them, but you've also given them an angle and outlook that works perfectly for them.

How to find the right journalist to pitch to

Now that your story angle is sorted, you need to find the right journalist to pitch to. Obviously, all agencies like mine subscribe to databases and services such as Gorkana, a media database that costs about £3,000 per year; and Response Source alerts, which costs about £1,500 per year. Both of these tell me what journalists are looking for. And both yield enough results and save enough time to be worth the investment, but they are not essential, so don't you go thinking that in order to do your own PR you need to subscribe to these tools.

Even with these tools, our best results are secured through old-fashioned approaches. Here is a step-by-step guide:

1. Get a copy of the publication you want to be in.
2. Familiarise yourself with that publication, and get a list of names of journalists who have done articles along the lines of your story.
3. Google those journalists, find them on Twitter and LinkedIn, and check that they are still there.
4. *Phone them* and check that they are the right person to pitch your idea to.
5. Follow up with an email containing the pitch.

If we can't get the name of someone specific online or in the publication, then we use another old-fashioned approach, which is phoning the publication, asking to speak to the editorial team, news desk or features desk, and saying, 'Hello, who would be the right person to pitch a story about ... ?', then getting that person's name and email address.

You see, both editors and journalists tend to pigeonhole themselves. It will be person A who covers this and person B who covers that. You are more likely to be listened to if you pitch to the correct person.

Tash's tips

Within journalism and PR, there is always talk of 'contacts' and, of course, it does help to know journalists and have great relationships with them. Those relationships make them more likely to consider your pitch properly or try to find a way to make it work for them. But following the process above will enable you to quickly build your own contacts.

The #journorequests hashtag, and other helpful hashtags on Twitter

Journalists love Twitter and use it to find information for articles they are writing and programmes they are creating. And that means you must be there, too. You don't, however, have to follow 1,000 journalists and spend all day frantically reading their tweets. Instead, there are a number of key hashtags (used to organise content around a certain topic) that you should follow in order to interact with journalists and influencers who are looking for you (but don't know you yet). Just search the following hashtags each day and see if there are any requests you can respond to.

- **#journorequests** This is used by journalists looking for information, case studies, expert quotes or products for articles they are writing.
- **#prrequest** is similar to #journorequests and was created for reporters to connect with information and experts.
- **#bloggerrequest** This hashtag connects website and brands with bloggers. It's helpful for targeting influencers.
- **#helpareporter** Help A Reporter Out (HARO) is a publicity service created in 2008 by public-relations expert Peter Shankman. Shankman started HARO as a Facebook page where journalists, writers and bloggers posted daily PR opportunities for anyone to access and respond to. Follow the hashtag on Twitter or sign up for emails at helpareporter.com.

What to say to a journalist when you pitch

Here's a step-by-step guide to pitching to a journalist:

1. **Find the name of a journalist** who has written something similar to what you are pitching. Or phone their main number and ask for the news desk, or ask for someone to speak to who works in news.

2. **Say (and this is now you talking to a journalist):** 'I am phoning from ... Who would be the right person to pitch a story to about ... ?'

3. **When you have established who the right person is, ask to speak to them.** This person may or may not take your call. If they do take your call, they are guaranteed to ask you to send an email. But you *must* make the call and personalised pitch, and find the right journalist. They get so many pitches each day that you want to be able to differentiate your pitch by saying on your follow-up email, 'Hello, nice to speak to you just now', or in the worst-case scenario leave a voicemail saying, 'Hello, I understand you are the person who deals with charity stories. I just tried to call but you're away from your desk.' Make sure you already have your email prepared so that it can be sent off as soon as possible after talking to the journalist while the idea is fresh in their mind.

4. **Talk quickly and confidently on the phone!** This is how journalists talk, and they hate it if people sound nervous or scared. Make yourself sound like them and that you know what you are doing. They also tend to talk bizarrely fast, so talk fast back to them. Get to the point quickly.

5. **If you're pitching to a local media outlet, stress your local connections**. This is so important. Local media outlets are only interested in local stories. They are not interested in anything else. You've got to have a local connection, to have grown up in the area, gone to school there, have your business there, or live there. There's got to be a local connection.

6. **Explain why you're topical**. Dive in on a debate, join a discussion, or create news through hosting an event. Make yourself topical. Survey your customers, or release statistics, or create a new catchy product that the local papers can promote.

7. **Apply a personal touch**. Say, 'I loved the article you wrote yesterday about … It made me think that you would be interested in …'

8. **There is no need to be scared of journalists**. If they are rude, just remember, they are fearful for their jobs and under serious pressure, so don't take it personally.

Here is an example email to a journalist or commissioning editor:

Hi [first name],

Good to talk to you just now/I just called and spoke to your colleague, [xxx], who said you are the person to speak to about [xxx].

As promised, here is the information I said I'd send you about [xxx].

[Then get to the point of what you are asking for]

Would you be interested in interviewing me or doing a story on this?

Could I write a guest article for you?

I have a lot of wonderful photos that you'd be able to use in any article. You can find out more about me on my website.

Let me know what you think.

Best,

[your first name]

[your website's URL]

MY STORY **Bradley Simmonds**: 'I've invested in PR to give my brand additional reach'

Bradley Simmonds is a health and well-being influencer on a mission to motivate and inspire people to improve their lifestyle through the power of regular exercise and a stable, nutritious diet. In four years, his following has grown to over 235k followers who love his 'Get It Done' approach.

Bradley, where did you start?

It all started four years ago. I'd been playing football for Queens Park Rangers on a professional contract, but I had to give it up because I had so many injuries. It was a big blow for me after wanting to become a professional football player. Things didn't work out for me, and I had to be realistic with myself and find a different route.

From being injured so much, I'd learnt a lot about the body, how it works and how to regain strength, how to regain fitness and all about nutrition. That took me down the route of becoming a personal trainer. I thought to myself that I could use Instagram to do something really positive, so I started posting videos, fitness pictures and regular posts on fitness and health.

I must have had only about 400 followers at the time, and

that was just friends and family from where I live, and I'm sure they thought: *What is he doing?*

Instagram messenger was a vital tool for you in building your brand, wasn't it?

Yes, I then direct-messaged every celebrity I could think of that had a good following, saying, 'Do you want to train for free in return for social media posts?' I even messaged Victoria Beckham and thought: *Why not? I am going to give it my best shot, and you never know who is going to come back.* It takes only one person to come back.

Out of about 100 I messaged, one girl, Sophie Hermann, from *Made in Chelsea* said yes. Within a few weeks of training Sophie, I was training eight of the *Made in Chelsea* girls, and they were all posting about me regularly. I managed to get to 10,000 followers within a few months.

Then, out of the blue, I got a message from John Terry, saying, 'Can you train my wife?' From there, I got a phone call from Jamie Redknapp and trained him and Louise Redknapp as well. I didn't know, but Louise had been following me, as she'd seen me training Lucy Watson from *Made in Chelsea*. There were so many eyes on me, and all because of Instagram. You never know who is following.

Of course, there was so much luck involved, but if you don't ask you don't get – that's my philosophy. Even now, if someone big follows me, I immediately direct-message them asking if they want training. If they say yes, then that's great, and if they say no, then that's no problem.

What's your strategy for growth?

To invest in the brand and get the help I need. When I hit 40,000 followers, I took on a manager, Issy from Insanity Group. What is great is that they negotiate ambassador roles, and they are so much better at it than me. Back then, I was agreeing to do things for £300 that the agency could immediately get me £3,000 for. Asking for money and knowing your own value is really hard.

I've also invested in terms of photography and videographers, and have a PR, Jack Freud, to help me with press coverage. PR really pushes me out and gets me on the radio, into magazines and allows me to express my philosophy to more people. The first time I got press coverage was when I first started working with the *Made in Chelsea* girls. We would train in parks and the next minute we would have paparazzi everywhere. The *Daily Mail* will literally stalk my Instagram feed and screenshot my Instagram stories and use them. Getting press coverage gives me credibility and new reach. Some of the best moments I've had have been having double-page spreads in *Men's Health* and being in *GQ* magazine. I never thought I'd be in *GQ* – it's iconic.

What's your long-term plan?
I don't want to become a celebrity. Throughout my career I have been asked to go on *Made in Chelsea* and *Love Island*, and I have constantly said no. I'd love to train actors for big movie roles, such as training the lead in the next *Black Panther* film. I'm 24 years old and buying my first house next month, which is amazing. I'd like to have longevity, own my own gym and healthy restaurants. I've got a book coming out – my English teacher would never have thought I'd become an author.

What's your advice to people starting to build their brand online?
So many people are worried about what's next. They don't take that risk and then they get stuck, and then one day they wished they had done something different, I would say: go with your

gut, get out of your comfort zone, because you can always go back into that comfort zone. Express yourself, challenge yourself, set big goals and really go for it, and be consistent and hard working, because if you don't have a good work ethic you won't go anywhere. And you will probably have to sacrifice nights out and going away. You have got to sacrifice these things to be successful. If I can do this, anyone can, it just takes hard work and consistency.

Understand, and use, the news cycle

When you're pitching a story, you must remember that you are doing so against a much more powerful backdrop: the news cycle (we're back to topicality again). This means that there are good and bad times to pitch, moments when you may have every journalist wanting to talk to you and other days when the same people couldn't care less.

In the story-brokering world, where I had my previous business, we would even see the value of a story (how much it was worth) dramatically rise and fall according to the news cycle. High-value stories would plummet because the storyteller hesitated about talking, and low-value stories would suddenly become worth thousands because the subject had become topical. This won't be the case for you in the Stand Out Online process, and the price of a story is irrelevant to you, as you're placing your story for free. *But* the news cycle will still affect you, in positive and negative ways.

Tash's tips

At various times, the news will be completely overtaken by a huge story, such as Brexit or a big disaster, and there will be no point in pitching. Even if you are pitching to a publication that doesn't particularly cover the huge issue in question, I would say that it's a bad time to pitch, and this is because all journalists, no matter what publications they are on, *love* a huge story. They'll all be distracted, overexcited and talking about nothing else. It's just not the right time for you to get their attention. Fridays, particularly Friday afternoons, are also not a good time to get a journalist's attention.

Now, if something comes into the news that you suddenly think, *I know about this*, then the very opposite is true. If what *you* do becomes topical, you need to ride this wave and pitch while there is interest there. One of my clients is a lawyer, and no sooner had we started working with him, when, through luck, offshore accounts were making the headlines. That was the perfect time for us to strike with his views, as he knows about this – and lo and behold, everyone is looking for 'experts to talk about offshore accounts'. He was on *Sky News*, literally, within a few hours.

Additional considerations when pitching

Much of what we have just covered applies equally to pitching to influencers and online media; however, there are a few additional considerations and best practice, which I've summarised over the final pages of this chapter.

- Make it personal and a good fit to that influencer. Refer back to posts you've read on their blog that you like.
- Make your pitch something you know they would *want* to write about, regardless of your pitch. It needs to resonate with the blogger, and refer to why it resonates in the pitch.
- Include great research, or make it funny, so that it feels like a good story.
- Products and stories that are particularly enterprising or show great initiative are more likely to be featured.
- Start by posting comments on the blogs that you want to guest post for or be featured on. Every professional blogger reads the comments posted on their own blogs, so this makes your name familiar to them. Establish a relationship without pushing your agenda: send emails saying you enjoyed their post or offering to help in some way without asking for anything in return. Finally, you can pitch for your own post.
- You might have to pitch multiple times before you are successful.
- Also remember that the better your relationship with the blog owner is, the higher the chance that your pitch and article will be accepted.

Here is an example email to an influencer:

Hi [first name],
   I'm a long-time reader of your great blog [blog name].
   I would love to write a guest post for you.
   Here are some suggested headlines:

- [Headline 1]
- [Headline 2]
- [Headline 3]

My previous articles have been published on:

- [URL article 1]
- [URL article 2]
- [URL article 3]

Let me know what you think.
Best,
[your first name]
[your website's URL]

Tash's Takeaways

- Make sure you have the strongest possible angle or hook for your pitch before you send it.
- There are seven key tactics to improving the strength of your pitch; even if you think your pitch is strong, check it against these and see if you can improve it.
- The #journorequests hashtag and Twitter are your friends when it comes to your media outreach strategy and creating a snowball of coverage.
- Whoever you are pitching to, you *will* need to keep pitching, and may even need to try many times in order to be successful.

Advanced Personal-Brand
Growth Hacking

The biggest and most visible personal brands tend to be supported by a very clear and comprehensive integrated and holistic online marketing strategy that includes social media, free downloads, list building, Google, Facebook and Instagram adverts, marketing funnels and product staircases. They seem to be able to reach everyone, but in most instances success has been achieved through a strategy that I call 'focusing on your own little world'. Essentially, it involves building an audience/database and continuing to increase its size, while retargeting those who are already inside that audience/database.

Your minimum viable audience

We are going to be talking about some of the more advanced techniques for doing the above in this chapter. But first, I want to share something Seth Godin wrote on his blog about searching for the 'minimum viable audience'. (I featured Seth in my previous book.) This concept follows the principles of the well-known business concept, the minimum viable product (MVP), a development technique in which a new product or website is developed and launched with only sufficient features to enable it to be used and to get feedback. The final, complete set of features is designed and developed after considering the feedback from initial users. Seth said:

> Of course everyone wants to reach the maximum audience. To be seen by millions, to maximise return on investment, to have a huge impact. And so we fall over ourselves to dumb it down, average it out, pleasing everyone and anyone.
>
> You can see the problem.
>
> When you seek to engage with everyone, you rarely delight anyone. And if you're not the irreplaceable, essential, one-of-a-kind changemaker, you never get a chance to engage with the market.
>
> The solution is simple but counter-intuitive: stake out the smallest market you can imagine. The smallest market that can sustain you, the smallest market you can adequately serve. This goes against everything you learned in capitalism school, but in fact, it's the simplest way to matter.
>
> When you have your eyes firmly focused on the minimum viable audience, you will double down on all the changes you seek to make. Your quality, your story and your impact will all get better.
>
> And then, ironically enough, the word will spread.

I see this very clearly when launching client's advertising campaigns on Facebook and Instagram. The particular power of these two networks is to retarget (that is, remarket to individuals) based on a particular action they've taken, and you do this using someone's email address or via having tracked them on your website using the Facebook pixel. If you are an e-commerce site, you would run an ad campaign with very precise messaging just for those who have added your product to their cart but not checked out. For a personal brand, you might run a similar remarketing campaign featuring precise messaging to those who have signed up for your webinar, but not attended it.

At the beginning of campaigns, the audiences are extremely small – so small that we will take time to manually add one or two emails into custom audiences on Facebook. (These are at the heart of Facebook's artificial learning and are fundamental for running successful ad campaigns on Facebook – more on this shortly.)

It's very easy to wonder why we are bothering. Because in the vastness of the Internet, what's one person? It's easy to think this way in the beginning when you are going wild with excitement over Internet marketing and imagining how you are going to reach the WHOLE. ENTIRE. WORLD.

But it leads to no results whatsoever!

Remember the value of a single person

If you think about it, one person in a one-to-one meeting, five people in a room, or 50 people in a room – every one of them is significant. Things are so skewed in our minds nowadays. We all think 50 likes on a photo is rubbish (in the online world) but 50 people is *way* more than came to my last birthday party, for example (in the real world). What makes a difference is when you remember that what you see as just a number is actually a real person. Stop thinking, *50 people! That's terrible*! And instead think: *OK, 50 people, that's a roomful. I have a chance here to give them a message*, and treat that one person who has signed up for your webinar with the same intent as you would the one person you might meet for a meeting. Focus on those people who are actually interested, rather than the bazillions you imagined you could reach on your first days, or even months or years, of promoting your business online (erm, if only it were that easy).

It's not about reaching everyone, it's about creating your own little world of people who are right for your offer and who are interested in you. And you know what? It's amazing how quickly it grows when you focus on just your own little world and really make your message great for them, and demonstrate to them how you can help.

Six months ago I was doing the above, building up custom audiences inside Facebook for two very different clients. Now we have 300,000 people either in or on the fringes of our 'little world' for the first client and 6,000 people on the other client's email list, which had stood at precisely zero when we began. From small acorns ...

How to build an email list

Email list-building – the process of collecting people's emails, adding them to a database and sending them follow-up emails/ newsletters – is standard practice for most experienced marketers, my agency included. Yes, emails are dead, yah-di-yah, it's about being able to reach people wherever they go. And email is still a place that people go. Just take a look at these stats published by HubSpot:

- Three-quarters of businesses agree that email offers 'excellent' to 'good' ROI (return on investment). (Econsultancy, 2016).
- Email use worldwide will top 3 billion users by 2020. (The Radicati Group, 2016).
- Gmail has 1 billion active users worldwide.
- Eighty-six per cent of consumers would like to receive promotional emails from companies they do business

with at least monthly, and 15 per cent would like to get
them daily (Statista, 2015).

Just looking at my inbox, why are companies like Amazon, River
Island, John Lewis and Groupon sending me so many emails?
Because they know that while some people will unsubscribe,
fundamentally email works.

For a personal brand, email marketing is about being able to
share news and latest blog posts and offerings, and often directing
people back to your website so that they can re-engage with you,
book your services, buy your products or whatever other action
you'd like them to take. The whole point is to keep people in your
world, up to date with what you do and engaged with your area
of expertise and your voice.

Three ways to build your email list from zero

Bearing in mind that everyone starts with capturing their first
subscriber and builds from there, here's where to start.

1. Put a newsletter sign-up form on your website.
2. Typically these are audio, written or videos that contain
   information that relates to what you do and that people
   want to access. If you're a beautician, that might be a
   download about skincare; if you're a fashion influencer,
   it might be a download about trends and must-have
   buys. Bear in mind that the opt-ins on your website will
   probably change over time, but you can always launch
   new ones and retire old ones.
3. Ask people you meet in person if you can add them to
   your email list. When you're out and about meeting

people, ask for their business cards and manually add them. Likewise, add existing clients and prospects to your list. Just make sure you have their approval.

GDPR - an important note

The General Data Protection Regulation (GDPR), which came into force in May 2018, affects every company and individual that uses personal data from EU citizens. If you're collecting email addresses and you send email to subscribers in the EU, you'll have to comply with GDPR – no matter where you're based.

GDPR touches several aspects of email marketing, especially how marketers seek, collect and record consent. There are plenty of resources online for GDPR compliance (and I'm no lawyer!), but effectively it involves collecting affirmative consent for all subscribers *and* adequately explaining to people how you intend to use their data. While these changes will likely slow down list growth in the short term, the positive is that you'll only be sending emails to subscribers who do want to hear from you.

How to get more traffic to your website

However fantastic your website is, by itself it can only generate limited traffic, and even then only if you are skilled at writing to meet search-engine behaviour and are blogging regularly. The good news about blogging regularly is that it has natural SEO benefits. Google likes websites that are authoritative and relevant, and regular publishing in the form of blogs shows both of these. One of the first strategies we put in place for all clients who are looking for more website traffic is weekly blogging.

Tash's tips

Think of traffic acquisition as a simple wash-rinse-and-repeat process – a never-ending cycle of publishing content, repurposing content and sharing content on social media, building your profile, getting in the media and becoming more known. Alongside optimising your site for the search engines, your focus should be on creating content that builds your social following and links to your site, and that motivates people to look you up online.

Embrace the fact that high traffic doesn't happen overnight

For most of us, understanding traffic is all about managing expectations. The key is to embrace the fact that traffic takes a while to build – and once gained, it needs to be actively maintained or your numbers will fall. There are exceptions: for example, a celebrity's website will always enjoy high traffic for as long as that person is famous. And, who knows, you might hit the news headlines and get wide media coverage. But, generally, it doesn't happen by magic, so, for your sanity's sake, see it as a game! Getting traffic is a bit like Tetris: it can have moments of immense frustration and also moments of immense joy.

Remember that traffic is not as complicated as it sounds

Despite all of this, traffic is not as complicated as it sounds. And that's because in the end there are only a few ways to generate it, so it's not hard to focus your energy on them:

- People google something related to your website's niche and one of your site's pages, or your blog pops up – it's all about content!
- People come across your site via something they see on a social media feed (triggered by one of their interests or shared by a friend) – again, it's all about content.
- People hear about you online, via an influencer or in the media and visit your website.

You can see how all the actions we are talking about throughout this book start to work together. You can also pay to promote your website's visibility:

- You can place ads on Google AdWords so that your site appears at the top of the search engine results.
- You can also place ads on Facebook, Instagram, Snapchat, LinkedIn and Twitter that will be shown to people.

Paying for traffic

There are many platforms for which you can pay for website traffic, engagement, videos, clicks and reach. My favourites are Facebook and Instagram. If you're not in a financial position to pay for traffic, you're going to have to focus hard on organic reach (and put your fingers in your ears every few months when a new story comes out about organic reach falling and algorithm changes). The bottom line is, however, that the Internet and our favourite platforms are getting busier and busier, organic reach is falling and the best and most visible personal brands are supported by paid traffic too, whether this is in getting more website visitors or social reach and video views.

In a typical Stand Out Online process – depending on what sort of business you're trying to build and what your outcomes are – I would recommend investing in one, or a mix, or all of the following:

- Google AdWords traffic
- Facebook/Instagram post boosts to your own custom audiences
- Facebook/Instagram ads to build email lists or fill webinars
- YouTube ads
- LinkedIn ads

You will get much further if you accept that organic reach *is* difficult (although not necessarily dead) and you can oil the wheels with a small investment in traffic and retargeting. If your budget is tight, I would recommend spending £5 or £10 a day boosting your content to three key groups of people:

1. Those on your email list.
2. Those who have visited your website.
3. Those who are already engaging with your content.

That way you can at least keep nurturing your own world of people, and you might want to reach them in two specific ways:

1. Just get your content in front of these people (known as reach campaigns).
2. Ask them specifically to do something, such as sign up to your email list/attend a webinar/visit your website/watch your videos (known as conversion campaigns).

Facebook and Instagram advertising: free training

As a trainer for Facebook's She Means Business campaign, I speak at free events both online and in the real world on how to use Facebook advertising for your business. Because the subject of Facebook advertising is so large and relatively complex, if you want to know more, please visit my website natashacourtenaysmith.com and you will find information about the next training event there.

You can also get plenty of information from Facebook itself at facebook.com/business.

Understand the product staircase

Most personal brands and businesses need to develop a tiered product staircase (ways to work with you) for service and product-based personal brands and edutainers. This enables prospective clients first to interact with them at a 'no brainer' price point, and then gradually drives them to buy more products at ever-increasing price points. This isn't a cynical ploy to get more money but a recognised sales technique that gets the most interested people to engage in a way that feels comfortable to them. Obviously, each tier in the staircase needs to offer more value, because if it doesn't, no one will progress to the next level. At each step, you are offering customers an opportunity to get more and more from you. That is a product staircase. You might also hear this referred to as front-end products, back-end products and upsell products.

You can usually see product staircases used most clearly by edutainers and coaches, where typically you might be invited to download a free guide or attend a webinar, then you would be sold a low-price introductory training course and then a higher-price programme.

Most people come into the edutainment space from a standing where they have been giving out free content and then graduating people into one-to-one coaching/consultancy/mentoring at a pretty average price point. When you look at the true pros in this space, they either don't do one-to-one coaching at all, or they do it at an extremely high price point. The price point for middle- or bottom-of-funnel offers for the true pros ranges from several thousands to tens of thousands of pounds. Meanwhile, the average newbie in this space misses out the entire middle of their funnel and doesn't realise that their one-to-one time (direct mentoring or training) should be their most expensive offering of all.

Tash's tips

For some people, the bottom-of-funnel activity can actually be turned into a done-for-you service or a service-providing agency. In reality, many people don't have the time to carry out the tasks needed to get the results that they want, and some, once realising the pro that you are, may ask you to carry out the work for them. Whether or not you want to do this is entirely up to you and, in itself, doing this work on behalf of someone opens up another opportunity for your personal brand: that of running a service-based agency.

Your staircase can always grow

On page 222 you will find a table that outlines a very simple product staircase. There are two things to remember:

1. Not everyone travels through the staircase in perfect order. You might have someone buy your most expensive product first, and then go back for some free stuff, and then attend a mid-tier event; however, *most* will progress in order.
2. Your staircase should always be growing and fluid, based on what customers want. It is vital to keep adding additional offers, particularly at the top of the funnel where people first encounter you. Keep switching up your opt-ins, changing your free webinars and listening for opportunities to develop your teaching further. If you've truly lived up to your goal to entertain, motivate, inspire and teach on one offering, you will have a group of customers keen to learn more from you.

You should, in theory, use a number of different income models, from selling back-end courses to subscriptions for your exclusive online learning club. Remember, the most successful online educators' personal brands command such respect that they can earn thousands of pounds for single one-to-one coaching sessions.

The product staircase

Type of content	Funnel position	Goal of content
Free content/free guides/books/ podcasts/free events/ free webinars	Top of funnel	To reach people, get them onto your email list, introduce yourself to them and make them think you're a person who they want to hear more from
Low-price product/ low-priced events/ membership club	Middle of funnel	To bring paying customers into your world at a no-brainer price point
High-priced product/ high-priced training events/level 2 membership	Middle– bottom of funnel	To bring these paying customers through to a high-priced offer
Extremely high- priced one-to-one coaching/lower-priced monthly membership/ mastermind/academy	Bottom of funnel	To bring the above tier through to your highest priced offer

Other Stand Out Online credibility indicators

Ever played Mario Kart? In that game (and in a lot of computer games), collecting coins helps you to unlock new karts, wheels and levels. You're playing the same game with a personal brand in that the more 'credibility' indicators you have – which we'll be talking about shortly – the more you are perceived at a higher level than your competitors. We've already discussed some credibility indicators, such as media appearances and guest articles. Here, we are going to focus on three more:

1. Book deals
2. Speaking
3. Awards and MBEs

What's interesting about all this is the non-linear way in which the Stand Out Online process works. You might want to seek these credibility indicators deliberately in order to gain more opportunity elsewhere. Or these may come to you as a result of the efforts you're putting in. These are credibility indicators *and* opportunities, and you might seek them out as both.

Book deals

Thinking about who will benefit the most from reading Stand Out Online (CEOs, founders, celebrities, entrepreneurs, experts), I am going to take a not-that-wild guess and say that the chances are you would love to be the author of a book. The reason I am so confident in saying this is that we all understand that books carry immense power when it comes to credibility. If I think about my own experience, since my first book *The Million Dollar Blog* was published, all sorts of good things have come about, such as massive growth in my digital marketing agency (Bolt Digital) to being asked by Facebook to be a trainer for them.

The three types of book publisher

When it comes to getting your book published, there are three main routes you can go down.

1. **Conventional publishing** A traditional publishing house commissions your book and they take on the financial responsibility for your book and its distribution, and they get their return on investment through book sales.

2. **Hybrid publishers** These publishers work to the same quality of production as conventional publishers but authors take on the financial responsibility for the publishing of the book.

3. **Self-publishing** This is when an author decides to become a micro-publisher and produce their own books. They take themselves through the entire process, including finding their own editor, laying out the book, getting it printed and listing it on Amazon.

There are pros and cons with each; for example, conventional publishing is clearly the most prestigious route to go down, but the process is slower than hybrid or self-publishing. If the purpose of your book is solely to give to prospective clients and in a very niche area, then you may be unlikely to get a conventional publishing deal, in which case hybrid or self-publishing could be the right route for you. Likewise, if you have a very large audience that you are confident will buy your book, you might want to self-publish it, as you will earn a larger proportion of revenue than you would if you went with a conventional publisher.

THE EXPERT'S VIEW Lucy McCarraher on hybrid publishing: 'A well-edited, well-designed book is a powerful tool for a business and personal brand'
Lucy McCarraher is the co-founder and managing editor of hybrid publisher ReThink Press, a leading hybrid publisher working mainly with business owners and experts.

What is ReThink Press?

We sit in the middle of traditional publishers and the process of self-publishing. We have a professional team of editors, coaches, ghostwriters and cover designers to help people get books written and published; however, the author pays up-front for these services. The vast majority of our authors are entrepreneurs who do not want to necessarily sell a lot of books. That is not what they are putting their book out there for; however, they understand that a well-edited, well-designed book can be a powerful tool for their business and personal brand.

Why does a book do that for a person?

There's a general perception that if somebody has the skill to write a book, and has a beautifully written and well-published book about their area of expertise, they are an authority on the matter. We also know that whenever anyone appears in the media as a pundit or an expert on a particular subject, they will almost always have been the author of a relevant book in that area. It just makes everyone think: *Yeah, this person is the expert on this; they have the book to prove it.*

When shouldn't someone write a book?
When they are right at the start of their business journey.
Although it's important as an entrepreneur, CEO or business
owner to have a book for part of your credibility piece, if you
are right at the start of the business journey, you might not have
the content to write a book yet. If you don't have clients you
can feature, if you can't talk about your experience over a
reasonable period of time, your book might not have the sort
of heft that is needed. We recommend the author's story and
experience should always be woven throughout the book.

How important are a book's looks?
We think a book's look is really important. Ignore the old adage
of 'don't judge a book by its cover' – of course you do, everyone
does. The things people look at first are the front cover, back
cover and then the contents page, so it's really important to get
those right. That's one of the issues of self-publishing: the books
just don't look right.

What happens to a person once they've published a book?
You cannot predict it, but the magic of putting your book out
there is that things do happen. I have never had an author
come back to me and say, 'I wish I hadn't wasted that time or
money I spent on getting my book out there; it's done nothing
for me.' Everyone comes back at some stage and says, 'Oh my
God, do you know what happened? Somebody passed on my
book to somebody else, who gave it to somebody else and now
I have been asked to do this and now I am on a world speaking tour!' What you can predict is that if you get a book out
to the right clients and prospects, you will absolutely increase
your business, you will get more clients and you will be able to
put your fees up. Some of our authors buy 5,000 copies of their

book just to give away when it comes out. Others buy 50 here, 50 there, but the important thing is to keep them in circulation, to make sure they are available. If you can think of anybody you want to get in touch with from your industry that you don't have a connection with, send them your book, because no one is going to put that to one side, and the book will end up sitting on their desks.

Is it always about sales?

Not if you are doing this for the benefit of your business and personal brand. It's a question of always travelling with five books in your bag, because you never know who are you going to meet, and instead of giving them a business card you give them your book. One of our authors is Marianne Page who has a book *From Process to Profit*. She has had people pick up books from Amazon and pass them on to other people, and she can absolutely identify clients who bring her £20k, £30k, £40k, £50k of business because they have just read her book on the beach on holiday, or found the book on Amazon by accident. Another author, Tim Farmer, the founder of TSF Consultants (the UK's largest provider of mental-capacity assessments to the legal profession), wrote a book about mental capacity called *Grandpa on a Skateboard*. Three months later, he came back to me and said, 'My business has doubled, and I don't know how to cope.' He'd been invited to the House of Lords and has sat on a government committee as a result.

How much does it cost someone to publish their book with you?

Publishing packages start at £5,000 plus VAT.

Speaking

Another way to be seen as an expert is to speak in public, whether this is sitting on panels, talking at events or filling auditoriums. It might feel daunting to find your first speaking gigs and, depending on who you are and where you are in your career, you may well have to speak for free before you get paid to speak.

THE EXPERT'S VIEW Dagmar O'Toole on public speaking: 'To secure a speaking agency, you must build some sort of "fame" around your personal brand'

Dagmar O'Toole is the founder and director of CSA Celebrity Speaker, one of the largest and most highly regarded speaking agencies in the world. Her business represents celebrities, prime ministers, CEOs, founders, Olympic champions, pioneers, neuroscientists, professors and change-makers, booking them for anything from £3,000 to multi-six-figure sums for speaking.

How do you choose whom to represent?

There are so many people who want to become speakers. Of 100 people who contact us, we probably accept around two. The first thing is, we only represent people with some kind of fame around them, not necessarily celebrity fame (although that helps) but industry fame. CEOs of big companies have this, founders of successful businesses have this, as do leading entrepreneurs. Authors also have a degree of fame. Next, we want every speaker to have done something extraordinary. They have to be able to differentiate themselves from others. Finally, all of our speakers have to be good storytellers – speakers are essentially storytellers, not lecturers.

What is being a good storyteller?

The best speakers have the gift of the gab, are entertaining and are able to get audiences emotionally involved. Some people already have great stories, because they have achieved amazing things; for example, they've climbed mountains or won gold medals, or even survived a tragedy – and there's an inspirational story in those things from which people can learn. But others don't have stories and they have to create stories; for example, one of our speakers is a former lawyer who wanted to become a motivational speaker. He didn't have any stories. Then a friend of his challenged him to become a jockey within a year, which he did and that became his story. He went through all the emotions of learning to ride and succeeding, and that became his story. He's since done other things such as learning diving, so he has created stories in order to become a great storyteller. You also have to have a great sense of humour and make people laugh. Plus, you must be willing to share personal details about yourself, especially nowadays. Your audience want to feel as though they know who you are, and as though you've shared your true self with them.

What is the motivation for people to become speakers?

It's about their personal brand and the way they're seen. Often, they are already speaking within their industry and want to speak to bigger audiences. There's also monetary motivation, and sometimes, when you really dig into it, you discover that at a younger age these people wanted to be performers, actors or actresses. They have inside them a natural drive to be in front of a crowd and hold an audience.

How much can speakers earn?

It's limitless. Our speakers start at around £5,000 per talk and go to high six-figure sums. We often see speakers grow, too: we have people who started with us at £3,000 per talk – now they get £20,000 or £30,000 as their brand has developed. It is in negotiating these bigger sums that an agency is invaluable; however, as a speaker you've got to choose an agent who really puts their whole might behind you, otherwise you'll end up frustrated that you're not getting enough momentum.

Depending on who you are, getting taken on by an established speaking agency might take a while to become a reality. Your motivation at first might be to speak to make your name known, to get in front of potential clients, to get photography of you speaking for the 'speaking page' on your website, or just to generate leads. But speaking for free can be equally as valuable in the early days of building a brand.

Seven steps to securing speaking gigs

1. Add the words 'public speaker' to all your biogs – on your website and social profiles. You can't expect people to consider you for speaking if you don't let them know you're available to speak!
2. Look for local colleges and universities. They may well be thrilled to have you and are a good place to practise speaking before going to wider audiences.
3. Google it! Search for events in your industry online or in industry media.
4. Host your own event – there's no easier way to cast yourself as the keynote speaker and get a ton of photography of you speaking than at your own event! These can be set up via Eventbrite or Facebook.
5. Run webinars. OK, so a webinar isn't usually perceived

as 'public speaking', but it's perfectly possible to present to 100-plus people on a webinar. Once you start doing these frequently and people get value from them, you'll find that you have the experience you can use to secure more talks.

6. Join a speaking agency. Whether or not you get accepted will depend entirely on your profile, your reputation and whether or not the agency thinks they will have a chance to place you as a paid speaker and earn commission.

7. Join Toastmasters International – a non-profit club that helps its members improve their speaking skills and has its own speaking bureau.

Awards and MBEs

Winning business awards and accolades, such as an honour or an MBE, is all part of helping to raise your profile, enhancing your reputation, making you appear more trustworthy and able to stand out from the competition. Awards also potentially carry PR angles and are definitely something to share on social media.

There are all kinds of awards that you can apply for. You only have to google 'business awards' to find some that might be right for you, and that's equally true whether you are a global organisation, an entrepreneur or a charity.

It might be nice just to win an award out of the blue, but such is the business of awards that whole businesses have sprung up – such as Awards Intelligence – that help people to apply for awards. The team at Awards Intelligence helps you find the right awards to apply for, gathers all the evidence you need, create your entries and help you become a multiple award winner without the hard work and effort of creating entries.

Honours

The crème de la crème of awards is the UK honours system, which recognises people who have:

- Made achievements in public life and/or
- Committed themselves to serving and helping Britain.

These awards include titles such as the MBE, OBE and CBE, and are reserved for people who have made life better for other people or are outstanding at what they do. Anyone can nominate someone for an honour, and although this can be done using private companies such as Awards Intelligence, you can also do it directly through the honours website at www.gov.uk/honours

All applications are considered by an honours committee. The committee's recommendations go to the Prime Minister and then to the Queen, who awards the honour. The process takes 12 to 18 months to complete, during which time all nominees are checked by various government departments, including HMRC, to make sure they're suitable for an honour.

Attributes for which people might be awarded an honour

People are awarded honours for achievements such as:

- Making a difference to their community or field of work
- Enhancing Britain's reputation
- Long-term voluntary service
- Innovation and entrepreneurship
- Changing things, with an emphasis on achievement

- Improving life for people less able to help themselves
- Displaying moral courage

Honours are given to people involved in specific fields, including:

- Community, voluntary and local services
- Arts and media
- Health
- Sport
- Education
- Science and technology
- Business and the economy
- Civil or political service

Tash's Takeaways

- The most visible personal brands tend to be supported by an integrated and holistic online marketing strategy that includes a number of elements *and* paid advertising.
- As a priority, online you should focus on growing your own world of people and techniques, such as email-list building and increasing website traffic.
- In the real world, credibility indicators, such as becoming an author or speaker, will also help your personal brand to grow.
- The icing on the cake is accolades, such as being on the Queen's honours list. Of course, it's crucial to act surprised when you learn of your nomination! You certainly didn't have anything to do with it yourself.

PART FIVE

Measure and Refine

'If you can't measure it, you can't improve it.' So said Peter Drucker, who wrote some 39 books on management. The journey to building an effective personal brand online can be a slow one, so how do you know you're going in the right direction?

It's very difficult to lose weight without keeping track of the numbers and making changes when you see whether you are succeeding or not. Likewise, it's very difficult to build and grow a personal brand without setting any objectives and measuring your progress. The answer is to take a long-term view and to define, measure and track success and make refinements accordingly.

PART FIVE

Measure and Refine

12

Know Your Numbers

My business partner at Bolt Digital, Steve Bolton, is a leading British entrepreneur, franchisor and philanthropist. He is also the founder of one of the most successful franchised businesses in UK history. Steve's personal mission is to 'mentor the world', and he has worked with thousands of business owners to help them break through to higher levels of success, both personally and professionally. This deep and broad experience gives Steve a unique perspective on the subject of measurement in business and in relation to digital marketing and the Stand Out Online process.

MY STORY **Steve Bolton**: 'Any founder, CEO or senior executive who doesn't take their personal brand seriously should be fired' Steve Bolton is a leading British entrepreneur. His franchised businesses have assets worth more than £300 million and a growing eight-figure company valuation. Steve is passionate about helping other people to achieve greater wealth, health and happiness, and he believes that the fast track to success is to 'stand on the shoulders of giants'.

I want to talk to you about measurement and numbers in business and in relation to personal branding. But first, how important has building your personal brand been in creating the success you have achieved?

My point of view is quite controversial, because I believe that any founder, CEO or senior executive who doesn't take their personal brand seriously should be fired. Literally, they should be given two verbal warnings, a written warning, and then fired if they don't fix it.

Wow! Isn't that a bit extreme?

Maybe, but here's how I look at it: basically, we are witnessing the biggest and fastest change in relation to communication in the entire history of human civilisation. When people living in caves first started grunting at each other and forming words, that process would have taken hundreds and thousands of years to develop and spread. Even the printing press in the fifteenth century was a massive positive disruption, but this took hundreds of years to spread around the world. Then radio, TV and the telephone came along, around 100 or so years ago. They are remarkable tools, but TV and radio were, and still are, one-way communication devices. The telephone has obviously always been a two-way device, but the ability to reach scale is not possible. It's a one-to-one, or one-to-few, device. All that changed with the internet about two decades ago. Then, around a decade ago, social media started to take hold, and the pace of change today is like nothing we have ever seen. And it's only speeding up.

Anyone in a position of responsibility in business, who does not appreciate that we are living through a radical transformation in communication that will affect every organisation and almost every individual on the planet is grossly neglecting their responsibility towards their stakeholders. There are two types of people and companies in this world to my mind: the quick and the dead. I see too many people saying, 'Facebook's for kids' or 'Why would I want to share a photo of my lunch with the world?' To me, people like this are similar to those who said, 'Computers will never take off' back in the 1980s and 1990s. They either adapt or they die.

What's the answer?

The good news is that there is still time for most people and most businesses, but the time bomb is ticking. Obviously, there are exceptions, as we can see in the retail sector. E-commerce will continue to decimate the high street, but if people act quickly and understand the shift, it is not difficult to turn a threat into a massive opportunity.

Did personal branding have an impact in helping you to achieve your remarkable success?

No question. In fact it's up there in my top three most important strategic and tactical decisions I have ever made in business. I started investing in my personal brand more than a decade ago. At first this was largely through offline channels because online was in its infancy; however, I pivoted to a more online approach several years ago, and it was a game-changer.

Let's talk about measurement. How important is it and how do you do it when it comes to personal branding?

Business is a game played by numbers. If you don't understand the numbers, you probably won't be in business for very long. Or, if you are, you are either very lucky or you won't be earning very much for a long time to come. I'm a great believer that you should mostly focus on your strengths in business. If you develop your weaknesses, you just end up with a lot of well-developed weaknesses; however, money and measurement are two areas that *all* entrepreneurs, influencers and business owners need to at least develop to the point where they know what's going on and can make decisions. Producing and being able to read a profit-and-loss account, cash flow and balance sheet are not only *must-have* skills for anyone in business, but they are also legal requirements for all limited companies to produce on a regular basis. It's really frightening to see how many people don't understand or produce these fundamental financial reports for their business, especially at the micro- and small-business levels – in other words, turnover up to £10 million per annum.

When it comes to the measurement of personal branding, the first thing I would say is that you need to view your personal brand as a business. Although it might not be a separate legal entity, there are still inputs and outputs that can be measured.

OK, so what are some of the key measurements, and how would you recommend that people track them?
Unlike financial measurements, like a profit-and-loss statement, measurement of personal branding can't be as precise; however, just like any real business, you have to invest in the roots before you can expect to produce the fruits. It's extremely rare for someone to start a business and for the profits to start flowing soon afterwards. The same is completely true for a personal brand. It takes time.

From my own point of view, here are some of the key metrics for measuring success from when I started out through to more recently, just to give a flavour:

1. The number of qualified leads generated for my businesses (more leads of a better quality) being the key measurable objective.
2. The number of partners (customers/clients) in the pipeline on a rolling basis (that is, your sales funnel adjusted for conversion probability).

3. The speed of conversion – based on increased trust that my online personal brand has produced. This is very underrated but very valuable.

4. Reduced cost of client/customer/partner acquisition based on people coming to you with existing knowledge of you, what you stand for, your expertise and enhanced positioning.

5. Increased referrals from a much deeper and wider network. You just never know where your content will end up and who will connect with it.

6. New opportunities are hard to quantify – it's much easier to measure backwards than forwards – but I don't know anyone who has got their personal branding right and has not had major positive benefits in terms of new opportunities.

7. Valuable connections. I am often quoted as saying, 'You are 67 per cent more likely to become the average of the people you spend most time with.' The reality is that a good personal brand will expand your network and bring you into contact with people who can help you and raise you to higher and higher levels of performance.

8. Staff recruitment is an often-overlooked aspect of personal branding. The success of any business is down in large part to the quality of the people. I shouldn't take it for granted, but whenever I am recruiting new staff members, I know they will do their research about the company and the people. They not only get great confidence from seeing that I 'get' and can operate well in the new digital landscape, but they have also been able to get to know me by watching videos, reading content and listening to my podcast, and it makes them far more likely to want to work with us.

These are just a selection of the key measurements that I would recommend people take into account.

Any parting thoughts?

Yes, building your personal brand is not a choice – it's a necessity. It is actually pretty simple to do, but that doesn't mean that it's easy; however, the rewards are remarkable once you get it right and, like most things in life, it starts with a decision and a commitment. Rome wasn't built in a day and neither are personal brands. But I assure you, if you start or expand now, in just one or two years' time you will be reaping the benefits in more ways than you can possibly imagine.

_____

Remember your goals

Back in Chapter 3, we talked about your vision and the five key primary goals that are on your wish list to achieve through your visible personal brand (page 51–2). Your examples might have included:

- Having your own online show watched by X number of people.
- Having been commissioned to write a book on your subject.
- Having social media audiences of X thousand.
- Having been on TV.
- Having been invited to advise government.
- Having been nominated for a Queen's honour.
- Having increased your income by a certain amount.

Even though you may always be the kind of person who moves goalposts forward, and forgets achievements within moments of them happening, reaching these clear, bold milestones is certainly going to be one way to measure success. But at the same time, you're probably not going to sign up to a social network and immediately have everything you want happen overnight.

Clearly, you will know when you arrive at one of your destinations; the answer is, however, how do you measure all the positive progress you're making along the way that will ultimately lead you to your destination? How do you check you're on the right route? How do you know when things are going right and when things are going wrong? How do you know what to do more of, and what to do less off? The answer is to track a number of metrics as well as your own actions on a monthly basis – and a simple Excel spreadsheet will work perfectly well for this.

Key metrics to track

Your own actions	Number of blogs/audio/videos published on own website
	Number of blogs/audios/videos published on other websites
	Number of social posts published
	Format of social posts published
	Number of emails/newsletters sent
	Number of engagement actions taken (i.e. comments/likes/shares that you've left for people you'd like to build relationships with) →

Soft stats (organic)	Social reach
	Video views
	Engagement
	Website visitors
Soft stats (paid)	Ad reach
	Ad click-through rate
	Ad cost-per-click
Hard stats	Website sign-ups (i.e. on email list)
	Emails opened
	Email clicks
	Webinar attendees
Real-world activity	Collaborations
	Media appearances
	Meetings with significant people
Clear success markers	Achievement of any of the goals listed in Chapter 3

Most social platforms, particularly Facebook, have very advanced information found in their analytics or insights section. Within Facebook you will find, on a post-by-post basis, feedback on what the post was, what media forms of content it contained and how well it did in terms of engagement, likes, clicks, shares and, ultimately, how many people it reached.

Effectively, your aim should be to understand what's working, learn from what isn't, and make refinements as you go. Measuring your key numbers will allow you to understand whether things are going in the direction that you want them to, or whether you need to try something slightly different (for example, a different style of content or a different tone of voice).

Let me give you an example. Typically, a video uploaded straight to Facebook or a Facebook live video attracts more attention than a URL that you've posted to your latest blog post. That doesn't mean that you should never post URLs again, as obviously you want people to visit your website, it just means that you should do it sparingly and make more videos or even use a different media format.

A good place to start is by posting a number of different media formats and styles on Facebook, from personal posts to educational posts, to posts about your strategies in your work, with the specific goal of seeing which ones perform best. However, bear in mind that if you start with a small audience, the data you have will be limited and you'll need to run further tests as your audience grows.

When to make refinements

What is clear is that not a single person I have talked to for this book got things right from the start. They all got started and faced a degree of awkwardness, then they learned and grew, and they made adjustments as they began to understand what worked and what didn't. You must do the same thing.

What to do before you make any refinements

You'll now see that there is a process that CEOs, celebrities, entrepreneurs, founders and influencers are using to build their personal brands, businesses, future and influence using the Internet. You've heard from a number of people from different walks of life who have been down this path already and who have shared their experience and wisdom. You now understand that the process is not always completely linear, although, certainly, planning and strategy is a must, content production and distribution is non-negotiable, and measuring and refinement over the long term are vital.

There is only one more thing to do and that is to start. Until you do, until you launch your Stand Out Online project, all of this will remain theoretical. The best way to learn is on the job, through doing it and through the process. Don't wait, don't over-analyse, don't get analysis paralysis, and definitely don't wait for permission from anyone else. Don't be scared, don't be shy, don't worry about the whats, hows and whens. Commit to content creation, commit to content distribution, and commit to making your dream a reality. It's not a get-rich-quick scheme – it's a journey.

Get out there and get started. And let me know how you get on.

Acknowledgements

Anyone who has written a book knows that it is a process that is both hugely exciting and equally daunting. It's exhilarating to get down on paper – in order – everything that is in your mind and that you've learned over two decades; yet it is also relentlessly hard work and painful at times. It is one of life's ultimate marathons, and I think I've realised I'm more of a sprinter! And all sprinters need support when taking on a marathon.

Thank you to Zoe Bohm and the team at Little, Brown firstly for commissioning *#StandOutOnline* and allowing me to write the book I always wanted to write, and secondly for always being so warm, supportive and not getting too cross when my manuscript (and edits) were late.

Thank you to my partner Ally Gordon, who listened and encouraged me all the way, and to my children, who accepted I had to devote time to this project and learned that checking the word count and telling me how much more I had to write was actually great fun.

Thank you to all the inspirational trailblazers I spoke to who have shared their stories of building their personal brands and standing out online, some of whom I now consider friends* (*waving to you Sean Vigue).

And finally, thank you to my business partner Steve Bolton for always pushing me out of my comfort zone – and for making me rewrite nearly the whole book in the last month. In doing so, you helped *#StandOutOnline* become even more valuable, impactful and a true game-changer for those who will read, learn and grow from it.

Index